
TITANS

Also by Tim Green

Fiction

Ruffians
Titans
Outlaws
The Red Zone

Nonfiction

The Dark Side of the Game
A Man and His Mother: An Adopted Son's Search

TIM GREEN

DOUBLE REVERSE

WARNER BOOKS

A Time Warner Company

The events and characters in this book are fictitious. Certain real locations and public figures are mentioned, but all other characters and events described in the book are totally imaginary.

WARNER BOOKS EDITION

Copyright © 1999 by Tim Green

Cover design by Stanislaw Fernandes

Warner Books, Inc.
1271 Avenue of the Americas
New York, NY 10020

Visit our Web site at
www.twbookmark.com

 A Time Warner Company

Printed in the United States of America

Originally published in hardcover by Warner Books.
First Paperback Printing: April 2000

10 9 8 7 6 5 4 3 2 1

For my wife, Illyssa, who eclipses all other things.

Acknowledgments

I would like to extend a special thanks to Lieutenant Mike Kerwin of the Syracuse Police Department for his valuable insights as a police officer and a fellow lawyer. Also I would like to give special thanks to Dr. Michael Parker for his insight into anesthesia and Dr. Barbara Conner for her expertise in emergency medicine.

Chapter 1

Trane Jones emerged from a small voodoo shop at the corner of Crescent and strolled confidently down Bourbon Street with his back straight, his head high, and a spring in his gait. He was full-framed at six foot four, and the biker boots he wore made him taller and more imposing still. Despite the late hour he wore a dark pair of Oakley sunglasses, and a black leather cap, worn backward, which matched his jacket but covered his trademark diagonal cornrows. It was a cool night in the Quarter. Before he could go ten steps people began to recognize him.

"Trane! Can I have your autograph?"

The boy was excited, a freckle-faced white kid about twelve years old. He looked like he came from a place like Nebraska.

"Fuck you," Trane said, scowling at the boy's parents and walking on without bothering to sign the kid's crummy piece of paper. Nothing pissed him off more than people grubbing for autographs.

Trane Jones wanted to forget about football. For any NFL player not involved in the Conference championship games, that weekend, like the Super Bowl, was an annoyance. All the hard work, the sweat, and the pain seemed futile when you realized that no one really cared about you quite as much unless you won a championship. Here he was, the NFL's best runner—the best ever, if you asked him—with records falling all around him like pigeon shit. But people still didn't give him the respect he deserved because he had yet to play for a championship team. He was a New Orleans Saint. It annoyed him to no end. It was the kind of mood that seemed to lead him to trouble, or trouble to him.

As he walked he spurned other autograph-seeking tourists with a deadly stare, refusing to stop or even slow his pace. He could have avoided the crowded street, but there was something satisfying about having the whole world point and stare and you just keep walking on by. Trane took a left on Conto and entered the dark bowels of the Quarter, leaving the crowded street behind. A handful of middle-aged drunks who'd just emerged from a bar followed him for a block but then thought better of it.

Trane snorted disdainfully as he passed the familiar signs that warned of high crime in the area, but all the same he caught himself absently touching the Glock strapped underneath his arm. Three blocks down he took a right between two battered redbrick buildings into a narrow, unmarked street. Halfway down the darkened street he came to a small storefront with a simple glossy black door and a large window painted entirely red except for the words etched carefully into the paint:

ELYSIUM: WHERE THE GODS PLAY.

Inside was a small anteroom lit by an orange lamp that suggested firelight. An elegantly dressed man in his mid-forties sat behind an important-looking antique desk. The man, Gaston, a half-breed, wore a thin European mustache and spoke with an accent.

"Mr. Jones," he said calmly.

"I want a banger," Trane said with a wicked white smile from behind the dark glasses.

"Of course," Gaston said, picking up a phone. "Please make yourself comfortable in the lounge, Mr. Jones."

Trane led himself through a dark wooden door into the smoky bar, where well-dressed men and beautiful women of every color mingled quietly together. Trane moved through the room and sat down at a small table in the corner. This was a club where unusual things were the norm, so it didn't seem to be any great surprise that Trane Jones had walked into it. Still, people couldn't keep from stealing a look his way. Trane let his tongue hang lazily out of his mouth so they could see the chrome ball he had pierced through it years ago as his trademark. Within seconds a perky redhead brought Trane a scotch. She ignored his tongue and he presumed she'd seen him there before. He returned her smile by wagging it at her and staring pointedly at her backside as she walked away.

Moments later a waif of a girl with snowy blond hair appeared from a door in the back and made her way to Trane's table. She was thin but adequately endowed. The skin about her neck and shoulders was a pale white, even against her simple white silk dress. She wore very little makeup, a touch of blush and a light pink lipstick. That and her big liquid brown eyes gave her face a childlike innocence that sent Trane's blood rushing.

"You my banger, baby?" he said.

The girl feigned timidity and brought her mouth to his. He held the back of her neck with his enormous hand and kissed her hard. She sat down.

"Drink?" he said.

Before she could answer, the redhead was back with a bottle of expensive champagne. "This is from Mr. Le Tousse," she said, displaying the bottle with dash.

Trane could see a balding middle-aged man in the background staring his way and puffing up like a peacock in his expensive suit. He was flanked by two striking black women.

"Tell him to fuck himself," Trane said casually, "and bring my little girl here a . . ."

"Manhattan," the blonde said in a heavy Russian accent.

"A Man-hat-tan, and another a this shit for me."

The redhead fought back a frown and returned to the bar with the bottle in hand. Trane gave the arrogant white man the finger and turned his attention to the girl. She was just what he liked. He'd have to remember to tip Gaston nicely.

After their drinks the girl asked in halting English. "Would you like go?"

Trane shook his head slowly and with a shameless grin told her, "I wanna just sit here and look and think about how I'm gonna tear you up . . ."

The girl managed a crooked smile and took another drink. Trane just stared. He could make even a girl like this squirm, and that somehow made him feel good.

Another drink, long and slow, and he said, "Now."

Without a word she stood and took him by the hand, leading him into the back and up a wide set of spiral stairs and down a long dim carpeted hallway to a room at the end. The room was Gothic, with high wood-carved ceilings and heavily draped windows that led to two separate wrought-iron balconies. Between the two windows stood a large sculpted four-poster bed draped with a diaphanous canopy. When the door was shut behind them, Trane hit the girl hard on the back of the head with his open hand, knocking her to the floor and sprawling her pale thin limbs onto the thick blue oriental rug. She got up slowly and turned to look at him. His eyes were lit with a strange glow, and her limbs began to shake.

"This for you," she offered.

Beside the bed on a dresser top was a Turkish water pipe. The girl lit it and inhaled long and hard before presenting it to Trane. The scent of opium filled the room, and the girl's dark brown eyes were soon glazed with indifference.

Trane beat her, then took her, then beat her again.

In the dead hours of the night Trane awoke to find the girl sitting on the edge of the bed with a needle in her arm. Half asleep, he watched her shoot her junk, and then took her hard one more time before collapsing for the rest of the night.

When the first beam of sunlight dropped across his face, Trane began to stir. The bed felt wet, wet and sticky. He bolted upright and rubbed his eyes furiously. A guttural moan clawed its way up his throat and escaped into the musty room. The bed was soaked in blood. The girl beside him was blue, stone cold.

Chapter 2

More than seventy thousand people felt the bite of the cold while a handful below shed steam under the blue lights that cut into the coming winter night. Clark Cromwell spit a gob of bloody phlegm between the bars of his mask into the frozen grass and sniffed with a wince. In the first quarter he had smashed the first knuckle of his left hand, dislocating the finger, and now it was starting to throb. The situation was desperate. They were seventeen points behind and there was less than eight minutes left in the game. It was the NFC championship. The winner would go on to the Super Bowl. The loser would go home.

The cold didn't bother Clark. He'd been raised in Alaska, and to him a chill wind seemed as much a part of football as a pair of shoulder pads. And while most people thought the game of football was tough, Clark had grown up hunting large game for food and cutting wood for heat. So to him, the toughness required to play the game of football seemed something less than it might to a kid who came from a comfortable suburb in middle-class America.

The play came into Mitch Faulkner's helmet from the sideline and the quarterback looked up desperately at Clark as he called it out. Everyone knew it was going to be a pass. Everyone knew Green Bay would blitz. They'd been blitzing all game, and the Los Angeles offensive line hadn't been able to do much about it. Faulkner had taken a beating. When the blitz came it would be Clark's job to take out the most dangerous man to the quarterback. That's what a fullback did.

"See if you can get two of them, Clark," Faulkner said under his breath as the offense broke the huddle and headed for the line of scrimmage. "They'll be coming."

"I got it," Clark said with quiet certainty. He might not be the best runner or receiver in the league, but at six foot one, two hundred fifty pounds, he was stout and powerful and possessed an unusual quickness that made him one of the best, if not the best, blocking backs in the NFL.

Clark eyed the formation and listened as Faulkner howled the offensive linemen's protection responsibilities through the mad din of the hostile crowd. Defenders inched toward the line like a bunch of kids trying to cheat at the start of a race. Faulkner barked out his last desperate adjustments, changing the pass pattern as well, then took the snap just before the play clock ran out. They came in a swarm, big and fast. Faulkner dropped back and Clark stepped up. He hit the strong safety squarely in the chest with his hands, stopping him better than a bullet. The pain from his finger shot into his brain, but the middle linebacker was coming fast. On instinct, Clark dove to his left and put his helmet into the bigger man's chest. He saw lightning bolts and felt an electric shock. Then everything went black.

When he came to, Clark was looking up at a circle of faces set against the black night sky. The pain in his neck was excruciating, like a buried knife. The rest of his body tingled but remained inert. He had no other feeling. He couldn't lift his head. His eyes filled with panic.

"Dear God," he said to himself. "Dear God, dear God, let me be well. In Jesus' name let me live. Let me not be . . . Let me move . . ."

"Don't try to move," someone said sternly.

"I—I can't move," he blurted out in a voice that he didn't recognize as his own.

After some time the doctors from the team and the paramedics tilted him carefully and slipped a board under his back. They pinned his head between two blocks of bright orange foam and tied him down with thick Velcro straps. Teammates and opponents looked on in horror. Grown men held hands and prayed. The seventy thousand fans, once raving, were eerily silent. A gentle rain of quiet applause broke out as he was wheeled off the field on the back of a golf cart. A rumbling ambulance waited in the concrete tunnel. Clark gagged quietly on the fumes as they loaded him in. He was crying and he didn't care. He prayed hard.

As they whipped through the wet, sleepy streets of Green Bay, Clark realized that the harder he prayed, the more he was beginning to feel.

"To glorify you, God," he said desperately under his breath. "My healing is your glory."

By the time they unloaded him at the hospital he could move his toes and his hands. Incredibly, the pain in his neck continued to grow, and little moans escaped from his throat when he didn't concentrate on staying quiet. By the time he was on the X-ray table, only his right arm, shoulder, and chest were still tingling. They hurt, too, but the rest of his body felt almost normal.

The doctors came.

"Your neck isn't fractured," one said, "but from your symptoms we know there is some nerve damage. We're going to take an MRI and have a specialist look at it."

"I can move," Clark said, wiggling his fingers and flopping his feet to prove it.

"We'll get this equipment off you, but try to stay as still as you can for now."

Carefully, with the help of some nurses, the doctor removed Clark's helmet and his shoulder-length blond hair spilled out onto the table. With razor-sharp shears they removed the rest of his equipment, cutting through straps and laces. They covered him with a sheet, then wheeled him into a dimly lit room and unloaded him onto a narrow table that protruded from the fat cylindrical MRI machine like a tongue.

"Would you like a Valium?" a young nurse asked.

Clark scowled. "For what?"

"You'll be in there for a while. You won't be able to move and it's tight. Valium will help you relax."

"I don't need it," Clark said resolutely. He didn't use drugs.

Twenty minutes after being encased in the MRI machine he regretted his decision. The walls of the huge machine were inches from his face and pressed against his chest, shoulders, hips, and ass. He couldn't move more than half an inch in any direction. The machine banged on with a terrible noise as they spoke to him through a headset that had been placed over his ears.

"How much longer?" he demanded after another twenty minutes.

"It could be a while," the nurse's voice said sympathetically. "Do you want that Valium?"

Silence.

"Just get me out," Clark said finally. "I need to get out."

Nothing happened. Then, without warning and with a whirr of mechanical wheels, Clark emerged into the glorious space of the open room.

The nurse appeared. "Take these, sweetheart," she said. "You're going to be in there a while and it will help."

Clark silently asked forgiveness and swallowed the Valium.

"It'll take a few minutes to work. Are you okay to go back in?"

"Yes," Clark said stoically. This time he knew what to expect, and by the time the claustrophobia began to creep into his mind the drugs had kicked in and washed away his worry.

The MRI took more than an hour, and it gave Clark time to think about what had happened and what might have happened. He knew that other NFL players had been paralyzed for life. Some recovered partial use of their limbs.

When they had the pictures they needed, the machine ejected him and he waited quietly for the doctor. Free from the restrictive machine, Clark found that his right arm, with some continuing pain and some weakness, was functional. The door suddenly opened and a new doctor, tall and gangly, smiled at him.

"Hello, Clark. I'm Doctor Devorsitz. I'm a neurologist. The good news first. Your spinal cord is not severed in any way. The bad news is that the cord was bruised and you've ruptured a disk between the fourth and fifth vertebrae. You'll need surgery to remove the damaged disk and fuse the two vertebrae."

"I . . . I'm going to be okay?" Clark asked.

The doctor pursed his lips and scowled before nodding. "The odds favor your full recovery, but I have to warn you that there are many things we don't know about the spinal cord. It can take some unusual turns."

"Will I be able to play?"

The doctor considered him as if he were a sideshow curiosity. "If the damage is no worse than it appears, and if your surgery is successful, then it's certainly a possibility. I believe people have suffered this kind of injury and played football again. Is that what you want?"

"Of course," Clark said. "That's what I am."

Chapter 3

Conrad Dobbins's phone woke him at a little after seven. He was in complete darkness.

"Hello?" he said, his voice scratchy and laced with annoyance.

"Conrad. I got trouble."

"What now?"

"Real trouble, man. I got a dead girl."

Conrad sat up and punched a button on the nightstand. A heavy set of curtains masking a massive semicircular set of windows opened to reveal the city of Los Angeles below.

"Goddamn! I told you, Trane. I told you and told you. Don't find trouble. Stay clean until I get this next contract *signed*. Two motherfuckin' months! That's all I asked you. Two motherfuckin' months! Who is the bitch?"

"Just a girl."

"Just a girl? Who? Your goddamn girlfriend? Some bitch? A hooker? The goddamn owner's goddamn wife? Who?"

"A hooker."

"Well that's something anyway . . . What happened to her?"

"I think she OD'd, but there's motherfuckin' blood everywhere. Things got a little rough."

"Police?"

"No. I'm at Elysium. That club I took you to."

"Goddamn, Trane," Dobbins complained. "Now I'm gonna have to call the goddamn Rocket and you know that ain't gonna be cheap."

Chapter 4

The chemical stink of a strong bromide disinfectant filled Clark's nostrils. For the past month that smell had punctuated the beginning of every day except Sundays. He was submerged in the hot tub up to his chin in the bubbling water. His arms floated languidly amid the bubbles, but he was in no way enjoying himself. The hot water still caused his neck to throb with a heightened intensity. He looked at the clock. Two minutes to go. He ground his teeth and tried not to watch the second hand.

When he emerged from the tub he was flushed pink like a boiled lobster. His long yellow hair was plastered in a dark web across his back and shoulders. He wrapped a white towel around his waist and lifted his weakened right arm over his head, stretching it out. By now, a handful of other seriously injured teammates were starting to straggle into the training room with sleep-rumpled heads of hair. They greeted one another with solemn nods. The trainers themselves had broken their huddle near the doctors' examination room and were waiting expectantly to begin a multitude of treatment regimens. Being first meant Clark got his treatment from the head trainer, Jerry Rhea. Not only was Jerry the best and most experienced of the staff, he was a good Christian man, and that gave Clark a certain amount of comfort. His treatment would stretch out over a three-hour period, much of it under the massaging hands of the trainer. The time went faster if you had something to talk about, and Clark always found conversation much more pleasant with someone who shared his fundamental ideas.

"Jerry," Clark said.

The older man looked up from the table where he'd just finished greasing up two electrodes. "Good morning, Mister Cromwell," Jerry said. The "mister" was Jerry's typically friendly sarcasm, but something about the trainer's smile struck Clark as being forced.

"How was the concert?" Clark asked.

"Symphony," Jerry corrected him. "It was Vivaldi and it was excellent."

Clark lay back. Jerry fixed the electrodes on either side of his neck with an elastic strap and wedged a wet rubber grounding pad under the small of his back. The frigid conductive gel under the electrode pads sent a shiver down Clark's spine.

"Tell me when you feel it," Jerry said.

When the needles of current bordered on pain, Clark said, "Okay."

Jerry backed it down a stop, forced another smile, and walked away. Clark followed the trainer with his eyes. The bad neck hindered his view, but he saw enough to detect a slump in Jerry's shoulders that wasn't normally there. There had been something about his tone of voice and his tight expression that disconcerted Clark. As much as anyone in the downstairs level of the facility, Jerry had his finger on the pulse of the team. He had no reason to be personally miffed at Clark. That meant something else was amiss.

The rest of the morning only confirmed Clark's initial

suspicion. It was nothing overt, but there were enough subtle signs: the other trainers not looking him in the eye, the equipment man offering him an extra pair of socks, the weight coach's distracted look when Clark asked about the starting date for the off-season program. So by the time Clark returned to his locker after a shower he wasn't surprised at all to see a note taped to his stool. Coach Gridley, the headman, wanted to see him.

Clark tried to tell himself that whatever happened was God's will. But as he sat in his scruffy jeans and a faded green golf shirt outside the head coach's office, worry gnawed away at his insides. An injured player was always on tenuous ground no matter how many good things he'd done in the past. And Clark was an expensive injured player. He'd signed a new multimillion-dollar contract only last summer. When the secretary told him to go in, Clark jumped from his chair and was through the door before the coach had replaced the phone on its receiver.

"Clark, sit down," Gridley said somberly. He was a heavyset, dark-featured man, young for someone in his position, but already his sagging jowls and eyes were marked with care from his serious intensity. He had none of the cheerful enthusiasm many people associated with a young football coach. He looked more like a draconian colonel in some third-world secret service.

Clark sat.

"How's the neck coming?" Gridley said in his low bass, looking pointedly at the still-bright scar traversing the length of Clark's neck. They had opened his throat from the front, pushing aside his trachea, esophagus, and muscles in order to get at the anterior of his spine and fuse the two vertebrae with a sliver of bone from his hip.

"Great," Clark replied enthusiastically, twisting his neck from side to side to prove it. There was no need to mention that his right shoulder and arm were still only about half their normal strength as a result of the nerve damage. Gridley, Clark knew, got a weekly report from the doctors.

"Well, I'm glad for that," Gridley said with a forced smile of his own. "Clark, this is the part of this job that I like the least, but you know as well as I do how this game has changed since free agency . . . Coaching a team is as much about accounting these days as it is putting in a good offensive game plan. I don't like it any more than most of the players, but that's how it is . . . Clark, I've got to release you."

Clark felt his stomach knot up. He had nothing to say. It was dizzying.

"I don't want you to think I don't want you as part of this team," Gridley continued solemnly, "but we just can't afford to keep you at your salary. I know you'll want to see what you can get on the open market, but I want you to know that I'm going to strongly recommend to Mr. Ulrich that we make a strong play to re-sign you. I'm sorry. I hope you understand."

It wasn't the money that bothered Clark. It was the rejection, to sit there and have to hear that he'd become too expensive, as if he wasn't worth everything he'd done for this team.

"It's business," Clark said with a scowl. "That's fine. I get that. And you're right. I will test the market. My neck is fine. I'm the same player you signed to a six-million-dollar deal last year. I can still block and run and catch, and I'm worth every cent of my contract."

Gridley inclined his head. "I'm not saying you're not worth it, Clark. I'm just saying that we've got salary cap constraints and Mr. Ulrich is determined to get a big free-agent running back. He's convinced, and he's right, that if we can upgrade our ground game we can win a championship.

"He's looking for places to cut the payroll. That's business. It's going to affect other guys on this team, too. Unfortunately," he added, with all the kindness he could muster, "you're hurt right now. I don't doubt that you'll be full go by next year. That's why I'd love to have you back. But on the market—and that's what this is all about—on the market, your price goes down. You know that . . ."

"I—" Clark began, but then closed his mouth and stood to go.

The coach stood, too, and extended his hand. Clark gripped it with his weakened hand and put as much into it as he could.

"Maybe we'll work something out," Gridley said. "I meant what I said, Clark. I'd like to have you back."

"Sounds good," Clark said, withdrawing his nearly limp hand.

In the main lobby Clark realized that a bevy of reporters, TV as well as newspaper, were clustered just outside the main entrance.

"Shoot," he muttered to himself. Word of his release must have already been leaked, and he didn't want to have to deal with any questions. He smiled sheepishly at the receptionist, who gave him a sympathetic frown, then made his way back through the offices to go out the side door by the players' parking lot.

Clark wasn't one to overuse his car phone, but before he had even started the engine of his Expedition he was punching up his agent's number, breathing so hard he was close to hyperventilating. He'd never felt this way before. It was like having a girl you loved tell you there was someone else, only ten times worse. It was a rejection so painful that Clark forgot to pray. He could only react.

"Caldburn, Baxter and Thrush," said the receptionist of the law firm Clark had dialed.

"This is Clark Cromwell," he said. "I need to speak with Madison McCall, please."

"Just a moment . . ."

Clark looked through the windshield at the Juggernauts facility, a modern smoked-glass configuration tucked up next to the three expansive emerald green practice fields. In the distance beyond the border of royal palm trees were the mountains that looked down on Orange County from the east. On a clear day it was a magnificent place to come to work. Apart from an initial two-year stint in Seattle, he'd been here for his entire NFL career. It was home, but now maybe it wasn't.

"Ms. McCall's office."

"Sharon, hi, this is Clark. I need to speak to Madison."

"She's in court right now, Clark. Can I help you, or do you want to speak with Chris?"

"Is Chris there?"

"I just saw him go into the conference room, but I'll let him know it's you."

While Clark waited, a long white limousine pulled into the circle in front of the Juggernauts main entrance. The reporters crowded around the car, and Clark felt a pang of shame at having thought they were waiting for him. He wondered if the receptionist had picked up on his foolish presumption.

"Hi, Clark," came Chris Pelo's cheerful voice. He was Madison's assistant, also a lawyer, who handled the nuts and bolts of the sports agency business they both ran for the firm. Madison was the real boss, but Chris was no slouch. Clark heard that Pelo had worked his way through law school as a police investigator.

"Chris, they cut me."

"What? Wait a minute, they cut you?"

"Just now," Clark said. "I just came from Gridley's office. Salary cap stuff, he said, my injury."

Clark watched three black men file out of the limousine. The last two looked like players, especially the last one. Clark knew by his size and the way he moved. The cornrows in his hair and the dark glasses reminded him of Trane Jones. Then, as the trio passed through the reporters on their way into the team's offices, Clark saw the distinct nickel-size scar under the player's left eye. It was Trane Jones. He was the free-agent running back, the reason Clark had just been cut.

"I don't believe it!" Chris said incredulously. "I talked with Ulrich just last week about your bonus money and he never said a word . . ."

"What am I going to do?" Clark said. He didn't mention Jones to Chris. He was afraid of sounding like a whiner.

There was a long silence before Chris regained himself. "We'll start calling around today! There are plenty of teams that would love to sign you."

"At a reduced salary," Clark complained.

"Oh, I don't know about that," Chris responded. "I don't know about that at all. Your neck is fine. The doctors will vouch for that. Your shoulder will come back. San Francisco needs a good fullback, and the Jets . . ."

Clark felt weak and materialistic talking about the money. He always told himself and everyone else it wasn't about the money. But it wasn't money he wanted for money's sake; it was the mark of how much worth a team ascribed to you. Every player wanted to be valuable to his team. Getting released, even if it was just to cram your salary down, was the ultimate sign of disrespect. It was what every player dreaded most.

In a way, Clark wanted to go to one of those other teams

that Chris was talking about, just to stick it in the Juggernauts' face. Let them sign Trane Jones, the derelict. Then let him get smashed in the mouth every other play without a good fullback to block for him. But after the initial adrenaline wore off, going to another team didn't seem like such a great idea at all. Clark didn't want to go anywhere. Los Angeles was his home. He liked it there. He liked his teammates. He liked his house in Rancho Palos Verdes, his church, his Bible study group, the coffee shop he went to. Besides, his team was close to winning it all. He knew that. They'd lost in the conference championship game, yes, but they were a young team and they had been just one game away from the biggest prize in sports: the Super Bowl.

"I don't know," Clark said. "Maybe Madison could call Ulrich when she gets back. Maybe it would be worth it to them to not have me going out into the free market. That would make sense for them. I could take a pay cut. Maybe we could get some incentives built in so if I had a good year I could get closer to my original salary."

"It's possible," Chris said dubiously.

"If they want me," Clark added.

"I'm sure they want you, Clark," Pelo said. "It's not a matter of not wanting you. Gridley said that himself. You know it."

"I don't know what I know," Clark said. "But I hope you're right. I've got to go. Will Madison be back anytime today?"

"She should."

"Well, ask her to call me, even if it's late. I really want to talk to her."

Clark started his truck and drove right past the reporters to a quiet neighborhood in Newport Beach. Tom Huntington lived there with his wife and their two young girls. Tom was a former Oakland Raider, a wild player who had lived life on the edge. Then, after almost losing his life to a drug over-dose, he had found God. Or, as Tom liked to say, God had found him. Since that day, Tom had worked to build a Christian ministry for professional football players in the Los Angeles area. Clark had heard of Tom's group, the Christian Players, during his days in Seattle. They were very active in doing good works in the surrounding area. And when Clark signed a contract with L.A., Tom had been one of the first people to greet him.

Tom's house was an impressive place with tall Doric pillars and a clay tile roof. In the back a pool sat nestled into a lavish jungle of landscaping. The arrangement of expensive Land Cruisers, Benzes, and Lexuses spilling out of the driveway and into the street wouldn't have raised a single eyebrow with the neighbors except that they knew it meant the Juggernauts faithful were meeting there as they did every Tuesday almost year-round. Sometimes the neighborhood kids would wait around outside and ambush the players on their way to their vehicles when they were flushed with goodwill. The only exception was during the five weeks of training camp, when no one had time for even a prayer meeting.

Inside the house, nearly two dozen teammates were spread out around Tom's living room, weighing down the tastefully plush furniture, each with his Bible in hand. They were reading Christ's parable about the sower of seeds. Clark sat down amid a flurry of good-hearted greetings. He knew by their tones that his teammates had yet to hear he'd been let go. Clark fixed his mind on the seeds that grew among the weeds, choked off by the cares and concerns of this world. That would be him if he let what was happening get him down. He couldn't do that. Clark bowed his head as he listened. He had to turn it over to God, his will be done.

After the closing prayer, Tom Huntington stood up to speak.

"I want to remind everybody that Friday night is the bachelor auction at the Century Plaza for St. Jude Hospital. I hope the married guys will come and bring their wives, just to support the event, and for you single guys . . ." Tom let loose one of his bashful chuckles. "Well, make sure you look your best. Every dollar you raise goes to a great cause. This is the kind of good work that we were talking about at last week's meeting. This is a great way for you guys to use your blessings as professional athletes to witness for Jesus. With all the bad things people see athletes involved in, this is a good opportunity to set an example."

There were nods and assurances of attendance as the players filed out into the afternoon sunlight. When Tom gave the call to duty, this group of players went. They were powerful Christians, each of them committed to giving 10 percent of their salary to Tom's ministry, the Christian Players. As a group they declared that if they ever did win the Super Bowl, they would use the opportunity to glorify Jesus Christ, to spread the word, and to let people know that it was the power of Jesus that enabled them to win the big one.

Clark hung back until the rest of his teammates had gone.

"You okay?" Tom said to him, giving his good shoulder a friendly squeeze.

Clark nodded but said, "They cut me."

The ever-present light that shone in Tom's eyes dimmed momentarily. "Are you okay?" he asked, narrowing his eyes with concern.

Clark nodded again and said, "I don't want to get choked off by the cares and concerns of this world."

"Yes," Tom said slowly, "that's right, but that doesn't mean we have to be completely unaffected by traumatic events, and I know this is a traumatic event."

"It's not like someone died," Clark said with a nervous laugh.

"No, but it's like part of you died," Tom said quietly. "Remember, I know what it's about. Sometimes you guys forget I was a player just because I'm skinny and worn out."

"I know you're a player," Clark said.

Tom had played wide receiver for the Raiders in the seventies until drugs and age had slowed him down. Since then, a maniacal regimen of long-distance running had left him thinner than he was as a player. That and a receding line of graying hair made him look nearly frail, one of the last people someone would guess as having played in the NFL. The only hint might have been the unusual intensity of his pale green eyes.

"No matter how strong your faith is, it still hurts," Tom said, hugging Clark.

"I know."

Chapter 5

Madison McCall took the dark-paneled elevator to the top floor of the building that was home to Caldburn, Baxter and Thrush. A handsome associate in his early twenties with close-cropped hair and a goatee tried hard to hide the fact that he was checking her out. She warned him off with a frown, but smiled inwardly. She was close enough to forty that it felt good to be mistaken for someone much younger.

In truth, Madison drew looks from men of all ages, even when she wasn't expensively dressed and made up for an appearance in court. Her height was just above average, but her long legs and strong posture gave her the appearance of being taller. Her frame, while athletic, had enough curves to steer well clear of androgyny. Her light brown hair was straight and silky, and by changing how she wore it she could present a different look for almost every working day of the week. Her nose was a little long, but it fit her face, and her eyes were an iridescent bottle green.

Madison's office was in the west corner facing the Colorado River and the Austin foothills beyond. It was the only top-floor corner office occupied by someone who wasn't a direct descendant of Caldburn, Baxter, or Thrush. Madison liked to feel that her office was the result of her prowess in the courtroom, but deep down she knew that it was more because of the money her sports agency brought into the firm's coffers than the clients she defended from an overzealous district attorney.

Outside Madison's office, her secretary, Sharon, sat like a protective gargoyle at her desk. Built like a fireplug, she wore her carrot-colored hair short and spiked. Before Madison reached the end of the hallway, Sharon was already on her feet with her mouth going strong. Madison walked past, absorbing the most important items on the move.

"The DA called and she wants to talk about the Vecchio matter," Sharon said, following Madison through the doorway to her office and into the expansive room. "Mr. Aguillar wants you to call him before the day is over, he says he wants to plead guilty and get it all over with; the Polt deposition has been canceled for tomorrow morning, so I moved your flight to L.A. up two hours, that will let you get in for dinner; and Chris wants you to try to use the extra time to meet with Armand Ulrich because they just cut Clark Cromwell; the dean of the UCLA law school called to invite you to a VIP cocktail party at her home on Friday night; and you're confirmed at the Hotel Bel Air for four days and nights."

"Anything else important?" Madison said as she slumped into her chair with a sigh.

Sharon caught her breath and said, "Nothing too urgent. That guy Cartwright from *USA Today* called again; just wants half an hour. He'll buy lunch. Everything else is right there in front of you: twenty-seven other phone messages, thirteen faxes, and four e-mails not counting the junk.

"Uh," Sharon hesitated, twirling a finger in her spiked hair. "Do you mind if I ask whether you won or lost? I mean,

I can usually tell by the way you look, but you look kind of neutral . . ."

"I guess I won," Madison said, giving her chair half a spin and looking out at the long green river snaking through the city, "but not the way I wanted to."

Sharon raised one eyebrow and held her ground.

"We didn't get a verdict," Madison explained, sensing Sharon's curiosity. "Before they could come back the DA offered me a plea I couldn't in good conscience refuse. I wanted to, because I think I would have gotten an acquittal, but when you're talking about the difference between taking a chance on jail, no matter how small it is, and guaranteeing just probation, you take the deal."

"Well, if anyone knows how hard you worked on that case, it's me, and I can't think anyone would blame you for wanting to get the verdict, especially since we all know the only kind of verdicts you get are the good kind."

"Thanks, Sharon," Madison said, spinning her chair back toward the room with a weak smile. "No calls and no meetings, please. I need to think."

"Coffee?"

"You're an angel."

"Yeah, people tell me that all the time. Still no milk?"

"I don't know," Madison said. Through her blouse she pinched the skin just above her waistband. The secretary rolled her eyes.

"Oh, what the hell, yes. No, no, don't. I don't need it."

"One fat-free coffee on the way," Sharon said with a disapproving frown, closing the door as she went.

Madison turned back to the river. After a few minutes of contemplation she looked up as the door opened, expecting coffee. Instead she got Chris Pelo. He crossed the room without an invitation and promptly hopped up on the corner of her ornately carved Louis XIV antique desk. His legs dangled nearly a foot above the oriental rug.

"Did you hear?" he said.

"About the Polt deposition, the Vecchio matter, or the fact that Mr. Aguillar wants to throw himself at the mercy of a merciless judge?"

"No," Chris said without missing a beat, "about Clark Cromwell?"

Madison chuckled quietly through her nose. "Yes," she said. "I heard. And now you want me to throw myself at the mercy of Armand Ulrich before I give my speech at the conference at UCLA on Thursday."

"He's meeting you at Spago at seven-thirty."

"Whoa! Did I miss something?"

"Not yet. You've got until tomorrow night at seven-thirty," Chris said with a juvenile grin that looked pretty silly on a vertically challenged Latin American ex-cop in his mid-forties. Unlike Madison's, Chris's age was more than obvious. His thin, wiry black mustache and an equally unruly thatch of dark strawlike hair were beginning to show random white strands, and his dark face had the look of old leather.

"And," Chris said, sliding a piece of paper her way across the corner of the desk, "here's a short list of ten contact calls I want you to make during the flight."

"Contact calls?" Madison moaned. "We haven't even signed the clients we've got contracts for this year."

"You can't start too soon with these college players. Same thing with free agents."

"Do you remember the days when you used to tell me all I had to do was step in and close the deals?"

"Yeah, your office was . . . let me see, down on twenty-three in those days, wasn't it?" Chris said, still grinning.

"Funny."

"Well, with the Polt thing postponed I figured you wouldn't mind. You have to be in L.A. anyway."

Madison thought about Clark Cromwell's situation for a moment, then said, "I don't remember studying these kinds of contracts back in law school, do you? The kind where one side can breach at any time and the other side gets to pound sand."

"Don't think of it as contract law. Think of it as the Uniform Commercial Code under the failure to deliver goods or services."

"You mean damaged goods," Madison pointed out. "It's like buying a lawn mower, running it down the side of a creek bed, and then refusing to make payments because the blade is bent."

"That's exactly what I want you to say to Armand Ulrich at dinner."

"You mean you don't want me to remind him that he was a player himself once?"

"That won't do you any good. They didn't make the kind of money back then that they make today. He has no sympathy. He'll tell you that in his entire ten-year career he didn't make half as much as he paid to last year's first-round draft pick in signing bonus alone."

"That could cause a shortage of sympathy."

"The more money people make," Chris said wryly, "the less sympathy they get. That's why I don't feel bad having you go to L.A. two hours early."

Madison gave him the finger and Chris laughed out loud.

"I knew all this exposure to the world of football would change you," he said.

"You forgot that I live with two football players. The only reason I'm doing it is because I like Clark Cromwell and I think it stinks the way they do this. It's exactly what they did to Cody."

Cody Grey was Madison's husband, a former player for the Texas Outlaws who was cut midseason in his final year after playing a series of games with a novocaine-filled knee for the good of the team. When he could no longer move well enough to make a tackle, that same team abruptly cut him.

"It's what they do to everybody," Chris reminded her.

"But Clark Cromwell?" Madison said. "That's like knocking down a . . . a Boy Scout, or pulling Santa Claus's beard. Why don't we just call some other teams?"

"I did," Chris told her grimly. "Believe it or not, I spoke to every team that has any real need for a blocking back . . ."

"And?"

"The Jets offered me minimum salary if he passes their physical," Chris said glumly.

"Minimum salary?"

"No one wants to touch him with this neck injury. They think even if he does heal that he won't ever be the same. He makes his living knocking into people with his head. No one wants to take the chance. Besides, he's old."

"Yeah," Madison said. "I forgot. He's thirty-one."

"That's old."

"So Ulrich is our best chance?"

"I think our only chance."

"And what makes you think he'll do anything more than what the Jets offered?"

"Because he's having dinner with you," Chris said, smiling big. "And you're a lawyer . . . and you're a woman."

"Now I've heard it all."

"How was the case?" Chris said, knowing by her reaction that she'd do what he'd asked and wanting to change the subject.

Madison threw her hands up over her head. "Lousy."

"I heard you got a plea without jail."

"I did," Madison sulked. "But I'm so tired of this kind of crap. I had a middle-aged accountant who walked into his daughter's home to find his son-in-law beating her with a piece of hose, probably not for the first time. My client hits this creep with a fire poker and breaks his neck. The DA was pressing for attempted murder and aggravated assault. I could have had that jury acquitting him with my opening statement alone. I think the DA knew it, so instead of going through with the trial she offers me third-degree assault, still a felony, but with the judge agreeing to suspend the sentence. It just burned me to have to stand there next to that man and hear him plead guilty to *anything*.

"There's almost a formula these days for what the DA will take on any given case," Madison complained. "No one wants to just try a case anymore and let it all ride on the jury. That's what I miss. It seems like a long time since I had a good courtroom battle."

"Maybe you're representing the wrong kind of clients."

"Meaning?"

Chris shrugged. "Just that in the last couple of years since you've gotten famous, you've had your pick of clients and you only seem to take the innocent-looking ones."

"I like to believe in my clients, thank you," she snapped, her back stiffening.

Chris nodded his head and said, "Then you'll keep getting pleas. If it's obvious to you that they're innocent, chances are the same will hold true for the jury, the judge, and eventually even the DA's office, although I admit it takes them a while. You need to take on some clients that are on the edge. Just something to think about."

"Maybe you're right. If trouble won't find me," she said sarcastically, "maybe I'll have to go find some trouble."

The next evening Madison was at Spago at the appointed

time. Ulrich was late. When he finally did arrive, he turned some heads. Ulrich was six foot eight, and while the distribution of his frame had shifted over time, he was still massive. An outdated seersucker suit and a broad blue bow tie did nothing to hide his bulk. His face and the shining bald dome of his head were deeply tanned, and he could easily have been the villain in a James Bond movie. His appearance and the fact that he was the owner of a highly successful NFL franchise made him a celebrity in a town of celebrities. In fact, Madison was certain that he had drawn as much attention from the other patrons in the restaurant as Oliver Stone had when he arrived twenty minutes earlier. Of course, Ulrich may have muscled in on some of the famous film director's notoriety by stopping at his table for a convivial five-minute chat.

Finally Ulrich sat down across from Madison and extended his mighty hand. "Madison," he said congenially. The two of them had dealt directly with each other during Clark Cromwell's contract negotiation less than a year ago, and Madison had insisted on his calling her by her first name.

"Armand," she said, returning his smile.

"I'm sorry about that," he said, inclining his head toward Stone, "but he's working on a film about the NFL and because he's in my backyard the other owners around the league seem to think I have some influence as to how we'll all be portrayed."

"They must not have seen *JFK*," Madison replied.

"Beg pardon?"

"If they'd seen *JFK*," Madison said, "they'd know that Oliver Stone does his own thing and everyone else be damned. I mean, the Pentagon was livid about how he made them out to be part of the conspiracy, but he went right ahead and did it anyway."

"Well," the owner said, unfolding his napkin, "he's a big 49ers fan, so I promised him he could meet the team when they play here next season. I'm sure Carmen won't mind. I had some associates of his as guests in my box for the Jets game last season."

"That's the way the world works," Madison said with a winning smile. "You do something for me, I do something for you."

"The lamb is particularly good," Ulrich said as the waiter handed Madison a menu. He ordered a bottle of wine before saying, "So what's that something?"

"Clark Cromwell," she said. "I want you to pay him like the player he is."

"You mean the player he was."

"No, I mean the player he is," Madison insisted. "He'll be every bit as productive this season as he has for the last eight."

"Of course you're confident in his *abilities*," Ulrich said leaning forward. "I am too. But he's not *worth* what he was. I'm sure you've learned that from the response he's gotten from other teams. So, you want me to pay him like the player he *was*. Am I right?"

"Yes," Madison said reluctantly. "But you know what he can do. You know what he will do, what he's done, what he's meant to this team."

"How could I forget?" Ulrich said, raising both eyebrows and giving her a twisted smile. "You reminded me day after day when we worked out his deal last summer. That's why I gave him a million-dollar signing bonus and over two million dollars in salary last year, and that's why it doesn't bother me to offer you three hundred and fifty thousand this year."

"That's an insult to a player of his caliber," Madison said flatly. "That's barely over the minimum."

"It's more than anyone else is going to give him."

The waiter returned and the two of them ordered, Madison intentionally not getting the lamb, even though it sounded good.

"I want you to give Clark a contract that's respectable," she said after the waiter had gone. "I don't want to have to dance around for the next six months negotiating. You know what kind of a player he is, and you know what kind of a person he is. This is the guy that parents point to as an example of what's good in sports. In today's sports world, he's an unusual and valuable commodity."

"Unusual, I'll give you . . . Valuable? Look around. It makes nice soft news, but people aren't interested in a good guy. People want a championship team. Period. The kind of person he is has nothing to do with it."

Then, in another tone of voice, a voice without passion, he said, "I've got to clear enough money under the cap to sign a major free-agent running back. This is about winning a championship, Madison. You know that. There are only two NFL owners who ever played the game, and it's very important to me to show the rest of them that if you played, you know what it takes to win. It starts at the top. I have the right coach, the right defense, the right quarterback, and an adequate offensive line. What I don't have is a runner, so I'm going to buy one. That's why I'm cramming down every salary I can. I can't pay Clark two point five million when I know I can get him for three-fifty."

"If you sign who I think you're going to sign, you'll need Clark Cromwell even more. Do you think you can have a team made up entirely of criminals and thugs and win a championship? If you sign Trane Jones, that's all the more reason to pay Clark a decent number and have a decent person to counterbalance what you'll have. The character of a team can be just as important as the talent," Madison said passionately. "You know that better than me."

The wine came. Ulrich tasted it and told the waiter to pour.

"I'll pay your client half a million this year, Madison, but I'll only do it on one condition . . ."

"And that is?"

"You owe me a favor."

"A favor?"

"Yes, something out of the ordinary. I don't know what, but I have a great respect for you and your abilities as an attorney. It would be worth it to me to know that if I needed you for something you'd be there."

"There are some things I don't do," Madison said.

"I'm not talking about something unethical," Ulrich said with an avuncular smile and a casual wave of his hand. "I'm just talking about something you might not prefer to do. Maybe the son of a friend gets into trouble with drugs and needs a good lawyer. Maybe my board of directors accuses me of absconding with money from the corporate treasury. I don't know what it is, a favor. That's what I want in return. Otherwise, you can take the three-fifty and better luck next time."

"A million," Madison said. "My favors are seven-figure favors."

Ulrich smiled so hard that two hidden crow's-feet broke out in the thick skin around his eyes.

"I can give you a seven in the figure, but not seven figures. I'll give you seven hundred thousand, but no more. You're right about Trane Jones. I'm going to have to make him the highest-paid player in the league to sign him, and I need all the cap room I can get."

"Seven-fifty," Madison said. "I'm talking about respect,

and three quarters of a million is respectable. Seven hundred thousand isn't."

"You have a deal, young lady," Ulrich said.

"Good," Madison said, raising her glass. "Here's to the perpetuation of decency in sports."

"Here's to . . . reciprocity," said the owner, and they drank.

Chapter 6

Conrad Dobbins's home was a massive contemporary structure perched on one of the highest peaks in West Hollywood. Four men including Dobbins sat around a glass patio table that seemed almost suspended in the night. The lights of Los Angeles flickered below. The men had been playing dominoes since just after dinner, and a warm breath from the distant Pacific never induced them to move inside.

Someone said, "Yo, I heard some shit went down in New Orleans."

"Conrad, shut that shit off, will ya?" Trane Jones said to his agent. There weren't many people who could talk that way to Conrad Dobbins, but Trane was one of them.

Conrad leaned forward and clicked off the 8mm camera that sat on the tabletop in front of him. He wore a thick gold medallion that clanked against the table. His head was bald and counterbalanced by an angry Fu Manchu mustache and beard. Like Trane, he wore sunglasses even at night.

"I got this young thing, pretty young thing," Trane said slyly, "and we're gettin' it on all night an' I wake up an' she's dead as hell an' motherfuckin' blood is everywhere.

"So first thing I'm thinking," Trane continued, the light

reflecting off the nearby pool's surface giving his evil grin an otherworldly quality, "is . . . I fucked that bitch to motherfuckin' death!"

Snickers from around the table, until Trane slapped down his last bone and snatched the stack of hundreds.

"Fuck you," muttered Lester Spinnicker in his booming bass. He was Conrad's top boxer at the moment, the number-one heavyweight contender.

"That's it for me," murmured Shawntell Christianson.

"Bitch!" exclaimed Dobbins.

"But that bitch really died from the junk, right?" Christianson said with a somewhat worried expression. He wanted to clarify the story. Christianson was the L.A. Lakers' sixth man and a soft brother. He knew the hard life from growing up in south Philly, but his grandmother's upbringing had indelibly marked him with a sense of compassion that none of the rest of them shared.

"Yeah, but how am I suppose to know that then?" Trane said, looking around the table to make sure his boys knew the gravity of the situation. "I'm thinkin' she had a goddamn *hemorrhage* from me just working it an' the bitch bled to motherfuckin' death. I'm tellin' ya, blood was all over that motherfuckin' bed."

"An' you—"

"Called my man," Trane said, looking into the agent's passive reptilian eyes. "What else?"

Everyone nodded in agreement, even the hulking figure of Zee, who stood just out of the lamplight leaning against the railing behind Dobbins's chair. In a crowd of top-caliber athletes, Zee was still imposing. He was massive. On his head was a short mop of Rastafarian locks, and a jagged scar hopscotched down the side of his face, heightening the intensity of his pug-faced scowl.

"'Bout a half hour later," Trane continued, "brothers was

comin' out of the motherfuckin' woodwork! They went to work like they was some kinda military task force—"

"Like *Delta Force* or something!" Spinnicker suggested.

"Yeah, like the motherfuckin' fuckin' *Delta Force*! They sealed off that buildin' like it was the motherfuckin' raid on Entebbe, guns everywhere."

"I saw that movie, man! That was the Israelis! They kicked some *ass*."

"And up backs this white van, right up to the motherfuckin' front door, an' they wrap that bitch up in plastic and cart her ass off like a motherfuckin' *rug* or somethin'. Then, the head brother—what'd you call that head brother, Conrad?"

"That was the Rocket," Dobbins said with the hint of a smile. "Rocket was my welterweight back in the seventies. Had a goddamn good punch but the motherfucker bled too much."

"Yeah, Rocket. Brother was like ice. A black motherfucker, black as tar. So the Rocket gets ol' boy Gaston—"

"The manager—"

"Yeah, an' just puts a gun right up to his heart and tells that motherfucker he didn't see nothin', an' ol' boy pees right in his motherfuckin' *pants* and starts blubberin' about his mama an' how she's countin' on him and then Rocket says, 'Shut the fuck up,' an' ol' boy does *quick*."

"So Rocket says, 'Who's this bitch's pimp?' An' Gaston tells him quick. And we get in the van an' go straight to where Gaston said the pimp was."

"Rocket don't care 'bout no pimp," Dobbins explained to them. "A ho an' a pimp and Rocket works it all out quick."

Trane nodded, but flashed Dobbins a scowl so he'd shut up and let him tell the story.

"So the bitch was an illegal alien," Trane continued, "from fuckin' Chechnya or somethin'. An' the only one really knows the deal with her is the pimp, an' Rocket just walks right into that pimp's place, one a them nice old places off Saint Charles Street, and me an' the other brothers waitin' in the van with the dead bitch in back—"

"Like a *rug*," someone said.

"Just *like* a motherfuckin' rug, yeah," Trane said with a grin so big you could see his gold-plated incisors. "And next thing I know the brothers is loadin' two more motherfuckin' bodies into the back!"

"The pimp?"

"And his bitch! Rocket, he just did 'em, bang-bang, and wrapped 'em up in motherfuckin' plastic."

"No muss, no fuss," Dobbins said with a satisfied nod.

"Shit."

"But this's what freaks me," Trane said. He stopped to take a swig from his drink and make careful eye contact with his cronies before going on. "Me an' those brothers go straight to where they're buildin' a casino on the corner of Canal an' Tchoupitoulas!"

"Downtown," Dobbins explained.

"Right in the middle of the motherfuckin' city!" Trane said.

"In the goddamn *day?*" Christianson wanted to know.

"Monday mornin'," Trane said. "So Rocket pulls into that site and backs the motherfuckin' van right up to a ditch. Then that boy hops out and gets into a motherfuckin' cement mixer, a *truck*. The brothers dump the bodies in that ditch. It's a hole, you know, with boards all around it."

"For the foundation," Dobbins said.

"Yeah, an' as soon as they're down in there the Rocket starts mixin' cement an' the shit starts shootin' right in over the top of 'em."

"And nobody's around?" Christianson said incredulously.

"Nobody right there. There was people working around,

but we was like in the corner of the site and there was a big motherfuckin' fence on the street side and a pile of dirt on the other an' Rocket just filled that ditch to the top. Then we get in the van an' he drops me off at my car an' that's it. Didn't say nothin'."

The steady hum of night insects filled the silence while the men gauged one another's reaction.

"I told him to stay outta trouble," Dobbins said, as if Trane wasn't there.

"We got paid," Trane said.

"Twenty million up front, biggest deal in the NFL," Spinnicker said with a wistful nod of his head.

"But that shit was *too* close," Dobbins complained. "I can't call the motherfuckin' Rocket every time. We were lucky it went off smooth."

"You got people in L.A.," Trane said casually.

"I got people everywhere," Dobbins admitted. "Anyone knows that, it's you. You cost me more favors than the rest of my clients combined."

"I make ya mo' money too," Trane said with a grin.

"Twenty million," Christianson repeated.

"He don't do too bad wit' me," Spinnicker complained.

"Yeah, you make me money," Dobbins said to Trane with disgust. "But one day you gonna go too far, an' then all yo' money an' all my connections ain't gonna be worth a rat's dick."

"Hey, I was doin' what I was supposed to be doin'," Trane glowered. "You said, 'You wanna bang a bitch around? Get you a ho.' So I get a ho an' she OD's. That's my fault? Fuck you."

Zee shifted behind the agent.

"An' fuck you, too!" Trane said, scowling at the enormous bodyguard in the shadows. "I'll take you out like a bitch!"

"Easy, man."

"Go cool, Trane."

"Chill."

Dobbins seemed unaffected. He looked up calmly from the domino he'd been twisting end over end.

"You're bad motherfucker, Trane Jones," he said with a deadpan face. "But that's the way I like you."

Chapter 7

"You're a good man, Clark Cromwell," Tom's wife, Vikki, said to him just before he walked out onstage at the ballroom of the Century Plaza. She knew what had happened to him with the team. Pretty much everyone did by now, so it was particularly embarrassing to go out there and have himself auctioned off with everyone knowing he'd been let go.

"They should have saved me till the end," he said, looking into her compassionate eyes. "I'm damaged goods."

"You'll probably bring in more than anyone," she said hopefully.

After finishing a list of his accomplishments and detailing the elegant evening in store for the highest bidder, the MC announced Clark's name. The PA system let fly with a little screech and Clark walked out onto the temporary stage amid polite clapping. He tripped just a bit on a duct-taped seam. His cheeks reddened.

He was wearing an ill-fitting rented tuxedo from a store that had donated all the evening wear for the bachelors being auctioned. The old man who'd tried to fit him became exasperated after an hour of fussing and finally used safety pins to gather up the excess material. Any jacket that could encompass Clark's shoulders and any shirt that could fit his neck were designed for a fat man. His legs, too, were cramped despite the fact that the pants, like the coat, were gathered together in the back by two industrial-size safety pins.

Standing there shifting uncomfortably beneath a horseshoe of pink and white balloons, Clark's attention was arrested by a woman. In a town where so many people were beautiful, she was the first to grab him by the throat with her looks alone. She wasn't flashy. He didn't go for that. She was pure and plain and simple, but still incredibly beautiful. Her blond hair was pulled back and unadorned. Her navy blue dress was unassuming. If she wore makeup, it was so slight it wasn't worth mentioning. If she were spoiled, you would never know by her ingenuous smile. If she were rich, the only giveaway was when she started to bid for Clark and kept bidding against a plastic-looking redhead in her mid-forties wearing an emerald green sequin dress.

The two women went back and forth, the redhead staring malignantly at the blonde, the blonde completely unfazed. When the auctioneer went from four thousand to five thousand, Clark heard someone in the audience gasp. There was big money in L.A., but only Mitch Faulkner, the team's quarterback, had brought in more than three thousand dollars.

At six thousand the redhead hesitated.

"Ten thousand," the blonde said in a quiet voice that seemed out of place.

The redhead pursed her lips and shook her head no.

Clark felt his face go hot.

"Ten thousand once, ten thousand twice, sold to the young lady for ten thousand dollars!"

Applause erupted from the crowd. Clark turned sheepishly and walked backstage.

"Clark!" Vikki was beaming. "You were great!"

Clark shrugged. He felt like a complete idiot. In the green room the players who had already been auctioned slapped his back and teased him mercilessly, accusing him of a setup.

"Bet it's his sister!" someone yelled above the din.

"You ain't that good-looking," barked Garvey, the center, who'd brought in a measly nine hundred dollars.

"I know that," Clark said in a subdued voice, unable to think of an appropriate response.

"He knows that!" Garvey bellowed. "What a pisser!"

Clark hid in the bathroom backstage. He let the reception get into full swing before stepping from behind the curtain and quickly mixing into the crowd.

"Champagne?" asked a young waiter with a tray full of long-stemmed glasses filled to the brim.

Clark broke out a guilty smile, nodded, and took two, wondering if he'd imagined it or if the kid had really winked.

His conscience delicately nagged him for having the wine, but only until the alcohol reached his brain. Then he felt much better, and his unusual indulgence didn't seem to be that big a deal. Emboldened, he began to search the room for his charity date.

She was standing with two other women not far from the bar beside a sixteen-foot column of the ubiquitous pink and white balloons. The other two looked more like L.A.—colored hair, tight dresses, heavy lipstick—real vamps.

They were talking.

"God, Angel, it's so you to do something crazy," Clark heard one of them say.

The talking stopped when they realized Clark was hovering behind them. The two other women eyed him up and down. One gave a quiet giggle. Clark tugged at his ill-fitting pants.

"Hello," said the quiet pretty blonde, extending her hand, "I'm Annie."

"Clark," he said, trying not to look at the two friends.

"Bye, girls," Annie said pleasantly, and they were gone.

"That was easy," he said. "'Bye, girls' and they're gone . . ."

"Old friends," she told him. "They're bored with me now anyway. They're from a different way of life."

"Can I . . . get you a drink, or . . . or something?"

"Oh, I already had one. That's my limit," she said cheerfully. "But if you want, you go right ahead."

"Gosh, that's so nice to hear you say," Clark told her. "I don't drink. I mean, I don't normally drink. I'm not drinking now. I mean, really drinking, but I had a drink. Well, I had two, but it was because I guess I was . . . I don't know. I don't really drink."

"Sounds like you need another one," Annie said, deadpan.

They both laughed. Clark suddenly didn't mind that his tuxedo fit poorly. He didn't care if his teammates saw him blushing. He wasn't even worried about the two glasses of champagne.

"Ten thousand dollars," he said.

"I don't usually do things like that either, but . . . well, it's a great cause and I'll be honest, it's not my money. It's my father's money. My father's dead, but he had a thing about charity or at least the appearance of charity. Part of his will reads that I have ten thousand dollars a year to give to charity. So every year I just kind of put it all in one place. When my friends told me about this action and it was for St. Jude, well . . . why not, I figured."

"Why didn't you just go right to ten?" Clark said with a crooked grin.

"Maybe I thought I could get two of you for five apiece?" she said.

"Or ten for one," he said.

"I only wanted one," she told him. Her eyes were pale green, almost milky, like the stones he'd seen in some Indian jewelry on a trip to Mexico.

A charge of power went right through his middle. It was one of those moments. He'd been expecting less than nothing from the evening, and now . . . She was beautiful beyond description.

"Do you realize," he told her, "we've been standing here for five minutes without looking away from each other's eyes?"

"Isn't that how people usually talk to each other?" she said.

"No, they don't," he said. "They look away, off to the side or at their shoes or watch or something, but people don't usually just look right into someone's eyes."

"Does it mean anything?" she said with a straight face.

Clark didn't know how to take her. He chuckled lightly and looked away.

"I broke the spell!" she said.

"No," he told her, looking back. "I don't think you did."

Clark had scheduled his date with the people from St. Jude for the night after the fund-raiser because he wanted to get it over with. Now he wished he'd had a little more time to prepare. He picked Annie up in a limousine only because it was part of the deal. He didn't want to seem ungrateful to the people who had worked so hard at the event. He wore a camel hair blazer, the same one he wore every season to the team's kickoff luncheon, the only formal jacket he owned. Underneath it were a pink oxford shirt and a pair of his nicest jeans with his ostrichskin cowboy boots. The restaurant where they were going was new but fancy. When he called they told him jackets were required, unusual in L.A.

The car pulled up to a handsome beachfront condo in Santa Monica and Clark went to the door. He was surprised to see Annie in the same dress she'd been wearing the night before.

"I don't really have a lot in the way of dress-up clothes," she said apologetically when they were seated inside the car.

"Really? Me too," Clark told her. "This is my only jacket. I never go to places like this. You probably know that from the tux I had on."

"That wasn't a custom tux?" she said, her eyes widening.

He looked at her closely in the dim light of the car to see if she was for real.

Finally she said, "I thought those safety pins were monogrammed."

He laughed. "Pretty bad, huh?"

"Look, just so you know," she told him seriously, "part of the reason I bid so high for you was the bad tux. Not just that, but that was the thing that gave me an idea that what's on the inside is a lot more important to you than what's on the outside."

"Yeah," he said slowly. "It is."

"I didn't really grow up that way," she told him. "It was one of those households where he who dies with the most toys wins."

"But not you," he said.

"No. I saw what it did and I promised myself I wouldn't have that."

Clark wondered about the damage, but knew enough not to ask. Instead he said, "I grew up with my dad for a while, in Alaska. When I was thirteen he died and I went to live with my mom in Portland. Clothes and things like that . . ." He shook his head. "No, she didn't go in for that stuff. I remember she used to get my sneakers at the grocery store.

She was the only person I ever knew who bought sneakers at the grocery store."

"I don't think my mother even went to the grocery store," Annie said. "That's how out of touch we were."

"My mom and my sister never seemed to care," Clark said. "It was like they were on some different wavelength. I tried not to mind, but for some reason, that kind of stuff, you know, drinking powdered milk because it saved the environment—"

"Saved the environment?"

Clark shrugged. "You know, less packaging. One big box could mix up about ten gallons. Think of the plastic we never used."

"I grew up on Diet Coke," Annie said. "No calcium, no vitamin D, lots of packaging." She smiled warmly at him. "But it must have been good in some ways to grow up that way."

"It was. I sure appreciate everything I have now. I don't worship things, but I appreciate having, like, my truck, or, you know, a dishwasher."

"That's a wonderful way to be," Annie said, the glimmer in her eyes letting Clark really believe it. They rode for a while, each in their own thoughts.

"How about you?" Clark said. "There must have been good things."

"I got a BMW for my sweet sixteen," she said absently, looking out the window.

Clark nodded to himself. That was something. "I had a Subaru wagon when I was sixteen. I bought it with money I made unloading fish at the market downtown. Then we had an ice storm one night and the accelerator froze up when I was starting it and it shot right down the driveway and into the street and I got broadsided by a delivery truck and flipped about ten times."

"Ten times?"

"Well, probably six, but it might as well have been ten."

"Were you hurt?"

"It scalped me," he said.

She looked at him funny.

"Cut the top of my head off like a divot of grass. It kind of hung there. It didn't hurt, but you should have seen my mom's face when she came out of the house after she heard the crash, screaming her head off. Then she saw me and passed out, right there in the street. And I was so worried about her I didn't even realize about my scalp until the paramedics showed up and the girl, she bent right over and starting heaving when she saw me. Then I realized I had blood running all down my face and I felt up on my head and felt my skull. It was all sticky with blood but I knew what it was and then I started freaking out."

"But you were all right?"

"Yeah," Clark said, proudly pulling back his hair to show her his hairline. "They sewed it back on real good and you can't even tell unless you look real close in the light."

"So that's not why you keep your hair long," she said.

"No. I just keep it that way."

"I like it . . ." she said.

The car pulled up in front of an antebellum-style mansion on Wilshire.

"So here we are," Clark said.

The driver hurried out to open the door for them, but before he could get there Clark was already out on the curb. He held out his arm for Annie and they mounted the brick steps. Inside they met the maître d's frown with expectant smiles.

"Cromwell for two," Clark said.

"I'm sorry, Mr. Cromwell," he said, barely hiding his disdain, "but we do not allow jeans at Le Bon."

Despite his frail build the man looked the part in his tailored European suit with his pencil mustache and slicked-back hair.

Clark fumbled with his words. His face felt warm, but he forgot everything when Annie erupted in French. He had no idea what she was saying but he knew she was chewing him out pretty good. It was as if she'd become another person altogether, rage seething from her imperious scowl as she barked. It was enough of a scene so that the people in the room immediately adjacent to the entryway stopped eating to watch. When she was done it was the maître d's turn to blush. He bent and mumbled a quiet apology before leading them to a wonderful table in the back by the window overlooking a courtyard fountain.

When they were alone Clark quietly said, "I'm sorry."

"No," she said, still scowling in the candlelight, "*he's* sorry." Then her face softened. "Can we forget about it?"

"Sure."

"I mean really forget it?" she said, then paused. "Most people can't, you know. People can't put the negative things behind them very easily. They seem to stick."

"I'm a Christian," he blurted out, looking at her closely to gauge her reaction. He was glad he had finally said it, that he had gotten it out. "That's, kind of, where everything starts for me."

"That helps you put things behind you?" she asked after a moment.

"If you don't think of your life as your own," Clark said eagerly, "if you give your life to God, then you trust that He'll take care of everything . . ."

"I've always been interested in religion."

"It's not just religion. It's giving your life over to God through His Son, Jesus Christ. Being a Christian isn't the same as being religious."

Clark was glowing now, excited, and Annie wasn't giving

him any indication she wanted him to stop. She definitely seemed interested.

"A lot of people aren't comfortable talking about it," he told her.

"Why? It doesn't bother me," she said.

"It used to bother me . . . I didn't want to think about it. It's like changing your whole life when you believe. It changes the way you think about everything. For some people that's harder than others. Some people, like our quarterback, Mitch Faulkner, they find their way almost without trying. Others need to be led by the nose. That was me."

"By your mother?"

"No, it was when my father died."

The waiter came and began to tell them about the menu. Clark looked at him impatiently. When he was gone, Clark told Annie everything that had happened. And as he spoke it seemed that it had been just weeks and not years ago.

Chapter 8

Along Highway 165, about seventeen miles from a town called Chinook Bend, a snow-encrusted school bus dropped Clark off, same as it did every other day. He shifted a canvas laundry bag full of football equipment over his shoulder and headed home. Today was the day the basketball coach swore he'd cut the locks off the lockers of the football players who refused to vacate their hallowed private locker room. The equipment had been waiting for this day in Clark's locker for over a month, and it stunk to high hell even in the cold. From the main road it was a half-mile walk in the dark and the cold, and a big wind was whipping down from the Crazy Mountains to the north. Clark tucked his nose beneath the rim of his scarf and leaned into a gust.

As cold as he was, by the time he reached the front yard he knew better than to go inside empty-handed. That could get you a wrench upside the head. He pulled back an electric blue tarp from the woodpile, sending a swarm of fat powdery flakes spinning off into the afternoon darkness. The days when it was light for twenty hours at a time seemed like another lifetime. Clark was only thirteen.

He secured the laundry bag to his back by crossing the

strap on his chest like a bandolier and loaded his arms with wood all the way up until the rough splinters scraped against the underside of his chin. On the porch he stumbled. Logs thundered into the front door. Two sticks into his cleanup the door burst open and his father filled the frame. The older Cromwell surveyed the mess from behind his thick black beard, quickly deduced what had happened, and disappeared behind the door without a word. Clark reloaded, then braced one side of the pile against his knee as he groped for the door handle.

Once inside he quickly shut the door, then set down his wood one stick at a time into the bin beside the stove. There was no other source of heat in the cabin, and Clark knew that if they ran out of fuel in the middle of the night he would be the one groping in the pitch-black for more. He removed his backpack and assessed his father. In one corner of the cabin was his toolbench, and there he sat, hunched over the barrel of his .454, methodically ramming a cleaning rod in and out of its bore. Clark didn't have to be told that he was expected to be up by four and ready to go. He had been raised carefully over the years, and it seemed that the more Clark knew, the less his father spoke.

Clark knew that beneath the placid surface of his father's weatherworn face he burned with rage. He had always been a reticent man, but when Clark's mother took his sister and left for Portland four years ago, something seemed to have broken inside him, leaving him with less feeling for all people—including himself, including Clark. Although Clark could not say why, he was fairly certain that, in part, his father blamed him for what had happened.

His alarm went off the next morning at 3:50. His father never used an alarm, but without it Clark knew he could easily sleep until eight o'clock. There was something about the dreary fall and winter months that left him wanting only to stay tucked beneath his warm covers, at least until a bit of gray light seeped in through the frosted windowpanes. But when they were going for moose, Clark knew oversleeping wasn't tolerated.

Clark hadn't been struck in months, but he suspected that was only because he hadn't given his father a reason. That idea inspired him to jump out of bed in a way that could have been mistaken for excitement. The real thrill of hunting had dissipated over the years as Clark began to realize that they did it out of necessity and not for sport. To Clark, killing a moose was like pulling down trees with the horses, then cutting them up and stacking the wood. It was merely a chore to ensure survival through the winter.

There was a steaming stack of book-thick pancakes on his plate at the kitchen table. His father was already into his second cup of coffee, and his plate was clean except for a few streaks of syrup. Clark wolfed down his breakfast with unfeigned enthusiasm and cleared the table. By the time he'd finished, his father was mounted up and waiting for him at the bottom of the front steps. A high-pressure system had moved in from Russia and the stars were so bright that even without a moon Clark could see the shadows of two horsemen mimicking them as they crossed the frozen creek bed and set out toward the Crazies.

By two o'clock the skies had clouded over and they were onto the blood trail of a gut-shot moose. The animal had been hit shortly after eleven. Clark's father was visibly irritated at not having killed it. To Clark it was impressive that the beast had been hit at all. The shot was well over three hundred yards and taken across a perilous ravine, which was why it had taken them so long to get to the blood trail.

The wind began to gust in their faces and the clouds to churn like a slow-boiling stew. The weather made Clark shifty. Every couple of minutes he couldn't stop himself from glancing up. Even more unnerving was his father's apparent disregard of the coming front. The older man seemed maniacally intent on the trail of blood, and he had that look in his piercing blue eyes that reminded Clark of the times when he drank too much and would sit staring at the fire, violently whittling whole sticks of firewood into toothpicks. Clark never got hit then. His father was a good man and only beat him when he did something wrong. But when he sat there staring and whittling like mad it was like walking by the cage of a snarling Kodiak, scary even though you were safe.

Before too long they stopped on a high ridge that overlooked a large wood. As his father scanned the trees below, Clark watched the older man's expression through the bank of steam that rose from his horse's neck. The wounded moose had clearly headed for the woods, where it would probably lie down. Halfway down the mountain the track crossed an expanse of snow and ice that spanned a chasm whose bottom was indiscernible. The horses were in a trot now, but they pulled up short of the ice bridge so his father could survey the trail. The frozen span looked solid, but Clark knew that appearances could be deceiving. He also knew that his father was anxious to get to the wounded animal before the light faded completely and the weather hit.

They were almost across when Clark's father stopped suddenly and looked back at their own trail. Clark looked, too, and saw clearly the black disk in the snow, one of the binoculars' lens caps, at the place where they'd stopped. Clark's father muttered a curse and violently reined his horse back toward it. Prophetic words of caution logjammed in Clark's throat. The debris of so many broken important moments between them over the past four years since his mother left kept Clark from speaking to his father as a rule.

When the ice sheared, it was with the horrible shriek of

Styrofoam being cut longways by a dull razor. Clark's horse reared, throwing him to safety, before plunging into the abyss that also swallowed his father along with a thousand tons of snow and ice.

Clark sprang to his feet and ran crazily up and down the length of the chasm perilously close to its lip. He screamed for his father until his voice was nothing. In a state of shock, he clumped down the mountainside, reaching the edge of the wood just as the heavy sky began to dump snow in earnest. As cold as it was, Clark knelt and stuffed a handful of powdered snow into his mouth. The tears and the walk had left him dehydrated.

No one would even think of looking for him until Monday, and it would take at least that long for him to make it home on foot. The snow would worsen too. The tent and sleeping bags were gone. He had some matches, but no ax to get enough wood for a fire that could last through the night. Elephant Lake was his only chance. He knew he was about five miles from the small round lake where they had often gone in the summer to fish for rainbow trout. There was a one-room cabin on the eastern shore. With the darkness and the snow, he had no idea if he could find it, but he had to try.

Within an hour's time he could see nothing. Snow swirled madly down at him in the darkness. He could feel it against his face and hear it whispering against the outer shell of his parka. He groped for an alternative to stay alive. If he found a big pine tree he could get out of the wind by burrowing under its branches, but he was afraid of freezing there without a fire. There was nothing else he could think of, so he pulled his hat down tight over his head and pushed on.

After another hour his legs began to tingle from the cold. They grew heavy. His fingertips were beginning to go numb. He suddenly entered another wood and the snow seemed to diminish, but the darkness was now complete.

Nothing looked familiar to him. He sat down to rest, know-ing he shouldn't. Tears welled fresh in his eyes as he won-dered about dying. It seemed to him that right before she left his mother had spoken more about dying than about living. She wasn't afraid to die. He knew that from the defiant tilt of her chin when she'd bucked his father.

She had found God. That's what she said, anyway. She had found God, and God wanted her to go to Portland and take his sister away from life in rural Alaska. Before she left, Clark's mother had imparted much of her wisdom about God to him. He knew from her that the only way to God was through Jesus. He knew from her that you were damned to eternal hell unless saved by Jesus. He also knew that God could perform miracles, that he was alive, and that through prayer he could be convinced to intercede in the misery of one's daily life. But even though Clark had listened to his mother's truths, he'd done nothing about them. He just never got around to it. His father, he knew, hadn't bought a word of it. But his father was dead.

Clark didn't want to die. He knew that. He didn't want to go where his father was. He was afraid, but not of the hell his mother had talked about. Hell was something he couldn't imagine. He was more afraid of nothing. That was tangible. That was terrifying: simply ceasing to exist, ceasing not only to breathe and pump blood through his veins, but also to feel and think altogether, and losing any awareness of anything one way or another. Clark closed his eyes and spilled tears. He prayed to God. He promised. He begged. And when he opened his eyes he saw a light.

That's how he would describe it again and again when witnessing the glory of God during prayer meetings in the coming years. He saw a light and the light was a cabin. Not the Elephant Lake cabin, but a hunting cabin more than three miles away, one he never even knew existed. He remembered three bearded men in flannel shirts and the orange hue of a warm fire. He remembered the black spots on the ends of his fingertips. He remembered the smell of cooking meat. He remembered crying more than he was supposed to. But most of all he remembered the deal he made with God.

"It's true," he said, his eyes glazed from the remembrance, "and I remembered what my mother always said. It's true. It was a cabin. I never even knew it was there and these three guys were there on a hunt . . . It's really true."

"You keep saying that," she said. "I believe you, Clark."

Clark paused to consider her, then said, "You do?"

"Yes. I do."

"Sometimes people don't like to believe what they can't explain," he told her.

"But you explained it," she said. "You said it was a sign from God, that it led you to him."

"You're right," he said.

"Thank you."

He grinned at her. "So that's basically it. After that I stopped trying to control my life and just turned it over to Jesus Christ."

"You said God before."

"What?"

"You said God, that you turned your life over to God."

"Well, God and Jesus are the same thing. Jesus is the Son of God, but he's God. And the Spirit of God, too. It's the Holy Trinity. The three are really one."

Annie looked confused.

Clark said, "The best thing really would be for you to talk to someone who's more knowledgeable than me."

"You sound pretty knowledgeable to me," she said.

"But I'm not. I'm not a biblical scholar. I don't know the original translations or anything like that. Tom does. Tom is my mentor in Christ. Tom Huntington. He was a receiver for the Raiders back in the seventies. He runs a ministry for the team. He's studied the original Greek translations of the Bible. He explains everything a lot better than I do. I'd love for you to meet him."

"I'd like that," Annie said.

The waiter came and asked if they were ready to order. Annie picked up a menu and looked through it quickly. So did Clark.

"Do you see anything that looks to you like a steak on there?" Clark said, red-faced again.

"Something close," she said pleasantly, and ordered for them both.

Chapter 9

Conrad Dobbins strolled off the eighteenth tee with Jack Nicholson, James Woods, and Lou Gossett Jr. It was an L.A. day. The sky was cobalt. The air was dry and breezy, the sun bright. Dobbins talked loudly to Nicholson about his next movie and laughed derisively along with everyone else about the director's sexual preferences. As they approached the stone patio jutting from the clubhouse, Dobbins was acutely aware of the stares they drew. When a preppy-looking white kid wearing a blue blazer and Docksides without socks approached the group, Dobbins was delighted with his wistful inquiry.

"Are you Conrad Dobbins?" the kid asked.

Dobbins could imagine the ire of the movie stars. It wasn't that they needed another autograph hound, it was that he and not they was being sought out in this exclusive setting. It was really sports that owned Americans' hearts. And wherever sports was king, Conrad Dobbins was an uncontested prince. While the major figures of sports had changed over the past twenty years, it seemed that a good deal of them had been and were still being represented by Conrad Dobbins. That meant he was connected. After all, it was the ringside seats in Vegas for the upcoming Spinnicker fight that had led to this golf game in the first place. It certainly wasn't friendship.

"I'm Conrad Dobbins," Dobbins said with gusto. He glanced furtively at his compatriots to gauge the level of their envy. Every actor he'd ever known was remarkably insecure.

The young man held out a folded piece of white paper and Dobbins reached expectantly for a pen.

"You're gonna have to get me a pen, boy," Dobbins said imperiously.

"No, I'm sorry, Mr. Dobbins," said the young kid with what might have been a smirk. "This is a summons to appear in court. You're being served."

Dobbins let out an ill little laugh and went another thirty seconds at least before he realized that the kid was for real. It wasn't that Dobbins hadn't been served before. He'd been served more times than he'd been audited, and that was saying something. It was the insult of being served outside the clubhouse of the L.A. Country Club. It was unforgivable.

"You better hope we don't meet at the wrong place at the wrong time," Dobbins said under his breath. The liquid hate brimming in his eyes quickly wiped the smile from the kid's face.

"I'm—I just work for the firm," he said with an apologetic nod before bowing out of the scene.

Dobbins stuffed the summons carelessly into the pocket of his bright red golf pants and tried to get back to the business of being important. But the day was already tainted. Over drinks and lunch, he had that hollow feeling that everyone was looking at him and seeing right through. The condescending glint in the movie stars' eyes ate away at him like some fast-moving leprosy. Still, through it all, he kept his head up and maintained an endless banter, the same as he would have done if the kid really had just asked for an autograph.

It wasn't until he was ensconced in the passenger seat of his big Mercedes sedan that Dobbins began to vent. Invectives spewed forth like a ruptured sewer line. When the cursing slowed to a trickle, Zee, who was at the wheel, glanced at him questioningly. Summonses and suits had rained down on Dobbins as long as Zee had been working for the powerful agent, but they'd always come from faceless entities, corporations, or government agencies. This was the first time to Zee's knowledge that a *client* had stooped to something as white as a lawsuit.

"Says I stole his money," Dobbins erupted suddenly in disbelief. "Stole his money!

"Gonna kill him now, Zee. Gonna kill that black-as-a-spade motherfuckin' no good pile of shit.

"Uh-uh," the agent continued, shaking his head. "Uh-uh. Can't let that pile a shit live. He lives, next thing you know, we got motherfuckin' brothers suing our ass every other day! Uh-uh. He's gonna die."

Zee silently agreed with a nod. There were plenty of former athletes whose money Conrad had handled loosely. Usually they could be disposed of with threats both veiled and direct. But Maggs hadn't gone away, and if he succeeded in a lawsuit, which he no doubt would, there would be others to follow. If every client Conrad had swindled suddenly sued him, Zee supposed there wouldn't be enough left over for him to get next month's wages. He chewed on the side of his mouth, contemplating just how he was going to kill Albert Maggs. It was always an interesting notion, how to kill someone. Zee liked to do it differently every time if he had the chance.

Dobbins turned his attention to his immense bodyguard. The man had the seat all the way back and reclined at nearly a forty-five-degree angle but still he appeared to have been crammed into the big sedan.

Dobbins remembered the first time he'd ever seen Zee. He'd come to him straight from prison in an ill-fitting suit and a pair of black sneakers. If it wasn't for Zee's reputation, Conrad might have poked fun at him. An associate of Conrad's who ran the south side of Memphis had vouched for his effectiveness and his intelligence. It seemed he had done some time on a technicality for an aggravated assault. The DA wanted to pin Zee for the murder of a man he bludgeoned in a nightclub, but no one ever found the body. The DA still held a grudge, so Conrad's friend said the best thing for everyone was if Zee left town. He had assured Conrad he was getting a topflight man, and his words were true. There wasn't anything Conrad had asked Zee to do that he hadn't accomplished with quick, quiet effectiveness.

Dobbins kept watching his bodyguard as they drove. When Zee stopped chewing his cheek the tip of his purple tongue popped out of the corner of his mouth. His eyes closed briefly as if he were warding off sleep.

"What you thinkin'?" Dobbins asked. Zee was the meanest human being he'd ever known. Conrad had a dog when he was a kid that might have been meaner. It bit everyone, including him, and was known to eat its own shit. Conrad killed it with a pipe one day when it locked onto a neighbor kid's leg and wouldn't let go. But that was a dog.

"Jus' how," Zee said languidly.

"How you gonna do it?" Dobbins asked, knowing the answer, knowing Zee contemplated killing someone the way most people daydreamed about an upcoming vacation.

"Mmmm," responded Zee.

"Well I want you to bring him to me first," Dobbins said slyly. "I wanna talk to that brother. I wanna know who else is in on this shit. Might be more than just him, an' we gotta know who . . . I don't mean just livin' an' breathin' either. I wanna *talk* to him, Zee. You got that?"

"Mmmm-huh."

Zee dropped off his boss, got into his own vehicle—a souped-up purple Bronco with polished chrome wheels—then went straight downhill to his own place. Ten minutes later he emerged from his grimy brown ranch with a black leather satchel. Zee took pride in his craft, and the bag held the tools of his trade. Before getting back into his truck, Zee looked up at the height of the sun and decided he had enough time for a drink or two.

He took a left on Sunset and drove until the real estate turned squalid. He stopped in front of a crooked hand-painted sign that hung at an angle above the door: MANNY'S SUPPER CLUB. Inside it was dark and musty, and a space fan in the back blew the smell of stale beer and piss toward the open door. Zee ordered a cold shot of Absolut and sipped away at one after another while he scowled and generally scared the shit out of the handful of hard-core drunks scattered up and down the bar.

When the plastic Colt 45 clock over the mirror read four, it was time to go. He paid for the drinks without leaving a tip. The sunlight in the street blinded him. South of the city, in an even worse neighborhood, he pulled into the dusty lot behind a body shop, exchanged a wad of cash for a stolen white phone company van, and headed east over the hills and out to Pasadena. He soon found himself in Maggs's neighborhood, an upper-middle-class development where the homes had more yard space than the places in L.A. proper. Zee pulled over across the street from the Maggs residence, a pale gray clapboard colonial with a spiffy blue-and-white Coldwell Banker FOR SALE sign sprouting from the center of the front lawn. Zee climbed into the back of the van, where he could see without being seen. He unfolded a lawn chair among the tools and coils of cable and sat back to wait for some sign of life.

At half past five Maggs's wife pulled up in a Volvo wagon with two kids in the back, one boy, one girl. Zee opened the little jackknife on his keychain and picked at the underside of his nails. Every so often he glanced up from the scrapings of yellow crud on the end of his blade to watch the kids play hopscotch on the sidewalk. By the time their daddy pulled up in his shiny white Tahoe the sun had already begun to dip below the bank of houses at the end of the street. The kids ran to the truck. A tall, lanky black man slid out of the driver's side and awkwardly bent to hug them. He took the kids by their hands and walked with an evident limp up the driveway, to the porch, and in through the front door. Dinnertime.

Zee grunted quietly to himself at the thought of something to eat now that the vodka was starting to wear thin. Someone had left a paper bag of little white powdered doughnuts on the parts shelf. The half-moon cellophane window told him the bag was still half full. Zee popped the doughnuts into his mouth one by one, then licked his fingers until the only trace was the white powder lacing his lips.

If Maggs went out, Zee would follow, looking all the while for the right time and place to snatch him. If he stayed put for the night, Zee would go in and get him, and that's why he needed the leather bag that contained the appropriate drugs for a job like that. He hoped that would be the case. There was nothing like going into someone's home while everyone slept. It was like invading another person's dreams. The feeling of power was complete. To look down at the sleeping face of a child or a woman, or even a man, and know that you could crush their windpipe and see the terror in their eyes as they became briefly conscious only to piss themselves before dying.

At eleven the lights went out, at twelve-thirty he moved the van to the front of Maggs's house, and by one Zee was on the move with his bag slung over one shoulder and his stomach growling angrily. His first stop was the phone box. It stood erect at the edge of the lawn. With a screwdriver and some wire cutters from the pack he quickly severed the phone line before marching straight up the driveway. If there was an alarm, it would call in to the security company when he went through the door. Without the phone line, no one but he and the Maggses would know they had a visitor.

As he approached the house, Zee heard the comfortable hum of air-conditioning units from the windows above. Nothing made a job easier than a good supply of white noise. When Zee was a kid they'd always go for the homes with air conditioners protruding from the windows. That usually meant that anything short of a gunshot wouldn't wake a soul. With a jimmy Zee quickly opened the side door to the garage, then with the same tool he quickly sprung the door into the house. Sweet silence signaled the lack of an alarm.

Zee crept upstairs and into the little girl's room. He set his pack on the floor and removed a Ziploc bag stuffed with a white rag that had been soaked in sevoflurane as well as a nose dropper full of Versed, a strong amnesic. Zee had no idea how or why the drugs did what they did; he just knew they worked, and he used them the way a simpleton might use a surgeon's scalpel to cut a slice of toast.

He stood over the little girl for several minutes, simply watching her breathe and timing it with his own. Then without any warning he broke the peaceful moment. From the plastic bag he removed the damp rag and with his big hand he clapped it over her mouth. Her eyes shot open, wide with horror at the sight of his huge face and the fetid smell of his toothy grin. This was the part he lived for. But in four seconds it was over. She was gone.

He let the sevoflurane rag lie over her mouth and nose for half a minute more before stuffing it back into the bag and sealing it tight. Then carefully he bled several drops of the Versed into her nose. She would wake up in the morning without any capacity whatsoever to remember the big dark bogeyman of her dreams.

The little boy was next, then came the tricky part: two for one, and the wife was facedown. Zee drew forth the rag with his head turned to the side. There was no odor, and he knew if he drew in much more than a whiff he'd be out cold himself. Carefully he laid the rag across Maggs's face. The former player emitted a quiet little moan and shifted his head ever so slightly before going comatose. Zee looked at his watch. He let Maggs breathe the drug for a good forty seconds before removing it.

Now he could do anything that he wanted to with the wife, and that made his heart race. The last one in a house was always the best. In this middle-class home, amid the narcotic hum of the air conditioner, he could create his own little version of hell. He could strip her and do things to her, make her afraid, make her beg, even make her scream, with no one who could help her. He actually sat down on the edge of the bed to turn the whole thing over in his mind, imagine it.

Of course, it was something he wouldn't do. He had a job and the job came first. A ravaged woman would prove that something violent had happened. The job called for wife and kids to wake and wonder where Dad had run off to. Zee let out a heavy sigh and took the rag from its bag once more, holding it at arm's length. With his free hand he began to rub the wife's leg. A little fun within the rules couldn't hurt. She slapped at his hand in her sleep like it was a mosquito. Finally she rolled over, sat up, looked right at him with eyes as wide as saucers, and screamed.

He pinned her under the covers and grabbed at her while laughter rolled up out of his belly and accompanied her shrieks of terror. He struggled to get the rag over her mouth with her fighting him like a hellcat, and soon his laughter gave way to anger and he had to check himself from smashing in her pretty face. Another minute of battle and he had her. Breathing hard, he got up off the bed and put away the rag before giving her several drops of Versed and tucking her back beneath the covers.

Without any additional nonsense he scooped up his black bag and crossed to the other side of the bed. He took out a roll of duct tape and used it to wrap Maggs up like a fly in a spider's web. As he shouldered the former player's angular body, Zee proudly figured that Trane would say it resembled the way someone would handle a rug. With Maggs's head thumping against the walls and doorways of the house Zee made his way back outside, locked up behind himself, and loaded up the van.

Chapter 10

After breakfast, Madison attended a roundtable discussion about media relations during a criminal trial, then delivered the closing remarks to the entire conference at eleven before heading back to her hotel. She changed into a faded pair of jeans and a short-sleeved black cashmere sweater, packed quickly, and checked out. A car took her south of the city to a restaurant just across the street from the beach. The theme was Tahiti: thatched roof, bamboo posts, war gods. On the second floor, in the open air, Madison found Clark Cromwell waiting patiently and alone. Sun and a breeze spilled in from the beach. He rose when he saw her and extended his meaty hand.

"You look happy," she said, at the same time signaling to the waitress so they could order.

Clark's big grin matched his blush. His long hair spilled around his bare, tanned shoulders. Dressed in a blue tank top, cutoff shorts, and sandals, and with muscles and veins bulging everywhere, he looked like a cross between a body-builder and a surfer. He wasn't an overly handsome man, but there was something endearing about his ingenuous grin and his striking dark blue eyes.

"I'm always happy," he said, looking at her directly.

After they'd ordered, she said, "Strong words for a man who's been cut from his team after having his neck fused together."

Clark shrugged in agreement, but couldn't stop smiling.

"Well, I know you're not smiling about this contract situation, so you must be in love," Madison said in an offhand way.

Clark's face went from a slight blush to beet red. He looked down at the place mat in front of him and fiddled with his silverware.

"How bad is it?" he said.

"The blushing or the contract?"

"Contract."

"I didn't want to leave it on your machine," Madison explained, "and I'm sorry I've been tied up with this conference. As I said, I met with Armand Ulrich on Thursday evening and we worked out a deal I think you'll— Well, not that you'll be happy with it. I know you were planning on about two and a half million this year, but given the circumstances . . . Ulrich pretty much wanted to stay with three-fifty, but I convinced him that with Trane Jones in their backfield, they'd need you as much for moral balance as they would for your blocking abilities. Anyway, I got him up to seven hundred and fifty thousand on a one-year deal."

Madison eyed her client carefully. The color in his cheeks had begun to dissipate, but his eyes had that incandescent quality that just didn't match the news of a substantial pay cut.

"That okay with you?" she said.

"A lot better than minimum," he pointed out.

"Well, it cost me a favor. I want you to know that. I wouldn't do it for everyone."

Clark knit his eyebrows and looked at her with concern.

"Don't worry," she said. "I didn't have to give up my firstborn, just a future 'favor,' whatever that means. Nothing illegal; I got that out up front."

"You didn't have to do that," he said.

"I wanted to do it, Clark," she told him. "Like I told Ulrich, you're the kind of person that's good for sports. It's getting worse, and I think any of us who are in the business should do whatever we can to perpetuate the career of someone who can play in the NFL or the NBA who's still a decent human being."

"Well, thank you."

"You're welcome," she said. "So, you going to tell me about Miss Right?"

Clark looked up at her, grinning again. "I've never felt like this," he told her. "I've had girls that I really respected and liked, and I've known women who . . . I don't know, who got me feeling . . . You know what I mean?"

"Got your blood up?"

"Well, I don't want to say lustful . . ."

"You didn't. I did."

"Okay, well, whatever it is, that physical attraction. The thing that just gets you . . . excited. I'll say that."

"Okay, so she's got your blood up," Madison said with a mischievous smile. She respected Clark's religious convictions, but she liked to tease him. It made him seem more human when she loosened things up a little.

"But I like her, too. It's what I've always wanted. But I just met her and I know that you can't . . . I don't know, is there love at first sight? Or second sight? Is that crazy?"

"People have been pawning it off since the beginning of time, so I think there's got to be something to it."

"Madison, I know you're my agent, but you're a woman. I mean, is this for real? Do things really happen like that? Did you feel that the first time you saw your husband?"

"Which one?"

"Oh," he said, flustered. "I didn't know. I just knew you were married . . ."

"It's okay," she said warmly, reaching over the table and patting the back of his hand. "My first husband, I fell in love with him pretty much at first sight. In fact, it was pretty much downhill after that, but I didn't know any better, despite being at the top of my law class, despite being determined to be a tough, sharp female attorney. I got burned. My first husband was . . . he was a bad person. No, he wasn't. He wasn't a person at all. He was an animal.

"Now, my second husband, he's a sweetheart, and I guess I fell in love with him at first sight, too, even though I didn't want to. In fact, the first time I saw him we argued—"

"But you felt that double thing I'm talking about," Clark said hopefully, "the excitement, but also that thing like, 'Hey, I like this person'?"

"Yeah," Madison said, looking past him into the hazy blue sky, remembering. Cody was a player himself then, handsome and with muscles like taut cables beneath his typically faded clothes. He was quiet and brooding, with a hint of danger about him, but even then Madison thought there was something softer underneath. He was the kind of man people talked about, but at the same time no one really seemed to know him. Her face softened with the nostalgia. She closed her eyes briefly against the brightness of the sun, then opened them. "I guess I did feel that with him."

"And you still do," Clark said, mangling a spoon.

"Yeah, I do. That's why I'm going to eat this salad fast and get on the road," she said as the waitress arrived with their food. "If I miss the two o'clock to Dallas, I won't get home tonight, and I've been gone since Thursday."

Clark raised his water glass. "Then here's to true love at first sight."

"Yeah," Madison said, raising her glass to his. "Just like the second time."

Chapter 11

The sun was a brilliant disk of heat in the cloudless sky. The air was thick from the smell of cut grass baking. It was the first day of minicamp. Beads of sweat broke out on the players' foreheads as soon as they began to stretch their hamstrings, doubling over, touching toes. They wore no pads, only shorts and purple mesh practice jerseys. Beside each man was his unbuckled helmet. The weight coach, dressed like the other coaches in tight purple shorts and a gray T-shirt, barked at them from the fifty-yard line. The other coaches wandered among the players, who were lined up in columns seven or eight men deep like soldiers at reveille. In this martial setting, even Trane Jones looked like he was part of a team.

When the stretching was over, the helmets went on and the team broke apart into smaller groups to run through drills specific to their positions. Linemen attacked padded sleds with mindless anger. Receivers made silent diving catches without bothering to celebrate. Quarterbacks threw whistling balls among themselves. And the runners blasted through the tickler, a cage of thick rubber appendages attached to industrial-strength springs that stung like mallets if you went through too slowly. The rookies always did. The second day was always their time to compare nasty purple welts in the shower.

Kemp, the running back coach, blew his whistle and barked the order to begin. Clark Cromwell led the way with a snort and pawed at the earth with his cleats when he was through. Trane Jones came next. He seemed to glide, moving so swiftly through the tickler that its bright orange fingers resembled flower petals in a breeze. Gulliford, who was now the backup tailback, banged through, then Wales, then Ossenmeyer. Then came Ike Webber, the fifth-round draft pick from Bowling Green, leading the rookies. The tickler tripped him up and battered his arms and legs as he staggered through, falling out the back end onto the hot grass. While Trane snickered, Clark helped the rookie to his feet and gave him a pat on the rump.

"That yo' punk bitch?" Trane mumbled casually.

Clark had heard Trane in the locker room, bragging alternately to some of the brothers about the prodigious size of his contract and his unit. But this was the first time he'd spoken to him directly. Clark turned and said politely, "Pardon me?"

"Yo' bitch," Trane said, clearly now and offensively.

"What?"

"I said, is that yo' punk bitch?" Trane said, grinning. "Yo' hand look like it lingered on the man's ass . . ."

Snickers. Everyone watched with interest. Do Good, some of them liked to call Clark. Would Do Good strike out or would he do good? Clark shook his head in disgust and on the whistle blasted back through the machine. Then he turned and stared. Trane ran through and stared right back, the nickel-size scar on his cheek bathed in sweat and shining like a new button. His dark eyes were flat and challenging, and he tapped the ball in his tongue against the metal bars of his face mask with a steady tang, tang, tang. Clark balled a fist and took half a step back.

The whistle blew and broke the tension. The running backs jogged en masse to the far end of the field, where the first-team offense gathered in a huddle. Clark was wedged between Trane and Featherfield, the team's shifty flanker. When Clark looked over through his mask the great runner was staring coldly. Clark looked past him as the head coach entered the huddle. Sweat stained Gridley's shirt and the dark hair protruding from his cap was plastered to his forehead. Clark thought about something else, the beach he was at yesterday evening, the cool breeze, the refreshing water. Heat always made him think like that anyway, like a mental mirage.

Gridley signaled for the rest of the offense to gather around the first team's huddle. "We talked about this already this morning," he began in his usual no-nonsense manner. "But I want everyone to be clear. With about fifty more yards on the ground in the championship game, we could have gone to the Super Bowl. That's the difference between you guys getting your asses on a Wheaties box or being the team that almost got there. This year, we'll get that fifty more yards, and this is how we're gonna do it.

"This series of plays is gonna be our trademark. That means every other team will study them and know them inside and out. But if we execute these plays, we can't be stopped. As a package they create deception that can't be defended against. Everything builds up to the double reverse. Every play in this package has to look before the snap count like it could end up being the double reverse. The play itself we might run twenty times all year. But just the threat of it, and the plays we can run from the trunk of the double reverse, will kick people's asses. You'll see, it's about execution.

"What I'm saying is," Gridley snarled, "if you want your

ass to be on this squad come September two when we kick off versus New York, you better know this package like your girlfriend's ass.

"Now let's see it work!" he barked, leaving the huddle.

"Or yo' boyfriend's ass," Trane said quietly.

Clark began to tremble. He fought the rage, but it was too much. He knew the drill with a cocky brother. If he kept letting it go, it wouldn't end, and he wasn't about to go through the coming year like that. He brought his far hand up and under the face mask of the star runner, twisting his own hips like a good fighter throwing a punch from the floor. Trane went up and off his feet, saw white stars, and was on his back before he could react.

Clark kept the fingers of his left hand clamped tight, put a knee in Trane's chest, and banged his face mask into Trane's.

"Enough!" he raged. "Enough from you!"

Trane choked and flailed his arms helplessly. Garvey, the burly center, and Featherfield grabbed Clark under the armpits and dragged him off.

"Let go, man!"

"Do Good, chill! Chill!"

They had Clark up over Trane and still struggling when Trane unleashed a kick to the groin.

"Fuck you!"

Clark went crooked in their arms and Trane was up off the ground now and on him like a cat with the fingers of one hand hooked into Clark's mask and the other whipping off his own twisted helmet with a violent jerk.

More players scrambled into the fray, but not before Trane was able to raise his helmet like a battle-ax and bring it crashing into the side of Clark's head. Clark collapsed in a lifeless heap, and it took four other players and a coach to subdue Trane, who was wailing like a banshee.

"Kill that motherfucker! Kill that motherfucker!"

Gridley began chewing out everybody.

"Goddammit! Goddammit!" He roared and pushed and shoved, and no one, not even Trane Jones, dared to shove him back or answer his curses with anything but sullen glares.

In less than five minutes they were practicing the double reverse, and no one who hadn't seen it would have known that anything had happened. Clark didn't show it. Trane didn't show it. Neither of them said a word to the other. Neither pushed nor shoved. Neither even bothered with a dirty look. That's the way it was in football. That's the way it had to be. It was over.

They had work to do, plays to learn and run and perfect. Besides deception, the keys to the double reverse were Trane's speed and Clark's blocking ability. With Trane split out to the right like a receiver, the quarterback, Faulkner, would drop and roll to the left. Featherfield would come from the left and take the handoff on what looked like a reverse to the right. From his spot at fullback, Clark would roll out in front of the quarterback. When the defense sensed the reverse, they'd all turn to chase Featherfield. By the time they realized it was a double reverse, Trane would be coming back to the left again with the ball. The defenders would be like spectators at a tennis match, their attention going this way and then that way and then this way again. In the confusion Clark could take the most dangerous defender and lay him out with a blindside block.

Over and over they ran the play. Over and over they ran a variety of passes and even some runs that all began with the players in the same initial formation that led to the double reverse. Over and over Clark bit into his mouthpiece: the irony of him throwing the key block on this play and so many other plays for a wretch like Trane Jones. But it was football. It was about winning, not personalities. They were in the same backfield, both essential to the running game that they needed to win a championship. Trane was the star, Clark the workhorse. They didn't have to like each other. They could even hate each other. It didn't matter a bit. All that counted was winning—on the field, anyway.

Chapter 12

Annie wanted to know. "What's wrong?"

"No, it's nothing really," Clark told her.

They were walking along the beach. The tide was out, and so was the moon. Surf hissed against the rocks. The sand was cool underneath their feet. Clark had known it would be that way, so Annie was wearing one of his sweatshirts over her cotton dress. Even pushed up onto her forearms, its sleeves nearly reached her fingertips and their perfect pink-colored nails. He liked the way she looked in his clothes, smaller and more fragile than she did in just her own.

"It's something," she said. "Look at the moon on the water."

"That's what I love most about coming here at night. That."

"So?"

"No, I just got into a fight today and I shouldn't have. I witness all the time to guys on the team for Christ and talk about what he's meant to me, how he's changed my life, and then I go and act that way . . ."

"What happened?" Annie said. She stopped and turned toward him. Her eyes were shining at him in the light of the moon.

"My God, Annie," he whispered, gently kissing her lips. "You're so beautiful."

"But what happened?" she said after the kiss.

Clark sighed and said, "I got into a fight with Trane Jones."

"You did? What happened?" she asked, an edge in her voice.

Clark looked away from her, up toward the high bank and the grass waving furiously in the ocean's night breeze.

"He said some things. I got mad. He said some more things. I got more mad. Then we were in the huddle during team period and I just lost it. I don't even know. I didn't think about it. I was out of myself. I just took him by the neck and threw him to the ground and then everyone broke us up. I don't know. It was the devil, I guess."

Annie burst out a choked sound, half a laugh, maybe? Clark looked at her, but she was somber. It was one of those noises that made him wonder if he'd heard anything at all.

"So then what happened?" she said as they started walking again.

"Then nothing. That's how it is. Guys fight. It's football. But this guy, this guy is bad. You've heard of him."

"I heard about his contract."

"He's the best runner in the game."

"But you took him by the neck . . ." Annie gave his hand a squeeze.

"I shouldn't have," Clark said.

"Sometimes that's the best way to make sure whatever it was he was saying he doesn't say it again. People like him—not that I know him—but from what I do know, people like him will just keep on you unless you get them by the neck."

"That's what I thought! Exactly."

"There were Christian soldiers, too," she told him. "There's a song, isn't there?"

"It's true," Clark said soberly. "Tom tells us that Christ is strong, not weak, and that we can witness for him by winning battles. Winning big games and getting big contracts isn't a sin as long as you use it for his will. That's what we do, the Christian guys on the team."

Annie stopped again and looked at him. "How do you use a big contract to do his will?" she wanted to know.

"We give ten percent of everything to Tom's ministry. He uses it for God's will. If we win the Super Bowl, we'll do the same thing with the fame, with the money. We'll use it to tell people about Jesus. People listen when you win the Super Bowl. Did you see Reggie White a couple of years ago when the Packers won their first Super Bowl in years? He witnessed for Jesus, and he was only one guy . . ."

"You're for real aren't you, Clark?" Annie said.

"Annie"—he took her face into the V of his hands—"I've been telling you, Annie. This is what I'm about."

Annie reached up and touched the hands that were on her face, then she touched his lips, then she kissed him.

"I want to be whatever you're about, Clark," she said to him in a husky voice. She pressed her firm body up against his, and he could feel all the parts of her he wanted to feel. Her chest was against his. Her hips pressed against his, and the blood rushed to his groin.

Nothing had happened between them. They had kissed and pressed against each other before, but that was all. Clark didn't want that. He thought Annie was special and he wanted to treat her that way. There had been times over the last few weeks when she'd seemed impatient with him, but the feeling passed and it was always just Annie there, smiling tenderly at him.

It wasn't that Clark was a virgin. He'd had his weak moments in college and even in the pros, moments for which he had to ask forgiveness the next day. But there hadn't been many. And with Annie, he wanted to do it right. He wanted her to know how much he respected her, how much he cared. There were times when he wasn't sure she liked it that way. It was never anything she said, but just a feeling he had. Still, he was determined to show her he was a man of God. How could he expect to lead her to Jesus if he didn't follow His precepts himself?

But Clark didn't think about any of that now on the beach with the fresh warm breeze and the narcotic sound of the surf and no one anywhere in sight and the soft light of the moon and her hips grinding up against him. Then her hands were on him, soft like silk, stroking him like silk, then her mouth, and Clark's knees buckled and he staggered. She pulled him down into the sand and he let her. Then she was on top of him, with her dress pulled up to the seam of flesh where her bronze thighs met the ghost-white bikini line on her hips. Clark couldn't keep his hands from searching up inside the soft cotton of his own sweatshirt for her breasts, and he couldn't help himself from groping for the feel of her bare flesh. And as she rose and fell he forgot about everything: tomorrow's practice, the devil, Trane Jones, God, even Jesus himself. There was only her flesh and his, and when Clark closed his eyes he didn't know if it was lightning coming in off the water that he saw through the lids or if it was what she did to him.

When it was over they lay together in the sand and Clark felt the dry grains in his long hair but didn't care. Annie spent the night with him and was still curled up asleep inside his big Juggernauts sweatshirt when Clark left early the next morning for minicamp. He was quiet so she could sleep, but on the drive to work he felt the heavy weight of guilt for what he'd done. He knew it wasn't right, and he knew that even the guilt couldn't stop him from wanting to do it again. The only way to have it all was to marry her, and that's what he would do.

Clark struggled to make the right blocks during camp. He struggled to remember simple things like the difference in his assignment when it was a double reverse instead of a double reverse pass. Gridley yelled at him all day and in the locker room. When Webber showed off his purple welts from the tickler, Clark only nodded his head and said, "Oh yeah, I know all about that," without even really looking.

Chapter 13

When Madison looked up from her desk she had to choke back a laugh. Chris had cleared his throat, drawing her attention away from her work. She recognized this sound, but was totally unprepared for the behemoth that filled the doorway directly behind her partner. On top of the giant's melon-sized head was a small sprout of Rastafarian locks. One of his eyes was foggy, like you sometimes saw in an old dog. There was no hint of a smile on his face, and he looked twice as imposing with Chris standing there in front of him throwing off the scale.

"Hello," Madison said, coming out from behind her desk and extending her hand to the giant.

"Yo," he rumbled and took Madison's hand in that awkward handshake that so many athletes used instead of the conventional straight-on job that she was accustomed to with the rest of the world.

"Madison, this is Amad-Amed Muhammad, who I'm sure you recognize," Chris said.

"Of course," she said cheerfully. She vaguely remembered Chris talking about a U of T kid who many were predicting would be next year's number-one pick, an offensive lineman of enormous proportions who could dunk a basketball and was as fast as a linebacker. Dunking the basketball she could imagine. Tall as he was, he didn't have far to go. The speed was another matter. Slabs of fat hung off his sides, hiding the waist of his red nylon sweatpants, and the only thing that marked where his face ended and his shoulders began was a large doughnut of blubber. He was big, but his appearance was far from athletic. If the bus in front of her could move as they said, like a racecar, then he really was something.

"How are classes going, Amad? Finals must be coming up."

Amad-Amed gave Chris a hard look.

"It's Amad-Amed," Chris said with a wounded smile that told her she'd been forewarned.

"Of course," she smiled. "Forgive me, Amad-Amed, I had a . . . I had a . . . there was a guy I knew in law school, a friend of mine whose name was Amad. I guess you reminded me of him . . . sort of."

Amad-Amed seemed to soften.

"*USA Today* is doing a big story on Madison in this Friday's edition, Amad-Amed," Chris said to bolster his partner's importance. "You'll have to look for it. Big color picture and everything."

"So you done Luther Zorn's last contract before he got hurt?" the player said in his low thundering voice.

"Yes. I did."

"The man," Amad-Amed said, shaking his giant head from side to side in what looked like amazement. "My man was hog-phat. I told my homeboys I was gonna talk to what agent was Luther's agent an' they all say, 'yeah boy, you do dat.' So . . . here I am.

"Boy was so *bad*," the giant lineman added.

"Yes," Madison replied. "He was very good."

"What I said," Amad-Amed mumbled with an affirmative nod.

"People are saying you'll be the offensive version of Luther Zorn," Chris said, looking up at the big man with a patronizing smile.

Madison hated this part of it. A big fat angry-looking kid in her office and the two of them, experienced, competent, respected lawyers turned into ass-kissing sports fans. It was time for her to get back to work.

"Well, would you like me to have Luther call you, Amad-Amed?" Madison said, not missing Chris's covert nod of approval. "I'm sure Luther would be happy to talk to you about our capabilities."

Amad-Amed's brief smile said it all. Madison made a mental note to call her old client, a former NFL superstar whose contract she had negotiated and whom she had also successfully defended in a murder trial.

"Well, Amad-Amed," she said, extending her delicate hand his way, "it was a pleasure meeting you. I hope we can be of service to you when the time is right."

"Yo," said Amad-Amed. He jerked his hand toward his face in some kind of sign that looked more friendly than obscene.

Madison walked them to her door. Everyone up and down the hall was gawking at the star lineman, and when he turned to go Madison silently shooed them all back to work.

"Big boy," Sharon, her secretary, observed quietly as she slid back behind her desk.

Madison was halfway into her next file with any thought of Amad-Amed Muhammad light-years away when Chris came barging back into her office and slumped down in one of the wing chairs facing her desk.

"Man!" he said.

"Tough one?" Madison asked, finishing the sentence she was reading before looking up to receive his answer.

"The Washington brothers are breaking my ass with this guy."

"The Washington brothers usually do," Madison said, stealing a look at the next sentence in her file. They were talking about two brothers from Detroit, African-American lawyers who'd graduated number one and two from Harvard Law School.

"'Keep your money with your people,' over and over. They hammer it into these kids. They try to make them feel guilty for having a white agent."

"Or a Latino?"

"Oh, that's even worse! They hate Latinos!"

"Come on," Madison said, looking up.

"It's true," Chris said defensively. "Not as an absolute rule, but you've got to know that these are two groups that don't mix. Oil and water. And with someone like the Washington brothers calling this kid every day to remind him, I don't know if we stand a chance . . . He's very pro-black."

"Meaning?"

"I'm just saying," Chris replied, "that our best chance is if Luther can blow this kid away."

"You mean you don't think he'll take my bungling his name and my inquiry about final exams as a sign of our innocence and our unassailable concern for his greater good?"

"Funny, Madison," Chris replied as he nervously massaged the bridge of his nose.

"Chris," she said, laying down her file and heaving forth a sigh, "let it happen."

"Meaning?"

"We've got clients, lots of clients. We'll get more. I know the Washington brothers are our competition, but what they're saying makes sense. It doesn't mean we give up on all the black players, but let's not get bent when we lose a few to the Washingtons. They're good lawyers and good agents. It could be worse. I'd rather lose a guy to them than someone like Conrad Dobbins."

"This guy is the big one though," Chris fretted. "He'll be the first pick in the draft. Most of our clients are veteran players. This would blow open the whole college scene; get the first pick of the draft, get a headliner contract, and then we can go after every first-rounder from UCLA to Syracuse."

Madison shook her head. "You know, running through my mind was why it doesn't matter, that we're big enough, we don't have to worry about getting more clients. And then do you know what I thought of?"

"What?"

Madison wore a sad smile. "The money. It's true. I'm ashamed to say it, but it's true. I just thought of the money.

"I can't help it. You can't help it," she said wearily. "Every year we do big contracts and we get a good cut. Then every year they get bigger, and bigger, and bigger, and so you find yourself chasing the next big player because you think how hard you had to work to get the guys you had last year. Now this new TV deal keeps driving up the salaries and you realize that even if you don't get bigger, even if you just do as well as last year in terms of players, you're going to double your money. But it never ends. It's more money, more money, more money . . ."

"Oh, come on, Madison," Chris said with a dismissive wave. "You're being too hard on yourself and me. We do good work for these guys. We get them good deals and we help them hang on to the money they make better than anyone else in the business. We're good for them. Yeah, it's good for us, but it's competition as much as it is the money.

We don't want to get beat by Conrad Dobbins or the Washington brothers or anyone else. We're competitors. We want to be the best at what we do.

"That's what it is. That's what this whole world of sports is about," he continued passionately. "Even with the players. You think it makes a difference to these guys if they make two million or three million? So they get one less Porsche. They buy a ten-thousand-square-foot house instead of fifteen thousand. It's not the money for the money. It's the money to prove that they're worth more than the next guy. That's you and me. We're competent competitive lawyers, not greedy agents."

Madison tugged on her lower lip and thought about that in silence for a few moments with her head tilted down toward her desk. From the expression on her face, Chris presumed she agreed.

Then she looked up and said, "Well, the *USA Today* article should help us. I talked to the writer about all the black players we've represented. Fact is, that's all he really seemed interested in."

"You never told me how it went."

"There's not much to tell. The guy's name was Darren Cartwright."

"I've seen his stuff. He writes columns mostly."

"Well, he said this was a big feature. They took a photo . . ."

"Great," Chris said. "I'll get a bunch of copies and send it out to all our prospective guys."

Then with a mischievous smile he added, "I'll send a copy to the Washington brothers while I'm at it. Meantime, how's your other job going?"

"If you mean my trial practice, don't ask. I hear you tell all these football players about what a big-time trial lawyer

I am, but I haven't had a big case to speak of since I can't remember when.

"Know what this is?" she said, picking up the file and handling it like roadkill. "It's the fourth DUI for the governor's nephew. You think that's gonna go to trial?"

"Well, you know what they say," Chris told her. "Be careful what you ask for. You might get it."

"From your mouth to God's ears."

Chapter 14

Dobbins ducked into the cabin and lurched toward the bathroom. He pulled the door shut behind him and latched it before digging in his pocket for a pill. The white tile floor swayed under his feet, and the smell of the disinfectant emanating from the toilet wasn't unlike what you got on an airplane. He gulped down his own bile with a crackhead's desperation. He was wearing a white nylon sweatsuit with white tennis shoes and a black silk T-shirt. Even the smallest chunk of vomit would be impossible to hide.

"Fuck," he said. He was damned if that whitey Lunden or any of his lackeys were going to see Conrad Dobbins chucking his shit up.

He found the pill and stuck his mouth under the spigot to get some water to wash it down quickly. When the son of a bitch asked him to meet on his yacht, Dobbins was determined to go just to spite the racist bastard.

"Do you mind going out on the water?" the son of a bitch had said to him.

"Fuck him," Dobbins said to himself out loud, just at the thought. He took several deep breaths and tried to refocus his vision outside the porthole at the few puffs of clouds suspended above the angry Pacific.

"Like a brother can't go out on the ocean," he muttered. "White fuck. How's he think we *got* here?"

Normally Conrad Dobbins wouldn't have bothered with someone like Kurt Lunden. Normally he'd just tell Lunden to contact him with a number. If the number was big enough, then they could do business. But that was before Maggs. And Lunden had hinted at a scheme that could get Dobbins out of some knee-deep shit. Lunden said he had an investment opportunity of vast proportions that could pay off exponentially. If the man was for real, it was just the kind of thing Dobbins needed.

After an ugly evening of questioning Maggs in an abandoned warehouse, Dobbins had learned that there was a groundswell building against him. Former and current clients were beginning to talk among themselves. The short version was that Conrad had lost tens of millions of dollars of his clients' money in bad investments. Most of the deals were speculative in nature. He had been given finder's fees. His clients had lost their money. His own wealth was intact and healthy, but the portfolios of almost every one of his clients were ailing badly. Even though Maggs was out of the way, Zee having slit his throat at the conclusion of their interview, that wasn't going to be an option if a group of his clients ever banded together. The unexplained disappearance of an old washout like Maggs wasn't going to generate too much heat. Zee had disposed of the body in a way that no one would find it. As far as the world knew, Maggs was just another has-been player who skipped town on his wife and kids. But Dobbins couldn't have Zee kill every client that revolted, and have them disappear, especially the more prominent ones.

There was a rapping at the door.

"Mr. Dobbins," came a voice through the wood. "Are you all right, Mr. Dobbins?"

Dobbins pulled the door open violently and glared at the silver-haired servant dressed in white-and-gold livery from collar to toe.

"'Course I'm all right, chump!" he said indignantly. "Why in hell wouldn't I be all right?"

"I'm sorry, sir," the servant said quietly, "but Mr. Lunden asked me to tell you he's 'on to one.'"

"'Bout time his sorry ass got a fish!" Dobbins said, mumbling as much to himself as to the frowning servant in front of him. "All I been hearin' is, 'sharks everywhere, so thick you have to fight 'em off.' Shit, we been drivin' this big bitch boat halfway to motherfuckin' Japan an' I ain't seen shit for sharks."

The two of them walked down the hall and out into the intense sun, Dobbins with his 8mm camera dangling from his wrist like a purse. Lunden was on to one. There was no mistaking it. The arrogant bastard was making more noise than a jealous bitch, and the other men ran around the deck like something important was happening when in fact it was just some fucked-up rich white asshole getting off on killing a fish. Dobbins looked sideways at Zee. The massive bodyguard stood silently beside the cabin door.

"Fuckin' pathetic," Dobbins mumbled as he centered the gold-nugget sunglasses on his face and brought his camera into play.

"Brothers an' sisters," he murmured just loud enough so that it would get picked up by the 8mm's audio, "this is how the oppressive rich white man spends his time after raping you for your hard-earned money. Watch on, brothers an' sisters . . ."

"Dobbins!" the man in question howled. "Come look at

this monster! I told you they were everywhere! It's a great white!"

Dobbins made his way through the throng to the stern of the boat and looked over the edge of the railing at the massive thrashing fish.

"Motherfucker's got some *teeth*," Dobbins exclaimed as he high-stepped backward.

Lunden gave him a hearty pat on the back and erupted with laughter. One of the crew hooked a gaff through the corner of the animal's mouth while another swung a boom out over the stern. A heavy hook and chain were lowered and latched around an eye on the back of the gaff's hook. Slowly the winch raised the enormous fish out of the water. It continued to thrash viciously and its pitiless eyes rolled malevolently in its head. Without thinking Dobbins backed well clear of the whole scene. The animal was at least sixteen feet long, and the more it struggled the more Lunden howled with laughter.

When the dangerous jaws were raised well above the deck, Lunden took a large machete from his silver-haired servant and lovingly unsheathed it. In a sudden flurry of activity, he stepped forward and with a series of vicious strokes laid the shark's belly wide open. Guts spilled out into the ocean in a brilliant pink cascade. Flecks of bright gore speckled the deck and railing, and as Lunden approached Dobbins he could see that the fisherman's white pants and windbreaker were also festively decorated with random blood spots.

"How 'bout a drink?" Lunden said, his face flushed with pleasure as he tugged his battered skipper's cap down tight and rubbed his liver-spotted hands briskly together.

The whole thing reminded Dobbins of sex. There was all this talk, all this buildup about shark fishing, and suddenly, after a flurry of activity, the whole thing was over. He followed Lunden up a set of steps and onto a large deck where a linen-covered cocktail table waited for them under an umbrella. Fresh drinks were already waiting for them. Zee followed the two of them up but stayed near the stairs and away from the table.

Kurt Lunden sat back in his chair and surveyed Dobbins over the edge of his glass. Dobbins popped a sliver of ice into his mouth, tasting the liquor, and surveyed right back. Lunden was over fifty, weatherworn, but tanned and in decent shape if such a thing was possible for a man carrying about forty excess pounds around the middle. He was a tall man with long legs and a barrel-shaped torso. The sandy hair on his head was long enough so that what had fallen out of the cap wafted gently in the warm ocean breeze. His blond walrus mustache was slightly crooked and drooped forlornly, giving him a roguish look.

Lunden's empire was built on toxic waste. In the mid-seventies he had purchased the largest toxic disposal site in the world in the Nevada desert, then secured contracts with almost the entire California defense industry. With those deals in place, he had helped finance a major political movement by Greenpeace and the Sierra Club to stiffen U.S. environmental laws. When that legislation started to get tough in the seventies and eighties, Lunden cashed in. After that he made and then lost another entire fortune in footwear. Zeus Shoes was a storybook success in the mid-eighties, but plummeted in the early nineties. Currently the company was reorganizing under chapter eleven bankruptcy proceedings. From the size and staff of the boat, Dobbins knew the toxic waste money didn't get away.

Lunden scraped a fleck of something from the edge of his bulbous red nose, examined it, then flicked it away before saying, "We can make a lot of money together, Conrad."

"That's why I'm here," Dobbins said, "to find out how."

"Not for the fishing?" Lunden said, smirking from behind his Porsche sunglasses.

"Bitch had some teeth," Dobbins admitted. "An' that machete shit was different . . . but it's all about money with me. You said ya had somethin' that was megabig. That's why I'm here. I'm the mega-agent."

"You're full of megashit is what you are, Conrad," Lunden said pleasantly. "But I've got an idea that's going to make us both more money than we need."

Dobbins said nothing. He just stared.

"The camera," Lunden said.

"Yeah?"

"Lose it."

Silver-hair appeared with a tray and waited patiently while Dobbins shut down the camera and tenderly turned it over to him.

"Careful with that," he warned.

"Now your guy," Lunden said, eyeing the bodyguard.

"Zee," Dobbins called out over his shoulder. "Go check out that fish."

When they were alone, Lunden rubbed a fingertip around the edge of his glass and began to speak.

"Zeus Shoes is in eleven right now, so the common shareholders are shit out of luck," he said. "I have some preferred stockholders that I'll cram down to common. The shares won't be worth much more than twenty-five, thirty cents."

"Piss-poor."

"But wonderfully piss-poor," Lunden said taking a drink. "One man's ruination is usually another man's fortune. Think of the multiples if I can get those shares to thirty dollars! That's three thousand percent, and I can do it. I've got the manufacturing facilities overseas, and with the Asian economy as sick as it is I can make product twice as cheap as before. I've got a distribution system and a sales force that can push the product out the door."

"But you ain't got product," Dobbins pointed out. "How about them fuckin' ice-cream color shoes! How in fuck did you ever think that was gonna work?"

Lunden shrugged it off. "You take chances, Conrad. You know that. Remember the band Ace Racers?"

"Ace what?"

"Ace Racers?"

"Fuck no."

"Exactly. They were going to be the hottest new teen band in the Western world. Disney and EMI sank ten million into the little shits. They had it all planned: albums, movies, television, it was all lined up. It was fail-safe. They were going to be the second coming of the Beatles and the whole fucking band was wearing ice-cream color Zeus Shoes. They were going to be the rage . . . you might say phat."

"Never heard a their sorry asses," Conrad grumbled.

"They died in a plane crash on their way into Tahoe in the winter of ninety-two, three days before their launch. It was page four news. EMI and Disney got some of their money back, but we were already eighty percent into production. We reshuffled our marketing strategy, but as you correctly pointed out, it didn't cut it."

"So what the fuck's all that gotta do with me makin' *money?*"

"Conrad, we live in an age where sex, drugs, perversion, profanity, and irreverence are the hot buttons to selling anything from razors to pizza to politicians.

"You've got a client that embodies all those things at the same time. Most people think that's not what you'd want a product to be identified with directly. They'll hint at it, but that's all. To come right out and sell something like that, people think that's too far over the top, too offensive. But they're wrong! A product openly identified with those things would sell faster than it could be produced, and that's what I'm going to do. I want to sign Trane Jones to an exclusive endorsement contract and I want to pay you, and him, with stock options. If my plan works, it could mean upwards of who knows, twenty, thirty million dollars. Apiece."

Lunden let that sink in before he continued.

"I want to design a line of shoes around Trane Jones and his reputation for being bad. After all, bad is good, isn't it, Conrad?"

"Stock options ain't worth shit if the stock don't go up," Dobbins pointed out. His voice was laced with derision. "You gonna have to pay me an' my man somethin' if you want a motherfuckin' endorsement."

"Conrad," Lunden said, removing his dark glasses and staring coldly at the agent, "your man isn't gonna make a dime in commercial endorsements without me."

Dobbins was struck by the intensity of the white man's light gray eyes. He knew Lunden had led a life of dissipation. It showed in the way the capillaries in his face were straining toward the surface of his sagging, wrinkled skin. But the incandescence of those eyes was that of a younger man, a maverick.

"He's got a felony record," Lunden said, ticking off on his fingers. "He's got a reputation for being abusive toward women. He's everything most companies don't want to come within smelling distance of. I'm the only person with the balls to take a character like Trane and sell that image. I'm offering the chance to make a fortune, for you both!

"You want to fuck around with me?" he went on, nearing anger. "I'll go get Dennis Rodman if I'm going to dump money into the front end. He'll do it and he's a big enough asshole to make this thing work for me. I'll pay for him up front because he's still accepted in the advertising world and there's some demand. But your guy? Come on, Conrad. He'd have to spend a year in charm school if he wanted to be a poster boy for the Hell's Angels.

"I'm taking a huge chance here. I'll get one shot to revive Zeus. If it doesn't work, I'm finished with shoes. If it does . . . like I said, there's big money in this. I mean big."

"I don't want no morality clauses or any shit like that," Dobbins said sullenly.

"Of course not," Lunden said with a disgusted wave of his hand. "The worse he is the more money we make. If he attacks his coach the way that basketball player did a couple years ago, the stock goes up. If he beats his girlfriend or spits in someone's face, it goes up even more. No, the only clause I might ask you for is an immorality clause."

Lunden chortled quietly at his own wit. There was a cry from below, and both men looked down as the crew prepared to cast off the enormous dismembered shark. Dobbins watched, but his mind was on the deal. He figured that besides his and Trane's own free options he could invest the rest of his clients heavily in the thirty-cent stock. If the white man's plan worked—and there was no reason to think it wouldn't—then all his problems would be solved in one simple deal. There was another shout from below and the shark's white-bellied carcass went spinning off into the wake in a boil of blood before sinking out of sight. Conrad smiled at the white man and nodded his head in a way that let Lunden know he had a deal.

Chapter 15

Clark knew that part of his mission as a Christian athlete was to evangelize his faith. Ike Webber was a perfect candidate for saving. A bug-eyed kid liked to please and worked hard, Ike was pretty quiet in a crowd. He'd grown up in a small Mississippi farm town by the name of Titus, and his country manners had never left him. Although African American and a client of Conrad Dobbins, he clearly felt out of place with the jive-talking crowd of Juggernauts players that included Trane Jones. Ike fell naturally under Clark's wing during the team's minicamp in late spring, and during the summer workouts at the Juggernauts facility he stayed there.

Clark had already discussed the situation with Tom, who was always eager for players to spread the word and expand his flock. Together they had prayed about it and decided that God would tell Clark when the time was right. After a long, hard workout on a Tuesday not too many weeks away from training camp, the young rookie asked for a ride home.

"Lent my car to my brother an' my cousin," he sheepishly explained in his quiet country drawl. "They dropped me off an' went to see Disney. They're visitin' me for the week."

"No problem," Clark said. He was sitting on the stool in front of his locker unlacing his sneakers. He looked up. "Hey, how 'bout lunch? I know a great Tahitian place down in Manhattan Beach. They got great spicy fries with vinegar. I'm meeting my girlfriend there, but come with me. I told her about you."

"Okay by me," Ike said, raising his eyebrows as if he were slightly surprised.

"I gotta shower and then get some treatment on my neck," Clark said, "but I'll be ready in about forty minutes."

"Okay by me."

Because Clark and Ike ended up in the showers at the same time as Trane Jones neither of them spoke. The star runner soaped himself shamelessly while he belted out a dirty rap song that had something to do with raping thirteen-year-old girls for one's own pleasure. *"Old enough ta bleed, old enough ta breed. Old enough ta bleed, old enough ta breeed . . ."* Over and over went the chorus.

It made Clark's ears hot, and he found himself wondering what Ike thought. Were Clark and a lot of his friends' distaste for rap and jive talk and loud bragging a racial thing or a religious thing?

There were a few black players in the Bible study group, but they talked and acted like whites. Clark didn't even think of them as black. Ike was somewhere in between, or at least he appeared to be. His dialect was more black than white, and sometimes if the morning was damp with fog he would wear a dark knit cap. He did not, however, wear baggy jeans that sunk halfway down the crack of his ass or sunglasses or thick gold chains or drive a foreign car that boasted the incongruent rims of a hot rod. But Clark could see those things coming if he didn't act fast. He'd heard Trane and Cushings, another Conrad Dobbins client, talking to Ike one day about a party they expected to see him at, so

Clark knew the temptation for Ike to fall into that way of life was very real.

In a way, the prospect of saving someone so close to the edge was even more exciting to Clark than what had happened with Annie. Annie was almost too easy: a wonderful girl with great morals and values who simply hadn't had the exposure to Jesus Christ and his teachings. Clark figured Ike was a different story altogether. There was no way, as a college athlete, that Ike hadn't been exposed to Christianity. Either the Fellowship of Christian Athletes or Athletes in Action were in every locker room he'd ever heard of. But for some reason the young runner was reluctant. It was up to Clark to find out why.

Clark got out of the shower as fast as he could, unaware that a tuft of foam was sliding down the middle of his back. Not that it would have mattered. He had to get out to keep from boiling over. There hadn't been a word between him and Trane since the first day of minicamp. That was nearly three months ago and just fine with Clark. He had nothing to say to Trane and didn't want to hear anything Trane might have to say to him. On the field and in the meeting rooms, it didn't matter. During those times, if they chose, players could go about the business of football without a lot of social interaction. Besides, Trane slept through most of the meetings. And when Clark was thrown into Trane's presence, like in the shower, he tried to ignore him.

After drying himself, Clark put on a pair of purple nylon shorts and went to see Jerry in the training room. Jerry hooked up the electrodes to Clark's neck and wrapped it in a cold collar.

"How's it feel?" he asked.

"Couldn't be better."

"Could've been better if you didn't have your vertebrae fused together," Jerry pointed out.

"Given the circumstances," Clark said. "That's what I mean."

"Ready for camp?"

Clark looked up at him from the table. "That's a whadaya call it . . ."

"Oxymoron," Jerry suggested.

"Yeah," Clark jibed. "Only a moron would ask it."

"Oh, come on, you guys are living the life," Jerry replied, turning up the juice. "All that money, all the time off. Where could you get anything like this outside of football?"

"Okay, I get you. But you know darn well there aren't a lot of people who'd do this for a living. Even for the money."

"There's millions who'd do it!" Jerry cried.

"They think they'd do it, until they had to go through it."

Jerry exhaled sarcastically. It was their ongoing debate, and Clark suspected the trainer did it just to get a rise out of him.

"Well," Jerry said with a puckered face, "is our neck going to hold up?"

"No problem with that," Clark said confidently.

"Uh-huh," Jerry said. "That's what I like to hear, no fear."

Clark snorted derisively. As if fear was ever an issue with him.

Clark would later describe lunch as a blessing from God. That's how he'd relate it to Tom, anyway. They sat upstairs in the open air. The ocean breeze gently rattled the dried palm fronds hanging from the roof. It was typically pleasant. Clark wore a pleated pair of tailored shorts and a brushed cotton shirt open at the collar. Annie wore a pretty summer dress, as if she, too, were going someplace important afterward. Ike, feeling underdressed in a simple pair of athletic shorts and a tank top, was soon put at ease by Annie's warmth and graciousness. She spent the first twenty minutes asking him about Mississippi, and Clark could tell that his teammate liked her.

After the waiter cleaned away the plates and set down two white porcelain mugs of coffee and one of tea, Annie said to Clark, "Why don't you ask Ike to come with us?"

"What?" Clark said, squeezing his lemon wedge so hard two seeds plopped into his steaming mug.

"Ask him," Annie said. "I know you want to share your faith with him. I can tell that."

Both men averted their eyes.

"Oh, come on, Clark," she said. "You're so obvious. Just ask him if he wants to come. Let him see what it's about. Let him feel the energy."

"It's not just energy, Annie," Clark said, feeling peevish as he spoke. "It's the Holy Spirit."

"Right! Let him feel it."

Ike looked at Clark now, puzzled.

Clark pursed his lips. Annie sometimes did things like this to him, going off with people in directions he couldn't antic-ipate. She wore the smug, delighted expression of a small girl revealing a polished stone to her friends. He put it down to her being raised in California. Where he was from people weren't that open.

"Annie's being baptized today," Clark explained with ob-vious hesitation. Then with more zeal he said, "Of course, you're welcome to come. I'm sorry, I haven't even asked you about your faith. Sometimes Annie moves fast—"

"Come with us," Annie said, her eyes gleaming as she reached across the table and boldly placed her hand on Ike's wrist.

"I could," he said, quietly glancing down at her hand. "I got time. I been baptized."

"When you were young?" Clark asked.

Ike nodded. "Yeah, my mom, she had us all baptized.

Then she died and Dad, he didn't go in much for church and all. We kinda got away from it, you know."

"Do you know if you were baptized by submersion?" Annie asked in a solemn tone. "Because some people think they're baptized, but they're not. Tell him, Clark."

"It says in the Bible," Clark patiently explained, "that to truly be born again you have to be baptized by submersion, put completely under water."

"I don't think that's how they did it in Titus," Ike admitted.

Clark looked anxiously from Annie to Ike. His hands were starting to sweat, and there was a spot on the left side of his upper lip that felt like it was being tugged toward the ceiling by an invisible string. This was it. He asked for strength.

"Ike, do you know Jesus Christ?"

Ike nodded that he did.

"I mean really know him," Clark said, exhaling the words, "as your Savior?"

"I think so."

"You don't then," Clark said somberly. "If you know him, you *know* it. If you don't, you just *think* so. But that's okay. A lot of people don't know him, *really* know him. I'd be happy to help you. It's not hard. It's a simple prayer. Believe me. Jesus Christ saved my life, He's saved Annie's, and he can save yours . . ."

Ike was listening. Clark could see that he was. It gave him strength to see that. Clark felt the power of the Spirit. It was what Tom talked about all the time. When you witness for Jesus, you feel the power of the Spirit.

"If you turn your life over to Jesus," Clark told him warmly, "acknowledge him as God's true Son and man's true Savior, then you're saved."

"That and being baptized," Annie pointed out.

"Yes," Clark said excitedly, "but you have to accept him first. That's how you change your life. It's not just me, Ike. It's Mitch Faulkner, Featherfield, Cobb, Deacon, McMann, Deuce, all those guys and lots more. Probably almost half the team is Christian.

"We're so *close* to the Super Bowl," Clark said fervently. "You know that, everyone knows. We think we'll win it, too. We think if enough of us have faith, God will help us win to glorify His name. We have a mission, Ike, we really do, and I know everyone would be really glad to have you join us."

That was it. Clark didn't know what more to say. It wasn't his nature to evangelize, to press. It was something though, as a Christian, that he had to grow into. Lead by example, that's what he'd always tried to do, in religion as well as in sports. But Tom made it clear that he needed to give more. "To whom much is given, much will be expected." If he closed his eyes and thought, Clark could hear the words in his mind the same way his father had once spoken his name.

He'd been given a lot. He knew that, and now Tom was charging him to give to others, to help save their souls. Clark had been pitifully negligent. Annie didn't really count. She was easy. He knew her and loved her, and he hadn't pressed her until he felt certain she had the same feelings for him. Then it was easy. But Ike, he was just a guy on the team. Clark wanted to evangelize, to reach out and grasp for wayward souls the way Tom taught them. He wanted to do what was right. But he didn't know what more to say. Under the table he wiped a sweaty palm against the pant leg of his shorts and then grasped Annie's hand.

Finally Ike spoke. "How?" he said.

Relief washed over Clark. He was almost too giddy to speak. Acceptance, this was the first and biggest step. Later would come tithing and real baptism, but Tom would take care of that.

"It's not hard," Clark said, the words bubbling out. "You just say this prayer with me, the prayer on the back."

Clark fumbled with his pocket and took out a credit card–size pamphlet. He flipped it on its face and laid it on the plastic tablecloth in front of Ike. In bold block letters on the back were the words that Clark believed could lead anyone to heaven. Ike read the words, moving his lips silently. Then he looked up at Clark, blinking.

"Here?" he said.

"It doesn't matter where," Clark told him. He held out his hands above the table, raising them palms up like a supplicating priest. Annie and then Ike each took a hand and then took each other's so the three of them made a triangle. Annie's fingers were warm and strong, and as they bowed their heads she looked triumphantly around the restaurant, noticing the people staring at them and smiling to herself as she watched the two men whose hands she held saying a prayer she had not long ago recited herself.

Ebullient with faith, the three of them snaked down the Pacific Coast Highway toward Newport Beach. At Tom's people were already waiting. Normally, women were baptized in bunches, but Tom felt that Clark, with his citywide, almost national reputation for good works, was an especially important part of his ministry. It was in honor of Clark that Tom was going to baptize Annie the way the players themselves were baptized: alone.

Clark had privately fretted to Tom about how the other wives and girlfriends would feel. But Tom had quoted the Bible, saying something about God giving as He saw fit, and that had put Clark's mind at ease. Clark believed, as they all did, that the Bible was the literal word of God, Him speaking to them directly and unequivocally. For her part, Annie seemed delighted to be singled out. At first Clark had worried that she wanted to put her thumb in the other women's eyes, but then he checked himself. He had too magnanimous a view of Annie to imagine her involved in petty jealousies. Besides, Annie had nothing to be jealous about. She was prettier and smarter and more vivacious than any of the other women in their group.

Tom welcomed Clark at the front door with a quick embrace and led them hurriedly through the center of the house to the pool.

"You're late, my friend," he chided over his shoulder.

Clark beamed and introduced Ike to Tom on the move.

"I was witnessing to Ike at lunch," he announced with a broad smile. "He's accepted Jesus as his Savior."

Tom pulled up abruptly and directed his luminescent eyes at Ike. "Praise Jesus," he said warmly. "Welcome."

Ike shook Tom's outstretched hand, and Tom pulled the young player to him and hugged him with a warm slap on the back. Then he turned his eyes toward Clark with a look that spoke of love, thanks, and admiration, a look almost beyond words.

Outside, nearly twenty of Clark's teammates and their wives or girlfriends stood clustered in groups around the pool. Their clothes were casual but expensive and stylish. Still, as she stepped into their midst, Annie stood out. The players themselves did battle with lustful thoughts while their wives looked fruitlessly for chinks in her veneer. Annie seemed to sense the focus of their attention, and it did anything but dull her.

Tom's backyard was luxuriously wide, with royal palm trees standing in a colonnade around the amorphous pool. Slashes of sunlight filtered through the upper reaches of the palm fronds and danced on the cut stone and the carefully manicured swatches of grass according to the whims of the breeze. Many of the players and their wives wore gold Rolex watches and fat diamond earrings that scattered the elusive rays of sunlight in a way that made the others blink.

Tom stepped forward and took Annie by the hand. He led her fully dressed in her pale yellow summer dress to the shallow end of the pool and walked her down the steps into the waist-deep water. The hem of the dress ballooned to the surface lilylike in the water. Suddenly possessed by the Holy Spirit, Tom, who stood waist-deep in his own clothes, began speaking in an indiscernible gibberish that the rest of them knew was tongues, the same miraculous venting of the Spirit experienced by Christ's first disciples thousands of years before. Clark had never spoken in tongues, but he'd seen other players do it. Once when they were losing to the Broncos by three touchdowns Featherfield broke out in tongues on the sideline.

When Tom grew quiet and emerged from his trance, he put one hand on the small of Annie's back and gently palmed her face with the other. After a quick prayer he submerged her completely in the pool as he blessed her soul and welcomed her with a cry into the kingdom of eternal life. As Annie waded up the pool's steps, flushed and dripping, the pale yellow dress clung indecently to her marvelous shape. While many of the poolside players could forestall a lewd grin by clamping down on the inside of their cheeks, there was no cure for their racing hearts. But Clark didn't see Annie like the others. He was well familiar with the voluptuous curves of her breasts and the flat luxurious length of her stomach. He saw only the complete salvation of the woman he loved, and he couldn't remember a happier moment in his life.

Chapter 16

Just after dawn Madison's husband, Cody, shook her from a deep sleep.

"Madison," he hissed, rocking her entire frame with his hand on her rib cage. "Madison!"

"What?" she said, then grumpily, "What!"

"There's no salt," he said with evident disgust. "I can't find salt anywhere."

"Salt?"

"Salt."

Madison sat up and used her fingertips to dig the sleep from the corners of her eyes. Their bed rested on a raised platform facing a big mullioned set of cathedral-style glass doors overlooking a golf course. The dark gray light in the sky told her she owned at least half an hour of sleep before her day had to begin. Cody stood over her in a drab cotton sweatsuit whose color matched the sky. His hair was tousled on top and matted with sweat around the edges. A bead of perspiration fell from the tip of his nose, leaving a dark blemish on the comforter.

Cody sniffed and wiped his upper lip on his sleeve. "Salt," he said again. "I'm makin' eggs."

"Cody," she snapped, "what makes you think I know where the salt is? If we don't have salt in the shaker, we don't have salt. Check the pantry."

"I checked."

"Then we don't have any."

"That's total bullshit," Cody said disgustedly. He wiped his face one more time on his sleeve and walked away.

Madison told herself he could go pound sand—or salt, for that matter. She shot back down into the bed and snapped the comforter up over her head to ward off the coming dawn. She wanted to get at least twenty of her thirty minutes back. That was something anyway. Instead, her mind began to chew on the subject of her marriage. She loved Cody, but they were so opposite.

Opposites attract. That she knew. They were attracted to each other. That was true. But from the beginning it had been tempestuous, and it hadn't changed. If anything it was worse.

The more money she made, the more notoriety she got, the more he seemed to expect that she play the role of housewife. If she brokered a twenty-million-dollar deal during the day, she knew damn well she better stop at the grocer's on the way home for a pint of heavy cream so she could make a chocolate mousse that night. Cody liked mousse, and it was one of the few skills she still possessed that proved she was a good little homemaker.

All week people had been talking about the coming of her big *USA Today* article. So today he was mad because in the commotion she forgot to make sure there was salt in the house. On the other hand, her training as a lawyer taught her to look at every situation from both sides. It had to be hard for Cody, she admitted, teaching and coaching at the local high school, a lifetime away from his days as a star player in the NFL when the money and the attention had been his.

She knew about his resistance to living a lifestyle that only her kind of income could support. Still, she found herself constantly circumventing that resistance, booking exotic first-class vacations, redecorating the house, buying herself new cars, new clothes, membership at the club, nice jewelry, even purchasing expensive clothes for Cody that he would only wear on special occasions. It wasn't that Madison was a spendthrift, far from it. She lived well within her means. But her means had grown substantially over the past few years since she'd become an agent. At the beginning it hadn't seemed to bother him as much. But lately his resentment had grown, and it sickened her to have to sneak around hiding the way she spent her hard-earned money.

As a statement of protest, Cody still drove an old pickup truck, typically dressed in ragged sweats, and battled her every time she made dinner plans at any place fancier than Pizza Hut. It was also rare for three months to go by without him suggesting that they move to a more modest neighborhood. And despite her mild protests, he typically cut the lawn the day before the gardener came, washed his truck and her car in the driveway on Saturday morning, and unloaded the dishwasher before Bess, their housekeeper, began her day at seven-thirty.

Still, Madison loved him with real passion. She admired his stubborn sense of pride, even if it confounded her at times. He was handsome and strong, although certainly not in the same shape as he had been during his playing days. He worked hard as a teacher and a coach and he cared about his kids. Most importantly, he cared about Jo-Jo, Madison's son from her first marriage. Cody had made him his own.

Recently they had begun trying to have another child, but to no avail. Madison knew that only added stress to their marriage. Cody hadn't mentioned it specifically and she wasn't going to bring it up, but for almost a year now they hadn't used any kind of birth control and still Madison wasn't pregnant. She was beginning to fear it was something with her, and she wondered now if Cody wasn't having the same sort of self-doubts. Maybe that's what was creeping to the surface in the form of anger over things like salt. It was something she'd have to talk with him about when the time was right.

Madison gave up on more sleep. She threw back the covers, showered, and changed into an olive business suit with a cream blouse before descending to the kitchen. Cody was there with the paper. So was Jo-Jo.

"Morning, Mom," her son said. He was ten, but tall enough to pass for twelve.

"Morning, love," she said, kissing him. "How were your eggs?"

Jo-Jo gave her a puzzled smile.

"Madison . . . I'm sorry," Cody said gently.

"Oh, don't worry," she told him, waving her hand and heading to the refrigerator for some orange juice.

"No, not that," Cody said with a frown. "This. I'm sorry." He tapped the newspaper in front of him. He'd pulled the paper apart and the sports section was on top.

"And the salt," he added.

"What's the matter?" Madison asked, closing the refrigerator door without her juice and walking back to the table. She had that sinking feeling inside and the buzz in her ears that was her sixth sense telling her bad news was coming, really bad news.

"Goddamn writers," Cody rumbled. "I oughta kick that son of a bitch's ass . . . Like Art Tally, one day he upended a writer who ripped him in the paper and put him headfirst into the trash can. Headfirst into a bunch of smelly ankle tape and gobs of snot."

Madison looked down at the cover of the sports page. Her

face, in color, filled the center of the three-column-wide page. The headline read: CASHING IN ON COLOR. Her eyes in the photo were only three-quarters open, the precursor to a blink. The resulting impression for anyone who didn't know her was of the face of a woman who was hard-hearted, almost sneaky. A little laugh of disbelief escaped her throat as she sat down at the table to read.

As she read, horror cinched down tight on her insides. It was all the more painful because she was caught totally off guard. She was expecting praise. A laudatory piece about a capable female attorney who reluctantly found herself embroiled in the lives and contract negotiations of NFL players around the country. A woman who served her sports clients much in the same way she served her legal ones. A woman who sometimes found they were one and the same.

This piece wasn't simply unflattering. It was harshly and cruelly defamatory. It suggested that she was nothing more than an opportunistic racist, that while she had cashed in on representing professional athletes, half of whom were black, in her private practice she provided legal services almost exclusively for whites. While the piece conceded that wealthy whites were the most typical clients for a lawyer who worked in an expensive firm such as Madison's, it pointed out that the pro bono work she did was also drastically skewed according to race. In fact the article said that the only black man Madison McCall had represented in a criminal matter during the last two years was Luther Zorn, a multimillion-dollar NFL star. "And even though Zorn was then a client of Ms. McCall's," the story claimed, "she would only do so after requiring him to put down one hundred thousand dollars as a retainer."

Of course she'd required a retainer, Madison thought; every lawyer did. And as to her pro bono work, she took pride in it. Most lawyers in her position shied away from doing anything for free. Pro bono work was something her father before her had always done, and it was a tradition she'd been determined to carry on. She had never considered the skin color of her clients. She simply looked at the circumstances and represented those defendants she felt she could most passionately serve. But this piece suggested that while she was perfectly willing to take 3 percent of an African-American athlete's ten-million-dollar contract, she was loath to represent a poor black wrongly accused of murder.

None of Madison's existing clients were quoted in the piece. The only client quoted at all was a bitter Jacksonville player whose bogus tax claims Chris had refused to sign off on and who had subsequently left them. The only lawyers interviewed were Madison's bitter enemies—a former DA whose career she had shattered by exposing his corruption, and various other liberal defense lawyers miffed at the attention she had gotten from past high-profile murder cases as well as the monetary rewards her agency work brought her. The piece was a total surprise. During the interview, the writer hadn't given even a hint that his story would be negative.

The phone rang. Cody got it. "It's Chris," he said grimly.

"Hello," Madison said, trying to add life to her voice.

"We'll sue," Chris told her. "It's libel. We'll sue them!"

Madison let out a heavy sigh. "Thanks Chris, but it's not. Twisted, misleading, unfair, yes, but look at it carefully. It cites facts. The damage is in the innuendo. How much damage is it, anyway?"

Chris was silent for a moment.

"Be honest."

"It's bad . . . I just think about Amad-Amed and the Washington brothers. They couldn't have asked for more."

"That's one guy, a junior," Madison pointed out.

"Yeah, but that's how it's going to go. You said be honest. The race thing is something we've been struggling against anyway. Now, with this . . ."

"Okay, we'll regroup," Madison said. "We'll write a letter of rebuttal to the paper's editor. We'll make calls to all our clients and prospective clients and follow up with a letter pointing out our side of this."

"Our side?"

"That I represent people according to the situation, not race. We'll get statements from former African-American clients I have represented: Luther for one, Yusef Williams for another. That was pro bono."

Three years ago, Madison had represented Williams, a youth at the time, and gotten an acquittal for a murder he didn't commit. She remembered it clearly because it was that service that had serendipitously helped her exonerate Cody in an unrelated case.

"That's good. Good idea," Chris said. "I'll get Sharon to go through your files and pull up every African-American client over the past ten years. I'll have the list by ten and we can go through it and try to contact them. This is good, a lot better than sitting around worrying about it."

"All right, Chris. Thanks. I'll see you at ten."

Madison hung up and turned to her husband. "How bad do you think it is?"

"In terms of what?" he asked, taking a sip of coffee.

"Recruiting new clients," she said. "Keeping the old ones."

Cody nodded solemnly and said, "Well, it couldn't be in a worse paper. *USA Today* is what players and coaches read. Most NFL guys wouldn't have seen it in something like the *Wall Street Journal*. But this . . . they'll see this. It won't hurt you with the white guys, but the black guys . . ."

Madison sat down and delicately massaged her temples.

"I don't get it," she said, distracted by his words despite the gravity of the situation. "White, black, what's the difference? NFL players are NFL players. Everything's equal. Blacks get paid like whites, whites like blacks. There's no color in sports on a team."

Cody snorted out air through his nose. "Come on," he said. "It's just like everywhere else. On the field maybe it isn't, but in the locker room, on the bus, in the hotel, the airplane? It's just like it is everywhere else. Blacks hang with blacks, whites hang with whites. For the most part they distrust each other."

Madison shook her head as if refusing to believe. "Come on," she said dubiously.

"Madison, you remember Carlester McGee? The linebacker for the Outlaws back when I was playing?"

"I heard the name."

"Yeah, well one night me and Carlester are having a beer; he and I didn't care what color a guy was, some guys are like that. But he tells me a story about how he couldn't get an apartment for himself and his wife when they were first married. They were still in school at BC and Carlester goes through the paper looking for places. He calls on the phone and asks if a place is still available. They say yes. He goes. Now he's as good a guy as you can ever find, but they see he's black, his wife is white, and suddenly the place isn't available anymore. He goes to another place, same thing, and another and another, and that's in Boston! It's supposed to be a liberal place.

"Most black guys I knew had a mess of shit they had to go through because of race. You'd think athletes are exempt from some of the normal prejudices, but they aren't. The same guy cheering Barry Sanders in Detroit on a Sunday afternoon might be having security follow him around his store on Monday because he's black and he thinks he'll steal something. That's the way it is. So when something shows up the other way, when someone black can say no to someone who's white, someone they don't know who needs *them*, it's not that hard of a thing to do. An article like this just makes it that much easier. I won't lie to you: This thing stinks bad, and it's gonna be tough as hell to overcome."

Cody got up and came around the table. He wrapped his arms around her neck, and she put her hand on his forearm.

"Not still mad about the salt?" she said.

"Blood pressure's too high anyway," he told her with a sympathetic squeeze.

Chapter 17

While summertime can be comfortable in portions of L.A., just over the hills to the north it's typically brutal. Like many summers, the one Trane Jones joined the Juggernauts was cruelly hot in the Valley, the kind that was good for sales in air-conditioning and space fans. Hot enough to make most people there daydream about what it was like in Malibu and how they might someday get there.

Kurt Lunden drove his Rolls up over the hills on Coldwater Canyon and wondered, in the languid way the rich sometimes do, why the people on the other side didn't get themselves out. The sun was at its zenith and soon the shadows of the hills would bring some relief. But for now the line of telephone poles up ahead was still wavering in the heat.

Beside Lunden in the front seat was Conrad Dobbins. The agent had left off fidgeting with the radio ever since Lunden had politely asked him to stop.

"Hey Conrad," Lunden said, glancing into the rearview mirror at Zee in the backseat. "You think I need a bodyguard?"

Dobbins snorted. "I'm a celeb and a brother," the agent

said simply. "I need my man Zee to keep people at a distance. You never know what kinda crackheads are out there. Nothin' worse to most white people than a black man with money."

Lunden nodded. He wasn't going to argue that one. He wove his way through the streets until they came to a high school in Studio City. Out back the parking lot butted up against a rusty chain-link fence that surrounded a football field and a track. Tired-looking bleachers flanked either side of the fifty-yard line, and amid the scrawl of graffiti a sagging press box bore the ghost of a purple tiger, the school mascot.

Trane Jones saw the Rolls pull into the lot behind the bleachers and roll slowly clear of them near the ten-yard line. It stood out like a white guy on an NBA team, something you couldn't help noticing, even if you weren't paying attention. And Trane wasn't paying attention. Laced to his chest was a canvas vest that looked something like an out-of-date bulletproof vest. Twenty-five pounds of lead had been sewn into dozens of pockets meant to distribute the weight evenly throughout the garment.

Trane held his chin high and gasped for more of the scorched dry air as he walked briskly back to the goal line. He was nearly halfway through a metabolic workout that gave him only sixty seconds between one sprint and the next. That meant he had to walk back to the goal line and get into position while the stopwatch on his wrist was running. No one was there to watch or goad him on. But to Trane the devil himself couldn't have spurred him on with any more sense of urgency than he already felt. He knew where he was in the hierarchy of life and he knew what kept him there. He was at the top. He was the best runner in football. To be the best runner in football Trane had to work. The drugs and the money and the women he enjoyed, but they all came at a price. Trane had seen it over and over, and he was damned if he would be caught in the same trap.

The sweat ran freely down Trane's forehead and into his eyes. He bent double and wiped his face with a length of towel that was tucked into the waistband of his shorts. The lead vest chafed at his armpits. Its weight made his once separated shoulder ache like a bad tooth. He took note and pushed it from his mind. If you couldn't tolerate physical discomfort, you couldn't play football.

Back at the line Trane glanced at his watch and bent down into a runner's stance. As the last seconds expired he dug his cleated shoes into the parched dirt and coiled his muscular legs. At the tiny beep from the watch he erupted into a storm of energy, dust, and speed. Straight ahead Trane ran, as if nothing mattered more on earth than reaching the forty-yard line. Sweat flew from his bare skin like a legion of insects and his lungs caught fire. The finish line and the distant memory of lunch made him nauseous, but that was something you got used to as well.

Over and over Trane ran the forty-yard sprint while the two men and the bodyguard watched from their leather seats in the cool air that blew from the dash.

"Works his ass off, doesn't he?" Lunden said.

"That's what I wanted you to see," Dobbins said proudly. "Trane may be a lot a things, but lazy ain't one of 'em. I don't want you thinkin' it's all about genetics. Jimmy the motherfuckin' Greek can kiss my black ass."

"Jimmy the Greek?" Lunden said quizzically.

"Sucker on TV that said blacks were bred for slavery an' that's why we're faster than whites," Dobbins explained.

"Yeah, I remember," Lunden said, nodding his head but saying nothing more. It sounded logical enough to him.

They watched Trane run another sprint.

"Why does he come here?" Lunden asked.

"Motherfuckin' heat."

"This is the place for it. But doesn't he run with the team? I thought they had trainers for this."

"Trane already did that," Dobbins replied. "He does what they all do an' then he does some more. Rest of the team probably out golfin' or sittin' by the pool. Trane knows that. That's why my man's here. That's why he *is* what he is . . ."

After his last sprint Trane staggered back to the goal line, unlacing his weighted vest as he went. When he reached the end zone he let the vest fall to the brown grass, then leaned to the side, vomited, and collapsed. The heaving of his naked chest was visible from the parking lot.

Lunden gave Dobbins a worried look.

"Naw," the agent said with a confident smile. "He'll be all right. He just run outta gas is all. I've seen this before."

For ten minutes the men watched Trane lie inert before he began to stir. When he rose he walked casually toward the big car that was parked next to his own red Mercedes convertible. His bulging muscles quivered like a horse's flank under his taut dark skin, an impressive sight. Dried grass stuck to his body from where he had lain, and the canvas vest, his soggy T-shirt, and a plastic gallon jug of water weighed down either hand.

When Trane could see the whites of their eyes, the three men got out of the Rolls and greeted him. Dobbins introduced Lunden as the head of Zeus Shoes. Trane knew the deal Dobbins was working on with the man called Lunden was supposed to be very big. Still he gave Lunden a bland look as he shook his hand. Lunden wiped Trane's sweat off of his hand on his pink golf shirt without apology. The dark fingerprints left a mark on the shirt that was reminiscent of smeared blood.

"Nice to meet you," Lunden said.

"Yeah, you too," was Trane's surly reply. He turned to

Dobbins for an explanation. The agent knew Trane didn't like people watching his workouts. He'd warned him more than once that he wasn't a racehorse.

"Little too hot out there for you," Dobbins commented slyly, his bald head already beginning to gleam with sweat. "Got yo' ass a little sick."

"Some of us sweat for a livin', Conrad," Trane said.

Dobbins emitted a little laugh and patted Trane playfully on the shoulder. "My man," he said, "you don' wanna know how many times I hadda sweat for *you*. Ha ha ha."

"I wanted to meet you in person," Lunden explained without being asked, "and I'm not big on lunch. I like to see people in their element. It gives you an idea what they're about . . . That was an impressive workout. Conrad tells me you do it every day."

"I do what I have to." Trane sulked.

"Glad to hear it," Lunden said, apparently unaffected by the player's boorishness.

"How 'bout we go get us a goddamn drink," Conrad suggested pleasantly.

"I'm gettin' a shower," Trane grumbled.

"How 'bout my place?" Dobbins said. "You get your shower. I get us some goddamn drinks. The sun goes down, an' we talk some motherfuckin' business, get us *all* rich."

Trane shrugged his assent and pulled his T-shirt on over his grassy, sweaty torso. "I'll follow you," he said, sliding into the front seat of the Mercedes.

Lunden nodded and they were off, winding their way down through the hills and then along Mulholland Drive to West Hollywood.

"You know where it is," Dobbins said to Trane with a grin when they got there. "Me and Kurt'll be on the deck."

When he first came to L.A., Trane had actually lived with Dobbins and some of his things were still in the guest bedroom. Fifteen minutes later he emerged from the house in an electric blue pair of silk pants with a black body top. Zee was making drinks at the bar, and Trane had him mix a vodka martini with two olives. He took that over to the table where they liked to play dominoes and sat down facing the view. Lunden observed him coolly and picked gently at the skin on the bridge of his nose. Dobbins had his 8mm rolling. He was narrating.

"This is a moment in time, brothers an' sisters, when a great white man comes into our midst and reaches out his hand across years of oppression to offer a partnaship, a *partnaship,* my brethren! The white man sharing with the black, both of them getting goddamn rich . . ."

"A bit melodramatic," Lunden pointed out. He reached down into his briefcase and brought three copies of a contract out onto the table.

Trane tapped the ball in his tongue against the edge of his glass and let a bit of the drink spill into his mouth. Dehydrated as he was, the alcohol found his brain in a matter of seconds. He didn't show any interest in the contracts, not because he wasn't interested but because he didn't want either of them to think they had something he wanted. That's how he liked to play things.

"Go ahead, Trane," Dobbins crowed. "Sign that deal an' make us all rich as Bill motherfuckin' Cosby."

Trane looked off away from the table at the city and the setting sun beyond. The sky was fading from pink to red.

"What is this shit?" he sneered before letting more of his drink slip away from the glass.

"What is it? What the fuck is it?" Dobbins said, his blood apparently up. "It's just the biggest motherfuckin' sneaker deal ever! You an' Zeus Shoes! Big as it gets! A megadeal from the mega-agent!" He took out his pen and laid it down aggressively on top of the contracts.

"Better not be any of that ice-cream shoe bullshit," Trane muttered as he picked up the contract to give it his own perusal, which consisted of reading six or seven random words per page and maybe locking in on a number or two. "How much?" he asked, turning to Dobbins with a smile. "I see a lot a shit, but I don't see how much."

"Maybe mo' than anything you're makin' playin' motherfuckin' football," Dobbins responded.

"Maybe?"

"Your compensation is in stock options," Lunden explained. "We build a line of shoes around you. If it works, Zeus Shoes stock will go up as much as three thousand percent. With the options I'm giving you, you could make twenty to thirty million, maybe more."

"Maybe? We got a lot a maybes in this fuckin' deal," Trane said slowly. "What if this thing ain't nothin' but funk! Then that's what we'll be gettin', motherfuckin' funk."

Lunden stared passively and waited.

"Hey, my man," Dobbins said glibly, "I told you all about it. We get nothin' if it don't work, but it will work! An' without this deal we ain't gettin' shit anyhow."

"What about those motherfuckin' shoes?" Trane shot out. "I ain't backin' no motherfuckin' *ice-cream* shoes!"

Lunden's mouth was hanging open now in a half frown, and Conrad Dobbins began to worry that the man was losing patience. He glared at Trane. He'd talked with him about the deal just yesterday. Nothing was wrong with it then.

"The shoes we've designed," Lunden said patiently, "are a line just for you. They capture your image—a bad image, frankly." He reached back into his briefcase and extracted five glossy prints. He handed them across the table.

Trane examined them crossly.

"We tested these," Lunden said, gauging the player's face. "In malls. What we do is put pictures of all the different shoes we're considering up on a two-way mirror. Then we watch the kids. It's simple numbers. We record the number of engagements and the amount of time they spend looking. It works. It's the same way NFL teams now find out what new logos they're going to use."

"Now this is some shit," Trane said, shaking his head and unable to keep from smiling at the array of black, gold, and white shoes, each adorned with the dark insignia of a screaming skull with demonic bloody teeth. "This shit's killer."

"What'd you say?" Lunden said, leaning forward.

"Shit's *killer*, the motherfuckin' shoes, man!"

Lunden smiled broadly now. "Bad is good," he said.

"Naw," Trane said, looking up with his evil grin, "it's *bad*."

"Yeah, we can use that," Lunden said with the appreciative smirk of a huckster. "Killer shoes. How good is that?" He looked at the agent, who was smiling too.

"Real good," said Dobbins. "Real *bad*."

Chapter 18

Trane knew all about being bad. He'd been bad from the get go. And not unlike Clark Cromwell, his fate had been sealed on a single day at an early age. It began with a call from the school. Trane had lit a roll of toilet paper on fire in the boys' bathroom. His mom hit him a few times with the toaster cord, but the blows lacked real passion. She went right back to making a toasted bacon sandwich with mayonnaise for her boyfriend, who was kicking back on their couch drinking a quart of beer.

Trane wasn't upset. He figured the suspension from school would give him an opportunity to make some money. There was a dealer named Scoot who'd pay him ten dollars to make a couple of deliveries. Trane knew how important money was. Money was everything. When he got bigger, Trane was going to make millions, but not dealing like Scoot. He was going to be a pro football player. He knew he could. He was the fastest kid in the hood. He was faster than the grown-ups. The last time he got chased by the cops, he had time to turn around and give them the finger.

The only football he played was in the street, but the real thing was coming. Next year he'd be in middle school and they had a team. There were some kids around whose moms put them into the youth league. Trane begged for that, but his mom said she wasn't having it. She said his father had played football and all it did was make him meaner than he already was. She told Trane he didn't need to get any meaner. But once he was in the seventh grade, she couldn't stop him. He didn't need her permission, and he didn't need any money to sign up.

There were other ways Trane made money besides running for Scoot. There was a strip club just across the highway in the middle of an abandoned industrial zone. Expensive cars came from the north side of the city. With a screwdriver and some nerve, you could jimmy the Mercedes symbol off the trunk of a car and get yourself five bucks for your trouble. The strip place had a security guard that roamed the parking lot. That's why it took some nerve. But with Trane's speed, it was easy money.

Since he didn't have to get up for school in the morning, Trane decided he'd go to the strip joint that night. He had a pair of sneakers on his mind. He'd seen Eric Dickerson in a pair of sneakers on an advertisement during cartoons. He planned to be like Eric one day, so the sneakers were important, but he was short by about twenty-five dollars.

He let himself out of the bedroom window around midnight. His mother and her boyfriend were passed out in the living room. Empty cans of Colt 45 stood among the bottles of Miller High Life in a loose crowd on the coffee table. Trane could have marched right out the front door without a hitch, but he preferred the window.

The air was hot and still. Trane paused in the narrow alleyway between his own brick building and the one next door to peer under the shade covering the neighbor's bathroom window. There was nothing to see but an empty toilet with the seat up. It was a quiet night until gunfire erupted a few blocks away. After a moment he could make out the distant mewling of whoever had been shot.

"Get me a gun," he muttered to himself, squeezing between the broken slats of a fence and into the backyard of his homeboy Nemo. Nemo lived with his granny. She couldn't hear a car horn if she was sitting on its hood, so Trane simply pounded on the back door. Nemo's face appeared briefly in the window before the hardware inside began to rattle.

"You ready?" Nemo asked, his eyes bright and shifting nervously in the night.

"Are you ready?" Trane said to him placidly.

Nemo nodded that he was, and the two of them set off for the highway. Trane was paying Nemo five bucks to keep a lookout and because trouble always felt better when someone else was with you.

Towering lights girded with sultry halos stood watch over the cars. The gleam of chrome and buffed black paint spoke of quality. It was always a pretty safe bet that Saturday night would bring people with money to the strip club. It was a good club. That's what people said. Where Trane was from, you didn't need a club to see a woman naked. Girls, they'd get naked if all you did was ask, some of them. He'd seen plenty of women naked, too, just stumbling onto their front steps, drunk, with their boobs falling out all over the place. He'd even seen a good-looking woman naked one day in the back of Abbot's Garage. She was with a dog and everybody came to see. Scoot brought him. The whole thing was nasty, but like the men around him, he really liked that naked girl.

"You keep watch, okay?" he whispered to Nemo.

"Uh-huh," Nemo said, grinning at all the fine automobiles lined up in the middle of practically nowhere. The two of them were lying on their stomachs in a culvert between the lot and the street.

Trane took a screwdriver out of the long pocket on the

right-hand side of his shorts. He stood to mark the location of the security guard, then ducked between a Town Car and a Mercedes coupe. With an expert flick of his wrist that barely chipped the paint, the emblem popped right off. The guard was heading his way now. He could see him through the windows of the Town Car. Trane ducked back down and scrambled to the edge of the culvert where his friend waited. A valet dodged into sight suddenly as if from nowhere, giving them both a start.

The man didn't see either of them though. He simply hopped into the Town Car and raced off for the entrance of the club.

"Shit!" Nemo whispered. "He almost got us!"

"Didn't almost get, my booty," Trane said disdainfully. "You just keep a watch."

They moved along the culvert to the farthest corner of the lot before Trane hustled back up over the edge and darted in between a long black Mercedes limo and a Corvette. For one lazy moment he peered at himself in one of the darkened windows near the back of the limo. He tilted his head and it looked bigger than he remembered. The sound of car doors slamming near the club's entrance broke his reverie, and he quickly went after the emblem on the trunk. It popped off with a pretty little click. Then he heard a click that jolted his groin: the hammer of a pistol being snapped back into its firing position. He froze.

"Little coon bastard," drawled the big man. He wore the most basic elements of a tuxedo: ruffled shirt, dark pants, patent leather shoes. Without their links the cuffs of his tent-like shirt hung forlornly from his elbows. His distended belly and the lack of suspenders had pushed down the pants to the point where he'd have to hitch them in order to take much more than a step. The top of his head was bald and shiny, and his nostrils flared like he was on something. Behind the steel-framed glasses his mean little eyes twitched like living raisins plugged deep into the dough of his face.

"You think you can do whatever the fuck you want, don't you?" The man glowered, jabbing the gun barrel at him through the air.

Trane had seen and smelled enough drunken people to know this man was. His knees began to wobble like Jell-O. A war whoop by the culvert drew his attention. Another man, younger and with long hair, also in the remnants of a tuxedo, came dragging Nemo into the light by a handful of hair.

"Got the little prick!" the younger man crowed. His face was much too thin for the big ugly features it had to carry, but when he opened his mouth his perfect teeth flashed brighter than the whites of Nemo's terrified eyes.

"We got us a couple of little ghetto monkeys," said the big one, licking around the edges of his lips and making up his mind about something.

"What are we gonna do with 'em, Josh?" the skinny one said with a nervous giggle.

"I'm thinkin' they're gonna suck our dicks," Josh said with a mean smile.

"Oh yeah." Skinny giggled. "They are!"

Everything happened so fast that the entire sequence would play itself out again and again in the smallest moments of Trane's later life. Sometimes, during the time it took the flame of a match to ignite a joint, or in the brief period between tying a shoe and standing up straight, he would see it all over again with remarkable clarity: Skinny would whip Nemo down and around on his knees and at the same time undo his pants. Instead of cowering, Nemo would take a vicious bite out of the man's exposed member, dirtying his mouth with blood. Skinny would throw him to the pavement, screaming. And in an instant Josh would spin and put a bullet into Nemo's head at point-blank range.

The noise of the shot would deafen Trane and before he could think about running the gun would be back on him.

"Kill that little fucker!" Skinny would howl.

Trane's hands would go up instinctively, mirroring the gun.

The barrel would roar an orange flame into the night. The bullet would smash through the second digit of his ring finger before hitting him squarely in the face. The impact would knock him back flat, and he'd stare up with blank eyes at the white light above him without being able to move a single muscle.

Outside himself he'd watch with calm fascination as the security guard, two valets, and a bouncer came racing up to see what had happened. He'd watch the two rich white men gesticulate wildly and pawn off their twisted version of what had happened. He'd watch the police screaming up the street under flashing blue lights.

He would remember not expecting to live, and in a way not caring. Then he would remember the phoenix of anger rising up inside him.

Half an hour later, an emergency-room doctor slapped up his X rays and said he would live. The impact of the bullet, attenuated by the knuckle, had only enough force to penetrate the nasal cavity beneath his eye. The men who shot him and killed Nemo didn't spend a single day in jail, but Trane gained power from the experience. He vowed never again to allow himself to be in a position of weakness, especially with a dirty white man.

Chapter 19

After lunch at Clark's favorite place in Manhattan Beach he and Annie doubled back to the truck for towels, chairs, and a cooler. Side by side they walked down a concrete path into the breeze with sandals slapping until they reached the hot sand. The beach opened wide and long before them. You could walk all the way to Malibu. And even right in the middle of L.A. it was spacious enough so that the two of them could lie in the sun without anyone else on top of them. Part of that, too, was that it was the middle of the week.

From behind her blue mirrored sunglasses Annie watched Clark unfold the chairs. Her arms were crossed, and she looked like she'd just eaten a bad piece of fish. She draped the chair with her towel and stripped off her shorts and T-shirt before mechanically slicking her skin with oil. Clark sat without speaking and nibbled the cuticle on his pinkie, wondering if any of Annie's recent behavior had anything to do with him. She seemed at times almost morose. Of course, in all fairness, she hadn't been entirely well. She had had some kind of lingering stomach bug over the last week or so, and that could explain why she seemed tired and grumpy more often than not.

Clark secretly rapped his knuckle against the stony shell in his shorts pocket. He was nearly giddy with the notion that what he had might be just the thing to pull her out of it. He pulled off his shirt. His muscles, tanner than they'd ever been, rippled with angry striations. Ghostly stretch marks shot out from his armpits before fading away into his massive pectorals. He was in the best shape of his life, stronger and faster than ever before. It was do or die for Clark. He had to recapture the confidence of the team—not so much the players, but the coaches and management. Right now they doubted him because of his recently injured neck, and he was determined to erase those doubts. If appearance had anything to do with it, he was well on his way. There were people now who saw him in a tank top at the mall and mistook him for a bodybuilder.

Annie seemed not to notice. Earlier in the summer she would run her hands over his arms and chest and bring a lemon to the beach for his hair. She'd halve it with a paring knife from the cooler and squeeze the juice onto his hair, letting it spill down the sides of his head for highlights. She had fussed over his hair back then. She had even convinced him to cut it so that now it stopped at his shoulders. He remembered how when they were in bed she used to beg him to swab her bare body with it, tucking his chin to his chest and rolling his head back and forth, up and down.

But sometime over the past few weeks the lemons had become a thing of the past, and it seemed that she didn't even notice when his clothes came off at the beach—or at the house, for that matter. The same couldn't be said for him. Even if he wanted to he couldn't stop staring at her. Now he caught himself looking up and down the long length of her golden body, remembering the feel of every dip and rise beneath his own bare hands. He sniffed hungrily at the air for even a hint of her skin braising in coconut oil. He found the scent and it caused him to shift in his seat and tug gently at his shorts in order to rearrange himself.

Clark lay back and tried to relax but couldn't. For one thing, training camp was too near. Life ended when camp began. There would be no languid moments on the beach, no cold bottles of Pepsi pulled fresh from the ice, and no erotic interludes before a late-evening dinner. For another, he was about to pull a big move. And even though he was confident it would make Annie happy, that it would pull her out of her slump, it was still uncharted territory.

"I love you, Annie," he said, leaning toward her so that his chair groaned audibly.

"I love you, too," she said, but it might have come from a can.

Clark got up and nervously walked toward the water. The sand began to scorch the bottom of his feet, so he scooted the last fifteen paces to the water and cooled them in the surf. He turned to see if Annie was looking. She wasn't. She was stone-faced and staring toward the sun without even a hint of a smile to keep the corners of her mouth from being pulled earthward by gravity. Still, in case she looked up, Clark surreptitiously took the shell from his pocket and dropped it where the sand met the water. Then he picked it up and held it high for her to see.

"Annie! Look!" he shouted.

Her head popped up from the chair and she saluted to block out the sun. Clark walked toward her.

"What?" she said irritably.

"An oyster shell," he said.

"Oyster shell? What do I want with an oyster shell? It's probably dead. You don't want to eat it."

Clark grinned nervously and shook his head. He held it

out to her and wondered if she could see the trembling that he felt coursing down his arm, in his throat, and in the middle of his chest.

"Open it," he said. "Just try and open it."

"Oh yeah," she said, propping herself up on her elbows. "Like there's a pearl. Like we're going to get a pearl . . ."

Still Clark held it out. Annie sat all the way up and looked suspiciously at him now.

"What is it?" she said apathetically.

"It's an oyster shell. Open it."

Annie held out her hand and Clark dumped the shell in her palm. She hefted it, and for an instant he was afraid that she might heave it into the water.

"I don't have a knife," she said, teasing him without pleasure.

"Open it, Annie," he said, losing his patience.

She separated the shell with her hands and a large diamond winked up at her.

"Oh, God," she said.

Her tone filled him with panic. He felt the vitality drain out through the bottom of his feet as surely as if he were a cask whose bottom had been breached.

It got worse. Her dismay turned to disdain.

"Did you really think this would *stop* me?" she said incredulously. "I'm tired of the whole thing, Clark. I was before this. That's how I am. I get tired of things, and this little game was just about over anyway. But to pull some cheesy little trick like this. Like you can stop me?"

"I . . . What are you talking about? I'm asking you to marry me," he said. It sounded pitiful even to him, a big strong man whimpering. He wished he could take back his words or at least the way he'd spoken them.

"You're *manipulating* me," she said, spitting the words, "or trying to. You got the wrong woman, honey. I'm not having a baby, yours or anyone else's. You think I'm falling for *this?*"

"I . . . don't know what the—what the hell you're talking about. What are you talking about? Baby? Are you . . ."

She was transforming now, right in front of him as she yanked her clothes on. The signs over the past few weeks hadn't been aberrations. She wasn't in some temporary funk. She was molting, shedding the outer layer of the person she'd pretended to be and revealing what she really was deep down. Had he stopped to think about it, Clark would have realized that part of him had known it was coming. That was why he'd been so nervous. The nervousness didn't come from asking her to marry him. Something inside of him had known the truth and he'd been afraid. Immediately Clark reduced the situation to biblical terms: it was satanic. Clark worked his lips in silent prayer, knowing full well that his sins had led to this. It was always the way. You sin, you pay.

Then it hit him in the face, dead center. She was pregnant. She thought he knew and that he was trying to marry her to stop her from—

"Oh my God, you can't." He grabbed for her, not with strength but with desperation. She shook his hands free and swatted at them.

"Leave me alone! You big dumb son of a bitch!"

His jaw went limp and his mouth sagged open. It was too much, too unreal for all of it to be happening.

"Annie, you *can't,*" he moaned, almost sobbing. "You can't do that. Annie, I'm begging you!" He groped for her again and dropped almost helplessly to his knees in the sand. She was dressed now and she shook free of him again, flailing her elbows and knees as if he were something poisonous. And then she walked. She just walked away from him on the beach, and by the time he realized she was really going it was too late. She was on her way up the concrete ramp and moving fast. He ran through the sand, then stopped when he saw her get into a cab. His mouth worked like an air-starved fish, dumb and gaping. He went back to his things and found the ring in the sand.

The chairs and cooler and other things he left. He never liked the beach. He remembered that now. As he trudged toward the street with his clothes in one hand and the ring clamped tightly in the other, Clark was acutely aware of his golden hair and his tanned bulging muscles and the way people stopped to stare. He was every bit the fool he felt. He had become something he wasn't to please a woman who was something she wasn't. His humiliation was only overshadowed by the horror that she was carrying his baby and was planning to murder it. That had to be his focus. He had to stop thinking about himself. That's how the trouble had begun. It was pride. He thought he was a handsome man and that he should have a beautiful girl. He thought his own faith was strong enough not only to carry himself, but to carry others. A fool, that's what he was—a self-centered shameful fool.

But Annie, she wasn't just a fool. She was acting out of pure evil. That was the only explanation for what she was planning. Clark had to stop her. He knew that. That was God's will, and sometimes His followers had to do His will on earth. You couldn't just take from God. You had to give back to Him. Clark would either stop her or he would— Clark didn't know what he'd do.

Chapter 20

It was late in the day and they'd been at it all afternoon. Madison sat across the conference table from Chris and the two young associates who worked under him. One was Billy Acres, a young African American fresh out of the University of Texas who'd graduated at the top of his law class. The other was Martin Woo, a Chinese man who'd gone through law school the way Chris had, working nights to pay for school during the day. They were a true melting pot, the four of them, even more of an aberration than they appeared because the firm to which they belonged was as old and stodgy as a plaid bow tie.

Yet despite the little group's unusual diversity, the problem plaguing them swirled around the accusation of racism. The table was piled high with files, and the four of them were assessing the damage of the previous week's nasty article in *USA Today*.

"So you haven't heard back from Amad-Amed?" Madison said. "That doesn't necessarily mean we're out. It's not like he's told us he isn't interested."

Chris shook his head doubtfully and said, "I disagree. With a player a couple of unreturned phone calls isn't anything to get hot about. But a week of messages and calls without any response means we're out. That's how they do things. These guys don't tell you straight out, they just avoid you until you go away. We're being avoided, by Amad-Amed and just about every other African-American player we're in the process of recruiting."

"Billy?" Madison asked.

The young attorney shrugged helplessly and pushed his black plastic glasses up higher on his nose. There was something he wasn't saying. His eyes went to the table.

"What?" Madison said.

Billy cleared his throat, started to speak, stopped, then finally said, "I'm a white brother to a lot of these guys. That's the word. I spoke to Barry Coltrian of the Ravens two days ago and that's what he said the word on me was."

"A white brother?" Madison said.

"Black on the outside, white on the inside," Chris explained. "Hey, we're going to get through this."

Everyone nodded in agreement, but it was more for show than a reflection of how each of them felt. The effect of the article had been devastating. Three existing NFL clients had outright fired them. None had called directly, but Madison had received phone calls from their new agents demanding they stop trying to contact the players. Seventeen other active clients weren't returning calls. Eleven more had talked with one or the other of them and had taken a wait-and-see attitude. Only two existing African-American clients had voiced their allegiance to Madison's group. Both of those had done so through Billy. The rest of their clients were white.

The heaviest damage, though, was with players who weren't clients, NFL veterans and college recruits like Amad-Amed whom they were trying to bring on board.

"Chris, what do you think about getting in front of these

guys?" Madison said. "I mean, we're sending letters and making phone calls, but maybe we need to just appear on some doorsteps and make them listen . . . Billy?"

"Maybe," Billy said.

Suddenly the door burst open and Sharon, Madison's secretary, stormed into the conference room.

"Sorry," she said, addressing Madison excitedly. "I know you said no calls, but Clark Cromwell is on the line and he says he has to speak with you. He says it's a life-or-death situation . . . Line two."

Madison lifted the phone from a small table by the window and set it down in front of her.

"Hello, Clark, this is Madison. What's the matter?"

"I've got to stop Annie from having an abortion—Madison, she's going to kill my child—I didn't even know—I asked her to marry me and she said I was trying to manipulate her, that she was going to have an abortion anyway—I didn't even know she was pregnant, but she is and I've got to stop her—How can I?"

"Clark, slow down. Collect your thoughts," Madison said authoritatively, hoping she could cut through his obvious distress. "I'm going to put you on hold for a minute and take this call in my office. Give me a minute, okay?"

"Okay."

Madison stood and offered no explanation to her group. "I've got to take this," she said.

She shut her office door behind her and sat down at her desk. She took a deep breath and picked up the phone, then swiveled toward the window to try and draw some tranquillity from the view.

"Clark, I'm here," she said calmly and patiently. "I wanted to talk in private. Now tell me again what happened. Tell me everything, but slowly."

Clark described for her Annie's unusual behavior over the past week or so, including her bouts of nausea.

"I had no idea she was pregnant. I don't know, should I have?"

"No," Madison told him. "How could you have known that? Take it easy on yourself."

He then described for her what had happened at the beach and how he'd gone to his place and then her place but couldn't find a sign of Annie.

"Clark," Madison said after listening carefully, "I'm sorry, but there's nothing I can do. I can try and get hold of her for you, but if you're asking if there's something legally I can do the answer is no. I can't."

"Can't?" Clark said incredulously. "Madison, this is murder. Abortion is murder and she's going to *murder* my child! What do you mean *can't?* There's got to be something. There's got to be!"

Madison let it sit, hoping he'd calm himself. "There isn't," she said finally. "There isn't."

"You're a lawyer . . ."

"And I know the law, and I'm telling you there isn't a thing that can be done."

Madison kept calm. There was no need to tell him how she felt about the situation. That would only precipitate an argument between them, and he was her client.

Clark made an exasperated, animal sound, then mumbled good-bye.

Madison took the phone from her ear but continued to hold it as she stared pensively out at the emerald river.

Chapter 21

Clark woke at 5 A.M. and tried desperately to get back to sleep. His neck was sore. That hadn't changed since camp had begun. His recent injury was apparently here to stay. But now he had much more to contend with than just a sore neck. Injuries had compounded on injuries. That was the way of camp. Air had to be let out of the cushions in your helmet and your forehead greased to fit your swollen head into its protective covering. Headaches were constant and monumental. Nickel-size divots of raw, oozing flesh pocked your ankles, feet, and hands. Constant pounding and constant taping all but guaranteed that a cut would take four weeks to heal. That was how long Clark had been in camp.

Dim light from the approaching dawn filtered in through a seam in the shades. The musty smell of the hotel room was so familiar by now that it felt like home. Clark examined a puckered scab on the knuckle of his thumb to test his four-week theory. Yeah, he remembered that one from the first day. He'd smashed it between two helmets and left a good-size hunk dangling from the noseguard's face mask. The scab was just about ready to come off.

Of course, on that first day of hitting Clark hadn't fussed

over a little cut. Even his painfully unsuccessful search for Annie was blocked from his mind. On that day, all he could think of was his neck. It felt good going into camp, strong anyway, if a little stiff. But it was only strong from six months of rehab. Six months of concentrated strengthening. Contact was the true test, slamming your head at a dead run into the helmet of another man. That was contact. That was what the NFL required, and on that first day Clark had no idea if he could still do it and survive. With every impact he had winced in anticipation of total paralysis.

He remembered how the team's medical staff and coaches had clustered around to watch him during the first contact drills, curious to see if he could hold up. His hands had been cold and damp and he had worried about them calling a play where he would have to carry the ball. But of course they'd given it to Trane, and Clark's first test was to run with abandon into the middle linebacker, Mallory, a blocky gap-toothed Irish kid from Notre Dame who had no more sense than God gave a carrot. Clark remembered digging in his cleats and coiling his legs. The quarterback's count seemed to hang in the air like smoke.

Finally it had come and Clark threw himself forward and into the linebacker without a single impulse from above the stem of his brain. When the impact came, Clark heard it and felt it and saw it. It was a dagger plunged into his spine. It was a bullet, a battle-ax, a tire iron. Mallory went flat. Clark staggered, but kept his feet and managed to get back to the huddle despite the good-natured cheering and excruciating backslaps he got from his teammates for springing Trane to the end zone on the first play of the practice.

Clark had then looked at Gridley and Jerry, who were standing shoulder to shoulder off to the side. He gave them a thumbs-up even though he wondered if he wasn't going to fall dead in the grass with his next step, the pain in his spine was so bad. He didn't fall though. He kept going and going, a regular pink bunny. That didn't mean the pain had diminished over the ensuing weeks. It hadn't. But Clark knew that constant pain was part of the game. There were things for that, and Clark was smart enough to know when God called time-out. Certainly moralistic self-denial didn't apply to the use of painkillers in the NFL.

At ten minutes past five Clark was able to put that scene as well as his dull throbbing injuries out of his mind. He flipped over on his side, ready to resume the incapacitating sleep that he had so reluctantly given up before rising to use the bathroom. But while his mind was strong enough for circumventing physical pain, the emotional issues plaguing him could boil to the surface suddenly and without notice. During the first week of camp he had been so distracted that only Halcion, the powerful sleeping drug, had enabled him to get any rest whatsoever. And while the initial anxiety about his neck was gone, other problems still tormented him.

For one, the team's running game that everyone was so intent on remedying had so far given a poor showing. The possible reasons were many, and Clark, like everyone else on the offense, worried that the blame would somehow be attached to him. The other thought Clark found himself constantly wrestling with—and in fact it was what kept him awake on this morning—was Annie. At random moments an image would pop into his mind of her sitting there on the beach with that sour look on her face. The resulting emotions were so tangible that Clark would involuntarily clench his fingers, teeth, and toes. That was what he struggled with now.

Against his better judgment Clark looked at the clock. It was almost six now and the sheets were damp and tangled. A shard of sunlight lay across his blanket, illuminating a small flurry of dust motes, and Clark thought about all the stuff that went into your body that you never saw. His mind was up and running now at a breakneck pace, so he flung aside his tortured bedclothes and got up to brush his teeth.

The other bed lay flat and empty, a reminder of how easy it was to lose your job in the NFL. Bill Brown, better known to L.A. fans as "Deuce," had been a possession receiver for eleven years. A flamboyant, undersized wide receiver, Deuce had made a name for himself with toughness and tenacity. But a competent receiver corps and a third-round draft pick out of USC left him as the odd man out. Three days ago, with his Jaguar XJ8 loaded up and the top down, Deuce had pulled out of the hotel parking lot swearing with his final words that he'd never do another day's work in his life.

Clark thought about that as he spit into the sink. It sounded good after four weeks of brutal training camp. But how long could you get along just surfing and playing golf and sleeping till noon before it drove you out of your mind? Clark was in no hurry whatsoever to end his life of training and competing. He'd take the pain and the sleeplessness, even the tormenting uncertainty—anything but life without football.

He looked into the mirror to check the progress of a deep cut over his nose, and the image of Annie flashed across his mind again like a poorly disguised subliminal advertisement. Then the involuntary question came: How could she? Sorrow leaked into his heart and formed a cold little pool at its bottom. During his days and nights of searching for her it had become acutely clear to him how little he'd really known about Annie. He'd never met her family, or even any of her friends. His search, if you could call it that, had consisted of calling her answering machine until it was full and haunting the places they'd been together. Most nights he'd slept in the seat of his truck across the street from where she lived, silently willing her lights to come on. They never did. If that apartment hadn't had her name on the mailbox he might have honestly wondered if she were anything more than a specter from his dreams.

At breakfast, Clark loaded one plate with pancakes and eggs and another with fruit. He was the first one to training table, so he said grace by himself then wolfed down his food, eating for survival rather than pleasure. If he didn't gorge himself during the rigorous days of camp he'd lose ten pounds in a week. Two practices a day combined with a rigorous regimen of running and weight lifting burned calories the way a blast furnace eats up tissue paper.

As he ate, Clark read through his Daily Bread pamphlet and tried unsuccessfully to focus on its message of letting Jesus take your worries away. Instead, all he found himself thinking about was Annie and antihistamines. He remembered a head cold that had afflicted him early in the summer. After he had sniffled for two days Annie had offered him an M&M-shaped pill just before bed.

"This'll clear your head," she'd told him.

"Antihistamine?" he had asked.

When she nodded he had told her his philosophy about things like that. "Tom says that when the body wants to purge itself of something, it does it naturally. If you stop the system, you're just keeping in the things that your body wants to get rid of. You cure the symptoms, but the problem stays."

"If you don't have the symptoms, then there's no problem," Annie had countered with a mischievous smile.

Clark had shaken his head and insisted that it was better to let the body have its way, to let the snot run freely from your nose and cough and wheeze the mucus up out of your lungs.

"You know, Clark," Annie had said, putting her pill back into her purse, "in the nineteenth century, the world's pre-eminent physicians would bleed you if you were ill. Kinda the same idea. They thought the body needed to purge its ill humors. Well, they were fools. No one denies that now."

Her words had hung there, inviting Clark to come to his own conclusions. She had done things like that from time to time, and Clark now presumed he should have sensed the broader implications. He should have known. But then, she had been baptized, and hadn't that absolved any faults she might have had to that time? It should have, and that was part of the reason why he just couldn't let it go.

Clark crossed the street that separated the Quinta Inn from the Juggernauts facility. The traffic at this hour was thin enough so that he didn't need the light, but a dirty stake truck full of Mexican workers roaring down the road forced him to move faster than he wanted so early in the day. In the training room, Clark wrapped a hot pack around his neck and jumped up on a table to get his ankles taped for the morning's practice. By the time he was done, a few of his teammates were beginning to filter in. Clark spent his extra time lifting weights, getting some of it over with in the hope that he could use the extra time he'd have after lunch for a longer nap. Glazed in sweat from the weights, Clark then dressed out in everything but his shoulder pads and helmet and went to the claustrophobic meeting room to wait for the morning meeting to begin.

Other running backs began to filter into the room showing varying degrees of discomfort. Some limped, some groaned quietly as they sat down—all were somehow afflicted. Kemp, their position coach, wandered in with a sixteen-ounce foam cup of coffee. The pungent aroma made Clark long for a cup of his own. Everyone looked at the clock. Being late was a finable offense, two hundred dollars a minute and two thousand flat if you went past ten. While most people outside the game thought that kind of money was a pittance, they didn't realize that NFL players got their blood up over a missing single in a forty-two-dollar per diem envelope.

Trane Jones came in last, moments before the red needle of the second hand reached the top of the clock. He slouched down in a chair in the back corner, ready to pull the bill of his cap down over his eyes the moment the lights went out and the film began. Kemp stood up. His fuzzy gray hair was rumpled and his eyes were baggy and damp from a coach's meeting that had lasted until 4 A.M. He cleared his throat.

"We got somethin'—" he began, only to be cut short by Gridley's barging through the door. The head coach, who appeared unaffected by his own marathon meeting, wasted no time on niceties. He marched to the front of the room, yanked down the screen, and took the floor. Kemp sat.

"We're not getting what I want out of the run game," Gridley began sternly. "You all know that. We talked about it before the scrimmage against Seattle, and we talked about it before this last preseason game against Detroit."

He glowered around the room, as if somehow each of them had taken part in some clandestine operation to sabotage the run game.

"That's what stands between us and a championship, gentlemen," Gridley said. He used the term only when he was really coming undone. "And now I know what our problem is . . ."

"It's not the running," he said triumphantly, his gleaming eyes passing over Trane Jones like the beam of a lighthouse beacon. "No. It's the run *blocking!* And I don't mean on the line, either. No. You men aren't where we need to be.

"You men," he began again, then dropped his tone and

said, "and look, let's not bullshit around, Clark, you aren't making it happen . . ."

Clark's face burned crimson and his ears rang as if someone had fired a pistol too close to his head. It took everything he had to return Gridley's glare. The shock of the situation left him without the ability to muster an ounce of defiance. His head spun like a tornado, and in its turgid gray walls he could pick out the fragments of little things that had happened leading up to this moment: a missed assignment here, getting beat in a one-on-one drill there, missing a couple practices because of a slight tear in his Achilles tendon. They were the same kind of little signs he should have seen with Annie but hadn't. It made him feel disconnected and dull.

"Now, starting today, I'm going to personally grade every contact drill you people do, every block you throw. And . . . if someone in this room can't start opening some seams for our runners . . . Well, I've already got scouts searching the wire."

Gridley went to the door, but instead of leaving he snapped off the lights and sat down next to the Beta machine. He clattered with the tape from yesterday's practice until Kemp finally got up and helped him guide it into the machine.

"Now, we're going to look at this together," Gridley said, hunching over in his chair with his head eagerly turned up toward the screen. "This is from yesterday. Okay, first play. Kemp, what's this play? Where's the script?"

Kemp fumbled in the dark with his papers and held the script up to the screen at an angle as he dipped his head.

"First play is . . . forty-four dive."

"Okay, forty-four dive."

A bird's-eye view of the field appeared and zoomed in on the area of the field where they were going through the inside run drill. The Juggernauts defenders were draped in loose-fitting red pinnies and showed the alignment typically used by the Giants' 4-3 defense. The film ran on. The offense came to the line and Clark got the handoff. He busted up through the middle of the drill and ran twenty yards into the end zone. Someone in the dark room cleared his throat, and Clark couldn't help looking back, in the hope of some contrite acknowledgment if not praise, toward the projector where Gridley sat.

"We're not going to win any championships building a run game around a forty-four dive!" Gridley roared, sensing the mutiny. "A shit throw-away play to run out the clock!"

No one said a word.

The next play was the double reverse. Trane went in motion wide. Clark led the way for Faulkner. Featherfield got the reverse. Trane took it on the double and was soon roaring up Clark's backside at full speed. The strong safety, who'd seen the play a hundred times throughout training camp, immediately broke for the sideline. Instead of sealing the safety to the inside as the play was designed, Clark got up under his pads and rode him full steam toward the sideline, thinking Trane could easily break back inside for a touchdown. But instead of working off Clark's improvisation, Trane tried to outrace the two of them to the sideline, where the safety knocked him out of bounds for a one-yard loss.

"Fucking pitiful!" Gridley barked. He began to rewind the sequence in slow motion and let it play back and forth as he spoke.

"Clark! What does this play call for?"

Clark knew where they were going and like a good soldier he simply took out his sword and fell on it.

"I'm supposed to block the safety back to the inside," he said flatly.

"Exactly! And where did you block him?"

"Outside."

"Horseshit! Cowshit! Bullshit! This sucks!"

Gridley was on his feet again and slamming the remote onto the tabletop, where it blew apart.

"Fix it, goddammit! Fix it!" he screamed. "Or heads will roll! Heads will roll!"

With that, the head coach stomped out of the room and slammed the door. Everyone sat in the dark for several moments silently examining their fingers and hands before Kemp got up and quietly and pathetically said, "Okay men. Let's fix it."

Clark looked back sympathetically at the older man and realized his ass was on the line as much as Clark's. The only one without apparent concern was Trane Jones. Gridley was either too scared or too embarrassed to put the onus on Trane. He was making more than everybody in the room put together, and even though the truth was obvious to the rest of them, it wasn't being addressed. If Trane spent a little more time paying attention to what the hell was going on he might be in sync with the rest of the team and they might actually get the run game on track. No one was chewing his ass up, though. No one was willing to say the emperor had no clothes. As the film began to run and Kemp did his best to sound authoritative, Clark stole a look back at Trane, who was splayed out like a dead man and breathing heavily from the efforts of sleep.

Chapter 22

Trane let his engine run. Phatt Momma's was the hottest club in L.A., and that meant there were valets to park VIPs' cars. Cubby and Leshay, two of his homeboys, got out of the red Mercedes with him, sunglasses on just like their patron and baggy pants hanging halfway down their asses. Homeboys were like pilot fish and Trane was the shark. They lived in his mansion with him, ate his food, and drove his cars. Their ride was free. Gold rope chains and medallions jingled together like sleigh bells. Cameras flashed from behind the velvet ropes, and Trane flashed back the finger, sticking out his tongue at the same time. He was into it. L.A. was his kind of town.

Inside, the music pounded their ears in thick waves. The flashing lights and smoke and the milling throng of people were like an acid trip. The head of security had a blond crew cut. He was a musclehead in a black T-shirt two sizes too small in the arms. He grinned foolishly at Trane and brought his hand briefly to his mouth to speak into his headset before leading them through part of the bar and up a purple set of stairs to the VIP room. Inside, there was less noise, but still enough so Trane had to lean toward Leshay and yell into his ear to get some drinks. Fresh cool air flowed through the room, a pleasant reprieve from the choke they'd been treated to downstairs.

Trane and Cubby tossed themselves down on a green leather couch in the corner of the room. Glass, floor to ceiling, allowed them to look out into the main bar and all its life forms. There were blacks and Mexicans, dykes and bikers, fags and muscleheads, hippies and suits, all crawling over the top of each other like a swarm of locusts. Leshay appeared with a short-skirted cocktail waitress in tow. She set down six ice-frosted tumblers of vodka, and after flashing Trane some hardware of her own, a chain link through her tongue, she walked away with her high round ass switching.

"Let that bitch suck my cock," Trane admitted. "Leshay, get that bitch right back here."

Leshay sipped the top off his drink before rising and pursuing the waitress. Trane took a mouthful of his own drink and watched Cubby snort some coke off the back of his hand then dust off his nose with a thumb. When he turned his head he was staring into the bronzed thighs of a goddess in a leather mini. His eyes groped their way up to her face and her long blond hair. Those features were equally impressive despite an angry little downturned lip. Her hair was blown out like the mane of a lion and her lips were painted the color of pink candy.

"That's my seat," she said.

Trane leaned back into the couch and let his elbows sink in the leather. He smiled up at her.

"Fuck you, bitch," he said in a friendly tone.

"Aren't you charming?" she replied with a false smile. "But that's my drink in front of you, so why don't you find someplace else?"

Trane noticed a drink marred by pink lipstick, a milky White Russian that he hadn't seen before.

"Why don't you sit right down on *this*, baby?" Trane raised his eyebrows above the tops of his glasses and wagged his pierced tongue at her.

"Here," she said, picking up her drink and dumping it into his lap. "This'll cool you down."

The girl snapped around to walk away, but Trane was on his feet with his hand on her upper arm before she could go a step. He spun her back fast and pulled her into his muscular frame so that he could feel her breasts against his abdomen and smell her tangy perfume.

"You're hurting me," she said, speaking in a quiet seductive whimper that let him know she liked it.

"Yeah, you want that, too, don't ya, baby?" he said, the words spilling from his mouth instinctively and without calculation.

She let him press her even tighter and looked up into his sunglasses with a crooked smile. "Maybe I do," she whispered in the same small voice.

He wasn't sure, but it seemed like she had flicked her hips against his leg.

"Let's go," Trane said, his own throaty voice thick with excitement.

"No," she said huskily. "Let's stay. Let's drink and dance and think about it . . . We can talk about it, about what you're going to do to me . . . I like to talk about it . . ."

Trane's smile spread even wider.

In the morning she was gone. Trane's blood raced just remembering. Him knocking her around, tying her up, her liking it all. Then for her to just be gone? He got up and parted the curtains. The driveway was littered with new cars, but they all belonged to him. She was really gone.

When had that ever happened to him before? It hadn't. Occasionally women had acted independent, even haughty. But none had followed through and simply left him before the sun came up.

"That was a bitch," he said to himself appreciatively.

Chapter 23

The sun shone beneath the clouds over the western lip of the Coliseum. Still, the rain fell with a steady hiss. Emerald cut grass clung to the soggy socks that sagged down the backs of the players' calves. Sweat mixed with the rain and washed sandy grit into uncomfortable spots between pads and skin. Even though the rain was warm, any wet weather was unusual for late September in L.A. Whether it would pass or not didn't matter anymore. The field was saturated. So was the tape wrapped tightly around every digit of Clark's fingers to reinforce his knuckles. Only eleven seconds remained on the clock, and it was running down. The Juggernauts were five points behind. They had no time-outs left, but they were on the 49ers' four-yard line.

Faulkner called the last play from the line of scrimmage. "Blue, blue, blue!" he shouted. The thinned-out home crowd was as quiet as the tension of the moment would allow. They knew their team needed to hear the play called by the quarterback at the line of scrimmage.

"Red Rover Cali strong! Red Rover Cali strong!"

The Juggernauts offense scrambled to their respective

positions. Trane Jones set up in split backs to the strong side of the formation, leaving Clark the spot to the left.

"You go weak!" Clark barked at him.

"Fuck you, motherfucker!" Trane told him as he anchored into his stance.

Clark jumped toward him. He'd push the dumb son of a bitch to the right spot if he had to. A quick glance at the clock told him if he didn't get lined up the clock would run out anyway. Clark jumped back to the weak side, the wrong place for the fullback with the play that was called. The weak back was the one who was supposed to go out over the middle and catch a pop pass in the end zone. The strong back was the one who had to pick up the blitzing linebacker.

Flustered, but knowing what his position on the field required of him, Clark got in his stance and planned his pass route. The ball was snapped. Clark raced toward the line between the guard and the center. As he burst through the raging wall of linemen and into the open space of the end zone, Clark saw from the corner of his eye that Trane had done the same thing. That meant the blitzing linebacker was unblocked. Clark spun, but too late. To get the pass off, Faulkner had to launch it early and high. Clark leapt and got his fingers on it, but the ball richocheted off and bounced uselessly in the wet grass. The whistle screamed in Clark's ears, ending the game.

On the sideline Gridley was in a fit. Clark tried to push the loss from his mind. He made his way to the middle of the field. Players from both sides were gathered in a loose circle. Clark knelt in a patch of gritty mud and held someone's hand and listened to the opposing quarterback pray out loud on behalf of them all. Even though everyone was equal in the eyes of the Lord, the star players typically led the prayers. Clark closed his eyes tight and tried to listen with his mind and spirit, tried to think of not being crippled and of other blessings. It was like trying to drive a big Lincoln up an icy driveway. Every time he thought he was there, he'd slip right back and start thinking about the game and what had happened.

He was going to be blamed. There was even an argument in his own mind for why he should be. But in his heart he knew it was Trane's fault. Trane was the one who lined up on the strong side of the formation. He should have stayed in to block. That was the play that was called. But the argument rang hollow. By now he was used to being the scapegoat.

"Amen," everyone around him said.

Clark felt pressure on his taped hand. "Amen," he said. "Good game."

Clark took out his mouthpiece and jammed it in between the bars of his steel mask. He turned his head up to the gray sky and blinked into the tiny drops that fell on his face. He opened his mouth and walked and tried to ignore the heckling of the few fans crazy enough to stay out in the rain just to shout obscenities at a team they called their own. One man with a thick black beard and mustache wearing gym shorts and a yellow Mickey Mouse poncho yelled so hard his voice split.

"Cromwell, you fuckin' bum! My goddamn grandmother coulda caught that pass! You *suck!*"

As Clark passed into the tunnel and underneath the worst of them he looked straight ahead. In the gloom of the tunnel the groundskeepers huddled together out of the rain like farm animals. Clark unbuckled his helmet but left it on in case anyone up top decided to throw something substantial.

Despite the fact that they'd won the first two games of the season, this loss filled the locker room with a sickening hush. Men stripped down in a silence broken only by the clatter of cleated shoes as the equipment men banged them steadily over garbage cans to knock off clods of grass. The pungent aroma of the rich green turf mixed with the damp smell of sweat. Clark's neck throbbed steadily. Other aches began to reveal themselves in his calf, his hand, his foot, knee, and biceps. He sat down stiffly and managed to shed his own gear before Gridley took center stage among his half-naked team. The coach looked like he'd been thrown off the bow of a ship and keelhauled. Not only was he drenched, he was battered. Yet his eyes were incandescent with intensity.

"The difference between winning and losing," the coach said in a voice ravaged from three hours of screaming, "is this small." He extended his pinched thumb and forefinger for everyone to see.

"And when it's this small," he continued hoarsely, "everyone has to be thinking the same way. Now, there were a lot of mistakes out there today that could have made the difference, but Clark . . . Goddamn, son . . ."

Everyone's eyes were on Clark. It was that same burning, sick feeling he'd come to know all too well lately.

"How in hell could you not pick up that blitzing linebacker? Hell, Mitch called the play because he saw that guy *coming!* It was a goddamn *touchdown!*"

"I was weak side," Clark said without shame.

"Clark, I don't give a shit if you're weak or strong or split wide like a fucking flanker," Gridley said wearily. "Do you think, with the game on the line, with your hands compared to Trane's hands, that I want you going out into the end zone and Trane staying in to block?"

Clark said nothing.

"Do you?"

"I ran the play the way it was called," Clark said, glaring right back at the coach.

"Goddamn it! Answer my fucking question, Cromwell! Do you?"

The silence was overwhelming. The media bumped against the big metal doors from the other side like cattle pressed into a gate. Other than that there was nothing.

"No," Clark said finally.

"Well fucking thank you," Gridley said indignantly, then knelt to the floor. "Let's pray."

Mitch Faulkner led the team in another postgame prayer thanking God for preserving the men He'd saved from injury and asking a speedy recovery for those He hadn't.

". . . and give us strength, Father, so that next week we may again know the taste of victory. Amen."

"Amen."

Clark got up and tore at his tape, brimming with disgust. Then the media came through the door and his locker was surrounded. Wrapping his waist in a towel, he turned to face them. Most times they didn't want to hear from him because they all knew he was going to use the opportunity to witness his faith just as he'd been taught. But today was too much for them to resist. How would the Christian lamb feel in the skin of a goat?

"What happened when you dropped the game-winner?" came the first question from a bold little woman wearing a yellow rain slicker. She stuck a Channel 7 microphone in his face.

"I dropped it. That's it. I lost the game." Clark spoke in a subdued but even tone and looked around defiantly at the rest of them.

"Do you think it was a good call?" said a crusty old newspaper reporter with pale, piercing eyes. "I mean, you're not known for your hands. Do you think it was an unusual play to call with the game on the line?"

Clark took a breath, pressed his lips together, and exhaled

through his nose. Mini spotlights from the cameras glared at him and the microphones bobbed ever so slightly, as if they were floating on the surface of a small pond.

"I ran the wrong play," he said. "That's it. There's nothing more I can really say to you."

"Will this cost you your job?" someone yelled from the back, arching onto his toes with his radio mike held up over the first line of reporters.

"If that's God's will, then I'll lose my job," Clark said with a bland face.

"Haven't you already been having trouble with the new offense?" someone else asked.

"No. I've been fine. I was fine in the first two games. No one asked me then when we ran for almost two hundred yards."

"Isn't that more because of Trane?" Another smart-ass in the back.

"I don't know, you tell me. That's all I've got to say."

Clark turned his back to them. That was it. No more. He refused to bite and they soon dispersed. Mark Mulligan, the slick-looking sports anchor from Channel 2, tapped him on the back.

"What?" Clark said over his shoulder.

Mulligan cleared his throat, "Uh, Clark, look, I'm sorry about everything, but my camera guy lost his battery. I'm really sorry, babe, but do you think you could give it to me again?"

"What?"

"Just the part about losing the game. Everyone's got it. I gotta have it, babe, or the station manager's gonna have my cajones in a jambalaya. I know it sucks, dude, but I know I can ask you. You're not one of these assholes . . ."

Clark turned to reenact his hara-kiri. He didn't even like this guy.

"So . . ." Mulligan said with a goofy smile, his pomaded hair shedding little drops from the rain like the back of a duck, "what happened?"

"I dropped the ball. I lost the game. I ran the wrong play. How's that?"

"Uh, yeah, okay, babe. Thanks."

Clark headed for the showers. There was an even bigger crowd surrounding Trane's locker. Trane was sprawled back on the stool in front of his locker, unit askew, wearing nothing but his sunglasses. By now, the L.A. reporters barely noticed. The cameramen just kept their shots high until the interview was over, then they'd sneak a wide shot to have something to show their friends and neighbors.

Clark couldn't help but hear Trane's subdued voice talking about the need for the team to have more mental focus.

"Ain't physical," he was saying. "It's a mind thing. We kicked their ass on the field. Beat their goddamn ass. We just gotta focus our minds."

Clark's urge to bust through the media and smack Trane's big mouth was so strong his arms trembled. Instead, he shook his head like a wet dog and went to the showers.

When he was clean and dressed, Clark picked up a bag of ice from the trainers and had them strap it to his neck. On the way out he held his breath past Trane's locker where the runner was contaminating the air with a heavy cologne. Outside the locker room the tunnel opened up into a waiting area where family and friends of the team were gathered, dripping and forlorn. Some of the wives and girlfriends were dry, however, meaning they'd found refuge in one or another of the luxury boxes that had been added on to the Coliseum during its renovation.

With his neck bound in ice his head hung forward so that his gaze could only come from the tops of his eyes. When he rounded the corner, his attention was drawn instantly to a ra-

diant blonde. In a crowd of stunning women, she jumped
out. She was a billboard. Her strong stomach was bare
below her top and golden brown. Her face, though heavy
with makeup, was exquisite. Her clothes, dark and stylish,
were at the same time revealing. She looked like an expensive whore. If Annie had a sister, this would be her. Drawn
by an unnameable force, he stepped toward her and stood
face to face, lifting his head against the weight of the ice
bag.

"Annie," he said dumbly.

"That's not even my name," she hissed at him with a
wicked grin.

For the second time in thirty minutes Clark began to tremble with rage.

"Hey girl."

Clark spun. It was Trane. He clamped a thick hand on her
upper arm and pulled her to him, sticking his tongue deep
into her mouth until its fat trunk pressed against her lips. She
went with it and the two of them moved through the crowd
as if Clark weren't even there. In that small moment he
thought he saw her hand move down to the outside of his
pants. He watched with his mouth agog as they left the
building. He realized that other people around were staring
at him and his face felt hot. He didn't know if it was because
of what had just happened or because he'd dropped the ball
and lost the game. He didn't want to know. He tucked his
head back down and pushed his way through the gaping
crowd.

Chapter 24

A hot wind lashed Angel Cassidy's golden mane. The car top was down. Her white dress rode low enough across her bronzed chest so that some middle-aged geek in a Porsche Carrera was trying desperately to keep up. The bald dome of his head bobbed up and down in her rearview mirror like an arcade target. Her fingers flexed against the leather of the wheel. With the hint of a smile she downshifted and shot forward at an angle between two slower cars, losing him. Angel didn't take to being pursued. She was the hunter.

She got off the freeway at Santa Monica Boulevard and bolted from light to light before turning onto Coldwater Canyon and weaving her way up into the hills toward the Bel Air Country Club. The sky was burning low in the west, barely red now and casting the deep purple shadows of night beneath the towering trees that lined the streets. At the club gate Angel slowed to a stop and presented her invitation with indifference. She was unaccustomed to asking permission for anything.

L.A. was her town. She'd grown up here, the daughter of a man many people considered to be one of the five most powerful people in Hollywood. He was dead now, but he had indoctrinated her at an early age into the society of entertainment tycoons and movie stars. She knew the most important things in life from the very beginning: power, money, and looks, in that order. The first two she enjoyed because of her father. The third she got from her mother, with a little fine-tuning from time to time from Dr. William Klimitz, the man everyone who was anyone used. In any other place, it would be considered unusual for a woman of twenty-six to have had half a dozen cosmetic surgical procedures, but this wasn't any other place.

Most people spent their lives pursuing those three essential elements of life. But since Angel already had them, she needed diversions. Her father always said there were two types of people in the world: those who created and those who destroyed. She was certain he'd never intended her to be a destroyer when he'd spoken those words of wisdom, but that's what she was. In fact, she delighted in destruction. It was her nature.

Even before she'd cared about makeup or clothes or boys, she had roamed the beach in back of their Malibu mansion just before sunset, searching for castles and sculptures other children had wrought from the sand. With her feet she would smash them, relishing the cool grainy texture of the walls, turrets, and towers between her toes. She could still see the pursed lips of her nanny looking on, prohibited by Angel's mother from reproaching her. And now Angel did the same kind of thing she had done to sandcastles, only with people. It was delightfully decadent, to smash a perfect marriage, or poison a once-loyal friendship.

A kid in a valet uniform gawked at her as she emerged from her Ferrari. That he was stricken meant nothing to her. She expected that, and it reminded her of the man who hadn't been stricken—not at first, anyway. It had taken a month just to get him into bed. Capturing his soul had taken even longer. She had had quite a time with him, even feigning a religious epiphany in order to have her way. The piquancy of that game made her smirk. Too bad it had turned so ugly at the end.

It wasn't that she hadn't been hated before. She had. But no one, she was convinced, could hate as vehemently as a zealot, and that's what he was. She wondered how he would react to her presence here tonight. After all, he was the guest of honor, and she was now playing the part of a rogue's bitch. He'd seen her before in her new role, outside the gates of the stadium waiting for her new man. She could never forget that visage of hatred when he'd approached her, called her Annie, and she'd told him that wasn't even her real name. Tonight might really set him off, though. After all, it was his night.

Inside the club, thousands of candles illuminated the ornate carvings of wood and stone that gilded every crease and border in the intricate architecture. The grandeur was impressive, even to Angel, and there was little she hadn't seen. Angel enjoyed black-tie affairs. The men were distinguishable only by their faces and frames. Dressed all the same, they were like drones, and it was the women who shone in brilliant colors with dazzling jewels, exactly the opposite of nature, where the males of most species were typically adorned with the brilliant colors and the females were muted and uninspiring.

From the top of the steps she searched the ballroom for her newest man. He was easy to find. He always drew a crowd. Even in this room, filled with Los Angeles's elite, he was the center of attention. Movie stars, entertainment executives, politicians, people accustomed to flocks of admirers—all craned their necks for a glimpse of Trane Jones. To Angel it was not surprising, but it was intriguing the way people fawned all over a man who was renowned for his despicable behavior.

She spotted him kicked back on a chair with his large sneakered feet splayed out on the dinner table amid the fine china and crystal glassware. A pair of silver-blue sunglasses hid his eyes, but his two large rows of teeth were bared in a fit of laughter. High on his left cheek, a round button of a scar rested like a smooth purple blight. Around him, dignified middle-aged people laughed in unison. They stood. He sat. It was his way of subordinating them.

Angel moved toward Trane and bumped squarely into the man who hated her.

"Hello, Clark," she said with a defiant little smile.

Clark Cromwell said nothing, but the left corner of his mouth twisted into a sneer, briefly giving him the appearance of a mild stroke victim.

Without another word, Angel moved off through the crowd until she was able to assume a perch beside Trane.

"My baby girl," Trane grunted, allowing his head to fall even farther back in order to meet her lips with his own. His tongue snaked lazily out of his mouth and into hers for anyone who cared to see it. Most of them did. Even a matronly old philanthropist with a chunky string of diamonds around her flabby neck couldn't help but stare at the silver ball bolted squarely into Jones's tongue about half an inch back from its pink tip. Meeting Trane Jones without seeing his pierced tongue would be like visiting Florence without seeing the statue of David.

"Hello, Trane," Angel said quietly after he'd retracted his tongue from her mouth.

Running her fingers through the slick cornrows of his hair, she took the opportunity to see if her most recent victim was still watching her. He was, staring malevolently from amid a cluster of pig-eyed politicians eager to make his acquaintance. Angel felt a wonderful chill scamper down her spine. Two dangerous men, and her pulling their cords.

It was almost eleven when a waiter slipped a note into Angel's hand without even a hint of who had sent it. Nor could she place the handwriting with any degree of certainty. Nevertheless, she was intrigued. It told her to be at the eighteenth tee at midnight. Angel looked around her to see if she was being watched. Trane had gone off with his agent, the python. She knew from an earlier conversation that tonight the two of them were to have a private audience with Dommer Graves, a big movie producer who was talking about casting Trane in his upcoming action flick.

Maybe Trane had sent the note, wanting to make up with her. At the end of dinner he had begun to talk dirty to her at the table, and she had thrown a drink in his face. It wasn't an unusual interaction between them. She'd thrown drinks before; likewise he'd cuffed her with his open hand. It was an exhilarating little game, and she knew that Trane liked to make some kind of a scene wherever he went anyway. The Los Angeles Charity Ball for Children was no exception, and she had been happy to oblige. It was part of her attraction to him.

She hadn't seen Clark since her entrance. Maybe the note came from him. Maybe he wanted to beg her to come back to him, as he had done over and over on her answering machine. Maybe he was over the initial shock and his desire for her had mastered his hatred for what she'd done. Maybe he'd begin to paw at her and cry and tell her he forgave her—pathetic, but titillating. Maybe she'd fuck him right there in the grass and then walk away, telling him to grow up.

Then again, maybe it was someone else entirely. Most women wouldn't consider acquiescing to this kind of mysterious note, but whoever sent it either knew her very well or

was incredibly perceptive. To Angel, a note like this was ir-
resistible. It spoke of secrecy and deceit, maybe even danger. She looked at her diamond Rolex. It was eleven-thirty.

Angel had another vodka martini and entertained the ram-
blings of Arnold Kassover, the man people were calling a
lock for next year's best actor. At ten minutes to twelve she
excused herself without an explanation. People were already
moving outside onto the back terrace. A white sliver of
moon had crept just above the treetops. Unlike the view
from the city below, the air was clear and the stars blinked
merrily.

Angel descended a stone set of stairs and made her way
past the last green. She stepped over some torn bunting,
remnants of the day's golf tournament to benefit the children. Her heels clicked along the cart path, and the noise
from the party soon became an indiscernible cascade, punctuated from time to time by the shrill laughter of one woman
or another. Angel wondered how her own laughter sounded
from a distance. She wasn't prone to laughing. Even so, she
thought it was strange that she couldn't recollect what she
sounded like when she did laugh.

She stopped short suddenly. Amid the rustling of the wind
high in the trees she thought she'd heard the whisper of her
own name. She spun around in a complete circle.

"Who is it?" she demanded.

"Angel," came the voice, again in a gruff whisper. "Don't
be afraid, Angel."

She relaxed. Then an explosion ripped the night and she
spun instinctively. Brilliant light filled her eyes. Fireworks.
A distant cheer went up from the clubhouse. She turned back
again to where she thought the whisper had come from and
he was standing there, only a few feet from her. She took a
sharp breath and a noise like a whistle escaped her throat.

She raised her hands above her head to break the impact

of the blow. Cold metal smashed down, snapping her forearm like a chicken bone, but her quick reaction had given her a chance to turn and flee. The next blow, however, hit her squarely in the back of the head, and it seemed to Angel that she tumbled forward in slow motion.

The night sky above the trees was a celebration of light. She lay on her back in a daze. He was grinning over her now, and she realized from the anxious smile on his face just how close she'd come to getting away. Standing over her, he took a half swing with the club, and she felt a sharp pain in her wrist. A tear rolled down the side of her face and her jaw worked itself slowly open and closed as if she were trying to speak. Then he raised the club over his head with both hands, bringing it down in the center of her forehead, splitting her skull with a terrific crack.

Chapter 25

Lieutenant Augustus Brinson drove his unmarked Caprice Classic through the parking lot without slowing and right out onto the cart path. He felt the big car slide but punched it and fishtailed back around onto high ground. He hoped the arcing brown tracks would offend some rich prick when they opened the hole again. That there was some dead woman just off the eighteenth tee didn't surprise Brinson in the slightest. It surprised him that it didn't happen more often. People always said poverty was the breeding ground for crime, but Brinson figured it was the other way around. Rich people had more time to fuck things up. They probably committed more crimes per capita than poor people. The difference was that few of them ever got caught, and those who did more often than not slid out of it on the slimy trail of some lawyer.

The Caprice lurched to a halt and Brinson got out onto the wet grass. His shoes were old and worn, so he didn't care when he busted up a little dried-up log of goose shit. At fifty-seven he was old for the force; the thin layer of graying hair plastered to the sides of his head proved it. His face was as big as a shovel and his chin rolled several times before melding directly into his torso, circumventing the need for anything by way of a neck.

The sun was out, but its light was fractured by the high trees overhead. The detective filled his lungs with a rush of pine scent that reminded him of bathroom spray. Without embarrassment he hitched his pants so the belt ran smack across the middle of his waist. Lots of fat guys Brinson knew either cranked their pants up high toward their armpits or wore them hidden below the bulk of their gut, kidding themselves that they were only a fifty-four instead of the full sixty-two like Brinson. He made no apologies for his bulk. He liked to eat and he liked to drink. Whole milk was a good thing.

"Mullet," he said, speaking to the assistant medical examiner the way card buddies will. Brinson looked off into the patch of blue sky and the white wisps of cloud that showed through the dark canyon of trees.

The ME was as small and dainty as the detective was big and sloppy. He didn't bother looking up from the notes he was jotting down in a ratty yellow spiral notebook.

"Brinson," he said.

"Whataya got?"

"Dead girl."

"Something new."

"Got a time of death for you," Mullet said, still writing.

"I got a dog in the seventh for you," Brinson said. He took a white pistachio from the right pocket of his gray blazer, shucked it, gobbled the meat, and popped the shell into a common grave in his left pocket. He did this with the precision of a habitual nibbler.

"I'm not kidding," Mullet said, offended.

"Every time I ask for time of death you guys make me wait three days then tell me you don't know. This blood ain't dry and you're telling me you got time of death?"

"He broke her watch. She raises her hands to protect her head," he said, raising his own hand and ducking as he presumed she had, "and the watch gets smashed. Twelve o'clock, just as the date's changing."

"He?"

"Women kill with knives, ice picks, and poison. You know that."

"What'd he get her with?" Brinson asked, peering past the ME to where the body lay. "A golf club?"

"Probably."

"I was kidding."

"I wasn't. Golf club has its own signature. I've only seen two of them before. Most people want to kill someone like this they do it with a baseball bat or a pipe or an ax handle. Then you don't know which is which. Just a blunt instrument. Golf club makes a big puncture wound. Check out her skull. Probably a big guy, too. Takes a lotta power to bust a hole in someone's skull. Besides, we're on a golf course . . ."

"Any witnesses hear someone yell 'fore'?"

Mullet shook his head sadly. Death was his business, but he didn't like to kid about it.

Brinson popped another pistachio and walked over to where the body lay. He lifted the sheet and peered at the dark cave of blood in the pretty girl's forehead. There was another in the back of her head. He picked up her clammy arm and looked at the watch. Her other arm flopped outward just below the elbow at an angle that made Brinson think of a chicken wing.

He straightened up and talked with the blue boys who had been first on the scene. They gave him the scoop on the Mexican groundskeeper who'd found her. They already had a guest list from the gala the night before. Brinson thanked them for getting the ball rolling and handed the grunt work over to Arnsbarger and Kelly, two of his sergeants, who had just pulled up in a maroon Concord. It was 6:30 A.M.

By eight they knew the girl. Annie Garron Cassidy was a rich L.A. society girl who'd acted in some movies as a kid but never made the big time. Daddy, the producer, was dead. He had left her enough money so she didn't have to do diddly. Mommy, the French nanny from marriage number one, was back in France. The boyfriend was Trane Jones, a bad customer with a history of violence. Jones had enough power in his swing to reach the green of a par five in two, or cave in a pretty girl's skull in one. Brinson had him in a hot white room by nine. The star player smelled like cigarette smoke and expensive scotch. He looked like roadkill in sunglasses. Even his fancy leather pants were rumpled and creased.

"Hard night?" Brinson asked, popping a nut into his mouth.

Trane looked at him wearily, thought about telling him to fuck himself, thought better of it, and simply nodded yes. He wanted to get in and out. He wanted a shower. He wanted some sleep. This was his only day off.

"You know your girlfriend is dead?"

"That sucks," Trane said with an uncaring shrug.

"When did you see her last?" Brinson asked.

Trane didn't hide the fact that his last glimpse of her was through a faceful of vodka. He didn't pretend not to have made a move to cuff her for dousing him, or threatening to "kick her ass."

"That's a love spat," Trane said. "That ain't nothin'."

He then told Brinson where he had been from that time on, right up until the detectives got out of their car in his driveway as he pulled up from a night so long it spilled into the day.

"You didn't wonder what happened to her?"

"Naw. Shit, we do battle, she gets her ass on home or wherever. That happened before. That ain't nothin'. Hot-blooded, that's her," he said, smirking in a way that discounted the fact that she was wearing a toe tag. "In mo' ways 'n one."

Brinson's face flushed with hatred. But instead of reacting he stuffed his emotions into some back corner of his mind and focused in on midnight. He asked Trane about his golf clubs, where they were.

"Fuck is that to you?" Trane said, annoyed.

"She was killed with a golf club. I'd like to see yours."

Through the haze of weariness and the lingering grip of alcohol Trane suddenly became alert. "I didn't do a motherfuckin' thing," he said angrily. "You arrestin' me? Am I under arrest?"

"No," Brinson said calmly. "No, we just wanted to talk to you."

"Go talk to yo' fuckin' momma," Trane said, rising from the chair and starting for the door. Brinson did nothing to stop him. When he was gone, Brinson looked at the glass in the wall and said, "Follow him."

Brinson sat for a second, then jumped up out of his chair and waddled out into the hall. "Don't lose his ass," he shouted to the detectives who were racing down toward the stairs. "Use a goddamn helicopter if you have to, but don't lose his ass!"

Trane took a quick peek into his car's trunk, then ripped out of the municipal lot with tires shrieking. By the time he hit the 110 going south, a maroon Concord had fallen in comfortably behind him. Trane didn't bother to check his rearview mirror. He figured a fat slob like Brinson was still trying to get his ass out of his seat. He drove south all the way to the Pacific Avenue exit before heading for the harbor. After winding his way through the streets he shot between two warehouses and pulled right out onto the docks where the big ships were berthed. At the ass end of a big tanker named *Metzaluna* Trane stopped and hopped out. As Brinson's sergeants pulled out onto the pier they saw him heaving a three-iron with both hands out into the murky water beyond the ship's rudder. They had him in cuffs before Brinson arrived. At 5:37 the divers brought up the club with enough blood stuck on the head to bring Trane Jones in front of the magistrate on a charge of murder.

Chapter 26

Sitting wedged between her husband, Cody, and her son, Jo-Jo, in a ratty T-shirt and a faded pair of jeans, Madison looked ten years younger than she really was. Her chestnut brown hair was pulled back by a simple band, making her neck and nose appear to be longer than they really were. She was annoyed with herself for breaking her own rule and watching football on a weeknight. Sitting through every Friday night high school game that Cody coached, as well as Jo-Jo's Saturday-morning Little League games, before forfeiting every Sunday afternoon to the NFL was more than enough. She'd told them both long ago that on Monday or Thursday night they were on their own. But the truth was, she wasn't watching for the football. She was like every other red-blooded American lawyer. She was watching for a commercial.

As stodgy as Caldburn, Baxter and Thrush might be, at the moment it was like every other workplace across the country, abuzz with the discussion of whether or not this particular commercial should be pulled from the air. In the spirit of true capitalism, Zeus Shoes, the company in question, had announced at a noon press conference that, despite the circumstances, it would continue to run its ads on Thursday night's prime-time football game as well as during other upcoming sports programming.

During a noon press conference on CNN, Kurt Lunden, the sandy-haired walrus who was the CEO of Zeus, said, "Zeus Shoes will not bow to the pressures of political correctness. This ad was created in the spirit of competition, not crime, and Zeus Shoes refuses to presume anything but the innocence of Trane Jones, unless he is proven guilty in a court of law. If that were to be the case—and we have no reason to believe it will be—then Zeus Shoes would reassess its ad campaign at that time."

Madison recalled the murmurs that had erupted from the crowd in the long conference room, her more liberal associates nodding with defiant chins while the conservatives wagged their heads like disappointed old dogs. She was one of the former. Of course she had a hard time believing that a rotten apple like Trane Jones, leaving a trail of smoke, hadn't created a fire. And of course she wasn't happy about the kind of mixed message Jones—and Zeus Shoes—might be sending to kids. But her entire legal career was based on the presumption of innocence. Despite the fact that Trane Jones had been arrested, despite his girlfriend having been killed—supposedly with a golf club that belonged to him—despite Trane's horrible past and everyone else's rush to judgment, it was Madison's place to presume innocence.

"This is it, Mom!" Jo-Jo exclaimed. He'd seen the commercial during previous NFL games, and had already put in his request for a pair of the infamous shoes.

Madison shifted her attention to the TV.

As the sun sank over a distant band of mountains amid a brooding apocalyptic sky, a lone motorcyclist raced down a single-lane highway toward the ground-level camera.

"When you run alone . . ." came the deep rich voice of the announcer, "you count on your treads . . ."

The camera cut to the spinning front wheel of a chopper with a big green, white, and black sneaker planted firmly on the peg just above it. Then it pulled out wide to reveal Trane Jones with a demonic grin kicking back spread-legged on his hog. The cape around his neck was a tattered American flag. His bare chest was a glossy sculpture marred only by a twisting mass of tattoos. His legs were snugly encased in red leather. The used-up stub of a fat cigar was clamped firmly in the corner of his mouth.

"And when you're headed for the top . . ." the rumbling voice continued, "you can't worry about the little things that get in your way."

The picture quick-cut to a pink stuffed bunny resting peacefully in the middle of the road. Jones's bike roared through the frame, which then cut to a low angle of the mangled, smoking bunny with the bike racing away toward a flat-topped pyramid bathed in golden light.

"That's killer," Jones muttered in a close-up shot of his face with the burning sky in the background.

The camera went wide again to capture the bike shooting up the side of the pyramid. Jones skidded to a stop at the top and dismounted. In the middle of the pyramid's top was a pit writhing with snakes. The ad cut to a shot looking up through the snakes from the bottom of the pit. Jones stepped to the edge of the pit, sneakers first.

"You fear no evil . . ." the voice intoned, "because you're as bad as anything on earth."

Jones pitched his cigar butt to the side and leaped into the pit, landing feet first. The writhing snakes morphed into scantily clad women, their bodies bathed in oil, each one groping for the football star. With the voluptuous young models draped all over his body, Jones flashed his trademark smile from behind his blue shades and urged, "Zeus Shoes . . . they're killer."

The final shot started in close. It was the satisfied, sleeping face of a beautiful brunette with her cheek resting peacefully on another girl's naked flank. As the camera pulled up, Madison could see that the bottom of the pit was now littered with the bodies of blissfully sleeping women. The camera lifted to a bird's-eye view of Trane pulling away from the edge of the pit on his demonic chopper.

"Zeus Shoes . . ." the announcer boomed as the screen faded to black, "they're *killer.*"

"Cooool," Jo-Jo said, drawing out the word to properly express the magnitude of the impression.

Madison sat with her mouth open while on the TV Mike Patrick waxed on about the beautiful blimp shot of Soldier Field in Chicago where the game was taking place.

"What'd you think of that?" Cody asked, tugging on her far shoulder where he'd draped his arm.

"Unbelievable," she said. "No wonder everyone's in an uproar. If this guy really killed that girl . . . I mean, I know they're saying those women are sleeping, but they could be—"

"Dead," Cody said with a solemn nod before turning his attention back to the game "I'm going to have to get me a pair of those shoes," he muttered.

Madison looked at him, her mouth still agape.

He looked back at her after a moment and grinned. "Kidding."

"That's not even funny," she told him, half-serious. "Did you see Jo-Jo?"

They both looked at Jo-Jo. He wasn't paying attention to them. The Bears were about to score.

"I imagine Zeus is going to sell some shoes," Cody pondered.

"It's unbelievable," Madison said, shaking her head. "Nobody cares anymore . . ."

The Bears scored a touchdown and kicked their extra point. The ensuing commercial brought Jo-Jo back into their midst.

"What do you think of Trane Jones?" Madison asked him, wondering about the practical effect of someone like that on a ten-year-old boy.

"He's killer, Mom," Jo-Jo replied candidly. "You heard the commercial."

Madison rolled her eyes. "Just because someone is in a TV commercial doesn't mean they're kill—" Madison checked herself. "Stop using that word, Jo-Jo!"

"Mom, it's just a word. It's like 'cool.' You don't know if he really killed anyone. You're the one always telling me, 'Don't judge this guy and don't judge that guy.' Come on, Mom . . ."

"Touché," Cody said under his breath.

"Great, Cody," Madison replied.

"Cody," Jo-Jo said excitedly, "did you ever play against him?"

"Trane? Yeah," Cody said, taking a sip from his nearly empty can of Coors Light. "I played against him when he was a rookie. That was before I even met your mom."

"Wow! Did you hammer him like Joe Montana?" Jo-Jo wondered. Cody was famous around Texas for knocking the star quarterback out of a big playoff game.

Cody looked at Madison with a wry smile and said, "Actually, I got kicked out of the game for slamming his head against the goalpost."

"Killer!" Jo-Jo exclaimed.

Madison was too interested in the story to protest her son's choice of words. This was one she hadn't heard.

"I was covering him on the goal line," Cody explained.

"The tight end picked me illegally, just slammed right into me to knock me off the coverage, and Jones scored. He slammed the ball in front of me and I got a little heated and called him a few choice words."

"Then?"

"Then he spit in my face and I slammed his head into the goalpost.

"He deserved it," Cody added matter-of-factly.

Madison got up from the couch with a slap on her knees. "Well," she said sarcastically, "I'm off to the bedroom to sew some clothes and make up a dinner recipe for tomorrow night. Maybe I can get you two a couple of beers and some raw meat to gnaw on while I'm up?"

"I'll take a beer," Jo-Jo said, lighting up.

"She's bullshitting," Cody said.

"Oh."

Jo-Jo watched his mom walk out of the room without another word, shaking her head

"They'll probably be asking her to represent the guy by the end of the week," Cody said under his breath as he finished his beer and turned his attention back to the game.

"You think?" Jo-Jo asked.

Cody shrugged and with a crooked smile said, "Why not? If I was accused of killing someone, I'd want your mom representing me."

"She already did," Jo-Jo said, reminding him with a smirk of how the two of them met.

"And she got me off, didn't she?" Cody said with a smirk of his own.

"You're crazy," Jo-Jo said, grinning.

"That's what they say."

Chapter 27

The next morning at nine o'clock Chris Pelo walked into Madison's office without knocking. Madison had undergone a transformation from the night before. Her glossy hair hung past her shoulders. A pinstripe suit and just a touch of makeup did more than make her striking; it gave her the appearance of a lawyer who was as intelligent as she was formidable.

"I just got a call from Armand Ulrich," Chris said, slumping down into one of the leather wingbacks that faced Madison's richly polished cherry desk. His feet barely reached the floor. "He wants us to fly to L.A. this morning. He wants you to represent Trane Jones."

Madison winced.

"You do owe the man a favor, Madison, and before you get started, you know as well as I do that if Ulrich is involved there's gotta be at least some reason to believe that Jones might not be the killer everyone is making him out to be."

Pelo toyed with his pale yellow outdated paisley tie and watched his partner carefully from behind his dark brown eyes, measuring the amount of resistance he was going to have to overcome. Madison looked up from her work with just the hint of a smile.

"I would imagine," she quipped, "that his reason has something to do with winning a championship, and not too much to do with Jones's reputation for moderate behavior."

"We both know what kind of man Ulrich is," Pelo countered. "He's one of the few people in this business where some things beyond a championship do matter."

"Let me get this right, Chris . . . I'm going to drop everything I'm doing because Armand Ulrich wants me in L.A. to represent one of the most reprehensible personalities that the world of sports has ever known? Okay," she said with mock enthusiasm, "when do we leave?"

"Right now," Pelo deadpanned. "He sent his Gulfstream Four and it'll be at the airport by the time we get there. And before you get sanctimonious on me, Madison, remember he's the owner of a team that two of our clients play for, as well as being the chairman of the NFL's competition committee. A working relationship with this man will mean a lot to us. And, it will help bail us out of the *USA Today* debacle. Besides, this is what you love to do. I know for a fact that you don't have anything juicier than a vehicular manslaughter on your hands right now."

Madison shook her head and said, "You forgot to mention that this will be the biggest legal circus since the O.J. trial."

Chris kept his lips pursed tightly beneath his rickety black mustache. A dark clump of his strawlike hair had fallen across his brown pocked forehead. He blinked before saying, "There's nothing wrong with notoriety, Madison. You don't have to pretend that it hasn't made us rich . . ."

"You're right," Madison said wearily, "We're rich. Rich enough, I think, so that we don't have to run off to L.A. at a moment's notice because Armand Ulrich thinks we're the right lawyers for the job and he's ready to call in some nebulous favor."

Chris only continued to stare.

"I know, Chris, but dammit, Trane Jones is so . . . so distasteful."

"Madison," Chris said blandly, "if you want me to count off all the distasteful people you've represented, I will. But you're the criminal lawyer. You're the one who's supposed to be telling me how everyone is innocent, and everyone deserves a legal advocate . . ."

Then he got excited. "Madison, this is what you've wanted. This is what we need!" Madison's partner got to his feet. "And you should be honored that out of every lawyer in the entire country, Armand Ulrich is calling *you*. After this, there won't be a high-profile case where you won't be the first person called. You've been complaining since Luther's trial about not having something like this to sink your teeth into . . ."

"Okay," Madison said after a long pause. "You hit me where it counts . . . right in my childhood dream. Let me call Cody to tell him I'm going, and I'll have to stop by the house to get some things in case we end up staying overnight."

The owner's jet brought them to the Orange County airport, which was only a twenty-minute car ride from the Juggernauts' newly constructed facility. The media, blocked off from the back of the facility where practice would take place later that day, had already staked out its territory beside the bronze fountain that was the centerpiece to a red granite courtyard in front of the team's offices. After passing through a security check comprised of off-duty LAPD, the car dropped them off around back. They were led to an abandoned locker room, and Madison knew by the lockers

filled with street clothes that the players must be in meetings. On the third floor, in a contemporary smoked-glass office that overlooked the three practice fields below, Ulrich
greeted them warmly at his cast-bronze desk, which was
sculpted by the same artist who'd created the fountain out
front. His voice was low and strong and seemed to lace the
room with vibration.

"Mr. Ulrich," Madison said with a warm smile, shaking
the older man's massive hand. Ulrich was polite but con-
strained. Worry marked the forehead beneath his bald dome.
The joviality that she'd seen in him the last time they met
was gone.

"I think everyone knows Conrad Dobbins?" he said
somberly.

Everyone did know Conrad Dobbins. He represented a
substantial number of black superstars in football as well as
basketball and boxing. That he'd spent time in jail for rape,
felonious assault, and extortion seemed not to matter to his
clients. He got them good deals, and he, like they, knew the
experience of having been repressed by the white man at
one point or another during their lives. Now, as Dobbins was
so fond of putting it, together they sought economic revenge. Madison knew he used the same powerful arguments
as the Washington brothers. But unlike the Washingtons,
Dobbins was an uneducated but streetwise con man.

The slick agent sat on the beige crushed velvet couch that
floated in the middle of the room facing the desk. He wore
an expensive cranberry suit. A diamond watch hung lazily
from his whip-thin wrist. In his hand was a compact 8mm
camera. He pointed it at Madison and Chris as if he was a
tourist at Disneyland. Madison remembered reading somewhere that the eccentric agent had taken to carrying the
small video camera with him wherever he went ever since
the Rodney King incident. She suspected more than any-

thing that it was part of his act, his created identity. Although Dobbins lowered the camera momentarily when Madison and Chris came in, he didn't bother to stand or even remove his sunglasses. He merely gave them a quiet imperious nod and then went back to filming.

"Hello," Madison said without emotion.

"I'm glad you've agreed to come," Ulrich said, shaking Chris's hand as well and directing them to the two chairs that flanked the couch before sitting back down behind his desk. The owner seemed neither to notice nor care that their whole meeting was being captured on tape.

The only other person in the room was Dobbins's ubiquitous bodyguard. Madison knew of him because it was so unusual for an agent to have a bodyguard at all. She had no idea what the man's name was, and no one bothered to introduce him. He stood against the wall like some forgotten appliance.

"I'm sure you know better than we do what it is we're dealing with," Ulrich continued. "We hope you'll agree to help us."

"Where is Trane?" Madison said. "If I'm going to represent him I'll need to talk with him."

"What you need," blurted Dobbins from behind his 8mm, "ain't what this is about." He began to preach in a singsong rhythm that was more of a performance for the camera than it was for them. "This is about a brother who's being falsely accused . . . This is about the struggle between a athlete an' the Jewish media, between a police state an' justice, between a black man an' the white establishment."

Madison cleared her throat and looked to Ulrich for guidance.

"Conrad," the owner patiently rumbled, "we already agreed on this. We all know Madison is the best person to handle the situation. You said so yourself so cut the crap. Our interests are the same on this one."

Dobbins stared at the owner for a moment before saying, "This time, they is."

"We have an alibi for Trane," Ulrich explained to Madison, ignoring the slight. "Conrad was with him at midnight in one of the second-story private rooms of the clubhouse at the Bel Air where the—where the girl was killed. Now, we want you to handle the case. We want you to handle the media, and we want you to do everything you can to make sure Trane can continue to play while the police are sorting this whole mess out. He's out on bail right now, but we're not even sure if he can leave the state. We play Minnesota on Sunday."

"I'll get with the judge right away so he can travel," Madison said. "So you know, it will probably require the team to post several million dollars in bail as well as pay for a federal marshal to accompany the team. I worked the same deal for Luther Zorn when I represented him, and actually used the California case against the old Rams player Darryl Henley as a precedent. It shouldn't be a problem.

"And since we seem to be speaking frankly with one another," Madison continued, staring straight into the lens of Dobbins's camera, "I might as well tell you that an alibi that consists solely of Mr. Dobbins's testimony is by no means unassailable."

"Go with it, babe," Dobbins said, his words accentuated by a series of clucks and chuckles he'd picked up during a lifetime of jive double-talk. "Least you speakin' truisms."

"Yes," Madison replied, "and I'll require a hundred-thousand-dollar retainer in advance with another three hundred if we go to trial . . . in advance."

"I'll be advancing the money, Ms. McCall," Ulrich said, clearing his throat. "The team will reimburse itself from

Trane's paychecks. I'll have a check for you before you leave today."

"I'm havin' a press conference at four this afternoon," Dobbins announced as he rose to his feet. "An' I want you there, babe. I'm gonna pronounce Trane innocent and that he's got the female phenom for a lawyer. You like that? Female Phenom?"

Madison didn't know what to say. Dobbins now had the 8mm camera's miniscreen turned out toward her so she could see what her own bewildered face looked like through his lens.

"Mr. Dobbins," Madison said, her face clouding over, "I need very much to speak with Trane. I need to do that, and I need to speak to the district attorney. A press conference is not high on my list of priorities."

"Well, you work for Trane now, right?"

"That's correct. I'll be working for Trane."

"Yeah," he said with a chuckle, "so that means you work for me, too. Me an' Trane, we one and the same." Dobbins grinned at Madison while she digested that tidbit. "He's workin' right now, babe. He's got a game Sunday. But he'll be here to meet with you after practice, then you both can meet me in the media room for the press conference at three."

With that Dobbins left the room, his silent hulking bodyguard in close tow. The three of them were silent for a moment before the owner spoke.

"I'm sorry for that," he said solemnly. "Now you know why some people have a bad feeling about agents. But, he's right about one thing: He and Trane are unfortunately one and the same. Trust me, Trane doesn't do anything without Dobbins's approval. I'm just glad he agreed to bring you on board as Trane's attorney. Truth is, he was eager to have you. It may have more to do with publicity than anything.

But whatever the reason, I'm glad you're here. I know you're competent from my own dealings with you, and quite frankly, I can't think of anyone who has the kind of experience you've had in representing athletes in these sort of . . . situations."

"Why do you think Trane Jones is innocent?" Madison asked abruptly.

Ulrich tilted his head down and poked at his thumbnail with a pen. With just his eyes he looked up and said, "I don't know if I do think he is innocent. From what I've heard, it doesn't look good. The police are being very quiet about the investigation, but from what I can gather, they've got his golf club as the weapon. He tossed it in the harbor down in San Pedro. His fingerprints and her blood are on it."

"What about the alibi?" Madison asked.

"Dobbins is the only one who was with him. He's acting as if Trane's exoneration is a foregone conclusion. I don't see it that way at all, but if he is going to get off, I'd rather have it sooner than later. I've got a PR nightmare on my hands. I've already got women's groups backing up my phone sheet. In the meantime I want you to make sure he stays out on the field on Sundays, the same way you did with Luther Zorn. Without Trane, we're just another playoff team. With him . . . we should be able to win it all."

"It's about winning, then?" Madison said.

"Yes," Ulrich replied, raising his chin defiantly. "Isn't it with you?"

"Sometimes."

Chapter 28

Brinson didn't like Bible-thumpers, and he knew that's what Clark Cromwell was. Besides being a homicide detective for the LAPD, Brinson was an inveterate Juggernauts fan. As a kid he had loved the Rams. He had pined for them when the team moved to St. Louis until the NFL gave L.A. a team of their own again. Since that time, no word in the sports page about "his" team had gone unread. So he knew all about Cromwell. He had read the quotes about how God did this and God did that every time Cromwell had a good game.

It was the same rhetoric he had heard from his sister when she was dying from leukemia. She'd gone to school in the east and married a classmate who was a Seventh-day Adventist. When she was diagnosed, they prayed. It was in God's hands, she'd told him. Both she and her husband were adamant that she would not receive the necessary bone marrow transplants to beat the disease. No one asked their two young girls how they felt about it, but Brinson could guess. Several weeks after the initial diagnosis he arrived at her bedside in a Boston suburb in time to watch her die a painful death. That sight, with her moaning and her husband exhorting God with all his worthless silent prayers, remained as an indelible scar in his mind. It convinced him that in fact nothing was in God's hands.

Brinson thought that people who held forth all that God-talk were really hiding some pathetic internal flaw. He thought Cromwell was hiding something, so he didn't feel any pity for the powerful fullback when the dry dusty air and the hot lamp started him coughing.

"So she was your girlfriend?" Brinson asked for the fourth time.

Cromwell looked to the ceiling, gave one more cough, and replied, "Yes, I told you she was. Was."

"What happened?"

Clark shrugged and looked down. "I told you, we just broke up. It wasn't working."

"How could you not have *hated* her?" Brinson asked, leaning forward like a confiding friend, goading him. "Your girl, throwing herself at that low-life Jones. She was your girl . . ."

"I don't hate anyone," Clark said, his eyes glowing. "God teaches us to love each other. She wasn't my 'girl' anymore anyway."

Brinson stared malevolently. He was round-shouldered and too obese to have enough juice to take on the big clean-cut football player in a fistfight, but bulky enough not to fear him either.

"Somebody didn't love somebody very much," the detective reminded Cromwell as he cracked a pistachio. "I've got a girl with a three-iron imbedded in her brain."

Clark frowned and nodded. He knew that already. "I heard it was Trane Jones's club," he said quietly.

Brinson nodded but said, "That doesn't mean it was him that did it . . ."

"Is that what this is really about? You think I killed her?" Clark scowled, deeply offended.

"Did I say that?" Brinson countered, raising his eyebrows innocently.

"No," said Clark sullenly, "you didn't. But your questions are . . ."

The silence hung brazing in the warm light.

"I appreciate your coming in and talking with me," Brinson said, suddenly as nice as he'd been when he'd first spoken with Clark on the phone that morning.

"Can I go now?" Clark said.

Brinson nodded, "Of course. Thanks again."

Clark rose, then stopped at the door to ask, "Don't you think Trane killed her?"

Brinson worked a chubby finger into his ear before saying, "He probably did. I just like to find all the facts. That's my job . . . Good luck Sunday."

"Thanks," Clark said, and then he was gone.

Brinson stared at the empty chair where Clark had been. He meant what he'd said about Jones, but something bothered him about Clark Cromwell. That self-righteous Bible-thumping soured him to no end. Maybe it was no more than that. He knew Le Fleur, the DA, didn't want him doing anything but sniffing out clues that implicated Jones, but he also meant what he said to Cromwell about being thorough. It wouldn't be the first time jealous rage had prompted a murder. In fact, to Brinson it seemed Clark Cromwell had a better reason to kill the girl than Trane did. After all, what was a drink in the face to Trane Jones? But then there was the fact that Jones was just a dangerous animal and dangerous animals didn't necessarily have to have a good reason to kill. No, he wasn't going to make a fool out of himself by heralding Cromwell as a possible suspect. He'd keep that angle to himself. It was enough to watch him squirm a little under the light. Chalk up one for the anti-Bible-thumpers.

Meantime, he'd gather the facts. Then he'd let the politicians figure out how justice was going to be meted out. That's the way it almost always worked. It was enough to make Brinson think fleetingly about retirement.

A detective by the name of Ball burst into the room and interrupted his reverie.

"Lieutenant, I got Jennifer Riordon. You want her?"

Brinson gave his man a puzzled look.

"The friend . . ."

It had taken them this long to track down someone who knew Annie Cassidy. It wasn't poor detective work. It was that the girl was a virtual phantom. Her apartment was bereft of letters, e-mail, or even an address book. It was strange, like she hadn't wanted anyone to know who she was. Her only relation was her mother. Brinson had spoken with her on the phone from France—a real bitch. The woman was uninterested enough that Brinson found himself feeling pity for Annie Cassidy, whoever she was.

It seemed Annie had only two friends, both women her age who had been on a trip to Hawaii at the time of the murder. One of them was this Jennifer Riordon. Ball opened the door and held it like the gentleman he wasn't. The girl Riordon walked through the door legs first. She had it all. She was so striking that he stood up and shook her hand with a clammy mitt and a deference that elicited a little snicker from Ball, who didn't appear to be in any hurry to leave.

"Thank you for coming," Brinson said with more authority than was necessary.

The girl, all six feet of her, gave Brinson a sullen vampire look and asked if she could smoke.

"Of course. Please sit down. Thank you for coming."

She hung her head to light a Kool and two sheets of shiny

chestnut hair blocked her eyes from view, giving Brinson free rein to scour the rest of her. Her bell-bottom pants hid only the shape of her ankles. The rest was on display, separated from the cop's eyes by nothing more than a thin layer of black stretch material. Her sleeveless V-neck top was skintight and also black, but judging by her demeanor Brinson didn't get the idea that the color of her clothes was because she was mourning. Her bare arms looked strong even though her creamy white skin suggested a sedentary life. She looked up much too soon and backed Brinson down with a malignant knowing grin that reduced him to a fat middle-aged cop in a cheap suit with breath that was less than minty fresh.

As he sat down, Brinson gave Ball an angry look and unceremoniously thumbed him out of the room. He reached for a nut, then checked himself and instead flipped through the pages of his legal pad and scratched the girl's name down on a blank sheet. He let his blood settle before he looked up and did his thing.

"So how well did you know Annie Cassidy?"

"You're talking about Angel?" she said, exhaling the words with a stream of menthol smoke that stung Brinson's eyes.

"That what you called her?"

"What everyone called her," she said. "Oh! Except Moose."

"Moose?"

"You know, from *Archie*. Archie, Veronica, Moose—the big dumb blond guy built like a brick shithouse?"

"That's Clark Cromwell."

"Whatever. I'm not a big sports fan."

"Was she?"

"Angel? Ha!" She said it with a short hard laugh that hit

Brinson like a jab. "She didn't know a football from a basketball."

Brinson frowned and said, "That's a little hard to believe. She went from one NFL player to another pretty quick. Isn't that what they call a groupie?"

The girl's cobalt eyes sparkled back at him disdainfully. "Yeah, right. Angel was a groupie. You're a regular detective. It was the other way around, Ace. Men were Angel groupies. She ate men up like snacks. She'd go out at night and grab a bag of whatever flavor she wanted, eat 'em up, then have another. Two or three in one night if she wanted. She was like a man that way . . . only when you're like her and you see something you want to fuck, you just get it. There's no chase with a man.

"You just snap 'em off the rack," she continued after another drag, snapping her fingers with a crack that wasn't unlike the sound of a dry tree branch breaking, "like a bag of chips at the deli counter."

Brinson felt an uncontrollable rush of blood. The concept was as beautiful as it was entirely true.

"I think that's why she got hung up with Moose."

Brinson's raised eyebrow asked the next question.

"She couldn't get him off the rack. He was a God-squadder. She had to practically rape him. We laughed about it. But even after she got him, she kind of hung on to him. We'd laugh about that, too. She'd say, 'Hey, he's a big bag of chips.'"

Jennifer puckered her purple-painted lips and sucked hard on her Kool, her laughing eyes narrow. Brinson reached into his jacket and shucked a pistachio before he caught himself and dropped the whole mess, contaminating his pocketful of nuts.

"Then he got stale," Brinson suggested.

"Now you're getting it, Ace."

Despite her sarcasm Brinson puffed up. "And Trane?"

"A stud."

"What was the nature of their relationship?"

She smiled at him some more and said, "You tell me, Ace."

"Did he hit her?"

Jennifer thought about that for a minute, then glanced up at the two-way mirror on the wall before biting her lower lip and silently nodding yes. "That was the flavor of the month," she said. "Like hot chips . . . real hot."

"She talked about that?"

"Yeah, she talked about it. Showed me the bruises."

"Ever go to the hospital? The doctors?"

"No. He got her once pretty good, though. She was in bed for about four days on nothing but painkillers. That was just once."

"And she went back to him after that?"

"You gotta understand Angel. That was what she did. She was in the movies when she was a kid. She was gonna be a big star. Then her dad died and she went through that awkward stage and her mom left. No one gave a shit about her then. She went to Juilliard in New York and worked on Broadway for a while. She got some bit parts and then came back here. She thought her father's friends and her looks and her experience would help her. But it turned out her father didn't have any real friends, and as good-looking as she was . . . well, it's a rough town. I think she just stopped after the first few months and said fuck it. She didn't need the money."

"So she just prowled around looking for men?"

"You could say that."

"Was there anyone else who might have wanted to kill her?"

"I can think of a few wives . . ."

"Anyone ever make any threats?"

"No, nothing like that. There were never any scenes or anything. Angel didn't stick around long enough for that. Not usually."

"Do you think Trane Jones killed her?"

"Of course he killed her," she said, stubbing out her Kool in the blackened tin ashtray that she'd been feeding.

"That doesn't seem to upset you all that much," Brinson said boldly.

She looked up at him, deadpan. "You don't know me, Ace. You got no idea what's goin' on in here," she said, making a gun with her fingers and touching it to her temple as if she was going to blow out her brains. "Angel was my friend. You'd call her that. But you don't build your world on someone like Angel. She was like the kind of girl that could've been gone the next day for good, or showed up in bed with your husband ten years from now. You don't build your world on that. She was my friend, though. We had fun. I just look at it like she took off. But if I can help you fry that son of a bitch Trane Jones I will."

Chapter 29

Madison was no stranger to celebrities. She knew what they did to people. Even she, who didn't pay much attention to movies or television or the music on the radio and the stars they all produced, could feel a certain excitement when she was in the presence of a true celebrity. Madison didn't know for certain why that was. She suspected that in a world whose complexity was growing exponentially, the few people who had a universal identity also carried with them an inherent power. She'd met Sean Connery, for instance, in a hotel lobby one night in L.A. She wasn't a big fan, but just his presence seemed to charge the entire room with an electric current. The same thing was certainly true for Trane Jones. When Madison asked for him at the team's office she could see that odd excited tilt of the receptionist's head. Trane brought that same kind of current with him wherever he went.

He was waiting for her in a small conference room. His big Zeus shoes were unlaced and sat plunked down on the polished cherry table like two bags of groceries. His red nylon sweatsuit was open to the waist, his hat backward, and of course his eyes were hidden behind sunglasses. He was cursing into a cell phone when Madison and Chris walked in, and he made no motion to get up or even acknowledge their presence. Madison and Chris sat down, and Chris could see that his partner was about to boil over. In his mind he could hear what she was going to say to him when this was over, if it got that far. It wouldn't have surprised Chris if she had gotten up and walked out. Trane talked on for three more minutes before giving one final "fuck you" and flipping the phone shut.

"What's up?" he said casually, his head lolling ever so slightly to the side.

"How'd you like to spend the rest of your life in a cell a quarter of the size of this room with a four-hundred-pound white child molester?" Madison said with a pleasant smile.

"Huh?" Trane said.

At least she had his attention.

"You heard me," Madison replied, staring at him without emotion. "Listen, you're the best runner in football? Well, I'm the best trial lawyer in football and anywhere else. Yeah, I'm a woman. Yeah, I'm white. But let's get over that right now. You want me to represent you and give you the best chance you've got to stay out of jail? Fine, I'll do it, but don't fuck with me, because from what I've heard you're going to need everything I've got to get you out of this mess."

"I didn't kill no motherfuckin' bitch," he said sullenly.

"Fine," Madison said with a curt nod. "You've established your innocence with me, now we've got to convince a twelve-person jury."

Trane stuck his finger up his nose and smirked knowingly at her. "Okay," he said, "you're my lawyer. Now what?"

"Now you tell me what the hell happened so I know what I'm dealing with."

"Bitch threw a drink in my face an' I should of hit her, but I didn't 'cause of all them society motherfuckers everywhere an' I wanna get that part in this other white boy's movie. Now she's dead, an' I didn't get to smack the bitch for wettin' me down an' the motherfuckin' law sayin' I'm the one that capped her ass."

Madison looked briefly at Chris as if to say, "How could you do this to me?" He smiled wanly.

"Who is this girl? How did you know her?" she asked.

"Angel? She was my bitch. Fine piece! Uh-huh," Trane said, shaking his head. "She was fine. Touchy an' bitchy, but a freak? Goddamn she was a freak!"

"Did you know her well?" Madison wanted to know.

Trane smiled at her big, his teeth like a picket fence. "Now you know I did . . . She was my bitch."

"That means your girlfriend," Madison said.

"You'd say that."

"Did you know her long?"

"'Bout two months. Didn't know much about her before that. Just after. Just about her an' me. Wasn't much to know neither. She was my freak. We'd go to clubs, dinner, wherever. She was with me most of the time. When she wasn't, I didn't know where she was. Didn't care. That ain't my way."

"What about that night?" Madison said. "Conrad Dobbins says you were with him. Was there anyone else there?"

"Naw, not then. We was talkin' with Dommer Graves about his next picture. Wants me in it. We talked. He left. Then me an' Conrad walked out on the balcony to watch the fireworks. Had a few drinks, bullshit about me bein' in pictures an' shit. That's it. We left about twelve-thirty, went to Phatt Momma's, party till I don't know when an' when I get back home the cops is waitin' for me and talkin' stink about me killin' her ass."

"And what did you tell the police?" Madison asked.

"Same shit I just told you. I didn't do shit."

"That's it?"

"Then I asked for a lawyer," Trane said with a big knowing smile. "I been through this shit before."

"What about the golf club everyone's talking about? Is it yours? Did you really throw it in the harbor?"

Trane's face grew sullen. His lower lip poked out red like a warning. "When they talked to me the first time, they asked me about my golf club an' said she was killed with a club. Shit, they say that an' I know they thinkin' I killed the bitch. So I walk outta there an' of course I look in my trunk to see what the fuck's goin' on. Then I see the motherfuckin' club layin' right there outside the bag an' blood all over that bitch an' I get my ass to that fuckin' pier as fast as I can move. I know it's a fuckin' setup if I ever seen one an' I don't wanna be no setup chump."

"Could someone else have gotten that club?"

"Shit, yeah," Trane spouted. "After the fuckin' golfin' everyone just leaves their fuckin' clubs in the fuckin' cart and take a bunch of motherfuckin' pictures an' any motherfucker coulda taken my fuckin' three-iron."

Madison digested his words, then said slowly, "But how could anyone else get the club in the trunk of your car?"

Trane scowled and said, "I don't motherfuckin' know. You the fuckin' lawyer. All I know is I ain't the one that killed the bitch . . . Maybe I left the motherfucker unlocked or some shit like that. All I know is, I didn't fuckin' kill her."

Madison chewed on the inside of her cheek for a moment and said, "Okay, I'm going to set up a meeting with the DA. I'll find out what they've got. Now, who handled your bail? Mr. Ulrich wants to make sure you can play Sunday, and I'll need to make sure your bail allows you to travel out of state."

"Tall white dude took care of bail," Trane said. "G-somethin', I don't know. Ask Conrad."

"The other thing: I don't want you talking to the media about any of this," Madison said. "And I mean anything at all. If a question comes up, you just say 'no comment.' If you feel the need to explain, just tell them your lawyer is advising you not to talk about the case until the trial is over."

Trane said nothing, and Madison wondered if he'd heard her at all. There was something frightening about him. He gave Madison the same feeling she had whenever she was around someone else's big dog. They weren't supposed to suddenly snap and tear out your throat, but if they did, there wasn't much you'd be able to do about it. The other thing was, like a big dog, Madison was certain that it wouldn't be wise to let him smell your fear.

"Are we okay on that?" she asked, sounding tougher than she felt.

"That's fine with me. All a buncha motherfuckers anyway."

"Good," Madison said, rising. "By the way, you can call me Madison, and this is Chris Pelo. He's my partner and he'll be handling our end of this investigation. We'll be looking into the facts of this case just as hard as the L.A. police, if not harder. Chris is the one who'll be handling that and he'll need your cooperation, so if you've got a problem with him for some reason or another you need to get over that, too. He's as good at what he does as you are at what you do and the things he finds are the things that are going to help me help you. Now, presuming I can clear you to leave the state, and I know you'll be going to Minnesota, but I'm going to need you for the day next Tuesday to go over this case in detail. Are we all together?"

Trane stood as well and towered imposingly over the two of them. "Yeah," he said, without paying much attention to Chris. "We cool."

"Good," Madison said. "Now, I know there's a press conference scheduled so I'll go get introduced as your lawyer and we'll leave. There's a lot of work to do before we meet with the DA."

Madison led the way out. A woman from the team's PR staff led them downstairs and into an anteroom behind the media room. Madison peered through an opening in the door behind the podium. The room was stuffed with cameras, microphones, and people. Men and women in suits were crouched on the floor in front of the podium scrabbling for space like nursery school brats fighting for the last cookie. Cameramen jostled and even pushed each other for a better angle. In front of them all was Conrad Dobbins, in the midst of a tirade and eating it up.

"—This is what the white establishment of this city tried to do to O. J. Simpson! Now Trane Jones, another black man, stands accused of a crime he did not commit!"

Here Dobbins took a large Zeus shoe from a bag at his feet and slammed it down on the podium. "They want Zeus Shoes to renounce his contract because they can't stand to see a black man succeed as a entrepreneur, an' that's what Trane Jones is! A black man who used his own equity to make a business prosper. Well, he is prosperin'. Zeus Shoes can't make enough. These shoes is selling faster than they can make 'em because while the great white establishment is condemning Trane Jones, the people of this country are sayin' NO! We don't believe the establishment this time! We know that all men are created equal! We know that all men are innocent until proven guilty!—"

Madison sensed her name coming up and was ashamed. That she would lend herself to this circus was disgraceful. But she was comforted with the thought that this was America, the same place that made Geraldo famous. This is what people wanted. And besides, there was no sense in her fighting it. She could no more have extracted herself than she could change her profession. She was a lawyer, a high-profile lawyer. Things like this happened. There was no sense fighting against the current. She'd need her strength for the battle ahead.

"—an' that's why Trane got's a woman for his lawyer, a famous woman, a defense lawyer comin' to the aid of the innocent be they black or be they white."

Madison leaned toward Chris's ear and whispered, "You couldn't have written that part of it any better."

"—the female phenom Madison McCall!"

Madison came out of the room amid not applause but more jostling and shouting among the media battling for space.

"Thank you Mr. Dobbins," she said sternly. "I am here to inform you that, yes, I will be handling this case for Mr. Jones. I would ask you not to solicit comment from him, but to direct your questions from this point further at me—"

The place erupted with reporters bawling questions. Madison held up her hands. During the melee, she wondered if she shouldn't push the Zeus shoe off the podium. It was sitting right there in front of her like a ridiculous prop. She wrestled with the notion until it was quiet again and too late.

"If you interrupt me again," she warned the reporters, "my part of this press conference is over. Now, as I said, I will handle your questions only at press conferences. As we proceed towards trial I will call these conferences only as I see fit. I have this statement to make right now . . ."

Madison took an index card out of her inside pocket and tucked the edge of it under the sneaker. She glanced at it, then looked up at the crowded room.

"I urge you, as responsible members of your profession, to remember that Mr. Jones is innocent. It is our intention to prove that in a court of law. Until that time, it is your duty and mine as responsible members of this society to remember that we have embraced the presumption of innocence.

This is what separates us from the injustice of the death squads that have and still do plague many of the societies in the history of man. This is an important right that I do not intend to let people forget. I hope you will do the same."

Madison left the podium amid a thunderstorm of questions. She presumed that would be it, but Dobbins was back at the mike immediately giving them more.

"Now!" he shouted. "My man himself is gonna come up here an' tell you the way it is! The truth! My man Trane!"

Madison was already through the doorway before she realized what was happening.

"Oh no," she said, going for her client until Dobbins's enormous bodyguard filled the doorway to block her path.

"Excuse me," she said, poking at a slab of fat in his back. He ignored her. It was too late anyway. Trane was in front of them all holding up the shoe with Dobbins nodding like a puppet beside him.

"I ain't no killer!" Trane said to them forcefully, and then after a dramatic pause and much more quietly, "But these shoes now . . . These shoes is killer."

Another storm of questions came crashing down on them, and Zee stepped aside. Madison bumped straight into Trane with Dobbins pushing from behind. They all got back through the door that Zee slammed in the faces of some of the more aggressive cameramen.

"What the hell was that all about!" Madison demanded, her fists clenched and her arms thrust down at her sides.

"You handle the legal stuff," Dobbins said to her wickedly. "I'll handle the marketin'. We got a lot invested in these shoes, babe. Just 'cause the white man is ready fo' a lynchin' don't mean we aim to stop sellin'. When this whole thing shakes out an' my man here is proved innocent, then you go home. We got too much invested. You do yo' job, an' I do mine."

Madison didn't know how to respond, and it didn't matter. Dobbins and Trane moved past her and Zee shielded them as if by instinct. They were gone before she could utter another word. On the other side of the door the news crews were still clamoring among themselves. Madison looked at Chris. He shook his head.

"What the hell," she said.

"Let's go get something to eat," he told her.

"What are we doing here?" she said morosely.

"You know how the players we work for are always talking about the shit side of playing in the NFL? Well, this is the shit side of being their agents."

Chapter 30

Madison had to stay in L.A. overnight. She missed Cody's win over West Lake Hills's archrival, Sam Houston High, and didn't stand a chance to see Jo-Jo play Saturday morning either. Gary Le Fleur, the DA, had been unavailable by the time Madison got hold of him on Friday afternoon. Instead he suggested they meet Saturday morning after his round of golf with the mayor. Madison wasn't in any position to bargain. At least, she reasoned, she would have the day at home Sunday, then a day to strategize with Chris in the office on Monday before flying back to L.A. for their next meeting with Trane.

Gary Le Fleur was a short, handsome man with curly black hair and a Roman nose. His muscular forearms and face were deeply tanned, and a small gold cross hung in the open front of his olive golf shirt. They found him sitting alone at one of a battalion of tables dressed out in green-and-white-striped umbrellas overlooking the water in front of the first tee. As they crossed the wide stone veranda Le Fleur splashed some Perrier over a wedge of lemon resting in a small glass of ice. He took a hurried sip before rising to greet them.

"Have you eaten?" he asked politely.

They hadn't, and Le Fleur had a waitress bring them menu cards. Chris used the opportunity to ask the DA to get him a special permit to carry his gun in California during his investigation.

"I never got over being a cop," Chris said with a friendly grin.

For Le Fleur it was no problem. Their talk took a casual turn. They might have been old law-school classmates caught up in a nostalgic tendency to debate the most recent events in the legal world. For a time Madison actually enjoyed quietly arguing over the recent Supreme Court ruling on the procedural limits of death penalty appeals. The air and the shade and the occasional distant pleasantries between golfers were soothing. The scent of lilies permeated the veranda.

But after she ordered a curried chicken salad, Madison cleared her throat and said, "So when do you foresee giving me a preliminary exam, Gary?"

Le Fleur poked at the lemon in his drink with a cocktail straw. A hint of a smile danced at the corners of his mouth. "I'm not even thinking about a prelim because I should have a grand jury indictment for you by the end of the week."

"You're going right to grand jury?" Madison said, unable to contain her surprise. "You don't even know if you have probable cause for the arrest."

"I'll tell you everything you need to know right now," the DA said somberly, laying down his straw and leaning his forearms on the table's edge. "Your client has a history of violence, especially toward women. I've got a friend of the deceased who says he beat her on a regular basis. By his own admission he had a confrontation with the victim on the night of the murder where more than a dozen witnesses heard him threaten her. He had motive. He had opportunity.

The only alibi he's got is the word of Conrad Dobbins, whose credibility as a witness is laughable."

The DA let those words hang for a moment.

"Then, we've got his golf club with her blood on it and him tossing it into the harbor. After being questioned by the police on the morning after the killing, he drove directly to San Pedro with the murder weapon in the trunk of his car. I think you and I should be talking about pleas, not probable cause. We aren't going to make the same mistake they did with O.J. We're going to try this in Beverly Hills where the murder took place and where the defendant lives. His jury of peers is going to look a lot different than the other guy's did. The city of Los Angeles has no intention of going through that same kind of legal humiliation again."

Madison absorbed what he was saying without any visible reaction. There was no doubt that the history of that infamous case was going to affect the politics in this one. Attorneys' careers were ruined in that one, political aspirations dashed. Sure, there were some book deals and some short-lived TV contracts for the prosecutors involved. They got their fifteen minutes of fame and then some. But the shame of losing that case with the defendant's blood and the victims' blood all over the place was something no real attorney could put a price on. It didn't take clairvoyance to know that every move Le Fleur made would be benchmarked against what happened in that case five years before.

"You've also searched my client's home," Madison said.

"Yes, we have."

"And I presume you haven't found anything else?"

"No."

"So how do you explain my client's having caved this girl's skull in with a golf club and not having a single drop of blood on his clothes or shoes? That doesn't sound good."

"He got rid of it somewhere."

"But when you arrested him he was wearing the same clothes he had on the night of the ball. You've got the wrong man, Gary. You should rethink this grand jury until you can answer that question a little better."

Le Fleur pursed his lips and shook his head. "No," he said. "I don't know where the bloodstains are. We're still looking. But the club is all I need."

"It seems likely, even probable to me," Madison countered, "that someone could easily have gotten hold of Trane's club, killed the girl, then planted it back in the trunk of his car."

"Yeah, that all sounds good," Le Fleur said, "but you can't explain that club away without someone else having his hands on the keys to Trane's car. That club was in the trunk, and there's no sign of anyone using anything but a key to get it open . . ."

These weren't the only flaws Madison saw in the DA's case, but they were the obvious ones that he'd be thinking about anyway. She wanted to raise them now, not to warn him of her strategy but to plant even the smallest seed of doubt in his mind. Madison knew that in some cases even the smallest detail could end up tilting the balance. Self-doubt was a detail, and not a small one.

"I'd hate to be in your shoes on this one," she said, baiting him even further. "The mayor probably reminded you this morning that you have to win this case to keep everyone from sinking. Am I right?"

She felt certain that's what would have transpired on this very golf course only hours ago. She could envision the mayor, an increasingly popular conservative icon with his own newsletter, talking tough about amoral professional athletes like Trane and how they needed to be put in their proper place: jail.

"The mayor, like myself, wants justice. Your client has a history of violence towards women. There's a clear pattern."

"I'll fight that admission."

"I'm sure you will, but California law is pretty clear on it. It'll go in."

"I presume you'll give me all the police reports?"

"Of course."

"I'd like their notebooks as well."

Le Fleur nodded his head and said, "I'm going to give you everything and then some. I'll have Lieutenant Brinson collect any notes from his men. I'll have those and every other document I've got copied by my secretary and available for you first thing on Tuesday. Don't worry. I wouldn't try to hide anything even if I had it, but I don't . . . The last thing I want is to have this thing turned over on appeal."

Madison let out a small laugh. "That's quite a presumption, that I'll have anything to appeal."

The DA tilted his head and raised one eyebrow as if to say he couldn't help it.

Madison pressed her mouth shut. There was really nowhere else to go. "So that's it?" she asked.

"That's it," Le Fleur replied. "Motive, opportunity, murder weapon, history. That's all I need not only for an indictment, but a conviction. People are fed up. They're fed up with athletes bludgeoning and abusing young women because they think they're above the law."

The DA suddenly turned bitter. "The timing of this case is in my favor, Madison," he said, twisting his mouth the way people will when they find a long black hair in their food. "It's time for the pendulum to swing back. This whole thing with Zeus Shoes, it makes me sick. We've got a young woman who was brutally murdered and your client is using it to sell shoes . . ."

Madison just looked at him impassively.

"I'm sorry," he said, raising his hand and running it quickly through his hair. "I didn't mean to vent like that."

Madison just looked at him coolly and said without rancor, "That's all right. While I'm on the opposite side of the aisle on this, I certainly understand your emotions."

Le Fleur nodded and stood to go. "I'm going to leave you to your lunch," he said. "Please, eat. You're my guests. I don't mean to be rude, but I've lost my appetite. I'll be in contact with you early next week. My hope is to convene the grand jury on Thursday and arraign your client on formal charges on Friday."

He shook both their hands and disappeared down the stone steps and around the corner.

"How about that?" Madison said when he was gone from sight.

Chris looked at her and shrugged. "The man's under some serious pressure."

Their food came.

"No sense in letting it go to waste," Chris said. He lifted a french fry from Madison's plate and bit it off at his fingertips. "Win, lose, or draw, this case is exactly what we needed . . . It's not ruining my appetite."

Chapter 31

Kurt Lunden sucked a long fat line of cocaine into his head through his nose. When the mirror was cleaned off he returned it to the top drawer of his desk. He needed some euphoria.

He pushed the intercom button on his phone and said, "Put him through . . ."

"Chu, what the fuck is going on? You told me you could deliver the units, and I need the fucking units!"

"Mister Lunden. I'm quite sorry, Mister Lunden. I got bad union trouble in Java. Bad union trouble, Mister Lunden. Bad bad."

"Chu, I got bad fucking trouble of my own. I got trouble out the ass. I don't give a shit about trouble. You give the fucking trouble to somebody else. You got union trouble? You get some people to talk sense to those union fucks. Talk sense. Use whatever you have to, Chu, goddammit; that's why you're there."

"You wanna use Lee Fung, Mister Lunden? You want Lee Fung to . . . to take care of union people, Mister Lunden? You tell me no Lee Fung unless I talk to you. You want Lee Fung?"

Lunden twisted the end of his mustache and chewed on his lower lip, thinking. Fung's name alone cut right through the cocaine and got him feeling shitty again. Fung was into the kind of shit that kept Amnesty International in business, but Lunden wasn't worried about his tactics. It was his price. If Fung caught wind of how much was at stake, he'd want a share of it. Unless Lunden could pull a move, which maybe he could do.

"Yeah, call Lee Fung. Offer him a hundred thousand dollars and go to a million, but don't go too fast. If he thinks we're desperate he'll want part of the action. Can you get it done for a million, Chu?"

There was a delay on the other end of the line. Lunden knew it was more than the overseas connection.

"Okay, I get it done, Mister Lunden."

"Chu," Lunden said, "you get me those units by the end of the month and you got a million coming to you, too. You got that, Chu? The end of the month."

Lunden put down the phone and looked at his watch. Dobbins was late. He was tempted to make himself unavailable to the son of a bitch. He couldn't do him any good anymore anyway. What was done was done. This thing would play itself out. The key would be selling the stock off at the right time before the orders outran the supply and the whole thing caved in on them. The other key would be not to let any of the other major shareholders know what was going to happen. If everyone bailed out, the SEC and the Justice Department would be all over his ass, and it didn't do you any good to make three hundred million dollars if you couldn't spend it.

The intercom buzzed and his secretary told him Dobbins had arrived.

"Send him in."

Lunden wiped his nose with the back of his hand, sniffed,

and stood as his secretary led the agent and his bodyguard into the room.

"Gentlemen, sit down, sit down," Lunden said, motioning to the black leather couch and taking a low matching chair opposite them. He slouched and grinned like an evil child who'd gotten away with a bad deed. He was dressed as always in a faded polo shirt, white pants, and Docksides with no socks, and he wore a rumpled captain's cap on his head. Lunden didn't believe in fancy expensive clothes. Real power was being able to dress comfortably no matter how it looked.

"Carmen," he said to the secretary before she'd left the room, "bring me those numbers from Wall Street." To Dobbins he said with a smile, "Conrad, everything we hoped for is happening. I wanted to tell you about it in person. This morning we broke ten dollars a share and we're still climbing. We're the hottest stock on the street right now. I'm targeting forty before I start to sell any of mine off, but I want you to know where you are so you can do as you like . . ."

Carmen returned with a folder and handed it to Lunden. He took out the top page and held it at arm's length.

"Right now you could sell your options for eight million dollars," he said, looking over the top of the page to see what kind of effect that had on the agent. "And that's just your personal stock. Trane's is the same. The clients you invested in have each made three hundred and thirty-three thousand dollars for every ten thousand they invested. You're looking like a pretty good financial adviser, Conrad."

Dobbins's grin was so wide that Lunden thought he saw the color of the agent's burnt orange suit reflected off his teeth. Dobbins licked his lips and said, "What's the maximum upside? I mean, I wanna know when to cash out."

"I think the media will keep Trane on the front page until about a week after he's indicted. After that, it will start to fade. Now, that doesn't mean the stock will fall, but it might. It will peak and valley along with the media attention. Right now everyone's talking not only about Trane, but Zeus Shoes. It won't stay like that forever. But when he goes to trial? There'll be another blitz."

"What you think's gonna happen if Trane is innocent?"

"Innocent?" Lunden said the word as if it was the first time he'd considered it. The truth was, they hadn't discussed it between them. It was enough that the murder and Trane's arrest was good for Zeus Shoes. "You mean after the trial?"

"No, before trial. My man, just so you know, didn't kill no bitch. I'm gonna prove it."

"You are?" Lunden said skeptically.

"Yeah, but I wanna do it at the right time."

"And you're asking me?"

"Yeah."

"If you could do something like that," Lunden said, narrowing his eyes and feeling the effects of the cocaine flooding back through him like an IV injection. "If you could, well, hell, I'd do it right when the media starts to lag, right when the stock starts to fall again. Then you could start it all up all over again. You know, rant and rave about racism the way you do. Get the whole media whipped up again. All of a sudden Trane Jones is a victim! The stock'll shoot up like a rocket. Shit, Conrad, you do that and I'm gonna have to find a way to make more goddamn shoes."

Chapter 32

Clark sat alone on the cold, damp sand encased in the early-morning shadow of a rocky cliff. In the distance a lone figure jogged steadily toward him along the water's edge. Clark turned his eyes to the high ceiling of clouds overhead. Underneath they burned orange so that their gray tops appeared to be the smoke of some chemical fire. The pungent smell of the ocean's nightly excrement, rotting fish and seaweed, wafted gently past Clark's nose on the tail of a warm breeze. He hugged his hairy blond knees one final time, then stood to stretch. The uncomfortable tugging against his knotted muscles distracted him. It was a pleasure not to think, not to be teetering on the mental precipice he'd been flirting with for the past half hour—no, for the past two weeks. Any quiet moment of contemplation seemed to exacerbate his tense, excitable condition. Peace seemed to come only at the price of some physical act, some exertion.

Clark stretched for five or six minutes, finally straightening his back just as the bright rays of the sun topped the bluff. The fire was snuffed from the clouds, leaving them cool and white. The mechanical chugging form of Tom Huntington was now close enough for Clark to see his eyes and the shiny glaze that always accompanied a bloodstream full of endorphins. Clark dropped in alongside and ran the last two miles with his spiritual mentor in silence. Clark knew he was welcome. "Anytime," Tom would say.

Tom ran the same ten miles every morning. Annie once suggested he was an addict. She said he'd simply gone from painkillers and alcohol with the Raiders to endorphins with Jesus. But Clark didn't like to think about that. He didn't like to think about Annie at all, even the things she had said—especially the things she had said. Still, he couldn't help himself. Even pouring out his heart to Tom three days ago hadn't helped him to shake her ghost.

When they reached the beach just down the street from Tom's house they slowed to a walk.

"Good run," Tom huffed, beaming at Clark.

"Yeah," Clark said, holding out his hand. "Thanks for havin' me."

Tom turned Clark's handshake into a fraternal embrace and patted him gently on the back. He did it the same way he always did, as if everything was as it should be. But everything wasn't. They walked up the beach, the sweat on their skin turning clammy, cooling down in silence.

"How are you, Clark?" Tom finally said with a hopeful smile. He grasped the back of Clark's thick neck.

Clark didn't speak, but his eyes brimmed with tears, and Tom turned his hold into a headlock, then hugged him tight, tighter than before. Clark could feel all the angles in his mentor's body as he stroked the back of his head like a small child. Clark began to cry silently, his body shaking, drawing his shortened breath in gasps. He felt himself slipping and unable to control it.

"Clark, Clark, Clark," Tom said, holding him by the shoulders at arm's length. "You have to forgive yourself. You have to."

"But my God, Tom. She's dead!"

"Come on, sit down."

There was a bench next to an empty lifeguard's chair and they sat down together facing the ocean. An older woman wearing a headset and waving a metal detector walked past them, stopping only to scoop a lug nut out of the sand with a truncated Clorox bottle. When she had passed, Clark swabbed his whole face with one violent downward swipe of his hand.

"I told you," Tom said quietly but forcefully, "God uses His people as instruments to do His will. You're one of His chosen people, Clark. Look what you've done with your life! Look what you mean to this ministry! Without you, there is no ministry. My work is nothing without you! You are the Peter of my church, the rock that it's built on. You're a sword of God, Clark. Sometimes He strikes with that sword. That's His will, not yours or mine. We sin. Of course we sin! But we're forgiven, Clark. You're forgiven."

"I want to be forgiven," Clark said desperately.

"You are, Clark. You are!"

Tom grabbed his leg and squeezed hard. They looked off into the postcard view of ocean and sky. Clark nodded to himself, willing himself to believe. A troop of gulls swept up the beach, screaming down at them. The birds passed by effortlessly and wheeled in descent a hundred yards farther down, where an old man and a boy with a bag of Tip-Top bread were scattering crumbs. Clark hacked up a clear gob of phlegm and spit into the sand before reaching into the front pocket of his sweat top. He took out a check.

"I want you to take this," he said to Tom. "I want to do what Jesus told the rich man to do in the parable. He said, 'Give away all your worldly possessions and follow me.' I want to give away my worldly possessions. I want to follow Jesus. I think that may be what happened to me with her. I was of the world, not of Jesus. She was a worldly temptation."

"She was a minion of Satan, Clark," Tom said bitterly. "I told you that. She was the devil trying to take you away."

Clark nodded that he knew this.

"I don't want all your possessions, Clark," Tom said, pushing his hand with the check gently away.

Clark insisted. "I want you to have it. I want it to go into the ministry. I don't need this money, Tom. I need my soul back, and I think this will help me get it. I'm not buying it. That's not it. I just don't want this money. I don't want things of the world."

Tom nodded now, too, and looked sadly at Clark, taking the check and unable to keep from noticing that the figure was so long it required two commas.

"My son," he said. "I will take this and I will use it to start a fund for our own church, a real church with stained-glass windows and a steeple and a bell. And you will be the rock of that church. You will be its Peter. You already are. But you have to promise me one thing . . ."

"I will."

"You have to forgive yourself for what has happened, and you cannot tell anyone about it. I know your nature. I know you want to shout your confession from the top of a mountain. But that's not what God wants. That's not what our church wants. We *need* you, and when you feel like punishing yourself for all that's happened, you have to tell yourself that it's the devil. It's Satan, and you have to tell him to get behind you because you are a man of Jesus and you are forgiven . . . Will you do that? Will you make me that promise?"

Clark grabbed at his face with his hand. He was slipping, but he shook his head violently against it.

"I will, Tom," he said, his voice muffled by his own hand. "I promise. I will."

Chapter 33

Madison and Chris flew to L.A. on Monday night. They got in late, which made Tuesday even more grueling. They devoted the morning to retrieving the police records from the DA and finding a suitable office to rent. In the afternoon they questioned Trane. He was hungover and surly, but they pressed him until the sun slanted directly through the window and continued even as it dropped out of sight behind the high-rise across the street. Of course the whole thing ended with Trane walking out the door. He said that if they needed more they could wait and talk to him after the next day's practice.

"I had enough of this shit," he told them. "I ain't no killer, an' I ain't no fuckin' lab rat chump motherfucker. That's enough of that shit for one day. I need a goddamn drink."

He slammed the door behind him.

"That was pleasant," Madison said, tapping her pen against the legal pad that lay on the table in front of her. It was fat with notes from the afternoon. Empty coffee cups and Styrofoam takeout boxes bulged from the wastebasket by the door. They were dressed casually, Madison in jeans and a white blouse and Chris in a faded black polo shirt and khakis.

One of Madison's bare feet was tucked up underneath her on the big leather chair. Her hair was pulled back into a ponytail. The gray room smelled like new carpet.

"When do you want to go through all these police records?" she said through the middle of a yawn.

"Now," Chris said, unable to suppress a yawn of his own.

"Now?"

"After something to eat," he said. "If we're going under the assumption that someone else killed Annie Cassidy then we don't want to wait. A murderer leaves a trail that tends to go cold fast. Most murder cases are solved in about forty-eight hours. The ones that get solved, anyway . . . We're already a week behind schedule."

"Fine," she said, "we'll do it after we eat. No more Mexican, though."

"You got something against Latinos? Hang on, let me put in a call to *USA Today*, I see another article coming on."

"Go ahead. There aren't enough Latin Americans in the NFL to hurt the business," she countered.

"Vicious," Chris said. "Wicked and vicious."

"Aren't you?"

"Why, because I pushed you into all this?" he said lightly.

"You didn't push me," she said, becoming serious. "Well, maybe, but I was going there anyway."

Chris looked at her with a defensive frown and said, "Just so you know, it's not all about money . . ."

"I know that, Chris."

"I mean, it wasn't too long ago when I would have asked you how you could represent someone like that," he said, nodding toward the freshly slammed door. "But I really understand something you said to me once. You told me that everyone deserved the presumption of innocence because sometimes they really are. Sometimes the evidence looks overwhelming, but when you get to the truth of the matter, it's something totally different. And if the truth is different from the way things look, then someone who is totally innocent gets punished, and that in itself is a crime and we, all of us, are the criminals.

"I thought you were crazy, you know that. I'm an ex-cop. In my mind every defendant was a guilty lowlife and defense lawyers just got them off. I thought that about Luther Zorn, remember? I mean, who would have thought he was innocent? Not me. Then it turns out he was . . . So I understand what you mean when you say, 'What if it were you and what if it were true.' Things happen, witnesses lie, people are framed, innocent people do get punished, and your job—our job—is to make sure they don't . . . Look, this guy's a lowlife. But the fact is I don't think he killed the girl."

Madison looked surprised.

"I don't," Chris said. "I mean, maybe he did, but in my mind, from being around you, I'm thinking that, sure, it's possible someone set him up. And the other thing? I don't think he's acting like he's guilty. If you're guilty, you kiss your lawyer's ass. You don't pull the same crap you pull with everyone else, because you know you did it and the only thing between you and a jail cell or the electric chair is that lawyer. I don't care how bad, how tough, how mean you are. If you're guilty, you kiss your lawyer's ass, or at the least you don't treat him like . . . like this shithead is treating us."

"Did you buy the story he told us about just finding the bloody club in his trunk after the police questioned him?" Madison asked.

Chris stroked his ragged mustache, thinking. "Yeah," he said after a moment, "I guess I did. That could happen. If someone wanted to make it look like Trane. That's what they'd do: Grab his club, kill the girl, and somehow put the club in his car."

"And if they grabbed it with a golf glove on then only

Trane's prints would show up. I know," Madison said. "But how did that club get into the trunk of his car?"

Chris shrugged. "I know. They'd have to have his car keys to do it, but it's possible. The club is easy. Like he said, he left his golf bag outside the pro shop after the tournament. Anyone could have grabbed his three-iron."

"But the car," Madison said. "I don't see how it could have gotten into his car. He said himself no one took his keys. They were in his pocket the whole night . . ."

"Did you know he ran for two hundred yards against the Vikings on Sunday?" Chris said.

"I read about it."

"Doesn't sound like a guilty conscience to me."

"God, this is funny," Madison said, shaking her head. "This is too much."

"What?"

"You think he's innocent?" Madison paused, then looked at him and said, "I think he did it. I don't think he's got a guilty conscience because I don't think he's got a conscience."

Chris raised his eyebrows.

"I know," she said, "not like me at all. But you're right. I'll represent him like he's innocent because he might be . . . I can do that with a clear conscience. It's not my job to be the judge and the jury. It's my job to advocate for him like he was my brother. I believe in the system. It's not perfect, but it's the best thing I've seen."

"What about a polygraph?" Chris asked.

Madison shrugged and rubbed the back of her neck. "I dismissed the idea because I thought he did it. I don't know now. If you think he didn't, maybe a polygraph can help. It can't hurt, that's for sure. It could help with the media. If we don't get something positive going there it's going to be tough to find twelve jurors who haven't convicted him before opening arguments. If he fails then we're no worse off. No one has to know . . ."

Chris exhaled loudly and said, "Well, we can put that on our list of things to do. I'm tired, but I've got to get through this stuff. If Trane really didn't kill her, the best thing I can do is to find out who did, or at least who could have. So Mexican is out. How about a pizza?"

"How about you call for pizza while I call home? Jo-Jo should be getting ready for bed and I want to say good night."

"How about anchovies?"

"Leave me alone, Chris."

He knew she hated anchovies. Madison slipped her shoes on and went into the empty office adjacent to their conference room. It was gloomy, so she put on the light and swiveled toward the window. Fifteen minutes later she was back in the conference room, where Chris already had half the police materials spread out over the long table.

"I didn't order anchovies, if that's why you're so gloomy," Chris said after glancing up at her.

"Don't worry about me," she said sarcastically. "I just did my best impression of a mother and a wife."

Chris didn't know how to respond to that so he kept his eyes on his work. When he finally looked up, Madison was still staring blankly at a gold-framed copy of a Warhol print, a close-up of some Lois Lane type with a word bubble saying, "Can you save me?"

"I can't," Chris said.

"Can't what?" Madison said, redirecting her attention.

"Can't save you."

"From?"

"From trying to be everything at once," he said. "It's not fair, you know."

"Why not?"

"Because there's no way a woman like you can be everything you want to be as a mother, everything you want to be as a wife, make a living, save the world, and still be home in time for dinner . . . At least I got you to smile."

"Thank you. You're right. It's not fair. But I want to do it all. I really do."

"You do damn good," Chris told her gently. "Wasn't that you I spoke to on Sunday afternoon, whipping up a batch of fudge in time for the Outlaws game? Fudge, for God's sake!"

"My mom used to make fudge."

"And wasn't that you I saw today, negotiating a lease, hiring a secretary, and hammering away at one of the most obnoxious personalities known to mankind, all in the same day? You do damn good. Don't let anybody tell you otherwise."

"Thanks, Chris. You're a good friend."

They looked at each other until the moment became uncomfortable. The phone rang and saved them. The pizza was waiting downstairs.

"I'll get it," Madison said. "I need the stretch."

When she returned Chris looked gravely up at her from the midst of his papers.

"What's the matter?" Madison asked, setting down the cardboard box on the end of the table. She popped the top and the warm smell of pepperoni quickly filled the room.

"Look at this. Read this," he told her, holding forth a one-page police report.

Madison read it. When she was through she looked up at Chris. He was staring at her intently.

Madison said, "You don't think . . ."

"You told me to look for whoever might have killed this girl if Trane didn't . . . If I didn't know who Clark was, yeah, that's what I'd think."

"But you do know who he is," Madison pointed out. Chris

had recruited Clark as a client and knew him even better than Madison.

"I do . . ."

"And?"

Chris took the report back from her and gave it a cursory glance. "Well, you and I know that he was pretty bitter about his contract being crammed down to make room for Trane in the first place. Now put this on top of that . . . I don't know. You'd almost think that if he were going to hurt anyone it'd be Trane. It depends on how serious he was about the girl."

"Real serious," Madison said.

Chris's eyes widened just a bit.

"If it's the same girl he told me about this summer," Madison continued, "and it probably is. It was serious. He told me she was the one."

Chris tugged on his mustache for a moment, then said, "From what I've read so far, they haven't found anyone else who might have had any reason at all to kill that girl."

"Do you think they're even looking?"

"Probably not too hard. When you got a guy tossing a bloody murder weapon into the bay and that same guy has a history of violence . . . It's just a natural presumption. By the way, nothing else I've read so far gives me any reason to believe that it wasn't Trane."

"You said you didn't think he did it."

"I said that was my instinct. It doesn't mean I'm right. I'm just saying that based on what's written here, the police have a pretty tight case as long as they can discredit Dobbins as a witness, and I doubt our friend the DA is going to lose much sleep over that one."

"Then we've got a problem."

"A conflict of interest," Chris agreed. "But then again, maybe not. Remember, the police haven't been spending a lot of time and effort looking for another suspect. There may be something more in these files, or I may have to find it on my own. If there's anything to find . . . Let me take some time and look into it."

"You mean under the presumption that neither Trane nor Clark is the killer?" Madison said, seeing the logic.

"Yeah," Chris replied, picking out a slice from the pizza and taking a mouthful. "Even though the chances of that are slim to none."

Chapter 34

Trane lay sleeping on his side in a tangle of burgundy satin sheets. The weather had been unusually warm, and an angry morning sun glared through the windows. The ceiling fan rested idly above the bed. Beside him lay a naked young girl, spread-eagled and facedown. Bleached blond hair fanned out like a peacock's tail across her back and gleamed like brass in the sunlight. A bead of sweat grew on Trane's temple until it was large enough to spill down the side of his face and drop against his nose.

"The fuck?" he muttered sleepily.

Eyes closed, he remembered the night before. A young agent, desperate to represent his movie career, had hustled him for two hours while the pretty little thing sat beside him in their booth sipping away at one margarita after another. Trane remembered the look on the agent's face when he asked for the wife. Even now it made him smile. Then he remembered what he'd done to her and the smile faded. A girl like that with a husband who would give her up was fair game for anything. He was tempted to do it again.

He opened his eyes and, fully conscious, he realized just how hot it really was, hot and stuffy. He rose from the bed and pissed long and hard into the white bowl, avoiding the bloodshot eyes lurking in the mirror. Back in the bedroom, the girl's still unmoving body sent a little jolt of panic through him. Last thing he needed was another dead bitch. He raised his big hand above his head and gave her bare ass a hearty slap. She stirred and whimpered, then dropped back into her drug-induced sleep. She, too, was warm and damp. Trane looked at the clock to see if he had enough time to mess with her, but it had stopped. Irritated, he slipped on a pair of canary yellow Jockeys and ambled out into the hallway. He looked at the digital thermostat. Nothing. He flipped a light switch inside his room. Nothing again.

"The fuck?" he said, more forcefully now.

"Cubby!" he shouted, shooting out of the master bedroom and through the house where he could scream up the stairway. "Cubby! Get the fuck down here! Cubbyyyyyy!"

Trane banged on the wall leading up the stairs and the noise reverberated through the mansion. Someone he didn't recognize rolled over on the living room couch and put a pillow over his head. Trane mounted the stairs three at a time and burst into Cubby's room, catching him in the act with the Jamaican girlfriend who'd moved in with him.

"Cubby, get the fuck off that bitch and get the fuckin' AC on, man!"

Leshay spilled out of his own room down the hall in a pair of boxers, his big afro looking like a poorly trimmed shrub.

"Wha's up, Trane?" he said, scratching himself with a yawn.

"Wha's up is you two no-good motherfuckin' brothers better get the goddamn AC on, bitch! I'm sweatin' my motherfuckin' ass off an' we got no motherfuckin' power!"

"Chill, Trane," Cubby said, rolling out into the hallway wearing his own pair of striped Jockeys and a surly look on his face. "I was hittin' it with my lady an' you just come in like a fuckin'—"

Trane cut him off with a backhand that knocked him to the floor. The girlfriend came shrieking out into the hallway and bent over Cubby. Trane kicked her in the ribs.

"Bitch! Get the fuck outta my house!" he roared.

She was howling now in a high-pitched wail. Cubby was on his feet and he started to beg.

"Trane, man, be cool, man. I'll get the AC on, man. Be cool. I'm sorry, man. I'm sorry. I don' know what happened. Maybe I didn't pay the fuckin' thing. I'll get it on, man. Chill."

"Chill? How the fuck am I suppose to chill when I got no fuckin' AC an' I got no motherfuckin' lights an' I got to go to the motherfuckin' courthouse today? How in fuck am I suppose to chill? Got a ten-million-dollar house an' I got no motherfuckin' power! Shut up, bitch!"

Cubby's girl howled even louder.

"What's goin' on?" came a voice from a head that had popped out of a doorway farther up the hall.

"Who the fuck are *you?*" Trane demanded, and the head disappeared.

Trane ducked into Cubby's room and pulled a Glock off the top of the dresser. He charged down the hall and burst into the room where the head had disappeared. Sitting around in a circle on the floor of the bedroom were four brothers heating heroin over a fat candle that was leaving a pool of red wax on the hardwood floor.

"Get the fuck outta my house!" Trane bellowed at them, leveling the Glock at the one whose head he recognized. The brothers were on their feet in an instant and scrambling for the door. Trane backhanded them randomly as they passed and pistol-whipped one. Then he marched through the upstairs checking the other rooms.

"I want every motherfucker outta this house!" he bellowed.

He opened the last door on the left and found his older half-brother, Dwayne, asleep with a fat, pasty redhead.

"Hey!" Trane shouted.

"Wha's up, Trane?" Dwayne mumbled sleepily, apparently unconcerned with the tirade.

"No fuckin' AC, man. My homeboys is gettin' slack as shit."

"I wondered why it's so hot," Dwayne said lazily and rolled over, pulling a pillow over his face.

Trane scowled at the redhead and shut the door. The rest of the occupants weren't so lucky. Except for his homeboys and their girlfriends who were stashed underneath their beds, Trane rousted them to a man with the Glock, giving them five minutes before he opened fire. He then walked out the front door and down by the gates. The big blue Town Car standing sentry lowered its driver's-side window with a low whine. The two security guards hired by Dobbins since Trane's arrest were having coffee in the front seat.

"The fuck are you brothers suppose to be doin'?" Trane said, glaring hard at them.

The first one, a tall, thin, tar-colored man with a pencil mustache, shrugged and looked at his partner, a slick, handsome mulatto with a short red afro.

"Trane, we asked you last night if you were sure you wanted these people to have entrance," the mulatto said.

"Well, fuck them," Trane said. "Get 'em out."

"An' fuck you!" he bellowed, giving the finger to the smattering of cameramen and photographers who skulked beyond the gates like jackals around a lion's kill.

By the time Trane was dressed out in a yellow three-piece suit with an electric blue tie the hastily closed car doors and squealing tires had faded to nothing. Cubby and Leshay were dressed, too, but that didn't keep them from capering about him like whipped puppies, pouring his Cocoa Puffs and splashing them with milk, buttering his toast, and cleaning up the ring his Coke can left on the mahogany dining room table.

Soon a black Suburban pulled up in the brick circle in front of the house and Trane piled into the backseat with Conrad. Cubby and Leshay sat in the very rear. Zee was sitting shotgun next to their driver. Trane related the morning's events and Dobbins nodded sympathetically, filming his client's complaints with his 8mm as they drove to the L.A. County Courthouse.

"My brother," Conrad said when they were almost there. "I want you to wear these." He held up a flashy pair of gold-and-black Zeus shoes.

Trane looked from his own blood-colored alligator shoes to the sneakers. "An' look like a fuckin' fool?" he barked.

"You ain't gonna look like no fool," Dobbins said passionately. "You gonna make a statement. You gonna show those white motherfuckin' reporters that just 'cause they tryin' to pin a rap on you that don't mean you gonna stop bein' *you*. You ain't gonna stop makin' money fo' yourself no matter what they gonna say."

Trane nodded at this logic and switched his footwear. He straightened himself and, pointing at Dobbins's camera, said, "What you gonna do with all that?"

"Gonna make a documentary for Spike Lee," Dobbins said with a grin. "Then the legend gonna live on forever . . ."

Trane sat back and said nothing. He liked the idea of being a legend, but he sure as hell didn't want to have to go to jail to become one. For the most part, Conrad's optimism was contagious, but it wasn't too hard to imagine the whole thing turning to shit and him actually ending up in jail.

"You gettin' me outta this, Conrad," he said finally, then turned to look for confirmation.

"I told you an' I told you, you ain't gotta worry!" Conrad said with a toothy grin as he patted Trane on his muscular back. "You ain't gonna do no time. An' we gonna make some *serious* cash, some righteous money. I promise that, ain't that right, Zee?"

Zee grunted that it was but kept his eyes on the road ahead where the courthouse had just come into view.

"You help Zee make a path," Dobbins told the two home-boys. "I'll be with Trane right behind you."

Reporters teemed like maggots on the courthouse steps. Trane had been indicted by the grand jury only two days before. Now he was being formally arraigned and would enter his plea to the charges in a public forum. It was a spectacle. The media pressed in on Trane and his entourage, only to be split down the middle by the forceful figure of Zee flanked by the homeboys. Cameras and microphones waved above them on sticks like Mardi Gras props. Men and women in suits and dresses shouted like barbarians. Trane hid behind his sunglasses with his head tucked into Zee's massive back. Conrad Dobbins was right behind him, wagging an accusing finger back at the media and reflecting their chaos with his camera whose screen was facing out at them.

The cameras, including Conrad's 8mm, were filtered out by the metal detector at the courthouse's security check. Anyone besides Trane and his entourage with hopes for a seat was already inside. Madison and Chris were there, too, waiting at the defendant's table on the opposite side of the court from the jury box. Beside them was a short, stout, balding lawyer named Paul Castle whom they'd enlisted as their local counsel to help them negotiate the intricacies of California procedure.

Trane marched down the middle of the courtroom with

his head high and a pimp's swagger in his step. All eyes were on him, and the look on his face suggested that he was enjoying himself. Despite Madison's earlier plea his clothes were as gaudy as a circus clown's, and he kept his sunglasses planted on his face. A bench in the front row had been set aside for Trane's entourage. Dobbins sat directly behind his client and patted him protectively on the back until Trane shirked him off like a bluebottle fly.

No sooner were they seated than the court clerk called them to rise for the honorable judge Sandra Douty-Bergenstien. She was a short, fiery-looking woman with olive skin and straight black hair that surrounded her head like a bell. Her face was fixed with what appeared to be a permanent scowl. She sat and banged her gavel with authority. The judge ripped right through the whole routine without so much as a pause to account for the high drama. Trane and Madison stood to enter the plea of not guilty, then Madison made her motions of suppression. Douty-Bergenstien whipped off dates to hear those motions in a way that let everyone know she'd been expecting them.

"Before I adjourn this court," she said, glaring out at the entire room, "I want it known that this will not be handled like a high-profile media circus. I will make my rulings quickly and I will expect the lawyers in this case, be they for the prosecution or the defense, to keep their comments within the confines of these rulings. This case will *not* become a mockery.

"I will not," she said, directing her gaze at Madison, "be steamrolled by any high-priced legal tactics and shenanigans. I know that as of now there is no DNA evidence in the prosecution's case. But should that arise, let it be known right up front that it will be processed by the Los Angeles County Coroner's Office, and the results of those tests will not be the subject of issue to the jury. That evidence will be binding, and before you even think about threatening *me*, Ms. McCall—and I know I've said this to you privately but I want to say it publicly—I will *not* be intimidated by the prospect of having my decisions overturned on appeal. And, I have no intention of letting you, Ms. McCall, or anyone, undermine the integrity of the Los Angeles Police Department or the Coroner's Office . . . Trial is hereby set for February thirteenth. This court is adjourned."

The judge banged her gavel again and then she was gone. The tumult began. Madison turned to Trane, but he was already on his way out, led by Zee and pushed by Conrad.

"Let's go," she said to Chris without hiding her disgust.

She felt more and more as if control of the entire case was slipping from her grasp. It wasn't anything obvious. Trane had given them the time that they'd wanted during the week. It was that he didn't seem to be as concerned as he should have been. Something didn't feel right. It was as if the whole thing had the quality of a play being staged by a troupe of community playhouse actors.

Outside on the steps Madison learned the reason for the group's hasty departure. Halfway down the wide gray steps Conrad Dobbins had set up an impromptu press conference to give his views on the proceedings. Trane stood beside him, grinning and looking like an irreverent fool in his three-piece canary suit and sneakers.

"I told him not to do that!" Madison said emphatically to Chris.

"We can't stop him now," Chris observed. "He's on a roll."

"Like a preacher," she said, spitting her words.

She shook her head. They stood on the top step, separated from their client now by a sea of reporters.

"Something's not right," she said. "We're going to trial, but it doesn't feel like trial . . ."

"You've never been involved in anything quite like this before," Chris pointed out.

"I've never been involved with these kinds of people before, you mean."

Just then, a group of cameras that weren't getting a good shot of Trane and Dobbins split off from the mob and went after Madison.

"No comment," she said, hustling now with Chris down the side set of stairs and out near the street, where a Town Car was waiting for them.

"What do we do now?" Chris asked, looking over at his partner's crumpled face as they slipped onto the freeway.

"We go home," she said sternly. "We go home for the weekend, and come back Monday ready to work."

Chapter 35

An unusual low front from Alaska dipped far enough down the coast to shed some rain on the Juggernauts' afternoon practice. In fact the clouds were so heavy they pelted rain in sheets. Chris watched from beneath a red-and-white golf umbrella that the PR director had lent him. There were no other spectators at practice. The media and everyone else had been banned since the murder of Trane's girlfriend. Armand Ulrich made an exception when Madison requested that Chris be given access.

"It's part of the case," she assured him.

And it was.

Chris watched the team run through plays over and over in the rain, as if nothing out of the ordinary was happening in the thick gray sky above. The players' practice uniforms clung to them like sopping newspaper, and their cleats kicked up cut wet grass with every step. Each man was decorated from knee to toe with thin green blades. Even though the field was well kept and sported none of the mud one would find on a high school or college practice field, the seats of the players' white pants were stained gray and brown.

Chris watched a double reverse. He knew the play and knew it was a staple of Gridley's new L.A. offense. Still, it was a thrill to watch the defense flow in waves, first this way, then that, and finally this way again, with Clark leading up the outside and leveling the safety with a bone-jarring thud. Trane Jones ran up the sideline, pointing at the defense and high-stepping into the end zone. With that last successful offensive play, Gridley called in his troops, addressed them, and then had them line up for sprints. Players helped each other strip to the waist, tugging violently at one another's soaking jerseys and shoulder pads and removing them in fits and starts.

Even though the rain made Chris feel cold, he could see that the running overruled any cooling effect the weather might have had on the players. Soon they began to glisten with a sweat that was slicker than the pure rain from the north. As they chugged up and down the field through shallow puddles and injured grass, Chris saw that every third or fourth man was bleeding from somewhere on his head or torso. Diluted by the rain, the blood ran in broad pink streaks. It was particularly noticeable on the white players, whose torsos and upper arms were as pale as shelled turtles from their constant encasement in shoulder pads and jerseys. No one besides Chris seemed to notice the blood any more than they did one another's sweat or the driving rain. It was just part of the landscape, something they were accustomed to.

Chris noticed that Clark and Trane ran with only a few players in between them and that there seemed to be some silent competition afoot. During the first several sprints Trane clearly took the lead. But as the drill wore on, Clark began to close ground and then actually take the lead. Neither of them did anything to indicate that they had recently murdered anyone. In fact, the entire practice, aside from the conspicuous absence of television and newspaper reporters, was unsettlingly normal. Chris had seen hundreds of practice sessions in his days as an agent, and this was just like all the rest.

Finally they were done, and at the sound of the head coach's whistle they came streaming past Chris toward the locker room. As the players passed him, Chris's nose was filled with the damp pungency of rancid sweat cut with musty rain. Some of the players stared at him curiously, wondering what a short little Mexican could be doing there in the first place with all the security they'd witnessed over the past few weeks. Others glared with malevolence, more than anything because he hadn't had to share in the lung-burning sprints. Still others ignored him entirely, huffing and puffing with their long faces and dripping like sad gargoyles migrating back to their perches of stone.

"Hey, Chris," rumbled Jeremy Plank, a big, fat offensive lineman from UT whom Chris and Madison also represented.

"Hey, Plank," Chris said in a voice that was friendly enough to let the kid know that Chris still appreciated him as a client but not so much that he'd stop to talk. He saw Trane Jones go by in an exhausted trance that didn't acknowledge him in any way. Then the coaches themselves passed, giving him the blank stares they gave anyone who had somehow slipped into their presence by working through the owner as he so obviously had.

Still there was no Clark. Chris glanced quickly after the remnants of the herd before he realized that Clark was still out on the field churning up more grass and more sweat in the downpour. Ten more sprints he ran on his own before he came gasping and staggering to where Chris stood. He seemed not to even notice him until Chris spoke.

"How come you didn't show up last Thursday?" Chris asked.

"Huh?" Clark said, the words clearly not fitting the scene. It was a Wednesday practice, hardest of the week and closed, yet here was his agent.

"I got hung up," he said, catching his breath. "What're you doing here?"

"Hung up," Chris said contemplatively.

"Yeah. Hey, I got a film meeting. You gonna hang out until after that?"

Chris thought about the question and wondered which answer would give him the best chance of a candid interview. He decided to play it nice. That was his thing anyway.

"Okay, I'll wait," he said.

"You gonna be upstairs?"

"No. I'll be right here," he said, plainly enough, not wanting to imply that Clark might try to duck him again.

"Okay, I'll see you in a few."

Chris moved out of the rain and under the roof that sheltered the double doors leading into the locker room. There was a bench there and he sat with his legs outstretched and crossed. After a few minutes the chill forced him to jam his hands down tight into the pockets of his windbreaker. It was half an hour before the players started to straggle out of the doors. They looked showered and fresh compared to the way they had gone in, and Chris retracted his stubby legs to let them pass. One by one and sometimes by twos they made their way under the overhang, then dashed across the parking lot for their cars.

When Clark came out he passed right by Chris in a flurry with his head down and a grim look on his face.

"Hey," Chris said, and he could see by his client's face that Clark had honestly forgotten he was there.

"Hey, yeah. Hey, Chris."

"Wanna get a cup of coffee somewhere?" Chris asked.

"How about we go to my place?" Clark said.

"I'll follow you."

Clark's home was in Palos Verdes. It sat high up on an enormous rock overlooking the ocean. As they wound their way up to the top with Chris following in his rental car, out over the ocean the tail end of the low front was ruptured by the sun and the rain that had fallen on the team's practice was quickly replaced by a shower of yellow light. Clark's neighborhood, a gated community on top of the rock called Rancho Palos Verdes, was one of the few places in Los Angeles where the homes had an acre or two between them. It was the only place where Clark felt he could find any semblance of sanity in a city that was such a far cry from the Portland suburb where he'd spent most of his youth. His house was a modest looking three-bedroom ranch with a red tile roof. It was the breathtaking view out the back that made it a multimillion-dollar home. Chris walked through the front door and looked straight through the living room out onto the glorious Pacific as it shed the storm.

Chris sat down at the kitchen table, which also looked out over the Pacific. Clark put on some coffee. They talked about each other's families, Clark's mom and sister and Chris's wife and five kids, until Clark set two steaming mugs down on the plank table and took a seat at its head.

"God has blessed you, Chris," he said with his warm smile.

"He hasn't been too bad to you either," Chris said, waving his mug in the direction of the marvelous view. "How old are you? Thirty-one? This is some place."

"It's nice," Clark admitted.

"Clark . . . I know you're probably not thrilled that Madison is representing Trane Jones in this whole thing, but I need to talk with you about it."

"I don't care who Madison represents," he said calmly enough. "She's a good agent. So are you. You've done good for me. I can't control the rest of your lives and what you do."

"You say that like we're doing something wrong."

"Wrong," Clark said, then pursed his lips. "I don't know. Is it wrong? Maybe, probably. But it's not my place to judge you. God will judge you."

Chris bit the inside of his cheek. He wasn't about to start defending his or Madison's actions, so he pushed ahead.

"Look, Clark, part of preparing for a trial is to find someone besides the defendant who might have killed the victim. That's just what you do. Now, look, you're our client. That's a sacred privilege. Neither Madison nor I could take any actions against you. We just couldn't. But I need to ask you about this case, about Annie Cassidy, not because I want to, Clark, but because I need to hear it from you that you weren't involved in any way."

Chris held up his hands before Clark could protest and said, "Now, I know you had nothing to do with it at all. But I've got to be totally honest with you. Of the obvious candidates for someone who might have done something like this? Besides Trane? You're number one, my friend . . . I need to ask you about Annie."

Clark's face grew pale and long. "Why?" he said, defensively enough to make Chris consider him silently for a moment.

"She was your girlfriend?"

"Was."

"Can I ask you what happened?"

Clark scowled now, and the dark look that crossed his face was something foreign to Chris.

"No. You can't."

Chris shifted uncomfortably.

"You're my agent, right?" Clark said.

"Yes."

"You're my lawyer?"

"I am."

"Then why are you asking me this?"

Chris sighed heavily and said, "If we prove Trane is innocent, the next person asking you these questions will be from the L.A. Police Department. Clark, sooner or later I think people are going to want to know a lot more about what happened between you and this girl."

"Not if Trane did it and they find him guilty," Clark said.

"No, not if they find him guilty," Chris agreed. "But it's my job, and Madison's job, to prove that he's innocent. I'm not talking about myself so much, but Madison? She's got a pretty good track record when it comes to these things."

Here Clark sneered maliciously. "Yeah, I know about it. Who doesn't? Funny, isn't it? You always told me that you and Madison were different. I don't see it . . ."

"Did you know a big part of the reason we're representing Trane is because Ulrich called in a favor Madison owed him from negotiating your contract?"

Clark shook his head that he didn't. This seemed to soften him a bit. "It's still bad business," he said.

"The team seems to be pretty accepting of it," Chris pointed out. "Even you. You haven't stopped blocking for him."

"That's different. In football it doesn't matter about the guys on your team. When you play, you play to win. If the guy's a criminal, that's his business. When you step on the field . . . then that's everyone's business. I'm not saying it's right. I'm just saying that's the way it is."

"But there's no love lost between you and Trane."

"Of course not," Clark scoffed. "I despise everything he stands for. If he— If he did what they say he did . . . then God will punish him. That's in God's hands, but he'll deserve what he gets. Everyone deserves what he gets. That's how God works it."

"You hate him though, don't you?"

Clark looked at him in a funny way and said, "You're the second person that's said that to me. No, I don't hate anyone. I despise what he stands for. I despise Satan in whatever form he takes, but I don't hate another human being. Christ teaches us to love our enemies."

Chris just took a sip of his coffee and looked calmly at Clark.

"I didn't kill her, Chris," Clark said.

Chris raised his brow and said, "Did I say you did?"

"No. You don't have to. That's why you're here, isn't it? Not for the way it looks, but for the way you think it might be," Clark said. "I know you used to be a cop. Of course I didn't do it. You've got to be kidding to even think it."

"Do you have any idea who did?"

Clark burst out in a short, powerful laugh. "Ha! Seems to me and just about everyone else that Trane did it."

"Besides Trane."

"Why, because he's your client?"

"No," Chris said seriously, "because I don't think he did it."

Clark knew by Chris's expression that he meant what he said. "I imagine there were lots of people who would have done it," he said.

"Lots?"

Clark shrugged and took a sip from his mug. Looking out at the ocean he said, "Annie wasn't what she seemed. She was an actress. She played a role with me. She probably did it with other people, too. She played with me the way you'd play with a toy. When she was done, she tossed me away. You don't act that way just once . . . Yeah, there had to be a lot of people that had it in for Annie."

"So you had it in for her?"

Clark turned his gaze to Chris and said, "The difference is, what kind of person are you? If she did what she did to me to someone else, maybe they'd do something about it. You know the kind of person I am. Do you really think that I would do something like that?"

Chris shifted in his chair. "No," he said quietly. "I don't."

"Then why are you here?"

"Because I have to ask," Chris told him. "I needed to hear you say it. If you didn't have a clear conscience, I'd know it. Trust me, even if I thought it was you . . . well, I'm not a cop anymore. I'm a lawyer. All it would mean to me was that Madison and I couldn't represent Trane. If I thought you did it, it would be a conflict that neither of us would want to deal with. But someone killed this girl, and I need to find out who."

"Why not just defend him by showing that it wasn't him? Why do you have to find someone else?"

"The evidence against him is strong," Chris said. "Maybe Madison can overcome that, maybe she can't. The best thing would be to find the person who really did it."

"Unless it was really him," Clark pointed out.

"Yes," Chris said after a pause. "Unless it really was."

Chapter 36

Kurt Lunden sat quietly in front of his computer screen. In his left hand was a tall, cool glass of gin and tonic. With his right he took the lime from the glass's lip and slowly sucked it between his twisted lips. When the juice was gone he dropped it back into his glass and raised the window shade with his free hand. The raging sun outside blinded him and he dropped the heavy material with a curse. The slow pitch and roll of the yacht had no effect on him. He'd been out on the water all week traveling down past Baha in search of sailfish on their southern run. Unfortunately, he'd spent more of his time in front of the damned computer screen than he had in his deck chair latched on to a big fish.

But now the time was right. He could feel it ready to peak. It was a sense he'd developed over the years. He knew he wasn't good at the market when it came to other people's companies. But when it came to his own company, with his own inside information, he knew when to make his move. Besides watching the Zeus stock, he had a satellite dish that gave him the latest fluctuations of the market. Things were happening exactly as he'd predicted. The media attention was starting to fade.

Lunden had watched with glee over the past three weeks while the whole cast of players were splattered all over the screen. But now the novelty was beginning to wear off. There were only so many television shows and so many questions Madison McCall could answer.

She'd been an ingenious touch, Lunden thought to himself. He'd give Conrad that much. Madison lent an air of credibility to an otherwise preposterous display of self-promotion. There was only so much the interviewers could tolerate of Conrad Dobbins and his shameless advertising of Zeus Shoes.

All that work Conrad had put into this thing, only to be left holding the bag when it all collapsed. Well, it would do him good. Dobbins had been screwing people his whole life, preying on simple-minded, ingenuous athletes. But Lunden wasn't an athlete and he wasn't a stargazer. He was a businessman through and through, and this was a business deal. Granted, he'd have to beef up his security after putting the wood to Dobbins. The agent was a vindictive bastard. Lunden knew that. But that was all part of the game, and Lunden had played it before.

He picked up the phone and dialed Tokyo direct. As many big deals as he'd done and as many risky schemes as he'd undertaken, his hands still shook. He gulped down the rest of the drink, ice and all, and felt the cold ache rush to his forehead.

"This is Gimble," said the banker.

"It's Lunden."

"Mr. Lunden, hello," the banker said, suddenly obsequious.

"When it hits thirty-three . . ." Lunden took a deep breath as the stock clicked up another sixteenth to thirty-one and seven-eighths, "sell it to the Japanese for thirty-one."

"How much, Mr. Lunden?"

Lunden could see the banker licking his dry thin lips. The commission on this deal would make him a small fortune.

"Sell it all."

"All five million shares?"

"Sell it."

"If you'd like I can conference you in," Gimble said. The sound of his fingers hammering away on a keyboard was audible over the phone.

"Good . . ."

Lunden stayed on the line. The stock hit thirty-three, hovered, bounced up an eighth, a quarter, and held. On the phone the conference line began to ring.

A Japanese-accented voice answered, "Hello?"

"Mr. Hagato, this is Arthur Gimble with World Trust. My client has given me instructions to offer you the five million shares we've been talking about at thirty-one dollars a share."

"Thirty-one? This stock at thirty-three."

"Mr. Lunden wants you to feel comfortable with the transaction, Mr. Hagato. Selling half his interest in Zeus is a partnership, and this is his way of beginning the partnership on a positive note."

There was silence on the other end.

Finally, Gimble said, "If you're no longer interested, Mr. Hagato, my instructions are to turn this offer over to our Hong Kong branch where we have an anxious buyer . . . Mr. Lunden of course insisted that you have the first opportunity."

"I buy."

"Good. I'll messenger the contracts over to you before noon."

Gimble disconnected the third line.

"Is that it?" Lunden said, his heart racing in his chest.

"That's it."

"Good job, Gimble," Lunden said and hung up the phone. Alone in his stateroom he sat and stared at the screen. He rang for another drink, and by the time it arrived the stock was back down to thirty-one. The Japanese were still getting a deal. A private sale was the only way for Lunden to cash out. If he tried to sell his shares on the market the flood of stock would cause the price to plummet before he could unload it all. Besides, the SEC would be all over his ass. It would be six months before people on the street learned that there was no way Zeus could fulfill its orders for the following year. When that happened, the bottom would fall out. But Lunden would be long gone by then, sitting safely on the sideline with his stock cashed out. Of course he had to keep that information to himself. Word of that kind spread faster than fleas in a pound. If everyone knew it, the stock would never climb out of its hole.

With half his stock now held by the Japanese, his only other objective was to sell the other half through a New York bank to a Saudi prince who had so much money he wouldn't even miss it when Zeus went belly-up. His strategy with each of the buyers was the same: Give them the impression that he was selling half his position to them to raise cash for some personal estate planning reasons. Neither knew about the other, nor would they until it was all over. The prince was a week away from the deal. If Dobbins could deliver the media surge he'd been talking about, the timing would be perfect. Lunden could easily walk away with three hundred million dollars.

The phone rang.

"This is Lunden."

"The fuck's goin' on, man?" Dobbins wailed.

"I was just thinking about you, Conrad," Lunden said flatly.

"You seen the stock? Shit's fallin' like rain, man. What the fuck's goin' on? I'm thinkin' about sellin'."

The agent's voice, laced ever so slightly with panic, brought a mean smile to Lunden's face. If Dobbins sold his and his clients' shares, the stock could go into a tailspin.

"Sell if you like," he said in a tone that questioned the agent's manhood.

"I don't wanna sell if the shit's goin' back to thirty-two! I wanna sell high. Motherfuckin' shit is down to twenty-fuckin'-nine! I just lost three million dollars, man, shit!"

"Conrad, I told you, when the media wears off, the stock will drop. You said you've got a plan. You can bring it right back. Then maybe you'll sell. If you do what you say you can, you'll drive the price right back up. I wouldn't sell it even then, though. I'm in for the long haul. This company could go to fifty."

"Fifty!"

"We've got a good product, Conrad. People love Zeus Shoes. Trane isn't going away. This thing could just keep growing. The media attention we've had is just the start. What you're seeing right now is profit taking. It will come back, especially if you tweak the media . . ."

Now Dobbins was chuckling on the other end of the line. "I'll tweak it, all right."

Chapter 37

On the fifteenth Sunday of the season the L.A. Juggernauts clinched a playoff berth. Madison and Chris were back in Austin shoring up the rest of their practice before heading back to the West Coast in the middle of the coming week. On Monday afternoon, Madison, who was going over her suppression strategy with her firm's best constitutional lawyer, got an urgent call.

"It's Gary Le Fleur," Sharon said, peeking around the corner of the office door.

"Excuse me, Richard," Madison said, picking up the phone. "Hello, Gary."

"Dammit, Madison, I thought you were a straight shooter. Well dammit, if I get the chance I'm telling you right now I'm gonna make your life goddamn miserable. Miserable! How the hell could you do this? I'm going to the bar, Madison! I'm telling you now, I'm going for your license! If I have anything to say about it, you won't try another case in this state! It's a disgrace to everyone!"

"Gary, what the hell are you talking about?" she said, floored.

"I'm talking about this tape! How in hell could you keep that from us! Why? Why would you do it?"

"Gary, Gary, back up," Madison said. "I have no idea what you're talking about. What tape?"

"It's all over the television. It'll be all over the newspapers by five. The tape! The goddamn Dobbins tape! Don't tell me you don't know about that!"

"I *don't* know," she said. "I don't know about anything. I'm telling you, I have no idea what you're talking about."

This seemed to confuse the DA. "He told the media he was turning the tape over to you."

"What tape?" Madison said, exasperated, "I've been locked in a meeting all day. I don't know what you're talking about, Gary."

The DA was silent for a moment. He considered the authenticity of her voice.

"Dobbins has a hi-8 videotape that allegedly proves Trane wasn't the killer," he said, a little more calmly. "If the tape is the real thing," he added. "I don't know. I'm suspicious of it, but goddammit, the L.A. network affiliates are all running copies of it and people in the media who've seen it are saying it's not something you can fabricate."

"I . . . I don't know about any of this," Madison said.

"Well . . ." Le Fleur said, his voice even now. "You better give Dobbins a call, because he's supposedly turning this tape over to you so you can have it examined by an independent lab. Hell, Madison," the DA said with disgust. "Like our labs are going to fabricate their findings! The whole thing's a goddamn disgrace."

Chapter 38

The squad room thundered with disapproval, but when Brinson walked in it got quiet fast. He shucked a nut and looked around before popping it into his mouth.

"Well, godammit, it's true," he said, chewing angrily. There was an eruption of murmuring. Brinson waited for it to pass before he continued.

"So you know," he said, "I saw the goddamn tape myself. We had our guy and their guy go over it and it's the real thing, goddammit."

There was another eruption of disbelief. Brinson held up his hands.

"I know, goddammit, believe me, I thought the same thing, but you guys have known me long enough to know that I'm not bullshitting you. I wanted to nail that asshole more than anyone but it ain't him. Not only is that video timecoded, the fucking fireworks go off in the background at twelve, the real fireworks. Our guy says there's no way someone could have created that on this film, no way. Trane Jones was on that balcony with his agent when our girl got whacked. Twelve midnight, gentlemen. His alibi is now rock-solid. We got zip."

"Could the ME be wrong?" someone asked. "Could the time be off?"

Brinson pursed his lips and shook his head. "No. The watch was smashed at the same time her head was caved in. There's glass fragments from the watch crystal imbedded in her brain. Everything fits, the time she was last seen and the ME's estimated time of death. I'm sorry, guys, but we been sapped. We got the wrong guy . . ."

"Now, I talked to the DA, and as you can guess, his ass is swingin' in the wind. He wants a killer. But I don't have to tell you that we got our asses burned here once and we ain't gonna let it happen again."

Brinson felt constricted. He grabbed the knot of his stubby knit tie and went at it the way a dog shakes a dead rabbit.

"So what I want is for us to go back at this thing with everything we got. I want every goddamn detail stretched and pulled at and turned inside out. Landover, you take your guys and Colt's and get me more on this girl. I want her goddamn life history. I want every boyfriend, girlfriend, lover, hairdresser, roommate, whatever—anyone connected to her who might have a reason to want to whack her. Cunningham, you and Greeb go over that party list again with your crews. Harper, I want your guys to go back over the employees' statements and question them again. What we've got, obviously, is a very clever guy on our hands, a guy who's not only capable of wasting this girl, but a guy who's good enough to make it look like someone else."

"Are we looking for a professional, Lieutenant?" came the question from somewhere in the second row.

"I don't know what we're looking for," Brinson said, his heavy jowls drooped in a frown. "I just know we're looking and we're looking hard. I got calls from the DA, the mayor, and the chief to prove it . . ."

"Now listen up you guys," Brinson went on. Although his

voice was gruff, his eyes shifted nervously. They were brimming with emotion. "I never said this to you, an' you know I been around long enough so there ain't much I ain't said, but I'm sayin' this now . . . My ass is on the line. I want you to know it. We don't come up with somethin' and somethin' good, I'm takin' the bullet for all the political shitbirds."

The room filled up with heavy silence.

"Now it won't be the first time some lieutenant takes one for the bosses, but goddamn I like this bunch, and I don't want to lose you . . . That's it."

Brinson couldn't help judging their reaction to his words as a measure of how much he was respected and liked. So of course the way they shot up out of their chairs brought a smile to his face.

"Kelly, Arnsbarger," he said through the din of scraping chair legs and shuffling feet. "Come with me."

The two sergeants followed him silently up the hall and into his own office.

"Sit down, boys."

Brinson handed them each a file folder across the desk. "Read this report," he said. "I interviewed this guy myself. I don't want to get crazy with this, but I think this guy might be over the edge. He's a big holy roller who says all the right things, but when you get down to it, his pretty white girlfriend was takin' the high hard one from Trane Jones."

"You think he's our guy, Lieutenant?" Arnsbarger wanted to know.

Brinson looked at his man calmly. "I don't know if he is. He could be. Whoever did it—and I'm like you, believe me— I find it hard to believe it's really not Trane, but I saw it with my own eyes . . . Anyway, it wasn't him, and whoever did it must have had access to Trane's golf clubs. That could be anyone at that tournament, but they also had to have access to Trane's car keys to plant that club in his trunk."

"But that means a friend of Trane's, and you said yourself that these guys hate each other," Arnsbarger said.

"But in a locker room," Kelly pointed out, "anyone could get their hands on another guy's keys. Just wait till he's in the shower or the training room or something and you grab 'em."

Brinson nodded at the logic. He'd been thinking the same thing. "And anyone could be Clark Cromwell," he said. "So what I want you two to do is turn this guy's life inside out. I want you to talk to every teammate, every friend, his family, his religious buddies, whoever, and find out what was going on between him and Annie Cassidy. I gotta believe that this guy blew a gasket when he found out she was bangin' Trane Jones, so get me a statement from someone who knows about it. I'm going to find the guy myself and see if I can't get him to sign a consent to search. If he gives it to me, we'll go through his place and see what we can find. If he doesn't, we'll need more than a hunch to get a search warrant."

Brinson looked at his watch. "The team offices should still be open. The players won't be there today, but you two shoot over there and see if Armand Ulrich will help us out with a list of the players' home phone numbers and addresses. Talk to the coaches and the trainers and find out who Cromwell's buddies are, then get started with his closest friends first. If I get him to sign the consent I'll radio you guys and get a forensics crew and we'll go through the house."

"You think this guy'll let us search his place, Lieutenant?" Arnsbarger asked.

Brinson pulled a nut from his right pocket and looking through its cleft at the greenish meat said, "This guy's a holy roller. He thinks he's God's right-hand man. If he didn't do it, he'll let us search. If he did . . ." The lieutenant shrugged.

"Who knows. If he did it he must be thinking he's pretty clever setting up Trane Jones the way he did. He might think the Big Guy will protect him from a couple of snoopy detectives and let us in anyway. I've seen crazier things."

Chapter 39

Brinson got in his car and headed for Clark Cromwell's house. No one was home. On his way down from the top of Palos Verdes, he got a call from Kelly.

"The trainer told me the closest guy to Cromwell is this guy Tom Huntington," Kelly said. "He's a former Oakland Raider who was a wacko, drugged out and everything. But I guess the guy found Jesus and now he's the religious guru for half the damn team. And by the way, they have their big prayer meetings on Tuesday afternoons at Huntington's house."

"You got an address for this guy?"

"Yeah. Ten twenty-nine Alexandria Court in Newport. It's not far from the beach."

"I'm on my way there," Brinson said.

"To talk to Huntington?"

"No, to get Cromwell to sign this consent to search while he's filled with the Holy Spirit."

Kelly let loose a guttural laugh and they both hung up.

Brinson waited on the street until players started spilling out of Huntington's house. It was a nice house, nicer than any of the twelve apostles had ever owned. Brinson would bet on that. He stared intently at the players through his little round wire-framed sunglasses from the front seat of his Caprice. Most of them noticed him but moved on without so much as a second glance. Brinson recognized them to a man and even knew what college each of them had played for. He was a true fan.

If it wasn't for the burgundy Expedition on the street in front of Huntington's house and Cromwell's religious fervor, Brinson would have thought the fullback had skipped the meeting. But finally, a good fifteen minutes after everyone else had gone, Clark appeared on the semicircular front steps of the house with a tall, lanky, gray-haired man whom Brinson presumed was Tom Huntington. He watched the men embrace, and then Cromwell went down on his knees. Huntington put his hand on the top of the player's bowed head and moved his lips in prayer. Brinson bit into a pistachio without shelling it.

"Fuck," he said, spitting shards of shell and slimy crushed meat into his hand.

The detective watched Clark get into his car. He waited until the player's truck was around the corner and down the next block before he pulled up alongside and motioned Clark to the curb. Brinson got out of his car and hiked his pants before sidling up to the Expedition.

"Hello, Lieutenant," Cromwell said through the open window. "Can I help you?"

"Fact is you can," Brinson said with a big smile offsetting his tiny round glasses. He leaned against the truck until his big face hovered menacingly just outside the window. "You can sign this consent form so I can have some men take a look through your house in a real decent manner. Or you can make me wait until I get a search warrant and then go through it the way they do in the movies. You know, when they cut open the mattresses and all that?"

Clark scowled at the detective's lighthearted threat. "Why?" he asked.

"That's a fair enough question," Brinson responded. "Because now that your buddy Trane is free and clear, you're the next best candidate for the job. You know what I mean?"

"You mean you think I killed Annie," Clark said, his upper lip stretching across his face in what Brinson knew was either rage or fear. The player's incandescent eyes made it impossible to know which.

"I told you before," Brinson said. "My job's to be thorough. That means I check out all the angles, even the bad ones. It's just my job. Like I said, you sign this, we go look things over real nice like, then we leave. You got nothing to hide, right?"

"Of course not," Clark spat. "But I should be able to have my privacy. That's a law."

"Fourth Amendment, to be sure," Brinson said. "The bane of police work everywhere, but you're right. You can wait until I've got a warrant from a judge, and the way this city feels right now about finding a killer, I bet it won't take me too long. Meantime I'll have someone following you every second of every day . . . figuring you've got something to hide, of course . . ."

Brinson stared for a moment and then slapped the form on Clark's dashboard, offering him a pen. "Better this way," he said.

Clark licked his lips, and as he signed he said, "I've got nothing to hide."

"Good," Brinson said, unable to let up. "I'm glad you feel that way."

He snatched the form back from Clark and suggested that he go get a drink somewhere. "A Coke or something. If you're allowed to have caffeine."

"You got a problem with me, Lieutenant?" Clark said.

"I got a problem with anyone who might have killed that girl until I know he didn't," Brinson said. "So, yeah, I guess I do got a problem with you . . . You got a key?"

Clark took it off his keychain and handed it to him. "Go ahead and look all you want. I didn't kill Annie," he said with a nasty sneer. "She brought whatever happened to her on herself."

"Meaning what?" Brinson said, his instincts perking up like a pointer picking up the scent of a bird.

"Meaning God judges us all," Clark said. "And God is just. He punishes the wicked and rewards the good."

"You saying she was wicked?" Brinson said, his blood rising. He wished he had a wire going.

"No," Clark said, suddenly calm again. "That's not for me to say. That's for God to say. I'm just telling you that if God felt she was wicked . . . it's His will either way. That's all. It's His will."

Brinson stared at him for a month-long minute. Then he brandished the consent form and said, "I'll get this over with right away. It won't take more than a couple hours."

"Fine, Lieutenant," Clark said. "I'll go back to Tom's house until seven. It's just around the block if you need to take me away in handcuffs. Otherwise you can leave the key under the mat."

Brinson snorted through his nose, uncertain now. "I'll make sure everyone's careful," he said, backing way down and feeling like a fan again.

Brinson didn't want to do any of the dirty work because he felt he'd do it with a jaundiced eye. He let his forensics people and his two sergeants dig through Clark Cromwell's underwear drawer and under his kitchen sink. But what he did do was stand in the middle of it all assessing Cromwell's lifestyle. The refrigerator was empty except for some milk, a few condiments, a six-pack of Beck's with one bottle gone, and several Styrofoam takeout boxes. The view out almost any window in the house was like something you saw in a magazine, and the pool out back was obviously cared for by a service. The living room was spotless, unlike the bedroom where the unmade bed and strewn-about clothes suggested a college frat house. In the bathroom the toothpaste tube lay uncapped beside the sink and the toilet paper hung all the way down to a pile on the marble floor. While the furniture was made of expensive wood and leather, the walls were bereft of anything more than a few chrome-framed Ansel Adams prints.

His people moved through the house like bloodhounds, sniffing and snooping and uncovering everything. The forensics people worked with magnifying glasses and screwdrivers while the detectives used their eyes and their intuition. Kelly found two drawers in the bedroom full of women's clothes.

"Must have broken it off on bad terms," he commented out loud. "She never got her stuff. Unless he's got a new one . . ."

Brinson put his hands behind his back and shuffled out into the main part of the house again to enjoy the view. That's when Arnsbarger called out from the garage.

"Lieutenant!"

Brinson moved fast, bumping his hip on the corner of the couch and almost upending a lamp table on his way into the garage. Both of the overhead doors were open and sunlight spilled in. Arnsbarger was standing in the back corner where the Sheetrock didn't quite meet the poured concrete foundation.

"There's something stuffed up in there," Arnsbarger said.

"Get some pictures," Brinson said to the tech who'd followed him in. After a few shots Brinson knelt down, testing the seams of his pants. He reached up under the wall. The tech whipped off a shot as Brinson extracted a thick gray Juggernauts sweatshirt. Clark's number, forty-three, was embroidered into the breast. The sleeves were speckled with brown spots of dried blood. In the large front pocket was the trunk key to a Mercedes.

Chapter 40

Since they missed the last flights out before the red-eye, Madison and Chris decided to spend the night in L.A. They were both worn out. After catching a 6 A.M. flight out of Austin they had spent the morning with the video experts and then the afternoon fielding questions from the media. Not that they were the center of attention. Dobbins had cornered that market.

Madison put her menu down. "I'll just have a glass of Merlot," she said.

Chris ordered, and when the waiter left he asked her why she wasn't eating.

"Truth?" she said.

"Yeah."

"It sounds like a cliché, but I'm sick over this whole thing," she said.

"Why? We got the hundred-thousand-dollar retainer and we got great publicity. Yeah, I know you didn't get to go to trial like you like, but there'll be other trials after this and the agency is going to be stronger than ever. You can't buy publicity like we got."

"I know," she said. "It's not pragmatic, but I can't shake

the feeling. Did you see Dobbins turn this thing into a racial crusade? I mean, saying that the only reason Trane was arrested was because he was black. And look, you know me. I'm the first one to cry foul when race comes into play, but come on. We won. His guy got off. But with his relationship with the girl, and the bloody club, and Trane's past, of course they're going to arrest him! Who wouldn't?"

"That's Dobbins's lifelong theme," Chris said.

"I guess it is . . ."

Madison's wine came, along with a cold Michelob for Chris. Madison took a sip and looked around them at the elegant dining room. They were staying at the Ritz-Carlton in Marina Del Rey, so there had been no reason for them to go out anywhere else for dinner. The people around them were dressed elegantly and spoke in low, intimate tones. The quiet ambiance made Madison miss her husband.

Out of the blue she said, "Chris, do you buy Dobbins's story about not knowing that piece of tape existed until he watched the film?"

Chris peered intently at her. "I don't know," he said. "I guess in all the excitement I didn't even really think about it. I guess yes. I mean, if this guy videotapes things all the time I doubt he's going home every night to review the tapes."

"But since he's videotaping things all the time, wouldn't you think he would have wondered before now, almost five weeks after the fact, if he had Trane on a video that would back up his alibi?"

Chris tilted his head and shrugged. "I guess. But none of us thought of it either. And why would he intentionally wait?"

Madison thought for a moment and then said, "The publicity?"

"I don't know, Madison," Chris said doubtfully. "I'll admit he loves the cameras, but let your top client swing out there in the wind for five weeks, the scourge of the world, just for some publicity?"

Madison nodded and they both turned their heads as a young couple burst out into a vociferous argument about having children. Everyone stared as the woman left the restaurant in tears and the man threw down his napkin and followed, shaking his head in embarrassment. Madison looked at Chris and shook her own head slowly.

"I'll tell you who made out—Zeus Shoes," she said casually as she took another sip of her wine.

"It's the American way," Chris said, raising his bottle. "It's just the American way."

"Excuse me, Ms. McCall?" said the maître d', a large white-haired man in a tuxedo who had suddenly appeared at their table. "I have an important call for you from your husband. Would you like to take it here?"

"Yes," she said, taking the cordless phone he offered her, trying not to choke on the word. "Cody?" she said into the phone.

"Everything's fine," he told her. "Jo-Jo's fine, everything's okay, but I just got a call from a guy named Tom Huntington. He says he's a good friend of Clark Cromwell. I guess the police searched Clark's house this afternoon and found a bloody sweatshirt or something and they want him to go in to ask him some questions. Clark is at this guy Tom's and Tom told him not to go. Clark had your number and this Tom called here wanting to know where you were. He says he wants you to call him right away. Are you okay?"

"Yes," she said, her heart racing, "I'm okay. I'll call him. What's the number?"

Cody told her the number, then said, "Let me know what happens, all right?"

"Okay. I love you."

"I love you, too, Madison. Bye."

"Bye."

Madison hung up and dialed Tom Huntington immediately. She knew who he was, what he did, and how close he was with Clark.

"Hello?"

"Hi, Tom? This is Madison McCall."

"Thank God you called. Are you in L.A.?"

"Yes."

"The police were just here and they want Clark to go in and talk to them. Clark let them search his house and they found a bloody sweatshirt and what they think is the trunk key to Trane's car. They think he killed Annie and framed Trane. He was going to go and talk to them, but I told him not to. I told him he had to talk to you first. Will you help him?"

"Of course I'll help," Madison said.

"He thought because you were working for Trane that you couldn't help him. I don't know. Is that a problem?"

"No. I'm Clark's agent and his lawyer already. As long as he's all right with it, it's not a problem for me to help him. There's nothing wrong with it."

"Should he go with the police?"

"No," Madison said. "You did the right thing. If they're going to arrest you, then you don't have a choice, but if they're asking then you don't want to talk to them without a lawyer. They're not still there, are they?"

"No, they left," Tom said. "But I've got the name of the detective . . . Lieutenant Brinson. He wants Clark to call him. Clark wants to. He wants to talk to them."

"Is he okay? Do you want me to talk to him?"

"I think the best thing would be if you could come over here. Can you come?"

"Yes. You'll have to give me about an hour, and I need directions."

Tom told her how to get there, and when she hung up she said to Chris, "Eat up. I'll meet you at the front desk. I'm going to book us for another night or two. I have the feeling we may be staying here."

Madison drove. Chris navigated.

"How do you feel?" Chris asked when they were out on the freeway.

"Mixed up," she told him.

"You can't say we didn't see this coming," Chris said.

"The suspicion of Clark we saw coming," she said. "But a bloody sweatshirt, a car key that might belong to Trane? Those are the two missing pieces of the puzzle. If that blood turns out to be the girl's, it's not good."

"You said he let them search the house?"

"Yes. He must have signed a consent."

Chris shook his head. It was a detective's dream, a consent to search.

"You said you had a good feeling from him," Madison said, glancing over at her partner. "How about now?"

Chris shook his head again. "If that's her blood . . . I don't know. I want to talk to him again. I had a good feeling, but then this whole thing. If that's his sweatshirt with her blood and if he's got the key to Trane's car . . . It's everything we were saying the police didn't have. What about his alibi?"

"I don't know," she said. "But we'll find out."

Tom's wife answered the door. She was a tall, attractive woman with short dark hair and large diamond earrings. Quietly she led them into the living room, where Clark and Tom were on their knees praying beside the coffee table. Madison stood uncomfortably with Chris until they were finished. Chris pretended to read the titles of books on a nearby shelf, but didn't miss a word of the prayer. It was guidance they were asking for, guidance and justice. Chris looked over at Madison's impassive face and wondered what she was thinking.

Tom rose first and gave them a subdued greeting.

"Hi, Madison. Hi, Chris," Clark said, his face drawn and tense.

They sat and Tom's wife offered them something to drink.

"Tea would be fine," Madison said, not because she wanted it but because she could see from the wife's anxious face that she was desperate for something to do. Chris was okay with nothing.

"I can't believe any of this," Clark said in obvious despair. "I can't believe Annie's dead. I can't believe you were representing Trane, and now it's me. He somehow got off, and now I'm the one they're saying did it. It's insane. It's really insane. But I know God will see me through."

"I'm glad you called me," Madison said. "We want to help."

"It was Tom's idea," Clark said. "I don't think I need a lawyer. I didn't do anything."

"If they found a bloody sweatshirt in your garage and it turns out to be Annie's blood, you need me. And you don't want to talk to the police."

"I do want to," Clark argued. "I'm going to. I didn't do anything. I don't care what they find. I didn't kill her. If I don't talk to them, they're going to end up arresting me. I don't want that. I'll talk to them and convince them I didn't do it. I don't want to be arrested, Madison. I don't want that. Not after all I've done, after all my life working to be the person I am, my reputation . . ."

"I know about all that," Madison said. "And I know how important those things are to you. But I'm a lawyer. I have to look at this strategically. My job is to protect you, and the police have ways of getting you to say things you don't really mean."

"But I—"

Madison held up her hand. "Let's talk about where we're at. If I can't convince you that it's not the best thing to do, then you can go talk to them and I'll go with you, but I'm going to ask you to sign a waiver saying that I advised you against it."

"Good. That's what we'll do," Clark said.

"Give me a chance first, Clark," she told him. "I don't want you to do that, and I think I can convince you not to, but if I can't that's how we'll handle it. For now, I've got some questions that I need answered so I know where we stand."

"Okay."

"First of all, where were you at midnight on the night Annie was killed?"

"On my way home," he said blankly.

"You left the party?"

"Yes."

"Weren't you the guest of honor?"

"I was, but all that was over. I was tired and I left about eleven-thirty."

"Was anyone with you, did anyone see you leave?"

"No," Clark said. "I was alone. I don't know if anyone saw me leave."

"A valet?"

"No," Clark said, shaking his head. "I got there early for the golf and parked it myself."

"Did you stop anywhere on the way home? For gas or something to eat?"

"No. I went home and went to bed. No one saw me. No one was with me."

Madison nodded somberly. "Okay. Tell me about her."

"About Annie," Clark said, looking over at Tom as if for guidance.

"Yes."

"She was my girlfriend. Then we broke up. When I saw her with Trane I was shocked. I was sick. But I didn't kill her. I didn't want to kill her. I was hurt, but I wouldn't kill somebody for that. I wouldn't kill anyone. It was her choice."

"When did you break up?"

"In the summer. Right before training camp."

"And you didn't see her, date her, since then?"

"No."

Tom's wife brought Madison's tea and she thanked her and took a sip before gently saying, "Why did you break up?"

Clark shrugged. "We just didn't get along anymore. I don't know. It was just one of those things. She wanted to go in a different direction."

Madison thought she saw a slight flush in Clark's cheek, and she watched him glance over at Tom. She looked at Chris to see if he'd noticed. His eyes had a knowing gleam and they were locked on Clark. He'd seen it, too.

"There must have been something," Madison said. "I mean, how did it end? Did you have a fight or something? Where were you?"

Clark sighed heavily. "Do we have to talk about this?" he said.

"This is what the police are going to ask you about, so you might as well tell me," she said.

Clark thought about that, then said, "We were at the beach. We were out on the beach and I asked her to marry me."

He looked up at Madison. She kept her face totally impassive, but Chris couldn't help narrowing his eyes. This was news to him.

"You didn't tell me that before," Chris said.

Clark looked at him guiltily. "It didn't come up, Chris. I didn't lie to you. It didn't come up."

"That's a pretty important point to leave out," Chris said quietly.

"Why?" Clark said defensively. "It's got nothing to do with anything. I asked her to marry me and she told me that's not the direction she wanted to go. She wasn't who I thought she was. I thought she was a Christian. I thought she wanted a family, a husband, a home. She didn't want any of those things.

"She was a liar," he said, his voice heating up. "She was a . . . she was a . . ."

"Whore?" Chris said, biting his tongue as he did, but the word had already escaped.

Clark's eyes were burning brightly now and his lips began to tremble. "Yes," he hissed. "She was . . ."

His eyes began to brim with tears and he clenched his fists. Then, speaking low and angrily he said, "But I didn't kill her. I wouldn't kill anyone."

Chapter 41

It's her blood."

"Thanks," Brinson said. He hung up the phone. He took a long swig of coffee. It was milky and rich from a heavy dose of sugar and cream. One of the advantages of being fat and not caring was that you got to eat and drink all the good stuff with a clear conscience.

"It was her blood," Brinson said. Kelly and Arnsbarger were sitting on the other side of his desk in the meticulously neat office.

"We gonna bring him in?" Arnsbarger wanted to know.

"No. He's coming in at one to talk to us," Brinson said. "This blood gives us enough to get into his locker at the Juggernauts, too. I'd love to find the shoes he was wearing when he whacked her. I want this thing airtight before we arrest him. I don't want another Trane Jones deal."

The detectives both nodded in assent.

"Kelly, you and Arnsey get ahold of the blues that are watching him and let them know it was her blood. Not that I don't trust them, but this'll give them some extra incentive to stay awake. I don't want anything funny going on now."

"You got it."

"Get going, because I want you both back here by one for the main event."

"We gonna sit in on it?" Kelly said.

"No. You'll be behind the glass, but I want six eyes and the camera watching this guy. I'm gonna try to break him."

Arnsbarger and Kelly left, and Brinson found himself drawn to a neatly framed five-by-seven photo of him and his sister. They were on the beach at Cape Cod. Behind them the sun was dropping from the sky in a swath of purple and orange clouds. The colors were faded now, but Brinson remembered the colors as vividly as they had once been. He had been thinner back then and had more hair. It had been a happy moment, and no matter how much time passed between his noticing it, the picture always took him back there. He smiled at the picture until it congealed into a lump of memories tainted by her death. Then the whole mess dropped into his empty gut like a dark turd. Nauseated, he removed a yellow legal pad from his desk and began to furiously scribble notes in black ink.

He was a lieutenant as much as anything because he could squeeze people. It was his gift. Still, for all his experience and talent, he liked to write things down and go over them again and again, looking for that elusive point that would be the key to breaking someone down. It wasn't that he wouldn't follow a blind trail that suddenly appeared during the course of an interrogation. He would. It was that he always made sure beforehand that he'd considered all the angles.

The angles kept him focused on his work. Even so, he found himself involuntarily drawn back to the photo. Once he even surprised himself with the words, "You were too good, Ginny. You were too good."

The ringing phone broke his reverie. It was Colt.

"Got something I thought you might wanna know, Lieutenant," the detective said.

"Shoot."

"I checked Annie Cassidy's credit card charges over the past year and didn't find too much out of the ordinary except an August first charge to a doctor at the Greer Clinic for a D and C."

Brinson knew the word meant something but he didn't know what. "DNC?"

"D *and* C, dilation and curretage . . . an abortion, Lieutenant. I went over to the clinic and found a blabbermouth nurse who let me know that she was only about six weeks pregnant. That's unofficial of course."

"Great job, Colt. Let me know if you find anything else."

Brinson hung up the phone and looked for the last time that day at his sister's innocent face. With renewed fervor he plunged back into his work.

At five after one the phone rang and Brinson realized he hadn't eaten lunch. The pile of broken shells spilling out of his little glass ashtray was no consolation. His stomach had become a living thing unto itself. It complained bitterly, tossing and turning like an insomniac. Brinson ignored it and answered the phone. Cromwell and his lawyer were downstairs. Brinson took a deep breath, underlined a few words, starred question eleven three times, and heaved himself up from the desk.

He checked to make sure his men were in place and went downstairs. His face set like granite, then revealed a grim sneer as he approached the lobby. Halfway down the hall he saw them standing there. Clark was obviously on edge. He wore sneakers, a navy nylon sweatsuit, and a FOX Sports cap pulled tight to his head. Despite the casual clothes he shifted uncomfortably the way someone would in an ill-fitting suit.

Brinson introduced himself to the lawyer and choked back a comment about life as a hired gun. The media would take care of that for him. He'd bet a pocketful of pistachios on it. How the hell could this woman really expect to go from representing Trane Jones to Clark Cromwell without a maelstrom of criticism? She couldn't. But that wasn't his business, so he kept his trap shut.

"Nice to meet you," he told Madison, proper enough without being mistaken for friendly. "Thanks for coming."

As tense as the situation was, Brinson still found himself considering the lawyer's good looks. She was taller than he thought she'd be, and the deep green color of her eyes as well as the length of her neck distracted him. On TV she had looked good enough, but TV failed to capture her true radiance.

Brinson pushed those thoughts from his mind and led the way to his interrogation room. There was a pitcher of water with three glasses on the table. The only people who got water were the ones who showed up with their lawyers. Otherwise they got what Clark got the first time he came, hot and dry.

The lieutenant went through the preliminaries of getting Clark to state his name and the voluntary nature of the interview. Madison broke in, wanting to make it clear for the record that Clark was there against her advice. Brinson wondered how that made the kid feel. Certainly it would heighten his caution. It didn't matter though. Brinson was glad just to have a crack at him.

The first thing the detective did was to establish Clark's time line the night of the murder. It was easy work. Clark rolled over and it was obvious that he had no alibi. Brinson took note of Madison's rigid jaw. She hadn't said a word so far, and he wondered when she would try to throw a wrench into his questioning. Obviously she was conceding the total absence of an alibi. Their eyes met across the table like card players, neither giving anything up.

Brinson moved on to the relationship between Clark and Annie. Here the player was more hesitant. His halting answers let Brinson know there was more to the story than he was letting on. But Brinson knew better than to press too hard when he came upon a sensitive subject. He wanted both the lawyer and the player to be as much at ease as possible. It was almost tender the way he asked about Clark's reaction to Annie's relationship with Trane. Brinson just knew the other two had to be snickering in the room beyond the glass. After fifty minutes of questioning, he paused to go over his notes to make sure there were no details he had missed before he got into it for real.

"How did that sweatshirt get in your garage?" he said, his voice now laced with hostility. "It's her blood on it, you know."

"I don't know," Clark said. "I have no idea."

"It's your sweatshirt, right?"

"Yes, but I have several of them just like it. Someone could have taken it from my locker. Annie had one of them. Trane could have gotten it from her."

"Trane?"

"He's obviously behind this," Clark said.

Brinson pressed his lips together in a skeptical frown and looked at Madison. She looked at her client, obviously as puzzled as Brinson.

"Let's not get into the possibilities, Clark," she said gently. "Let's just answer the questions as the lieutenant asks them."

Clark nodded.

"What about the key to the Mercedes?" Brinson said. "Didn't you take that from Trane's locker?"

"Never."

"It just showed up in your garage with the sweatshirt?"

"And I have no idea how they got there," Clark added. "I never touched them."

"Was there someone at your house who might have put them there?"

"No," Clark scoffed. "No one who's been at my house would do that."

"Did someone break in?"

"Maybe."

"Did you report a break-in?"

"When they did it, I didn't know about it."

Brinson nodded doubtfully. "Tell me about your religious convictions," he said suddenly.

Madison shifted in her seat and said, "That's totally irrelevant here, lieutenant."

"I don't think that it is," Brinson said, not taking his eyes off Clark. "What are they?"

"I don't think you should get into that, Clark," Madison said.

Clark looked at him calmly and said, "I'm a born-again Christian. You know that, Lieutenant."

Brinson nodded. "Yes, I know. I know about Jesus being your personal savior. I've heard all about it. I've seen you say it on TV. I've read it in the paper, too. But what about the Bible? How does the Bible fit into all this?"

"The Bible is the word of God," Clark said, glowing proudly now.

"You mean it's man's interpretation of what God wants," Brinson said, knowing full well that he was being contradictory.

"No, the Bible is God's *literal* word. He used the men who wrote it the way we might use a typewriter. It's God's word."

"So when it says 'an eye for an eye, a tooth for a tooth,'" Brinson said, "that's God's word."

"Of course."

"Lieutenant," Madison interrupted, "we did not come here for a discussion in theology. I would appreciate it if you kept your line of questioning to the matter at hand."

"Oh, but it is, Counselor. It is," Brinson said patiently and with a strange smile.

"So if someone killed, let's say . . . your child," Brinson said, staring intently at Clark and pointing at him with a pistachio he held pinched between his thumb and his index finger, "then they would deserve to die."

"That would be God's will," Clark said, frowning emphatically. "We can see that over and over in the Bible. But God gives out justice as He sees fit, Lieutenant. Jesus said turn the other cheek."

"But you believe that if someone killed your son that God would have justice, isn't that right?"

"In His time, yes."

"How about abortion?" Brinson said.

"Good God, Lieutenant!" Madison burst out. "This is enough."

The word seemed to have hit Clark upside the head with the force of an iron bar.

"What about it, Clark? Is that murder?"

"Of course it is," Clark hissed. "It's the most brutal form of murder."

"And she murdered your child, didn't she?" Brinson said, forcefully, keeping his eye contact with Clark, ignoring the lawyer's protests, moving in for the kill.

Clark shook with rage. Madison grabbed him by the arm.

"That's enough!" she said, standing and tugging at her client. "Clark, let's go. This is enough. No more. Lieutenant, you're way out of line."

Clark shook her off, his eyes locked on Brinson's. "You know," he said flatly, his eyes filling up with pain.

"I told you before, it's my business," Brinson said. Then, quietly but forcefully he whispered, "She killed your baby, Clark. She sucked it out of the womb in pieces with a stainless-steel tube. What does that *do* to you?"

Clark let out a primordial bellow and leaped across the table at Brinson. Brinson bolted back. Clark missed his neck but got hold of his shirt and tore it wide open. Brinson's pale flesh spilled out into the open. Kelly and Arnsbarger burst through the door and grabbed Clark by either arm.

"It was God's will!" Clark bellowed. "It was God's will, if that's what you want to know! She got what she deserved! She got what she deserved!"

"Clark!" Madison's scream pierced the melee as she grasped the front of his sweatjacket and shook him with surprising strength. "Stop it! Stop it!"

Clark went limp. He was shaking and tears streamed down his face.

"You're under arrest!" Kelly shouted, forcefully pulling one of Clark's hands behind his back.

"No he's not!" Brinson ordered with an outstretched hand. He was gasping for breath. "He's not. Let him go."

The two detectives dropped Clark's arms and Madison looked fiercely at Brinson. The overweight detective was pulling the remnants of his shirt together with one hand and steadying himself on the back of his chair with the other.

"That was wrong," she said, seething.

"Take him," Brinson snarled back at her. "Take him outta my sight."

Chapter 42

Coach Gridley addressed the team first thing Wednesday morning. His eyes were bloodshot and each had its own puffy gray satchel to contend with. He needed a shave.

"This team has overcome tremendous distractions this season," he began in the rough morning voice of a smoker. "I thought we finally had all this bullshit behind us . . . but we don't. For those of you who don't know, Clark Cromwell is now being investigated for the death of . . . of that girl."

Gridley looked around the room at his silent team and their scowling faces.

"Clark won't be here today," he continued. "I don't know what to say to you all except to tell you the facts and to tell you to keep focusing on the game the way you have since this whole thing began. Now, we've got to go out to Buffalo this week and it's going to be cold and nasty. We win this game and we've got home field throughout the playoffs. We all know what that means . . ."

Everyone did. Home field during the playoffs gave a team a distinct advantage in reaching the Super Bowl. The emotional edge of a home crowd often made the difference in lifting a team up over the top. The season's final games were a time when everyone was mentally worn and physically battered.

"We've got a lot of work to do to prepare for their thirty-four defense and we can't afford to be thinking about all the bullshit going on outside this facility. Like I said, you've done that well so far and you've got to keep doing it. We've got the thing with Trane behind us now, and that's a goddamn relief. Hopefully the same thing will happen with Clark, I don't know. It seems like the police have their heads up their asses but we'll just have to weather it. Ossenmeyer, if Clark doesn't practice this week, you'll start in Buffalo. As far as the media is concerned, you guys just keep treating those whores to silence à la mode. I don't want to see any comments on this bullshit. You just do your jobs and talk football. We've got a championship to win."

For Trane the day went like any other. He slept during the meetings, then practiced hard when it came time to go out on the field. At the end of the day he headed for the weight room to do his upper-body lift. He went through the machines with a steady intensity that even the hardest-working of his teammates admired. While he might slack off on the mental preparation for a game, it was a rare day when someone outdid him in the physical realm.

After a shower, Trane found himself alone in his section of the locker room with Ike Webber.

"Hey, Ike!" he said, loud and sudden enough to make the younger player start. "Come here, brother. You an' me gotta talk."

"Wha's up, Trane?" Ike said with a nervous grin. Trane rarely spoke to Ike, and most times when he did it was to poke fun at him. "Country Brother" is how Trane referred to the young runner. Ike never said anything about that. Trane was a star. He held a place in the NFL's hierarchy that

Ike dreamed of. Even his mild insults to the coaches were tolerated.

"Wha's up is you, brother," Trane said with a sneer. "I wanna know if you're a brother or a motherfuckin' Oreo, a white brother. You a white brother, Ike?"

Ike bit the flesh beneath the inside of his lower lip. Trane just talked that way to people. It wasn't anything to get offended about. It was just his way.

"I ain't white," he said. "I ain't white, Trane."

"Then how come you walkin' all over hell with them white-boy Bible motherfuckers? That's a white man's bullshit."

"Naw," Ike said. "They're good people, Trane. They got Jesus."

Trane snorted. "They do what they do. They ain't no better than you or me. That's a white man's thing. Been usin' that shit fo' two hundred years to keep the black man his slave."

Ike twisted his face in protest but said nothing.

"What you need is to spend some mo' time with the brothers," Trane said, slowly drying his privates. "An' I got just the thing. Tonight's gonna be a big motherfuckin' party at Phatt Momma's. Zeus Shoes is celebratin' my innocence. That's where you need to be."

"I don't do that stuff, Trane," Ike muttered.

"You don't do drugs. You don't do alcohol. But you sho' as hell like a freak. I know that. An' I got a sister that's gonna do shit to you that you don't even wanna *know*. Yeah, you like that. I see that smile . . .

"Besides, Conrad gonna be there, an' he don't want you actin' like some white boy. You gotta spend some time with your brothers if you wanna be a brother. Conrad, he don't wanna represent no white brothers."

"Okay, Trane. That sounds okay. I'll check it out."

Trane's warm broad smile made Ike feel good. It was like an unexpected burst of sunshine on a gloomy winter day.

"That's what I like to hear, brother. An' the shit starts at eight so don't be late."

Chapter 43

Conrad Dobbins snickered to himself. Most people could be bought for next to nothing. He'd closed multimillion-dollar deals over inside information he'd purchased for the price of putting a fifty-thousand-dollar addition onto someone's home. He'd obtained information that cost people their lives for the price of a used Mercedes convertible. It was laughable. So when he got a call from Sergeant Arnsbarger, he wasn't caught off guard. Ten thousand dollars in a paper bag was all it cost him to keep abreast of the wheres and whys of the Annie Cassidy case. Ten thousand dollars. Dobbins was looking at thirty million.

"He's over the edge," Arnsbarger said.

Dobbins was on a lounge chair beside the pool looking out over the smog-cloaked city. The sun's brilliant rays were blocked out by a large cloth umbrella. A fresh drink sat quietly sweating beside him on a little cocktail table. On his other side, just beyond the shade, lay a twenty-six-year-old dancer facedown without her top.

"You gonna nail him?" Dobbins wanted to know.

Arnsbarger was quiet for a moment and Dobbins could

hear traffic in the background. The cop was calling from a pay phone.

"I should probably be asking you," the detective said sarcastically.

"What I wanna know is if you got enough shit on this motherfucker to put his ass in jail right now?" Dobbins said, reaching out for his drink and taking a slow sip before putting it right back in the center of its wet ring.

"Maybe," Arnsbarger said. "Maybe not. The lawyer seems pretty sharp. I hear she doesn't lose. You know that. She was with Trane. He could go down, but he might not. I've seen good lawyers get people off with even more against them. We've all seen that."

"What about Brinson? Is that fat son of a bitch sold on the white boy?"

"Oh yeah, Brinson was onto him from the start."

"Good. That's all I need to hear."

"Okay, hey, if you need more stuff, you know, in the future . . ."

"Yeah, I'll keep you in my mind."

Dobbins snapped the phone shut and tapped its shell against his teeth before setting it down beside the drink. With his left hand he reached over and felt the curve of the dancer's ass where it met the back of her thigh. He stroked the tiny white hairs growing there even though they were too fine to be felt. Then he gave her a little slap that made her start up with a small shriek.

"Go on, bitch," he said cheerfully. "I need to talk to my man. You go on inside an' I'll be in there real soon."

The girl rose shamelessly from her chair, exposing her naked breasts and even adding a little arch to her back. Conrad and Zee leered together. The bodyguard stood resting his bulk against the wrought-iron railing that kept the agent's guests from falling to their death.

When the girl was gone Dobbins said, "Put yo' fuckin' eyes back in yo' motherfuckin' head an' come over here, Zee."

Zee adjusted his sunglasses and grumbled something about his eyes being right where they should be, but did as he was told all the same.

"S'up," he rumbled, now standing directly in front of Dobbins's chair with his feet spread shoulder-width apart and his hands clasped firmly behind his back. The man was so large he obliterated the sun.

"What's up is you, brother," Dobbins said congenially. "I got somethin' that you gonna like. I gotta job that's gonna take all your motherfuckin' abilities, an' I know you like that . . ."

Zee knew what was coming. "All his abilities" meant someone was going to have to die. It also meant that he was going to get paid, and paid big. Being a bodyguard was fine, but when there was something special to be done, his deal said that he got bonuses, big bonuses. It was the kind of money a professional deserved. A few more jobs that required "all his abilities" and he wouldn't be working for anyone but himself. He already had close to a million dollars socked away in a safe-deposit box. Zee fingered the medallion that hung from his neck on a thick gold chain. The medallion never left his neck. Behind it he had adhered the key to his deposit box. It was his passport to freedom. His face broke out in a nasty smile now, because after this job he might just have enough to break out on his own. Maybe he'd have a bodyguard of his own.

The first time Zee went into the gated community of Rancho Palos Verdes it was in the bed of a pickup truck full of Mexican yard workers. For a hundred bucks the boss let Zee ride around with them for the day all through the neighborhood.

Hiding beneath a Green Thumb cap and armed with his own weed whacker, Zee had free rein inside the exclusive community. And while it was true someone couldn't just drive up and pass through the gates, the community's intricate web of horse trails made it accessible if only you were willing to crash through some underbrush. Under the cover of a stolen municipal water truck, Zee pulled over at a park outside the community. He pushed through the dark underbrush until he emerged onto a horse trail that he knew would take him to within a hundred feet of Clark Cromwell's house.

Dobbins had alerted him that there would be police outside watching the house, but that was no problem either. Zee knew how to get in through the back. With the stars shining brightly and a half-moon in the sky, negotiating the wood-chipped trails wasn't a problem. Less than twenty minutes after leaving his van Zee was lurking in the shadows of the neighbors' lawns. At one house he stopped to watch a young girl doing her homework at the kitchen table. In the next room her mom, with the same long dark hair pulled into a similar red ribbon, sat twisting her ponytail as she talked on the phone. Zee felt the thing he liked buzzing up inside him. He could wait right there until these rich white fools went to sleep and then snuff the life out of them. They felt so safe in their home behind the gates. But he was real and he could end it for them in a terrible way. It was an alluring thought, but business was at hand.

If he did this job right he'd have more than enough money so that he wouldn't have to work. With this deal he'd be making more money this year than some of Conrad's richest clients. With the money he already had in the box and the money he'd get from selling the new options Conrad had promised him, Zee wouldn't have to work like he did. With money like that he could go down to Mexico where the value of a human being was supposedly much less than it was in L.A. He had a notion that he'd like to make some movies down there, and he knew just where he could sell that kind of thing. But first he had to take care of business. He moved through the shadows with a stealth that belied his size. Before climbing a neighbor's tree that would let him drop down inside Clark's wrought-iron fence, Zee stopped to check out the cops. They sat in an unmarked car across the street. One slept with his head against the window while the other read a book, glancing up every few moments at Clark's house. When the one cop's head went back down to his book Zee shouldered his black leather pack and swung himself up into the tree.

Chapter 44

Clark sat watching the phone as it rang. It rested in the middle of his coffee table surrounded by a regiment of empty beer bottles. Normally the sight would have filled him with guilt. But now his head swam in alcohol and the mess and the annoying sound of the phone didn't seem to matter all that much. He had bought a case of St. Pauli Girl at the grocery store on his way back from the police station. His intention had been to only have a few to settle his nerves, but he had ended up drunk. In an abstract way it was shameful, really. He knew you couldn't be drunk and have the spirit of God. The two didn't go together.

The phone didn't stop. He knew it was Madison. She had said she was going to call him and he'd promised he'd be there.

"I am here," he slurred out loud to himself.

The phone stopped. Clark's spirits continued to fall from one level to the next without apparent end. Nothing seemed to matter anymore. Not God, not Jesus, not football, not anything. He was so alone it made him ache. His head lolled against the back of the couch and his eyes drooped shut. The room began to spin.

"She deserved it," he heard himself mutter before he plunged into a stupor.

Madison pulled on a pair of faded jeans. She haphazardly tucked one of her husband's soft cotton undershirts into the waist and cinched down her braided leather belt. She crossed the hall and knocked on Chris's door. His phone had been busy. She assumed he was talking to his wife. Chris came to the door looking even more destitute than Madison in a pair of washed-out red running shorts and a moth-eaten T-shirt. He looked so out of place coming out of a room in the Ritz-Carlton that Madison had to stifle a grin.

"I, uh . . ." she stuttered, "I'm going to drive over to Clark's."

"Clark's?" he said, looking at his watch. "Madison, it's ten-thirty."

"I know. But I've called five times and haven't gotten an answer. I'm worried about him."

"Worried? Like what?" he said.

"I don't know. I told him I'd call him. He said he'd be there. I don't know, Chris. That was a lot today. I . . ."

"You think he'll do something?" Chris said.

"Maybe."

"Hang on," he said. "Let me get dressed."

Chapter 45

Trane hadn't lied. The VIP lounge was like a Hollywood magazine turned inside out. Weaving in and out of the celebrities was one beautiful woman after another, page after page. They were all there to celebrate the exoneration of an innocent black man. Ike wandered self-consciously through the crowd and the noise with a glass of Coke in his hand. Finally he lit on the corner of a leather couch next to two stunning Asian girls with short skirts and long glossy hair. After a disinterested assessment of Ike they turned to each other and chattered away in a language that was beyond his recognition.

Trane appeared, much like the appearance of royalty, in a black tank top and lots of gold. He had his typical entourage, a handful of homeboys and Conrad Dobbins in a deep purple suit talking and gesticulating boisterously. All heads turned, and the Asian girls stopped their conversation to point and stare. The small crowd broke out in spontaneous applause that rose to a level above the thumping music. In return, Trane wagged his tongue. Without being asked, a cocktail waitress brought the star player a glass of chipped ice swimming in good scotch. Trane casually massaged the girl's rump as his way of saying thanks. Ike watched this and shook his head dubiously. Maybe this crowd was too fast for him. Despite his affinity for women, Ike was like flypaper. He just sat and waited for them to come to him.

After most of the crowd had paid their personal tributes to the guest of honor and his agent, Trane spotted the rookie through the crowd. Grabbing two women on his way, he crossed the room and filled up the rest of Ike's couch with himself and the two women. The Asian girls were pressed into the other corner now, where they lit up cigarettes and pretended not to gawk. Suddenly Ike was a close personal friend of Trane's and the taller of the two flashed him a discreet smile. Ike felt the thrill of Trane's power and hoped it didn't have anything to do with the devil.

"Hey, little brother. What's up?" Trane said, holding his fist out so he and Ike could touch knuckles.

"Hey, Trane. Just chillin'."

"How 'bout these two?" Trane said, grinning lecherously and jerking his thumb toward the two girls he'd brought with him. "Fine freaks."

Ike nodded that they were indeed fine freaks. They were thinner than he really preferred, but their faces, one light brown, the other milky white, had that magazine quality.

"My boys!"

Conrad Dobbins was suddenly in their midst. Beside him stood a Middle Eastern man wearing a suit and slicked-backed hair. Next to him was a man who looked so dissipated and shabby that Ike suddenly felt like he fit in. The man's crushed and dirty cap sat at a crooked angle on his head, and his sun-scorched face reminded Ike of a poor rural farmer. Only an eighteen-karat gold Cartier watch and a diamond pinkie ring suggested he was something more.

"Ike, my man," Conrad said, slapping hands with the

young player, "This is Mr. Kurt Lunden, owner an' founder of Zeus Shoes and our partner . . ."

"An' this," he continued with a flourish of his hands, "is Prince Fasad, my man from Saudi Arabia, the newest partner in Zeus an' the man that's payin' for this party."

"Nice to meet you," Ike said politely. He could see that his agent's eyes were glassy from liquor.

Dobbins turned to the prince and the sneaker magnate with a playful grin and said above the din, "How 'bout this boy? He's a polite country motherfucker, but he's gonna be a star. Boy's got moves and hands!"

Dobbins sat down on the arm of the leather couch and tucked Ike's head in the crook of his elbow. "It's good to see you, little man. My man Trane was tellin' me you was hanging with that motherfuckin' Bible crowd an' that ain't no way to live in this town."

Ike shrugged bashfully but didn't bother to defend himself. His agent was talking without listening.

"Bible shit didn't do that Cromwell motherfucker no good, did it?" Trane said mischievously, arching his eyebrows. "That cat blew a fuckin' fuse an' put my bitch on ice."

Conrad let out a careless drunken chuckle and said to Ike, "Yeah, an' ain't suicide a motherfuckin' sin, Ike? Bible don't go fo' no suicide . . ."

Ike looked at him seriously and shook his head. "Naw," he murmured. "That's a sin."

"Well . . ." Conrad said with a devious grin, "we may be sinners o' one kind, but we ain't suicidal motherfuckers so I guess you're with the right people tonight."

Lunden grew sour-faced on that note and excused himself and the prince for a drink.

Trane glowered. "Fuck's his problem?"

"Aw, don't mind that," Conrad said, waving it off. "That

motherfucker made us too much money to care about his goddamn manners. Made you a little money, too, Ike! Shit yeah, I got you in on that Zeus Shoe stock *early*. We're all doing good on that."

"When'd I get in?" Ike said hopefully.

"Shit!" Dobbins replied, taking a long swig of his vodka tonic. "You got in same as the rest of us . . . at thirty motherfuckin' cents!"

Ike was no *Wall Street Journal* subscriber, but even he knew the stock was way beyond that now. "How much of that did I get?" he asked. He had no idea what was happening with his money, just that Conrad had invested it.

"About ten thousand shares," the agent said.

"Man, that's about three hundred thousand," Ike said, beaming. "That's phat as a hog, Conrad."

"That's why you with me," Dobbins said. "That's why all these athletes is with me."

Even Trane had to nod his assent to that one. He was looking at ten million dollars on the deal and, like Conrad, hoping the stock was on its way to fifty.

"Man, everybody loves those shoes. Almost everybody I know back in Titus already asked me to get Trane to sign a pair. It's a good investment," Ike ventured.

"It's mo' than that," Conrad told him after taking another large gulp of vodka and signaling one of the homeboys to get him a refill. "It's about orchestratin'! That's what it was. We *massaged* that motherfuckin' stock . . . That's the only way to make real money. That's how the white man does it on Wall Street, but now we're doin' the same damn thing in L motherfuckin' A."

Chapter 46

Zee dropped to the concrete beside the pool and looked
warily around as he backed himself into a clump of high
shrubs. After a moment he worked his way around the landscaping until he had a good view of the glass doors from
where most of the light was emanating. He squinted and
peered hard through the night. It looked like Clark was
passed out on the couch, just lying there spread-eagled in
front of the glass doors. The white fuck was dead drunk. It
was too easy.

Slowly he stalked around the pool and across the open
space toward the glass. He knew that even if Clark were
awake he would see only his own reflection since all the
light was coming from inside the house. Still, he was cau-
tious. Five feet from the door he could see that it was open a
crack. The phone rang and Zee froze. His blood surged with
adrenaline, but the shrill ring elicited no response from
Clark. A smile sneaked onto Zee's face and the corners of
his eyes crinkled merrily. He wasn't going to have to wait
around in the bushes until 2 A.M. He'd be home in time to
watch a *Twilight Zone* rerun at midnight.

Nevertheless, Zee continued to move carefully and quietly as he shed his black satchel. He set it on the concrete in front of him without taking his eyes off the comatose player. He undid the leather flap and felt through the various metal tools for the cloth rag sealed inside a plastic Ziploc bag. With his other hand he automatically felt into a side pocket for the little dropper of Versed. He found that and tucked it into the front pocket of his pants.

He straightened up and walked heel-to-toe toward the glass. Slowly he wrapped his fingers around the edge of the slider and pulled it open wide enough so that he could move inside. Clark's nose twitched and Zee froze again. Clark passed his hand across his face before it fell back to the couch. Zee was in the danger zone, too far in to go back, not close enough to get an immediate grip on his victim. There was still a good eight feet as well as a coffee table between them. He stayed still for a full minute before beginning to move again. The thrill was beginning to mount, and Zee let it wash over him. With a cat's patience he crossed the floor and skirted the low table.

When he was standing over Clark he held the plastic bag at arm's length and extracted the rag soaked in sevoflurane. Giddy now with confidence, he stuffed the corner of the empty bag in his pants pocket, then reached down with his free hand to take a sip of Clark's half-finished beer. As he lifted the bottle it clinked softly against one of the empties. Zee's eyes shifted to Clark's face. The player's eyes split slightly. Zee dropped the bottle with a crash and swung the toxic cloth toward Clark's face just as a foot shot straight up into his groin.

Clark was up and on top of the bigger man, pummeling his face for all he was worth. But drunk as he was, the blows weren't nearly as hard or as accurate as the one jab Zee shot up under his chin. The punch knocked Clark sideways and into the coffee table, shattering both wood and glass. Clark recovered quickly though, and before Zee could get off the floor he was back on top of him with his hands planted firmly around the bodyguard's neck. The rage flowed through Clark's body and out his hands, strengthening the death grip he had on the enormous killer.

Zee bucked away under Clark, but the player's grip only grew tighter and his knees were pinned to Zee's sides the way a cowboy rides a bull. With his eyes bulging and his head starting to spin, Zee suddenly felt peaceful and composed. With his left hand he groped about the floor until he touched the damp cloth rag. He grabbed hold, then crammed it into Clark's face. Clark's eyes went wide, but still he held on to Zee's neck. Zee fought against the chokehold to remain conscious. He knew the last one to go would be the one to live. Zee gurgled desperately for air. Then everything went black.

Chapter 47

Madison leaned on her horn until the guard came back out of the guardhouse frowning angrily. He was a rail of a man with a heavy black mustache and dark curly hair that grew out from under the edges of his cap like untamed shrubbery.

"Listen, lady," he snapped, narrowing his beady little close-set eyes. "I'm not gettin' an answer. You're not on the visitor's list, and if I don't have approval from Mr. Cromwell you can't go in. That's my job, lady."

Madison was burning now. They'd been waiting more than fifteen minutes and she had seen how nonchalant the guard had been about the whole thing, talking and joking with someone on the telephone, letting several other people in before trying Clark's house a second time.

"You're not going to have a job if something's wrong and you keep me from going in there to help," she said menacingly.

The man crossed his arms and smiled in a way that let Madison know this wasn't a job he was particularly fond of anyway.

"I'll run through that arm if you don't raise it," Madison said calmly.

"And I'll have the police right behind you, lady," the man jeered. "So you go right on ahead "

Madison looked over at Chris, who tugged his mouth down at its corners and shrugged helplessly. Madison probably wouldn't have done it but for the guard's smart-ass grin. With an I-told-you-so nod of her head she threw the rental car in gear and punched the accelerator, leaving the guard with a wonderfully stupid look on his face. They could hear him screaming at her as the wooden barrier snapped into three fragments and they drove off down the road.

Zee's eyes rolled forward in his head and he blinked. He realized his tongue was hanging out of his mouth and he retracted it. Clark was lying on top of him with his hands still gripping Zee's neck. Zee slapped the player's arms away and staggered to his feet. The phone was ringing. Zee shook his large head and shifted his weight unsteadily back and forth, swaying like a mortally wounded buffalo as he collected his wits. When the phone stopped ringing he went into motion as if on cue. He took the dropper of Versed automatically from his pants pocket and tilted Clark's head back. Two drops went into each nostril. Once it was done, Zee absently wondered why he even bothered. There was nothing to remember when you were dead.

He shook his head to clear the haze and grasped Clark under each arm. He dragged the player's limp body into the garage and hauled him up into the front seat. There was no need for a hose. It wasn't a large space. He'd just gas the whole place. The keys were in the ignition. Zee fired up the truck and walked back into the house, closing the door tightly behind him. Carefully he looked around the shambles of the living room, trying to think of any sign he might have left. Amid the beer bottles he saw the sevoflurane rag, and beside the couch was the plastic bag. He stuffed the rag into the bag, sealed it, and put them into his back pocket.

Because his head was still spinning, he sat down on a chair to look over the scene and think. The last thing he wanted was to leave something behind. It had to look like a suicide. The smashed table could be explained by a fit of rage on the part of Clark, but the rest of the mess had to be straightened up. It was obviously the result of two big men in a scuffle. With that thought he rose and began slowly to pick up the mess as best he could, straightening the furniture and putting the beer bottles back up on what was left of the coffee table.

Within minutes Zee had altered the scene from the site of an obvious brawl to a quiet place where one man had simply gone off the deep end. That's when the doorbell rang. Zee looked toward it and felt a lump of panic form in his chest. He did one last visual sweep of the room and let himself out through the back slider without bothering to close it behind him. The doorbell rang over and over again. Zee could hear it as he ran past the pool. With the help of a deck chair he got himself up into the shadows of the tree he'd come in on just as he heard a shout from the front of the house.

Chapter 48

Chris shook his head as they wound their way through the streets of the exclusive neighborhood.

"We're in trouble," he said.

"This is an emergency," Madison told him.

"Madison, what emergency? The guy hasn't answered his phone."

"Call it intuition," she said. She was shaking now and didn't know whether it was intuition or simply the residue of a foolish act.

"There's the police," Chris said, pointing to the darkened sedan across the street from Clark's house.

"They won't have far to go to arrest me," Madison quipped. She pulled directly into the driveway. Chris noticed the police perking up.

"At least they're on their toes," he said. "If something had happened they probably would have known about it."

"If Clark was gone," Madison pointed out, "then they would have followed. He must be inside. So why wouldn't he answer the phone?"

"Madison," Chris said as they piled out of the car and hustled up the walk, "the guy's upset."

"But he knew I was going to call. He said he'd be here," she reminded him.

Madison rang the bell once politely. When there was no response she rang it again and again, maniacally. Chris looked over at the policemen. They were both alert now and peering curiously out at them. Madison rattled the door handle. It was locked.

"Come on," she said, starting back down the walk. "Let's check the back."

Walking quickly past the garage, Madison thought she heard the low rumble of a truck motor. She looked at Chris.

"His truck," she said.

"Maybe he's getting ready to go out?" he said.

"With the door shut?"

Madison pounded on the garage door.

"Clark!" she yelled. There was no response. She rounded the house in a sprint, climbed over the gate like a high school track athlete, and dashed into the back by the pool. The sliding door was wide open and Madison saw the destruction in the living room. Beer bottles were all over the coffee table. Two of its glass panels were shattered and the wood was fractured as if someone had tried to kick it in. A small noise of panic escaped her throat. Something was so wrong. She made her way past the mess and into the garage with Chris right behind her.

The door leading into the garage was shut, and when Madison opened it she was overwhelmed by the stench of fumes. She stepped back, flipped on the lights, and drew a deep breath. She plunged into the noxious space and searched frantically for the garage door opener. It was on the wall next to the door. She punched it desperately. As the door slowly opened, Madison made for the truck. Clark was slumped in the front seat, completely inert. Madison opened the door and began to tug at him. Chris was beside her, and together they pulled his body out onto the garage floor. Madison couldn't hold her breath any longer, and without thinking she took a large gasp of fumes and began to choke.

Together, she and Chris began dragging Clark's body outside onto the driveway. The detectives were out of their car now and running toward them. Madison fell to the pavement, choking and gasping, and Chris was doubled over as well.

"He's not breathing. You check his heart," said the first cop, who immediately began mouth-to-mouth resuscitation.

The second detective felt for a pulse in Clark's neck and found none. He began CPR.

"Is he dead?" Madison asked frantically.

The detective working on his heart looked up at her doubtfully. "Call an ambulance," he said.

Chapter 49

Brinson walked in through the garage and took a cursory look around. Arnsbarger and Kelly were already there, leaning against the doorframe that led into the house.

"Want us to turn the place upside down?" Kelly asked.

"Again? No, just photo it up," Brinson said.

"Should we look around at all?" Arnsbarger said.

"Yeah," Brinson said. His detectives stepped back so he could lead the way up into the house. "We can see if there's a note."

"Guy tied one on," Kelly said, looking over Brinson's shoulder at the mess of beer bottles on the broken coffee table.

Brinson snorted disdainfully and gobbled down a pistachio. He walked into the kitchen, looking casually around without messing the place up. Usually when someone checked themself out they left the note out in the open if they left one at all. Besides, his men would sniff around like hounds on a hare. They knew their business. Brinson walked back into the living room and let himself out through the open glass door. Out back the trees hissed in the wind. Brinson could smell the ocean—a nice way to live. If Brinson smelled anything in his own backyard it was the sour hint of the nearby landfill. And it seemed that once summer rolled around there was never enough breeze to do more than elicit an occasional tinkle from the wind chimes his wife had hanging from the eucalyptus tree.

It never surprised Brinson when he was investigating some sick crime in the home of someone who lived so well. No life could be that perfect. Something always had to give. Brinson knew that when people live as good as Clark Cromwell, something's got to give. More times than not they begin to think the rules no longer apply. They drive down the freeway in their big expensive vehicles and see a truckload of sweaty laborers or the masses of white-collar midlevel managers all struggling for a nut, and most of them just can't stop themselves from feeling a little superior. That's what Brinson figured happened with Clark Cromwell. The guy thought he was above it all, like he had a hotline to God.

Brinson couldn't keep himself from indulging in a smirk. The look on Cromwell's face that morning had been a slice of bliss. That shocked and horrified look was all about him realizing that he wasn't so high and mighty and that despite his holier-than-thou beliefs, he was going to pay the price for what he'd done—just like the next guy.

Chapter 50

Clark had a dream about Annie. They were holding hands, walking down the beach, in love, but arguing about the name they would give their child. The argument turned bitter, then ferocious, then Annie began to hit him, tight little fists to the face.

He woke with a start and had no idea where he was. He didn't feel well and he had the sense that something was wrong, although he didn't have the energy to lift himself from the bed to ask. There was a nurse standing over him, and then Madison's face appeared, then Tom's.

"Where am I?" he said. His words were garbled by the tubes that had been snaked up his nose.

Madison smiled nervously. "You're in the hospital, Clark."

"Clark," Tom said, his voice choking with emotion. "Clark, we love you. We're here for you, Clark. God forgives you."

"What do you mean? What do you mean, Tom?" Clark said, his words coming out slow and sluggish.

Tom reached out and put his hand on top of Clark's head

as if he were a small boy. "I mean He forgives you," he whispered.

"I know," Clark said slowly. He raised his left arm and looked quizzically at the IV attachment. "But why am I here?"

There was a long silence. Madison looked at Tom.

"You . . . you fell asleep in your truck," Tom said. "You had carbon monoxide poisoning."

"No," Clark said, "I didn't. I wasn't in my truck. I was . . . I don't know where I was. I was home, wasn't I?"

"Do you remember this morning?" Madison asked. "Do you remember the police interview?"

"Yes," Clark said, his face darkening.

"Then you went home," she said.

"I had a few beers," Clark admitted. "It wasn't good at the police station."

"You were in your truck in the garage when I found you," Madison said.

Clark looked at her, then at Tom. Their faces showed more than concern. They showed pity, even fear.

"Oh no," he said, struggling to raise himself from the bed. "No. No, that's not what happened. I don't remember, but that's not what happened. I wouldn't do that. I wouldn't do *that!*"

A doctor who was in the room stepped forward. "It's all right," he said, calmly putting his hands on Clark's shoulders and pushing him back down into the bed. "Everything's all right."

"No," Clark said, beginning to struggle feebly against him, "it's not! It's not all right! I didn't do that! I don't know what happened, but I didn't do that!"

"That's okay," the doctor said patiently. "No one's saying you did anything. Just lie back—"

"I won't!" Clark said, pushing the man's hands away and

swinging his legs over the side of the bed. Even groggy he was strong enough to overwhelm the doctor.

"No, don't do that," the doctor insisted. "Don't do that. You have to stay in bed."

Two attendants came through the door. They were strong, wiry men, bigger than the doctor. Clark looked to Madison and Tom. Neither said anything. They just stepped back out of the way, and that scared him more than anything. Clark ripped the oxygen tubes out of his nose just as the men grabbed him by either arm. They were like pythons: The harder he fought against them, the tighter their grip became. The doctor turned away for a moment and then came back toward him with a needle.

"No!" Clark screamed. A jolt of adrenaline cut through his fog. He twisted one arm against the grip of one of the attendants and partly freed himself. He stiff-armed the little doctor, shooting him backward into some monitors and knocking over the oxygen tank.

"Hold him!" the doctor said, his formerly kind face now awash with hostility.

The attendants got him again. Still he struggled, and a menacing growl escaped him as he watched the doctor defiantly bare the needle and inject the drugs into the meat of his leg. He felt its sting and fought maniacally, gnashing his teeth and spitting locker-room invectives at the little bastard.

"You little fuck! I'll kill you, you little *fuck!*"

The Haldol hit him like a wave. Just swoosh, it washed over him, and suddenly nothing seemed to matter.

"I'm okay," he said slowly, relaxing his arms against the grip of the attendants. "No, iss all right . . . I'm okay . . ."

"What are you going to do?" Madison asked the doctor, who was pushing his glasses back into place.

"I'm transferring him to seven-B," he said, calmer now. "The psych unit."

"Oh," she said, glancing over at Tom. "Of course . . ."

"We'll do an evaluation," the doctor said.

"Of course."

A nurse poked her head in through the door and said to Madison, "Are you Ms. McCall?"

"Yes."

She looked from Clark, who was now lying passively in his bed, back to Madison and said, "The police are out here and they would like to speak with you."

Madison pressed her lips tightly together when she saw Brinson in the hall talking quietly with Chris.

"Lieutenant," she said coldly.

The enormous cop rotated toward her with a curt nod. "Ms. McCall."

"They're moving him to seven-B," she said. "For evaluation . . ."

Brinson nodded. "Have they got him sedated?"

"Yes."

"Good. When they're done with him, I'm going to arrest him and take him into custody."

"Is that necessary?" she asked.

"Yes," he said, "it is. I'm working right now on getting a judge to arraign him. I want him restrained and under a suicide watch. The last thing I want is for him to get out of it that way."

Madison looked at him with disgust.

"Not quite the Boy Scout we thought he was," Brinson said, not wanting to give in to Madison's stare.

"He's disturbed, Lieutenant," Madison hissed. "Who wouldn't be? But before you go casting aspersions, just remember who he is . . . one of the finest people in this community. All you have to do is ask."

"Fine on the outside," Brinson countered. "That doesn't always mean fine on the inside, Ms. McCall. This is L.A. This guy had an alcohol level of point one three and traces of a benzodiazepine, probably Valium, so he's not as lily-white as you and everyone else thinks."

"He's disturbed," she said. "Can't you leave it alone at that? You have to *arrest* him, Lieutenant?"

"That's the way it is, Ms. McCall. We're the police. We want to know what happened," he said. His fat face was droopy and bland. He cracked open a nut he'd pulled from his jacket pocket and, pointing it at Chris, said, "You can ask your partner here about that. He knows. He was a cop."

Madison turned away from him without speaking. "Come on, Chris," she said.

The two of them walked down the hospital corridor together but didn't speak until they were alone on the elevator.

"What'd he mean, 'they want to know'?" she asked Chris as the doors closed in front of them.

"He meant they want Clark to go to trial. They want to see him convicted of killing Annie Cassidy. They want to either win or lose," Chris said with an apologetic shrug. "In police work, a suicide is like a tie."

Madison thought about that until they walked through the hospital's doors into the midnight air. A tepid breeze coming in off the ocean was freshening the day's smog-stained air.

"Where are we now?" Chris said.

"I don't know," she said. "Where?"

"I guess we were wrong," he said, sadly shaking his head. "I guess maybe I believed him because he believed himself . . . It's that religious stuff, you know. He's so whacked-out on it that I think he really believes he wasn't responsible for killing her. You know, God using him to get back at the girl for killing his baby, like it wasn't him that was doing it. Like God was using him the way you use a puppet. I don't know. The whole thing is crazy. Obviously he's crazy . . ."

"My God," Madison said as they crossed the parking lot to their car, "to see him that way in there . . . It was like he really didn't remember trying to kill himself."

"It's probably too painful," Chris said, getting into the car. When they were under way he asked, "So . . . you going to go with insanity on this?"

Madison shook her head. "I don't know. I'll see what the reports come back with. We'll get our own evaluation. It's getting tougher and tougher to get a jury to buy it."

"*Is* he insane?" Chris asked.

"I don't know," Madison said. "Is it crazy that someone could convince themselves they killed another person because God wanted them to? I guess it is, but murder is always crazy."

Chapter 51

Ike woke up swamped with guilt. He'd done it again. What Trane had said to him was true. His weakness was women. Chalk up one for the devil. He said a quick prayer asking for forgiveness and slipped quietly out of bed so as not to wake the lovely brown-skinned girl next to him. As he drove to the practice facility the details of the night revisited his mind in dirty little snatches. Ike shivered and wondered how he could ever resist such temptations. He couldn't. He was a damned sinner.

Ike switched on the radio and found 102.9, the Christian station. He listened to a pop band sing about Jesus, electric guitars wailing.

"Naw," he said out loud. Church gospel was something he liked, but if they were going to try and put electric guitars with Jesus, he'd rather just listen to the real thing. He punched the tuner until he heard Snoop Doggy Dogg rapping about life on the streets. That's the way he pulled into the players' lot, with his car windows buzzing from the vibrations of the bass. When he shut off the engine the silence left an emptiness that immediately backfilled with guilt.

Inside, Ike's teammates were strangely subdued. It was as

if the whole team had been out freaking last night and they were sharing Ike's shame. Since he was just a rookie, Ike didn't bother asking anyone what was up. He'd know soon enough, and if he asked, odds were he'd get a fabricated line of bullshit or some kind of sarcastic remark. He undressed in silence, scratching himself and feeling his stomach flop as the notion of disease settled into his brain. How did he know that girl didn't have AIDS or something? The itching persisted, and Ike checked the big clock on the wall to see if he had enough time to grab a quick shower. He didn't, so he pulled on a pair of shorts and fretted all the way to the training room, where he hopped up on a table so Jerry could tape his ankles.

Jerry looked like someone had shot his dog. Ike said nothing, but he worried that the trainer's absent way of wrapping his ankles might lead to a sprain. Again, he kept quiet because he was a rookie and a rookie had no place questioning the head trainer about his tape job.

When Jerry finally looked up from his work, Ike saw that the older man was misty-eyed.

"You're a Christian, aren't you?" Jerry said.

Ike nodded that he was.

"You make sure you say a prayer for our boy," Jerry said in an uncharacteristically emotional voice. "He needs our prayers."

The trainer slapped Ike's ankles, sending him off like a ship from the yard before beelining for his office in the back. Ike hopped down and looked around, wondering what in heaven's name Jerry was talking about. Ike didn't even know Jerry *had* a boy. Ike needed to find another rookie. He left the training room and scanned the lockers. It was five minutes before the hour and his teammates were beginning to hustle toward the first meeting of the day.

"Yo, Manny," he said quietly to a fat rookie noseguard hobbling past on crutches. "Wha's up?"

"With what?" Manny said.

"Man, everybody's acting like someone died," Ike whispered. "Did Jerry have a son died or somethin'?"

Manny looked at him stupidly. "Naw, man," he whispered. "Your boy Clark Cromwell tried to ice himself last night."

"Whaaa?" Ike said in disbelief. "When?"

Manny shrugged. "I don't know. Ten o'clock, that's what they said. But his lawyer found him and they brought the boy back to life."

"Ten o'clock?" Ike said.

"That's what someone said," Manny told him. "Man, we gotta go! We gonna be late an' get our asses fined."

Ike's guilt about last night slipped away. Suddenly the girl and his weakness seemed very small. Instead he sat through the day's meetings in a frightened daze. If what Manny said was true about the ten o'clock time, then Ike had a serious problem on his hands. Conrad Dobbins had been talking about Clark's suicide attempt around nine, an hour before it happened.

Chapter 52

Madison and Chris went to their office in L.A. Each of them had enough business to keep busy on the phone all day, but underneath it all was the waiting. They knew that by the end of the day Clark's mental evaluation would probably be done, and if Brinson held true to his word he would then be arraigned and confined in the county jail. As Clark's lawyer, Madison had to be present.

At ten she went outside to make a brief statement to the press, pointing out that nothing was conclusive. The fact that everyone knew Clark had tried to kill himself made it difficult, even for her, to maintain the pretense of his innocence. Presuming guilt in the wake of a suicide attempt was a natural reaction.

Neither Madison nor Chris bothered to watch her press conference on television. Chris went through the papers, but Madison didn't have the stomach even for that. She had put a personal moratorium on newspapers since the week before, when *USA Today* had slammed her for being a hired gun going from one defendant to another in the same murder case. Besides, she knew what they would do with the present circumstance. They'd twist it and sensationalize it.

They would harass Clark's mother and his sister. They'd find old classmates and teammates who'd be willing to say Clark was always a little odd. In short, they would condemn him.

At five they headed for the hospital. As they stepped into the elevator on their way to 7B, someone shouted to hold the door.

"Madison, Chris," said an out-of-breath Tom Huntington as he slipped into the elevator. "Hello."

"Hi, Tom. How's Clark?" Madison said.

Tom's face was flushed. He was either disturbed or excited or both. "We need to talk," he said under his breath, glancing furtively at the handful of other people who were also on the elevator.

They got out at the seventh floor, and Tom led Madison by the arm to an empty lounge area. He leaned forward and, still holding Madison's arm, said, "Clark didn't do it. He didn't do any of it."

Madison and Chris glanced at each other. "What do you mean?" Chris said skeptically.

"What I mean is this," Tom said, his eyes aglow. "This whole thing was a setup. Clark was framed. For the murder of Annie Cassidy, and for his suicide. That was no suicide. Clark wouldn't kill himself. I knew that. I doubted at first, but I prayed on it and I *knew*.

"No," Tom went on, waving his hand in the air, "I know what you're thinking, but it's not just that. Do you know Ike Webber? He's a backup runner on the team."

"Yes, we know him," Madison said.

"Well he's a Christian," Tom said. "He's been wayward. A good soul, but sort of lost. Clark brought him into our fold and I think he's close to recommitting himself to Jesus Christ, but he's not there yet. Anyway, his agent is Conrad Dobbins!"

Tom looked at them as if he expected some kind of response. "So," he continued, "Ike was at a party last night, a party for Trane held by Zeus Shoes, and Ike heard Dobbins talking about Clark's suicide. He was talking about sin and sinners and saying that Clark was no better than any of them, that suicide was a worse sin than the carousing they did."

"Suicide?" Madison said. "How did he know?"

"Exactly!" Tom said, gripping her even tighter. "It was just after nine when that happened. Ike remembered because Trane had told him to be there at eight and he remembered when Trane and Dobbins got there. Just after they got there, Dobbins was sitting with Ike and talking about Clark's suicide. He knew!"

"Because he was behind it?" Chris said.

"Exactly!" Tom said. "Clark wouldn't kill himself!"

"How?" Chris said. He looked from Tom, who had no answer, to Madison.

"Knock him out somehow?" she said.

"And he doesn't remember?" Chris said dubiously. "How could that happen? Maybe the whole thing with Dobbins was a coincidence, or maybe Ike Webber has his times mixed up. He was at a party, don't forget, maybe drinking. It seems a lot more likely . . ."

"You're wrong," Tom said vehemently.

"Chris," Madison said, "remember what Brinson said to us? He said Clark's alcohol level was point one three and then he said there was something else in his system, a benzadaza-praline or something like that. Remember? Because after that he said it was probably Valium. I thought it was strange when he said it, but then I was thinking that Valium is something NFL players certainly have access to. They give them to guys when they go into those MRI machines because they're so big and the tube is so small. I just figured

Clark had one lying around and maybe took it to calm his nerves. But Valium is sometimes used as an anesthetic, isn't it?"

Chris shrugged. So did Tom.

"What if Clark was anesthetized? With Valium or something like it?" Madison said. "That could be how they got him into the truck."

"But he'd remember!" Chris said. "Somehow someone would have to get that drug into his system."

"What about an amnesic?" Madison said. "Some anesthetics have those properties. They give them to people if they wake up during operations or if kids have to have something done. Jo-Jo had that one time when he had to have his lip stitched. They gave him something and he never remembered getting the stitches."

"That's got to be it!" Tom said. "I'm telling you, Clark would never kill himself. That's it."

"Remember the coffee table?" Chris said.

"With the beer bottles?"

"Yeah, but that table was trashed," Chris said. "I mean, maybe Clark did it himself . . ."

"Or maybe it was smashed during a scuffle," Madison said.

"They got him down, sedated him, and gave him that stuff you were talking about," Chris said. "Do you think whatever it was is still in his system?"

"I don't know," Madison said, heading for the ward, "but we'll find out."

Chapter 53

Zee sat at the bar just inside the glass doors. From his perch on a stool he could clearly see his boss as he chattered on the phone, ensconced between two simpering dancers or models or actresses or whatever they were calling themselves. A cold bottle of Smirnoff sat in front of him on the rich maple wood, sweating a puddle big enough to reach Zee's drink. Gently he slapped at the pool with the bottom rim of the glass, seeing how far the splattered droplets could reach. His head throbbed and his neck felt like it had been throttled with a bike chain.

To make matters worse, he'd heard on the radio about Clark Cromwell's rescue from death. It was big news. The bitch lawyer had saved his ass. The good part was that more than ever, people figured Cromwell killed the girl, and Zee had been lucky enough to put the drops in his nose even though at the time he thought it was a mistake. He knew for a fact that Clark would never remember a thing. No one ever did with that stuff.

Conrad hadn't been happy about his failure to take the white man out. But Zee had argued that dead or alive, he'd still managed to make Cromwell look guilty, and their tracks had been covered just as effectively as if the player were dead. After a mild verbal lashing over the phone, Conrad acquiesced and told Zee to come to work. Zee was in no mood for work, and he tried to get out of it, but Conrad had screamed at him like a bitch when he suggested a day off.

"You gettin' paid, ain't ya!"

Well, Zee was there in body only, not in spirit. He'd been sullen ever since he arrived, even though Conrad seemed not to notice. As a further protest, when he did arrive he'd plunked himself down at the bar with his bottle of vodka, and that's where he'd remained for the entire afternoon. He could damn well guard the agent's body from the bar as well as he could leaned up against the railing out there in the fading sunlight. When someone came in through the front of the house, though, Zee spun himself around on the chair for a better look.

"The fuck happened to yo' ass, Zee?"

It was Trane. He peered at the bodyguard through the gloom that was settling in on the interior of the house now that the sun was low in the sky.

"You lookin' like the fuckin' Michelin man with a goddamn tire stuck in his throat," Trane said with a sarcastic snicker.

Zee only stared malignantly.

"Don't gimme that look," Trane said with a dark stare of his own. "I ain't no street chump that looks away from that shit. Yeah, I know all about you. You some kinda killer or some shit like that. I know how that shit goes, kill some chickenshit chump when he's good an' scared. But I ain't scared of that gangster shit . . ."

Zee continued to glower.

In a more friendly tone Trane said, "Man you got a chain mark on yo' neck that looks like they cut yo' head off an'

sewed that shit back on . . . Where is that big motherfuckin'
chain you always wearin'? Somebody hang ya by it?"

Zee felt for his neck. It was swollen and sore and lacer-
ated where his thick gold medallion had dug into the flesh.
But Trane was right. The medallion was gone. He never took
it off. On the end of its thick, heavy links was a fat gold disk
with ZEE written in one-carat diamonds. Stuck to the back
was, of course, the key to his safe-deposit box. He was so
used to having the chain around his neck that it felt like it
was still there even though it wasn't. Zee tried to think
where he might have left it. He remembered treating his cuts
with some salve when he arrived home the night before,
then taking a sleeping pill to get some rest. He hadn't taken
the chain off then, and now that he thought about it, he
didn't remember seeing it. In a panic he remembered checking around Clark's living room . . . until someone came to
the door.

"Fuck me," he said, suddenly realizing where it must be.

"Naw," Trane said, sliding behind the bar and pouring
himself a Smirnoff from Zee's bottle. "I had a fat bitch last
night."

Zee seemed almost not to hear him. He stared into the
space that hung over the bar. A sick chill ran through him
from top to bottom. It was all over. He would be found out.
The medallion would give him away. And if they found it,
they would have his key.

All the money he'd put away, the funding for his new life
in Mexico where he would be the boss—all that would be
gone. Zee felt the floor shift underneath him. Everything
that had mattered only a few minutes ago suddenly didn't.
He swallowed hard, but like a surge of vomit the panic rose
up out of his stomach, making his lips twitch. Conrad would
flip him in for the whole thing—Clark, that Angel Cassidy
bitch, maybe even Maggs. When Conrad found out about

the medallion he'd do more than just stand by and watch Zee take the fall. He'd help it along. Zee had been around his boss long enough to know that much. Conrad was a shark, and if he smelled blood on his own mother he'd turn on her and tear her to bits.

"Said I *had* a fat bitch last night . . ." Trane said, emboldened by Zee's silence.

Zee's head shot up and in an instant the insult hit home so hard it made him flinch.

"The fuck you gonna do 'bout that?" Trane said with a nasty smile, casually pouring himself another drink.

Zee flipped the Glock out of the waist of his pants and slid back the action with the smooth confidence of a short-order cook flipping an omelette. The forbidding eye of the gun's barrel stared into Trane's face. His drink went down the wrong way, and his face contorted with the effort it took not to choke.

"Who's a bitch?" Zee said menacingly. "You is . . . bitch."

The shot blew a hole through the back of Trane's head the size of a bread plate and sprayed the mirror behind the bar with scarlet gore. Trane's mouth worked open and closed in disbelief.

"Bitch!" Zee growled again, and the player's body collapsed in a heap behind the bar.

"The fuck goin' on!" Conrad screamed as he charged in from the terrace. "Zee, goddamn! The fuck you doin' shootin' off a damn cap in the fuckin' house?"

The agent had no idea. In the gloom he didn't see the blood-spattered mirror. Zee stood still, the gun at his side, a dark sentinel beside the bar. Conrad stopped halfway across the room to let his eyes adjust. He wanted to see his man's face. His instincts already told him that rushing into the house had been a mistake.

"Zee?" he said, more calmly now. "The fuck, Zee? S'up?"

"I ain't up," Zee said, and as he raised the gun, "an' you goin' down . . . bitch."

In rapid succession Zee ripped three shots into Conrad's chest, pummeling the agent back into a chair where he flipped over and lay twitching and bleeding on the carpet. Zee crossed the room and walked calmly out onto the terrace. Out of the corner of his eye he caught the flash of color as the girls ducked behind the poolside bar. He walked quickly and found them cowering under the sink. Like schoolgirls they closed their eyes and covered their ears when they saw him round the corner with his gun. Carefully he shot them both in the head. The shots echoed off the back of the house and faded into the sprawling city below, swallowed up like gumdrops.

Zee went back to the house and checked the kitchen. He had seen Juanita, the housekeeper, go out for groceries a couple of hours ago, but he wanted to make sure she hadn't come back. The house was empty. Zee walked out onto the driveway, glancing all around, and got into his purple Bronco. With tires squealing he shot out into the winding road. Down the hillside he raced, checking in his rearview mirror every five seconds and expecting any moment to see a squad car with its lights flashing and its siren wailing. His mind switched channels to Mexico. He could just go. But he'd have nothing. He could start over again. But he'd never have the chance to make the money he did with the Zeus deal. He thought about Clark's house, the crime scene. What if the medallion was still there?

The idea ate away at his brain like a fast-moving cancer and soon it had a hold. What harm could it do to go back? It would be dark by the time he got there. He could see in, and if someone was in they couldn't see out. If the house was dark . . . The medallion could easily be lying there on the floor amid the mess. If the police *had* found it, wouldn't

Conrad already have known? Through the whole deal he knew Conrad had been getting information from the police. Wouldn't a big gold medallion with diamonds spelling ZEE and a key stuck to its back have gotten a rise out of the cops?

It was worth the chance. If he got the key, he could get his cash and be across the border by tomorrow afternoon. He could see it, a place in Baja on the beach, not too far from Tijuana, young brown-skinned girls lolling around his pool, *his* pool. *He* would be the boss. It was worth everything. It was worth dying for.

Chapter 54

Brinson was sitting at a plastic table on the screened-in porch in the back of his house. His clammy feet were bare but he still wore his slacks and undershirt from the day. The sound of crickets in the lawn was so pervasive that he no longer noticed. He was reading the sports section under a bare bulb that hung from a chain. In front of him on the table was a big cookware bowl soiled with sauce and the very few strands of spaghetti lucky enough to escape his maw. Red stains marked his white tank top like splatters of blood, and the kitchen was filled with the small sounds of his wife cleaning up.

Brinson took a swig from a longneck bottle of Pabst Blue Ribbon. He was deep into the sports, away from all the wild front-page speculation about Clark Cromwell and Brinson's own exhausting quotes of "no comment." It was comforting to know that despite all the tabloid coverage of the Annie Cassidy case there were still articles in the sports page that dug in to the viscera of the game. The big strategic question for the team was how well the double reverse offense would work without the recently reliable blocking of Clark Cromwell. Brinson was so engrossed in the story about the offensive strategy for the upcoming game in Buffalo that he never heard the doorbell. Only the shuffling of feet in the kitchen and his wife's insistent calling disrupted his concentration. He looked up and blinked at the dim forms of Madison McCall and Chris Pelo. He felt violated.

"This is my home," he said, pulling his bare feet in under his groaning chair. "What do you want?"

Madison tried not to notice the detective's enormous belly messy from dinner or the stolen packs of Sweet 'n Low jammed into an old sugar bowl in the middle of the battered table. She felt like an intruder. At the same time she was fascinated with the sense of being in the cramped lair of an animal too big for its hole.

"We need your help," she said.

"Call me tomorrow at nine," Brinson replied curtly, with an exclamatory snap of his paper.

"You've heard of an equivocal death investigation," Chris said, stepping out onto the porch.

Brinson slid into detective mode. "Investigating an apparent suicide with the presumption of murder," he shot back. "What about it?"

"That's what we're going to do," Chris said.

"We want you with us," Madison added.

Brinson snorted so hard that his belly shook, rattling the sports page. "For Cromwell?" he said disdainfully. "Lawyer's tricks. If you'll excuse me, I'm reading the paper."

"You said there were traces of a benzodiazepine in Clark's system," Madison said. "You presumed Valium."

"Typical for a suicide," Brinson added.

"Yes," Madison said with a quick nod, "but there are other benzodiazepines."

"Anesthetics," Chris said.

"Amnesics," Madison said. "We've had his blood sent out for tests to find out exactly what it was that was in his system. But it would make sense. He didn't know what happened to him, Lieutenant. He couldn't remember!"

"You're suggesting that someone knocked him out, then put him in the garage to die?" Brinson said skeptically. "That someone tried to murder him?"

"That's what we have to presume," Madison said. "We won't know about the exact drug until tomorrow, but we're going back to Clark's house and we want you to come with us."

"If we find something," Chris said, "we want you there. We don't want anyone saying it was a lawyer's trick."

Brinson stared at them coldly. "I'm off work," he said flatly, then directed his gaze back down at the paper as if they weren't there. His wife ducked meekly back into the kitchen.

Chris gave Madison a helpless look.

She pursed her lips and said, "What are you afraid of, Lieutenant?"

Brinson kept his eyes on the paper, but the corners of his mouth pulled into a frown.

"What personal tragedy would it be for you if Clark Cromwell were innocent?" she said bitterly. "Does it scare you to think that someone who's constantly being described in your sports section as being so good really might be? Is that it? In your cop world of bad guys and lies and deception is it too much to think that a person who gets as much press as he does could be the real thing? Is that it, Lieutenant? Is that why you're afraid?"

Brinson just stared at his paper. He didn't bother to pretend he was reading it. He just stared and boiled.

Madison waited.

After two long minutes she said, "Come on Chris, let's go find a cop who cares more about the truth than his own goddamn prejudices . . ."

They were in the kitchen when Madison heard the scrape of Brinson's aluminum chair against the concrete porch.

"Wait," he said, and that was all. Madison watched him disappear through the other side of the kitchen. His wife glanced at them furtively, then silently went back to her dishes. In a moment Brinson returned with his shoes on and a windbreaker over the top of an enormous gray-green golf shirt. He was tucking a pistol into his belt as he came.

"We'll look," he growled. "I don't want no tricks . . ."

Madison gave him a satisfied nod. They left the house together and got into separate cars.

"What was that about?" Chris said when they were alone.

"Just something I saw. I thought there was something when he questioned Clark," Madison said, "a kind of joy in watching him come undone. Then at the hospital yesterday I was sure about it. But I think Brinson is basically a decent honest cop so I figured what the hell, if he does have any emotions I might as well play on them. We had nothing to lose . . ."

As she drove, Madison thought about Clark. When they had gone to his room with Tom he was pathetic. It was a frightening notion. They could drug you into submission and it was worse than leather straps and a straitjacket. Clark had simply stared at them listlessly, his face sunken and gray. His mother and sister, down from Portland, were nothing but tears and gloom. While Tom prayed and Madison tried to cut through Clark's fog with some piercing questions, the two women fretted and cried. Tom was the one to explain to them in his self-assured way that Clark didn't try to commit suicide, but had been the victim of a terrible crime. Even though it did nothing for the women's condition, Madison hoped he was right.

Their theory about Clark being anesthetized had been met with almost total disbelief by the medical staff. Still, at

Madison's insistence they had sent his blood off to determine exactly what benzodiazepine he had in his system, and one of the younger residents actually admitted that an amnesic would do just what they were describing. All in all though, it had been a depressing visit, and unless she and Chris could come up with some concrete evidence it was unlikely that Clark would be freed from his medical restraints anytime soon. As Brinson had said only a day before, they wanted to keep him alive.

"So they can kill him," she said out loud.

"What?" Chris said.

"I was just talking to myself, thinking that the police want to keep Clark alive so they can kill him."

"Don't start with me about the death penalty," Chris said.

"I'm not . . . Do you think we'll find something? I mean, wouldn't the police have found anything there was to find last night?"

"Not necessarily," Chris said. "I'm sure they thought it was a suicide. They would've been looking for a note, or Valium, or the beer bottles, but not much else. They already went through the place once with Clark's permission. No, if Clark struggled with someone there could be hair or fibers or who knows what else. There are plenty of things the police could have missed."

"Well," said Madison as they pulled up to the gates of Rancho Palos Verdes. "We'll see."

The guard wasn't the same as the one from the night before and Madison wondered whether or not she was going to hear from anybody about running the gate. The barrier had already been repaired, cobbled back together with pieces of raw wood.

"We're with Detective Brinson," Madison explained, pointing back to the lieutenant's car as she rolled down her window. "Police business."

The guard went back to Brinson's car and after a moment let them pass. At the house, Chris and Madison pulled into the driveway and waited for Brinson to haul himself out of his Caprice.

"You first," Brinson said at the door. "I don't want to violate anyone's Fourth Amendment rights," he added sarcastically.

Chris gave Madison a look. She dangled the key and just as sarcastically said, "I have my client's permission. Do you want another signed consent?"

Brinson gave her a grumpy snort. They walked into the house and Madison fell back behind the two men. The lights were on just as they had been.

"This is how the door was," Chris said, pointing to the open slider.

Nothing had been disturbed and Brinson wondered what kinds of things he and his men could have missed. Although he was skeptical, the notion of an equivocal death investigation interested him.

As if reading his mind, Chris said, "How thoroughly did your men go through the place?"

"Nothing," he said. "I just had them sweep for a note and photo the place up."

"Could we have someone dust this slider for prints?" Chris said.

"Tomorrow we can," Brinson told him.

"And the bottles?"

"Tomorrow."

The three of them stood there in a cluster.

"Well," Brinson said. "Investigate."

Chris nodded. "If someone assaulted Clark, they could easily have come in through this door. He was drinking, obviously, and his response would have been dulled. He wouldn't have even seen them coming. It was dark out and the lights were on in here."

Chris looked at Brinson to see if he was buying any of it. His face was still stony with skepticism.

"There would have been a fight," Brinson said. "Even if he was drunk, you don't just take out a guy like that, even with two or three guys."

"That's why the table's smashed," Chris said.

"Yeah?" Brinson said, pointing to the beer bottles lined up on the coffee table. "Pretty neat-looking scuffle."

"Maybe they straightened up?" Madison suggested.

"Let's see what else we can find," Chris said, getting down on his hands and knees and poking under a chair. He brought out a bottle.

Brinson rolled his eyes.

Chris moved on to the smashed table and examined the jagged edges carefully.

"Probably broke it in a fit," Brinson suggested.

Chris ran his hand under the table, looked up, and said, "This looks more like someone was thrown down on it. The wood is splintered on the underside on either end. Can we have your techs check this glass for fibers and hair?"

"Sure," Brinson said flatly.

Chris felt underneath the couch and his eyes lit up.

"Look at this!"

He held up for them a large gold medallion. Dangling from it was a thick gold chain that had been snapped in two. Sizable diamonds glittered at them in the lamplight.

"Zee," Madison said.

"Look!" Chris said, rising and triumphantly pushing the medallion toward Brinson's face.

Brinson frowned, then scowled as he eyed the medallion, then said, "This . . . this is something."

"There's someone out there!" Madison said, abruptly pointing through the opening in the glass doors.

Brinson and Chris wheeled toward the glass. Chris flipped a bank of switches on the wall and the pool area was ablaze in white light. Brinson had his gun out, and he slid through the open doors in a crouched firing position. Chris followed with his own gun.

"By the tree!" Madison said, but by the time Chris and Brinson looked there was nothing but shadows.

When Zee saw the woman pointing at him he panicked. He heaved himself back up into the tree just as the lights went on. His eyes shot back to the house. He'd seen them through the glass holding up his medallion. He was on the verge of attacking when he was discovered. The sight of two drawn guns made him retreat instinctively into the tree, where he hugged its large trunk twelve feet up, hiding his bulk from the men below. From his perch he clenched his teeth and thought as hard as he could. His head hurt. So did his neck. If he dropped down out of the tree with his gun blazing, he'd be lucky to make it out of there alive. Alive. His head swam. He wanted to stay alive. Before it seemed like the money was worth dying for, but now that didn't seem right. The medallion, the money, none of it meant anything if he was dead. It meant even less if he were captured and put in jail. If they saw him, he'd fight it out. If they didn't . . . Zee waited patiently, listening as the two men worked their way through Clark's backyard. When he heard their voices recede into the house he scrambled down and dropped quickly into the darkness of the neighbor's lawn. Quietly, and looking back to make sure he wasn't being seen, Zee began to run.

*   *   *

"I . . . I thought I saw something," Madison said, feeling somewhat foolish standing there beside the pool in the peaceful breeze of the night.

"Maybe you did," Chris said, even though he and Brinson had checked the bushes around the pool, slowly and carefully working in tandem as if it were something they did together every day.

"If there was someone, they're gone," Brinson said, puffing from the effort. He reached for the medallion and, taking it from Chris, said, "There's a key taped down to the back of this thing."

"Meaning?" Chris said.

"Nothing," Brinson said, "Just a key."

Madison knew from the detective's face that he was a believer.

"There was a stock deal between Conrad Dobbins and Zeus Shoes," she told him, relating the other details that Ike had revealed to Tom Huntington. "A lot of his clients made millions of dollars on options when the stock went through the roof. I think that's what this is all about. I think Dobbins sent Zee to kill Annie Cassidy. They made it look like Trane, then proved him innocent, and shifted the blame to Clark. By the time Trane was cleared by the videotape, Zeus Shoes was already the biggest thing going. Think about it. No one knew about Zeus Shoes. Then the murder, the media barrage, the controversial commercial—it was all planned."

Brinson nodded. "It's possible," he said. He was businesslike now. "I'll take this and I'll call in a car to keep an eye on this place until the morning in case you did see someone. We'll reinvestigate the scene and sweep it for everything. Meantime, I'm going to go pay a visit to Conrad Dobbins and see if he wouldn't like to come in and have a little talk."

Then to Madison he said with a twisted smirk, "You may want to give him a call."

"Why's that?" she said in surprise.

"Won't you be representing him now?" Brinson said.

Madison pressed her lips together but suppressed a biting reply. "Fair enough, Lieutenant," she said with a sigh, and for the first time she saw the big cop smile.

"Just kidding."

Madison and Chris could see Brinson jawing into his radio as they followed him through the winding streets.

"I'd like to be there when they talk to Dobbins," Chris said.

"Maybe I *should* represent him," Madison said, glancing at Chris out of the corner of her eye.

"That's a good one, Madison."

Brinson had disappeared ahead of them as they drove, apparently in a hurry to get his hands on Conrad Dobbins. But now as they pulled up to the guard shack they could hear the loud wail of Brinson's horn. The gate was apparently stuck. Madison pulled up behind the detective and as Brinson got out of his car Chris did the same.

"Something wrong?" Chris asked.

"Goddamn guard must be sleeping!" Brinson said gruffly. Chris joined him and they made their way to the sturdy-looking brick shack.

"Shit," Brinson said at the threshold.

Chris looked down and saw a crimson pool of blood trickling out of the shack and onto the brick pavers. He, like Brinson, drew his gun instinctively. Inside, the guard lay slumped on the floor under the glare of a small fluorescent light. His throat was slit. As the scene registered in Chris and Brinson's minds, the night erupted in gunfire and smoke, and each of them felt a hail of bullets rip through his rib cage.

Chris spun into the fire and tried to level his gun at its source. In the darkness by the gate he could make out the large dark form of Zee behind the flashing gun. Then everything went black.

Madison saw Zee's daunting shape as he emerged from the shrubbery beside the gates like an enormous phantasm. She jumped from the car, but her scream of warning was drowned out by the shots. Zee descended on the prostrate bodies of the two men like a hungry spider and groped about them with his hands. Madison felt as if she was in slow motion, and in that oozing moment she felt her own instinct to run overcome by something deep and fierce inside her. Instead of fleeing, she moved toward the danger. When Zee saw her he spun her way and leveled his heavy pistol. The gun broke the night with an angry click and Zee flung it down, reaching behind him into the belt of his pants for the sticky knife.

Madison saw Chris's gun on the ground at the same time Zee brandished the blade. She dove for it as he slashed. She got the gun and sprang backward. Zee slashed again, moving toward her now. The knife ripped through Madison's T-shirt, leaving a bleeding gash in her abdomen. She shrieked and fell backward to the ground, fumbling frantically with the gun. Zee loomed over her, his dark angry face twisted with rage. He drew back his blade for the lethal blow. As it came, Madison fired up into his face and he reeled backward away from her. His gory face spouted blood. A gaping hole had opened below his eye. He came at her again with a ferocious roar. She shot him again in the chest, wincing as the hot flame lit the barrel of the gun. Zee staggered but started for her again. Again she shot him, and again. Finally his legs collapsed underneath him and the killer let out a sad-sounding groan as the life was torn from his enormous frame.

Epilogue

It was the biggest game of their lives, and the Juggernauts were down by four. With time nearly ready to expire, everyone expected the unexpected. Still, even the cameraman lost the action momentarily when the Juggernauts offense ran their trademark double reverse. The quarterback rolled left and handed off to Featherfield running right, who handed off again to Ike Webber going back to the left. But the Miami defense was well coached. They closed in on the play with the focus and discipline of a championship team. When Ike reared back and heaved the ball downfield it was the first time anyone had seen the play. There wasn't a soul in the end zone except Clark Cromwell.

Clark pulled the ball from the night sky and knelt down in the rich green grass to pray. Around the world people watched. It was a moment that would be remembered in the same breath with names like Montana, Namath, and Franco Harris. It was football history.

Around the living room Madison, her family, and friends erupted into a raucous celebration. Madison and Cody had planned the gathering as a combination Super Bowl party/welcome-home bash for Chris Pelo. Chris, still in a wheelchair but getting better every day, celebrated with a slow smile. With his index finger he signaled Madison to lean close.

Through the din he said in a low, raspy voice, "Think of the advertising opportunities . . ."

Madison grinned at him and said, "You *are* feeling better."

He gave her a halting thumbs-up and opened his mouth so his wife could fill it with a salsa-laden chip. He chewed slowly and deliberately, glad to be chewing at all, glad just to be alive. Brinson wasn't as lucky. Although Chris's wounds had appeared to be the more dire of the two, the detective's heart had stopped in the middle of emergency surgery. He never knew that Conrad Dobbins and Trane Jones had gotten what they deserved, killed by Zee, the monster they had unleashed on so many others. And he never knew that Madison had exacted revenge on that same man. Chris didn't think about that. He hoped Brinson was in heaven. Maybe it was Clark praying on TV that got him thinking that way, Chris didn't know. Whatever the reason, he found himself praying for the dead cop.

Madison left Chris with his wife and his thoughts and crossed the room to where Cody was finishing off a Coors Light that, judging from the expression on his face, had somehow gone sour.

"What's the matter?" she said cheerfully. "You wanted L.A. to win."

"Just that," Cody said, gesturing toward the TV in disgust.

"What?"

"That," he said, "That praying on TV bullshit."

"Why do you say that?"

"Ah, it's all a ruse," he said. "Like God cares who wins or loses the Super Bowl. Listen to this guy. 'God was with us.

We were destined to win for the glory of Jesus . . .' I don't like it."

Madison thought about that to herself. She knew Cody wasn't highly religious, but she also knew he was no atheist.

"I guess some people could find it offensive," she said.

"Religion's between you and the Man upstairs," he told her sullenly.

Madison nodded her head. "I guess I believe that too," she said. Then, pointing to the TV set and the weary but ebullient figure of Clark Cromwell as he hugged Ike Webber, she said quietly, "But I'll tell you something about that man right there . . ."

"What's that?"

"No matter what you or I or the rest of the world thinks, to him this was more than a game. And you know, after all he's been through I can't really blame him. Anyway, I guess you have to respect him . . . because that's what he believes."

THE SPRING RAIN WAS LIGHT AND FRESH. THE AIR WAS WARM. A sliver of sun had torn through the hem of the western clouds with the promise of better weather soon. Bright sprouts of grass had recovered from a chilly Texas winter and they blanketed the lawns in a shimmering lime green. The trees lining either side of the busy street were exploding with new buds. But, Bob Bolinger didn't notice any of that. The heat was getting to him. The air pumping out of his car vents was tepid at best. He needed Freon, among other things. He also needed a date. He knew that. It had been almost five years since he had found his wife in bed with his ex-best friend.

Bolinger looked at his watch. Quitting time. He loosened his tie, slid down in the driver's seat, and relaxed for the first time that day. Like Houdini, he squirmed out of his old gray blazer, keeping one hand on the wheel and noticing for the first time a week-old mustard stain on the jacket's sleeve. Maybe he'd get in a quick nine holes before dark. Then he could shoot on over to The Romper Room, have a couple of scotch and sodas and a burger at the bar, and who knew? He might get lucky. What was that lottery slogan? You gotta be in it to win it.

Then the call came in. Bolinger cursed out loud but gladly took it. The last thing The Romper Room needed was a mangy old cop on the prowl for some love. Anyway, this call was important. Apparently, a young coed, a law student, needed a body bag. He wondered fleetingly if his ex-wife would ever end up in a body bag. He cast that whimsical notion aside and ran a hand up over the top of his bristly gray crew cut, scratching the back of his leathery neck.

From the tone of the call, it sounded like a messy scene. Bolinger spun the wheel and turned his unmarked cruiser back against the grain of traffic. He shot up Guadalupe and into the old homes near the university. The University of Texas was as big a part of Austin as the state capitol itself. So, when a body turned up anywhere near the campus, all kinds of noses got out of joint. No one liked the idea of anyone dying young.

There were already six squad cars and an unmarked at the scene as well as an ambulance with its lights still flashing. The patrolmen were well into the process of sealing off the area. Bolinger didn't have to show his badge as he dipped under the yellow tape. They knew who he was. The crime lab techs arrived at the same time jumping out of their van and invading the scene like paratroopers. They spilled around Bolinger and he let them. He was in no hurry to get inside. He wanted to take in the scene. The house was an old two-story surrounded by towering oaks. The multiplicity of mailboxes told him the place had been split up into three apartments. A cracked driveway led to the detached garage at the back of the house. The girl's apartment was back there on the ground floor. Bolinger met his best friend on the force, a detective named Farnhorst, on the back steps. He was the first suit on the scene and his honey-colored skin had a green cast to it.

"I heard it's ugly," Bolinger said.

Farnhorst looked down at his boss. Bolinger was only five-foot-six. Tears welled in the bigger man's sad looking eyes and this puzzled Bolinger.

"Goddamn, sergeant," Farnhorst choked. "Goddamn."

"Anyone see anything?" Bolinger asked. His square-cut chin was protruding and his dark brown eyes bore into his friend like deadly weevils. Bob Bolinger did his job without emotion.

"Nothing yet. No one home in either of the other apartments. The paperboy found her and called 911 out of his mind. I guess she'd leave the money on the kitchen table and he'd just walk in to get it if she wasn't home." Farnhorst let Bolinger pass and said quietly, "Her name was Marcia Sales . . ."

Bolinger could smell the gore the second he walked through the door. When he saw the body he took a deep breath.

"Holy shit," he uttered.

A tech snapped off a shot and stepped to the side. The girl lay on her back in the middle of the floor, naked. A thick band of duct tape encircled her head covering her mouth. Her eyes were frozen wide with horror. Blood was everywhere. Bolinger moved closer.

"Watch it sergeant!" cried a scowling tech as he darted toward him. Bolinger sidestepped a bloody organ he couldn't identify and crouched down next to the body. There were bruise marks around her neck and Bolinger found himself involuntarily hoping that was how she died. On the couch were what he presumed had been the girl's clothes. Oddly, they were folded. That told him she probably got naked on her own and that she knew whoever did this pretty well. Carefully, he poked through the clothes. There was no underwear or bra anywhere and Bolinger wondered if there was a reason or if it had simply been the girl's style.

There was a scuffle in the entryway accompanied by Farnhorst's bark. Bolinger looked up to see a large man with long dark hair who looked part Native American. He pushed his way into the living room. Bolinger stood up to face him. Before he could speak the man who wore faded jeans and cowboy boots froze in his tracks and let out a maniacal howl that made Bolinger reflexively draw his gun. The man's face was contorted and he pulled at his own hair. When Farnhorst and his partner got hold of either arm, the man burst into a wild flurry of arms and legs. Farnhorst, who weighed in at about three hundred pounds, went flying like a lawn chair. The other cop went sideways into a lamp and they both crashed to the floor.

The maniac's howl turned to a blood-curdling scream and he shot toward the door. Bolinger was after him with Farnhorst and his partner in tow. The man bolted out the door and down the driveway, screaming all the while.

"Stop him!" Bolinger shouted.

Halfway down the drive two patrolmen brought him down like a pair of linebackers. But even the shock from his head hitting the pavement did nothing to take the fight out of him. He bucked the patrolmen up into the air and spun himself around. As he rose, one of the cops took out his baton and struck the back of his neck. As he went down the big man yanked a revolver out of the other patrolman's belt. Bolinger was two steps away on a full run when the man jammed the gun into his own mouth.

Instinctively, Bolinger dove for the pistol, jamming his fingers between the hammer and the chamber just as the man pulled the trigger. Bolinger cried out in pain but didn't let go. With his other hand he grabbed for the gun and wrestled for it but the maniac had clamped down on the barrel with his teeth for all he was worth.

When Farnhorst hit the guy with mace Bolinger got a good shot of it, too. Blood was running freely down his hand now but still he kept his fingers jammed beneath the gun's hammer. With his eyes shut tight against the burning mace, Bolinger rolled with the punches until he realized that he'd been separated from the melee and he alone held the gun. He rolled over on the pavement and sat up coughing and crying from the mace. His eyes cleared enough to see that even with a set of cuffs on his wrists and another shot of mace the Indian continued to struggle violently. Bolinger could only think he was whacked out on PCBs.

Before he knew it, the guy was up again and surrounded by four policemen, two wielding their batons. Blood streamed down the man's face from his nose and his eyes were swollen half-shut, yet still he screamed. Abruptly, he dropped to his knees, hung his head, and let out a dismal sob. Then he dropped on his side and cried almost as violently as he fought.

"It was Lipton!" he bawled. "It was Lipton! She said she was afraid! She told me she was afraid of him! Lipton! Oh my God, Lipton!"

And then his words were so garbled that Bolinger couldn't understand him. Carefully the cops loaded the man into the back of a cruiser and let him sit.

"Shit," Farnhorst said, helping Bolinger to his feet. "You all right?"

"Yeah," Bolinger said, stooping down to pick up a wallet from the ground. He leafed through it.

"Donald Sales," he said to Farnhorst, holding the wallet up and wiping the tears from his face on his sleeve. "Girl's father?"

Farnhorst shrugged, "Jesus, I guess. You think he was the one who killed her?"

"I have no idea," Bolinger said, his lips pressed tight. "Take him in and chain him up to the floor so he can't hurt himself. Let him sit for a while and then I'll talk to him. He said something about someone named Lipton."

"Sergeant?"

Bolinger spun around. It was Alice Vreeland from the ME's office. She was a stubby redhead and the best they had.

"Rough day?" she said.

Bolinger shook his head. "Didn't start out that way, but it looks like that's how it's ending up."

"Looks like the photos are finished," she said, eyeing the cameraman who was loading his equipment back into his van.

"When the crime lab is done you want me to remove the remains, or is there anything else you need to see?" she asked.

"No," Bolinger said. "I've seen enough."

At six-foot-five and two hundred sixty pounds Sales was an imposing man. Cuffed and chained to the floor with his face swollen and bloody and his pale eyes burning with hate, he looked downright scary.

"Cigarette?" Bolinger said.

Sales nodded and Bolinger stuck one into the man's

mouth. Sales sucked greedily when it touched the prof-
fered flame. Besides being big, Bolinger guessed that,
cleaned up, Sales was a handsome man. His tan skin had a
reddish cast that suggested Native American blood somewhere close by in the family tree. Bolinger already knew
that Sales was a decorated veteran who'd served in South-
east Asia and that since his return he'd been self-employed
as a carpenter who specialized in building docks around
Lake Travis. Just after he'd arrived home from the war,
Sales had been arrested in separate incidents for disorderly
conduct and an assault charge. Both had been thrown out.
The red flag was that Sales had undergone treatment at the
VA hospital for Post-Traumatic Stress Disorder. It wasn't an
uncommon thing for veterans, but Bolinger knew it wasn't
an uncommon thing for psychopathic killers either.

Bolinger lit a Winston of his own and looked candidly at
Sales through the smoke.

"You want to sit down?" the sergeant said.

Sales jangled his chains and snorted disdainfully but sat
down anyway on the cell's concrete floor. Bolinger sat on
the bench against the wall. Beside him, he put down a tape
recorder whose rectangular red light glared accusingly at
Sales.

"What brought you to your daughter's apartment?" he
asked quietly.

"Ha!" Sales barked. His face crumpled in pain and tears
began to stream freely down his face. He shook his head
from side to side as if it could make everything go away.
"Ha! My daughter! Oh God! Oh my God!"

Bolinger waited. In ten minutes, the big man's crying
subsided enough for him to take a deep breath and say,
"We were supposed to have dinner together. I was taking
her to dinner . . ."

"We did that," he explained sadly, looking directly into

Bolinger's eyes. "I promised her that if she went to law school at UT I wouldn't be around all the time. I only live an hour up the road. But I told her I wouldn't always be checking up on her. When she was at San Angelo State I used to drop in on her a lot . . ."

Here, Sales looked at Bolinger to see if he understood. Bolinger didn't have kids, but his brother did so he nodded with commiseration.

"Yeah, so I stopped doing it but we'd still see each other pretty regular. We were going to dinner . . . Oh God!"

Sales started to shake and cry again. When he was quiet Bolinger said, "Where were you before?"

"Home," Sales said dully. "I finished a job after lunch and took the rest of the day off to work around the house."

"Anyone with you?"

Sales shook his head.

"Anyone see you?"

"My house is out in the middle of nowhere," Sales said. "No one ever sees me."

"Would you sign a consent that allows us to search your house and your truck?" Bolinger said.

Sales looked at him, mystified. "Why?"

Bolinger shrugged and held out a consent form with a pen.

"Ha!" Sales erupted. "Ha! You think I . . . Ha! I told you who did it! It was Lipton. Her professor, he was after her. I told her I'd talk to him but she didn't want that. He gave her the creeps."

"Give me that," Sales said in disgust. "I'll sign anything. You can look anywhere you want for anything you want, but you better have someone go get this guy!"

Bolinger talked with the father for over an hour, pumping him for every bit of information from every angle he could think of. At the end of that time he excused himself and reported to his lieutenant.

"I'm letting him go," he said.

The lieutenant raised an eyebrow. The father was all they had. They could book him and hold him on assaulting an officer and resisting arrest. They didn't need to let him go anywhere. They could sit on him for another day if they wanted unless he started barking for a lawyer. But Bolinger cut through all that. He was a man who'd built his reputation on instinct.

"He didn't do it," Bolinger said. "He's calmed down now and if he blows his brains out, then he does. But I don't think he will. I think he just lost it. If I book him then I'll have to deal with some lawyer and I'd rather be able to talk to this guy straight. He may be able to help to us. I don't know."

The lieutenant nodded and said, "You going to go home and get some rest?" It was after ten and Bolinger had gone on duty that morning at seven.

"No."

"Didn't think so. What next?"

"The professor. According to Farnhorst, the girl's criminal law professor is a guy by the name of Eric Lipton, a well-known academic. Besides teaching at UT, he travels all around the country giving seminars on defendant's rights. He's the one the father thinks did it."

"Holy shit," the lieutenant moaned, "a law professor. That'll be fun. Anything prior on him?"

Bolinger shook his head. "Clean as a whistle."

The lieutenant paused for a moment before asking, "You ever look at the crap that builds up on the inside of someone's whistle?" He'd spent the first two years of his career in the traffic division.

"No," Bolinger said, "but I'll take your word for it."

Professor Eric Lipton lived in the fashionable neighborhood of Terrytown. It was where a lot of the old money lived, expensive real estate directly adjacent to the wide placid stretch of the Colorado River running through the center of Austin. Lipton's place was a big white contemporary speckled with glass cubes that allowed light without compromising privacy. A wrought-iron fence surrounded the property. Although it was night, a bevy of landscape lights illuminated the house and the lawn that sprawled under carefully manicured trees cut into geometrical designs. It was a big money place and Bolinger could tell by the shape it was in that Lipton was the kind of person who squeezed his toothpaste out of the tube from the bottom up. Little white gravel stones crunched under Bolinger's tires as he pulled into a semi-circular drive and underneath a tall flat-roofed portico supported by a cluster of narrow white columns.

Lipton came to the door in a white satin sweat suit and expensive leather Polo slippers. His glare was hostile. He was a tall angular man whose figure suggested that of a swimmer. He had none of the usual stoop for someone of his height and age. His hair was a wavy faded blond, flowing back from his face as if he'd just come out of the wind. His skin was tan but its orange tint told Bolinger he was the kind of person who'd spent time under an ultra-violet light. His high rugged cheekbones, perfect teeth, and the weathered skin around his bright blue eyes reminded Bolinger of the tennis pro who tried to teach him how to serve on his last vacation in Fort Lauderdale.

"Can I help you?" the professor said with a disinterested sniff.

Bolinger knew that's not what he meant. The last thing on earth he wanted to do was help. Something about the professor didn't smell right.

"Professor Lipton? I'm Sergeant Bolinger," the detective said. "One of your students has been killed and I wanted to ask you some questions about her. Would you mind coming downtown with me?"

Lipton looked him up and down. A light airy laugh spilled from his mouth.

"Do you know my area of expertise, sergeant?" he said snidely.

"Yes, sir. I do."

"Then you shouldn't have even asked if I would go with you. This is my world sergeant. My view of the police is a . . . an adversarial one . . ."

"However," he continued as if he were lecturing a class, "I don't wish to insinuate a hostile or secretive nature. You can come in sergeant. You can ask me whatever you like. I'm a reasonable man . . . I'll give you five minutes."

Lipton looked down at his watch, marking the time, then said simply to Bolinger, "Anything more would be a waste of my time and yours. My knowledge of Ms. Sales is quite limited."

"How did you know it was Marcia Sales?" Bolinger said, his blood racing and his eyes narrowing at the sound of her name coming so unexpectedly from the professor's mouth.

Lipton's eyes flickered with panic for a moment, nothing more. Then he said calmly, "Why sergeant, you told me."

"No," Bolinger said with a crooked smile. "No I didn't."

"Get the hell out of here!" Lipton said, flaring up angrily. "Don't you come here to my home making insinuations! You forget that I know my rights! I'm not some street thug. I don't have anything to say to you! You want to talk? Call my lawyer!"

The door slammed in Bolinger's face, but still he smiled. He had his man.

A slip of the tongue wasn't much. Bolinger knew that getting a warrant based on that alone might not float. But it was enough for him to stake out the house. And, he was confident that by the middle of the next day the crime lab would come up with something. When they didn't, Bolinger felt his stomach sink.

"Cleanest crime scene I've ever seen," was what the crime lab's captain told him.

Bolinger had twenty men working under him on this one and so far, no one had turned over anything concrete. He knew it was Lipton. But he needed something concrete. A hunch never convicted anyone. That took hard evidence.

Ten minutes later Farnhorst burst into his office with a mammoth grin.

"Got what you need, Bob!" he said, waving a paper triumphantly in the air. He slapped it down on Bolinger's desk and said, "Did a computer cross-check on the area and I came up with this!"

Bolinger followed the detective's thick finger to the spot on the page that chronicled a code ten-seventeen, a hit and run property damage. Apparently on the day before at two-thirty in the afternoon, a woman whose car was parked on the street opposite from Marcia Sales's address witnessed a maroon Lexus sedan back out of the driveway and into her car. The driver, who she couldn't identify, sped off without stopping but the woman got the license plate number as the car tore down the street. The car belonged to Lipton.

"Yes!" Bolinger said, slapping the paper. "Get me a warrant, Mo. I want the house and the car turned inside out and I want him under a light before lunch."

Bolinger closed the door to his office, then opened the window before taking out a cigarette and lighting up. He rubbed his eyes and gulped down what was left of his coffee, taking time to crush a few bits of grind between his teeth. Sleep was something that would have to wait. This was how it was done, classic detective work. Most homicides were solved in the first forty-eight hours or they weren't solved at all. He knew when he saw him that Lipton smelled and now he had him.

Earlier in the morning, Alice Vreeland had confirmed for him that the girl hadn't died of asphyxiation but from having some of her insides cut out. She bled to death. She told him he was looking for a pretty sharp knife.

"Sharp enough to shave," Vreeland had commented.

"By the way," she had continued, "I've got to go back to the house. I thought they had everything, but I can't find her gallbladder. No one picked one up, did they?"

Bolinger rubbed his eyes some more and wondered again at her macabre comment. Unsure of whether or not she was trying to be funny, he hadn't reacted. Now he wondered if, instead of an oversight, there was some reason the gallbladder was missing. He had never heard of anything like it, but he'd never seen a body like that either, half choked to death and then split open like a butchered cow. Bolinger shuddered at the thought. An image came screaming into the forefront of his mind. It was the look on Don Sales's face and the sound of his horror when he walked into that room. How deep must that pain be?

Bolinger picked up the phone. He wanted to give the father something, an offering of condolence. The only way he knew to do that was to show how hard he was working to pin down her killer. He wanted to call Sales and tell him about the apparent hit-and-run. Then he thought better of it. He'd wait until they had Lipton in the bag. There was no reason to build the man's hopes on circumstantial evidence. Who knew? They might get lucky and find the knife with the girl's blood all over it, although from the cleanliness of the crime scene, he doubted it. Whoever killed the girl knew what they were doing. A crime scene that clean was almost unheard of.

Bolinger worked up some paper. It was nearly two hours before Farnhorst returned.

"We got him, Bob," he said triumphantly. "Guy was getting ready to take a little trip. He booked a ticket to Toronto and was already on his way north on 35 towards the airport when I caught up with the surveillance team to bring him in. When we tried to pull him over he made a run for it. Wrecked his car, then hopped out and ran into some woods. He didn't get very far. Had a couple bags packed, his passport, and about twenty-thousand dollars in cash."

Bolinger stuck a pen in his mouth and started to chew on it, "Shit, good job."

"But this is what you're really gonna like," Farnhorst said holding forth a plastic bag containing what looked like women's underwear.

Bolinger took the bag and looked at it quizzically.

"We found this stuffed into the bottom of his duffel bag . . ." Farnhorst said. "It's a woman's bra and panties . . ."

"There's blood on them, Bob," Farnhorst said quietly. "I wanted to show you before I send them to the lab . . . I think they might be hers."

To read more, look for *The Letter of the Law* by Tim Green.